For Gina + Patrick —
who found
Enjoy this
Just like "Jour ...
love
aunte Em —

Mary George, Her Book

Marilyn Anne Pate

PUBLISH
AMERICA

PublishAmerica
Baltimore

ISBN: 1-4241-5056-6
PUBLISHED BY PUBLISHAMERICA, LLLP
www.publishamerica.com
Baltimore

Printed in the United States of America

To Terry— Prince of Pages, Husband Extraordinaire, and Head Cheerleader. You are both the wind beneath my wings and my anchor.

Acknowledgments

Many thanks to the staff of Larson Memorial Library, Pinetop-Lakeside, Arizona, the Navajo County interlibrary loan system, the Apache County Historical Society, the Ramah, NM Pioneers Center & Museum, far flung family members and friends who shared oral and written stories. The letter from William George asking to be released from his mission is quoted verbatim.

Three books were helpful for background material:

Mormon Settlement in Arizona, James H. McClintock, 1921

Take Up Your Mission, Charles S. Peterson, 1973

Mormon Country, Wallace Stegner, 1942

Prologue

Bluewater, New Mexico, 1965
Tom's dead.

Saturday morning he was out back working on the railroad tie house he started ten years ago. Ken, our packrat son, had stockpiled in our side yard, a load of surplus ties from the uranium mill at Ambrosia Lake. Tom wanted to make a house with them because he felt like building something enduring and tie houses are warm and snug in the winter. He'd never forgotten the cold New Mexico Zuni Mountain winter in Ramah when his family nearly froze to death. They lived in a shack built of warped green lumber. Many mornings they brushed the snow off their bed covers before getting up. The wind blew so hard through the cracks that they couldn't keep a lamp or candle lit.

When I went to the kitchen door to call Tom in for lunch that day, he sat on the tie house steps enjoying the pale February sunshine. My orange tabby cat, Marmalade, snoozed in his lap. He put Marmalade down and stood. Tom wasn't six feet tall anymore, and his stride had turned to a shuffle but as he approached the backdoor I saw, with the eyes of my heart, the used-to-be-young, handsome cowboy, husband, father, rancher and stubbornly hopeful miner whose El Dorado was always just over the next ridge.

"Feeling creaky today, Mame," he said.

His pet name for me was Mame. No one else calls me that.

"You need a hot bowl of split pea and ham soup. Come in and wash up. Hot water's in the basin on the dry sink."

We sat at the table, said the blessing and started to eat when there came a knock on the front door. Three kids from the new trailer park stood on the porch. They were looking for work to earn spending money. The uranium boom has brought a lot of outsiders to Bluewater.

The children were clean and spoke politely, so I said, "Come back in a month and help us get our garden ready for spring planting."

I started back to the kitchen and felt uneasy. Tom usually called out, "Who is it, Mame?" He liked his old friends to come and visit. There were no sounds from the kitchen; no slurping of soup or clink of butter-knife on the dish. It was as if all the air in the house had whooshed out the front door leaving our home empty and silent. I caught my breath and without going into the kitchen, knew I was alone.

While I answered the door, he had rested his head against the pie cabinet next to his chair. As quickly as a cloud covers the sun, Tom died. I sat beside him at the kitchen table, held his big rough hand in mine, put my head down, and cried. He was ornery, stubborn, impatient and an enthusiastic dreamer, but he was my Tom. I grumbled about him, but nobody else had better say a word against him or they'd get a good tongue lashing from me. It's hard to remember when I didn't know and love him seeing as we met when I was nine and he was twelve.

The folks who came for his services have gone. I face living alone for the first time in my eighty-eight years. Maybe I have four or five years left, but how will I fill them? I sit with my arms across my chest in the old oak rocker feeling barren and abandoned. The only sound in the empty house is the creaking of the rockers, back and forth, back and forth. Each creak carries me across time and space to where it all began.

Chapter One

Mendon, Utah Territory, Spring 1885

"Henry, it's the chance we've been waiting for," Uncle Bill said.

"I hope your news has something to do with keeping warm," Father answered his brother and held his large callused hands toward the warm stove. "I'm sure tired of these cold Utah mountain winters. What's got you stirred up?"

"The Church has called Jane and me to go on a mission to Arizona Territory. I told Bishop Reid we'll go gladly, but we'll be happier if your family comes along. They propose I supervise the planting of citrus groves and act as missionary among the natives." Smiling broadly through his dark curly beard, Uncle Bill rose from his chair and paced the room. He was so excited at the prospect that he couldn't sit still.

"We'll leave in June and travel to St. Johns on the Little Colorado River. Twelve Mormon families are already there—not enough saints to carry on the work of Zion. We both have seven children, so that makes eighteen of us. The Mormon population will swell to roughly two-hundred souls," my uncle said with a laugh in his voice.

It was a cold drippy March afternoon. I sat very still in my corner reading my Sunday School book. If they knew I was listening they might send me away. My face felt hot and my heart thumped so hard I thought it would jump out of my chest. I was happy and scared at the same time. We'd lived in Mendon for all of my eight years. The only time I'd ever left was when Father took me on an overnight trip to Logan. Now, Uncle Bill was inviting us on a grand adventure.

Father said, "Have to talk it over with Elizabeth. Sounds good to me, but you know how touchy she can be." ·

"Well, got to get along. We don't have time to waffle about this. You must decide pretty quick," Uncle Bill said as he pulled on his coat and opened the door.

Father looked up and saw me, "Mary, isn't it time to get supper started? The boys will be home from school soon. Don't say anything about Arizona to your brothers. No sense in getting things all riled up. May not happen."

I couldn't go to school with my brothers, but Mother had taught me to read and write. She didn't feel like some folks did, who thought girls learned what they needed to know by helping at home. The reason I couldn't go was because Mother needed me at home. I had two older and four younger brothers and Mother wasn't well.

I slept on a cot in one curtained corner of the kitchen/parlor. The boys slept in the loft and our parents had a separate back bedroom. Later, after we kids were in bed, I heard Father telling Mother about Uncle Bill's plan.

I strained to hear my parent's discussion, but drifted off to sleep only to be wakened by Father's angry voice.

"Elizabeth, this may be our only chance to make a new start. The summers here are so short that it's impossible to raise enough to get us through the summers, much less the winters. I want to go with Bill and Jane."

"Arizona's so far away. I'd have to leave all my family except for Jane. I don't know if I'm cut out to be a pioneer. Living on the trail for four months scares me," Mother said.

I heard tears in her voice. Soon she was sobbing, blowing her nose and pleading with Father. "Don't make me do this. I'll go if you demand it, but I'm sure no good will come of it."

"I have to decide soon. Other folks are lining up to be included in the party. Let's sleep on it and I suggest you pray about this wonderful opportunity."

After they closed their door, I lay awake for a long time. How had two such different people ever fallen in love? Father was outgoing and optimistic. He loved meeting people and swapping stories. Reading church books was all right, but poetry and novels bored him. Mother found it hard to meet new people, liked poetry and novels. She enjoyed reading about other's adventures, but didn't like change in her own life. When life piled up on her, she disappeared into a fog and took to her bed for days at a time.

Aunt Jane, Mother's older sister, told me Mother was known as high-strung when she was a teenager. I didn't understand what high-strung meant, but I guessed it was being sort of touchy and persnickety. She was fussy about her clothes, wore a clean, white apron, and brushed and braided her long golden hair each day.

She was just tall enough for the top of her head to reach Father's chest, but when she was angry she was a towering thundercloud and I was a fearful mouse trying to get out of the rain. I never knew what was going to set her off. One day it was all right to sit reading in the sun on the back steps. The next day she'd yell, "Mary George, you are the laziest girl in Utah. Get in here and finish the ironing." I tried to be good and follow the rules, but the rules kept changing. I felt she blamed me for her sadness. Father was easier to be around.

I envied my two older brothers, Lester and Reuben. They spent more time with Father. While they worked cutting firewood, plowing, planting or taking care of the cows and horses, they laughed, sang, and told funny stories. William and Roy, who were just younger than me, went to school, helped with the animals or weeded the garden. In addition to the housework, I cared for toddler, Richard, and baby Parley. He was my favorite because last October I'd helped Mother give birth to him.

Sometimes, in late afternoon, I'd go to the barn and watch the boys do the milking. I'd talk to the cows, lean against their silky sides and smell their outdoorsy mountain meadow perfume. They chewed their cuds as warm frothy milk squirted into the pails.

A family of cats lived in the barn and I liked chasing the kittens. Cats had to earn their keep by catching mice. Dogs helped herd the sheep and cattle and chased away hungry mountain lions, bears and wolves that hunted in the nearby canyons. The cats and dogs weren't pets and were never allowed in the house. No matter how cold it was, they had to sleep outside or in the barn.

I wished I had a kitten of my own to bring into the house. An orange tabby took a shine to me. She wound herself around my legs, meowed and let me pick her up to scratch behind her ears and cuddle her while she purred. I named her Marmalade.

One afternoon while I romped with the kittens, Mother called, "Mary, get back in here. Times a wasting, no time for you to be playing around. We have to get the bread started. Foolish girl. Those cats aren't going to bake bread for us."

We baked twelve loaves of bread twice a week. I liked the feel of the spongy, silky dough. Kneading was fun if I was mad at Lester or Reuben. I'd pretend I was punching them instead of the dough. Churning butter and kneading bread had made my arms and hands strong. I embarrassed Reuben when I beat him at arm wrestling. I preferred outdoor chores—feeding chickens, gathering eggs and working in the vegetable garden.

I didn't like doing laundry. We scrubbed dirty clothes on washboards in tubs filled with hot water heated over stone fire rings in the yard. I had to be careful not to get close to the fire or I might singe my skirt. The lye soap stank like wet ashes and stung my raw knuckles. After rinsing, we wrung them out. We twisted the small stuff by ourselves, but it took two of us to wring sheets, overalls and tablecloths. We hung the wet clothes on a line strung between two posts, and when there were too many things for the line, we draped them over bushes or fences. On Monday—washday —Tuesday—ironing day—we didn't do anything else. Every day we cooked, served and cleaned up after meals.

We sat around the big kitchen table three times a day. Father made Mother mad when he ate his dessert first, before the rest of his dinner. He believed you should have as much fun in this life as you could and eating dessert first was one of his pleasures.

"Henry, you set a bad example for the children. How am I supposed to teach them the right ways when you persist on doing things backwards?"

"Elizabeth, I like my pie when I'm hungry—not after I'm full of food. Children, do what your mother says and save your pie until after your meal. When you grow up you'll have the privilege of eating pie whenever you want," he said with a grin.

Evenings after prayers, we knit socks, caps, scarves and mittens. Mother taught the older boys how to knit, but Father said his hands didn't fit the needles so he read to us from the Bible or the Book of Mormon as we knitted.

Sometimes Mother and Father told us about their wagon journeys from Missouri to Salt Lake City.

Father had been ten years old and his job was to help with the horses. They could never leave the horses unguarded. Indians followed the train hoping to find a horse left untended begging to be stolen.

Hunters rode out every day to find game for the traveling village. If they returned empty handed there would be only a small ration of bread or biscuits for supper. The travelers frequently went to bed with hungry, grumbling stomachs.

The boys hunted for small animals and were told to hunt with a buddy and stay alert as to their whereabouts.

"Henry, be sure you see the cloud of dust the train makes as we move along so you can find your way back," his father told him.

Father's cousin, Sam, went hunting by himself and didn't come back. His family never knew if he'd become lost and died of starvation, had an accident or been kidnapped by Indians.

Mother told the story of her two-year-old sister, Emmy, who fell out of the family's wagon and was killed by the big wooden wheels. They buried her on a hill over looking the Platte River.

She remembered lying on the ground, wrapped in a blanket, under the wide, dark prairie sky, when a shower of falling stars lit up the night. "None of us had ever seen anything so glorious. It was beautiful and fearsome. The man in charge of our train said it was a manifestation from God that proved we were blessed and would all survive the journey," Mother said.

Finally, my mind quieted and I drifted off to sleep wondering where Arizona Territory was.

Several days later, Father called us together after supper for our daily prayers and readings. I liked his deep, clear voice. He was a robust, fair skinned man who sunburned easily so always wore a hat when outdoors. There was a hat line across his forehead—white above and reddish below. His beard was neatly trimmed and his straight black, silky hair brushed his shoulders. He stood next to the fireplace and rested his elbow on the mantel.

"Children, your mother and I have decided to move to Arizona with Uncle Bill's family. The trip will take three or four months and we aim to leave in early June. We'll sell our belongings to raise money for the trip. You may take a few personal treasures, your clothes and your bedding. It will be a hard journey, but we'll be sustained by our faith in God. We'll be helping to build the Kingdom of Heaven on Earth," Father solemnly told us.

I was jubilant and wanted to jump up and shout Halleluiah! Instead, I sat quietly, gripping one hand with the other. I was tired of housework. I wanted some excitement before I reached eighteen, got married and settled down.

After Father's announcement about our move, Mother said, "Idle hands and people who eat dessert first only serve the Devil. I guarantee there won't be any disagreements about what to eat first when we're on the trip to Arizona. We'll be lucky if we don't starve."

Chapter Two

Utah Territory, June 1885

Mother must have done a lot of praying in the next few days. She surprised me one morning by saying, "My mother told me, 'If you have to eat a frog, don't spend too much time looking at it.' Let's get on with what we have to do and not dwell on our misgivings."

Father said we could bring only a few of our belongings. It was hard to choose. I borrowed Reuben's quill pen and wrote "Mary George, Her Book" inside the front cover of my catechism book—my only book and my most precious possession. If it went astray I wanted the finder to know it was mine. I packed the button head doll Mother had made me, two everyday dresses, my Sunday dress, four sets of underwear, a coat, a sweater and two pairs of shoes. That's all. We each had a bedroll. Mother, Richard and Parley would sleep in one of our two wagons. The rest would sleep on the ground.

A family from Logan bought our place. The thought of strangers living there saddened me. I asked Father if I could bring Marmalade. "Cats don't belong to people, but to a place. If we took her, she'd try to find her way home. We don't have room or time to fool with her. What would she eat? More likely the coyotes would eat her."

I loved my father and was closer to him than to Mother, but I didn't like all his decisions. Girls and women were as smart, worked as hard and did as much for the church and family as men, but we weren't allowed to have a say or make decisions. Leaving Marmalade was the hardest part of the move. Maybe I'd get an orange striped kitten in Arizona.

Mother and Aunt Jane spent three days baking trail crackers. They were hard, tasteless and lasted for months. The church furnished a list of provisions to take. We packed dried food—fruit, vegetables and meat in gunny sacks. Flour, sugar, and salt went into barrels. Mother dried herbs, made awful tasting tonics for stomachaches, and salves for skin ailments. Father organized emergency feed for the animals and his tools. We expected to buy things we needed at settlements along the way.

The evening before we left, Uncle Bill called a meeting. He was Bishop for the move and was responsible for our moral and spiritual health. The Church provided a guidebook and map. Father and Uncle Bill told us the rules for traveling and showed us the map. Our route was marked with a black line. I crowded in between my cousins to get a look. I saw Brigham City, Ogden and Salt Lake City, all of which I'd heard of. Then came places that were new to me—Pleasant Grove, Provo, Springville, Birdseye, Pigeon Hollow Junction, Manti, Circleville, Panguitch, Orderville, Kanab and Lee's Ferry.

We'd cross the Colorado River at Lee's Ferry. It was a formidable barrier, not a gentle guide showing us the way. South of the Colorado, the map was almost blank. A few Indian settlements, vaguely marked rivers and not much else made Arizona Territory look like an empty cupboard.

We prayed for guidance and a successful journey, then bedded down next to our wagons. It was a long restless night. After a hasty breakfast, the men and boys hitched teams of mules to our four wagons. Father counted noses and we started for Brigham City where we were to meet three other families. Four young men looking for adventure would travel with us and help drive the wagons and herd the animals.

"With our worldly goods and supreme confidence in our God and cause, we depart to spend the rest of our lives in places unknown," Father pronounced.

I swallowed the lump in my throat and blinked back the tears. I wouldn't have been so scared if Marmalade had been with me.

The three-day journey to Brigham City was a picnic. What fun to be out of doors, with no floors to sweep, no laundry to scrub, or butter to churn. Making butter was easy. Mother poured our cows fresh milk into the churn, tied it to the wagon and let it slosh until butter formed. The weather was warm during the day and comfortably cool at night. Clouds floated across the sky, but no rainstorms dampened our spirits. We were in a festive mood as we traveled down the mountains into the valley.

Father brought his fiddle, Cousin Amos his banjo and the rest of us banged on pots, pans or tapped sticks together during the songfest each evening after prayers. I especially liked to sing "All is Well" and "The Battle Hymn of the Republic." I was proud to be a pioneer on a journey of discovery and adventure.

Our train grew to more than forty people and twelve wagons when we met the Smith, Richards and Selkirk families. We were a moving village. The men discussed, voted and organized the trip. They followed guidelines the Church provided for pioneers traveling to colonize the far reaches of Zion.

Captain Jack Morgan was hired to be our guide. He was rough looking and smelled of tobacco, smoke and sweat, but was friendly and took good care of his animals. Buster was a strange looking horse with dark brown spots on his tan rump. I'd never seen an Appaloosa before. Brownie was a sad looking bloodhound. He hated bears. I liked him and he often walked beside me.

For the first time I was out of the mountains and could see them. I couldn't keep my eyes off the rock walls, high peaks, cliffs and canyons of the Wasatch Range. The shifting cloud shadows, changing colors, and silver, tumbling streams were dreamlike. I'd been transported into a book of wondrous fairytales. When my chores were done, I liked to walk away from the hustle and bustle of camp and daydream of what other magnificent things I might see in the coming months.

When I turned away from the mountains, the Great Salt Lake glistened in the afternoon light.

Why is it here? Why is it salty? I wish I could swim in it. I've heard you can lie on the water and float with no effort, but the boy who told me is a big tease so I don't believe him.

I was overwhelmed with my smallness as I stood at the bottom of that bowl of beauty between sky, mountains and lake.

After three days in Brigham City we headed south. Mother insisted I wear a sunbonnet to protect my complexion. My dress had long sleeves and a skirt that reached my shoe tops. I wanted to dress the way the boys and men did, but Mother said I mustn't forget I was a girl. Even though we were on the trail, we would be ladylike. She always looked clean and crisp with nary a hair out of place or sunburn on her nose. Every evening she spread a tablecloth over our portable plank table as if we were in town—not traveling through the boondocks.

I envied Sister Selkirk and her girls. They wore a new kind of garb called bloomer dresses. A short knee length skirt covered a pair of bloomers gathered at the waist and ankles. The Selkirk girls straddled a horse with ease.

We aimed to travel ten to fifteen miles a day, with Sundays off for rest and worship. I helped with my little brothers, made bread and did laundry, but they were fun when done out of doors. Everyone, except babies, toddlers and the sick had jobs.

Mother didn't feel well and spent most of her time resting in the wagon.

How can she rest in the relentlessly jostling wagon? Is she in the family way again? I hope not. Parley's weaned, so I watch for signs she's having her monthly. She and Father aren't sleeping together so maybe there'll be a breather from babies for a while.

She made a back sling for Parley so I could carry him when he wasn't napping. He was eight months old and after I'd carried him for five miles, felt like he weighed a hundred pounds

While I walked, I remembered his birth.

That afternoon a cold wind raced down from the mountains. Heavy gray clouds scurried across the sun and the sharp cold air stung my nose and made my eyes water while I hurried to the pasture and herded our three milk cows into the barn. I coaxed the chickens in with the cows so they wouldn't freeze in the drafty chicken coop. A snowstorm swallowed our valley and I was alone in the house with Mother and three little brothers. Father, Lester and Reuben were in the canyon with Uncle Bill and his boys cutting firewood. Before they left they knew a storm threatened, but thought they'd be home before dark. We had plenty of wood in the wood box, buckets of water in the pantry and food in the kitchen. Surely the storm would let up by morning. There was no hint of what was to come.

Before supper, Mother said, "Mary, the baby's coming. You'll help deliver this child. Do what I say and all will be well. You're eight years old and it's time you had a sister." We knew the baby was due soon, but there'd been no sign her time was at hand. There was no way to get to Aunt Jane's. I'd get lost in the white out once I stepped off the porch.

I fed William, Roy and Richard and put them to bed. I'd watched when Richard was birthed, but Aunt Jane had been in charge. This time I was on my own and was as scared as a tenderfoot on a runaway horse. I said a "Lord help us" prayer and took a deep breath.

We gathered the clean flour sacks, old towels and sheets Mother had prepared. I heated water and scalded the bread bowl to use as a wash basin. Mother put on a loose fitting gown.

We sat near the stove while she read aloud from a book of poems. At ten o'clock she lay down on her bed. As Mother's pains came closer and harder, my heart pounded and the palms of my hands were both icy and sweaty.

I am about to deliver a baby. I'm barely eight and I've never done this before. God, help me do this right.

Near midnight I saw the top of its head and prepared to catch the baby. After one more contraction, he was born. I wrapped him in a warm blanket, held him close and sighed with relief when he took a breath. He looked right at me and grabbed my thumb. I put him on Mother's belly and, following her instructions, I cut the cord. Next I made sure his mouth was clear, washed him in warm water in the bowl, wrapped him in a clean towel and lay him beside Mother. She delivered the afterbirth.

My parents had decided if it was a boy he would be named Parley Parker after two church leaders.

When I have a boy, I'll name him Parley. I'll choose a different middle name though because Parley Parker sounds old-fashioned.

After we cleaned up, I fell asleep on my cot. The next thing I knew Mother and Aunt Jane were talking quietly in the brightly lit room. The sun reflecting off the snow told me the storm had passed. Aunt Jane had snowshoed over and was surprised to find Mother with a baby in her arms.

Two days later the woodcutters returned. Aunt Jane invited us to supper and everyone celebrated the birth of another strong boy. I was proud I'd helped bring him into the world, but why couldn't he have been a she? Even if we never had another girl, I thought it was time for Mother to stop having babies.

When I spoke my opinion, everyone laughed, and Father said, "Mary, one day you'll learn it doesn't work that way."

As I walked the trail with Parley on my back, I thought about my life.

When I get married things will be different in my house. I won't have so many children. Mother's only twenty-six but she acts old and tired all the time. She makes me feel I'm to blame for her unhappiness.

For the first time I had friends my own age. When Sarah, Rhoda, Roxie and I were free, we walked together. We sang, gathered wild flowers, tossed stones into the creeks, giggled and talked about which boys we liked and which ones we detested. We thought Josh Blake was the handsomest of the wagon drivers. He was too old for us, but my, he had the most beautiful green eyes and thick dark lashes. My cousin Amy set her bonnet for him.

One afternoon, after setting up camp, Mother asked, "Mary, want to walk with me? The boys are napping and I feel like stretching my legs."

We looked for mushrooms in shady damp places, skipped stones across a pond and speculated about Arizona. She laughed at my wishes to have lots of kittens and talked about the big pretty house we'd have. I always loved Mother, but even more so when she was playful and happy. She skipped and chattered like a blue jay with a full pinecone.

Even when she was playful and happy I felt uneasy. I never knew how she'd react, so I watched her carefully to guess what kind of mood she was in so I wouldn't get a tongue-lashing. When I did something really dumb, like knocking over a pail of milk or letting the coals on top of the dutch oven go out I knew I was in for it.

"Mary George, when will you learn to pay attention to your job? You are careless, lazy and stupid!" She slapped my face, stalked to the wagon and wouldn't speak to me for two days. She was either as high as a hawk soaring between shadow and sun in the canyon dawn or deep in a dark well of despondency.

I asked Aunt Jane, "Why does Mother get so upset over every little thing? I never please her. Something must be wrong with me."

"Mary, you ask a question we've never answered. She's always been touchy and easily angered. It's not your fault, honey," she said as she hugged and held me while I cried into her abundant bosom.

The country changed. From a distance the low, round hills were golden mounds of velvety pillows. As we came closer, we found they were dry and rocky—not velvety. Stickery, prickly grass and shrubs caused their color. We had to feed the animals some precious oats. For three days while crossing the mountains south of Provo we had no fresh water. The water in our barrels ran low. It was our first taste of hardship. As we descended into Long Valley that runs through the center of Zion, I saw the welcoming, silvery ribbon of the Sevier River.

"Elizabeth, we're going to camp here for several days. We'll fish, hunt, and rest the animals and ourselves. It'll give you and Mary time to wash bedding and clothes. All are in need of a bath. If we catch a mess of fish, we'll have a fine supper of fried trout. We'll smoke and dry some to take along," Father said.

"It'll be nice to be under the trees next to the river," Mother replied. "I'm so jostled by the wagon that I dream about it at night, even after we've stopped moving. How many more days 'til we reach Orderville? I look forward to visiting my Cousin Ionia and her family. I wonder how the United Order is doing."

"Two more weeks to Orderville. The Order is having a rough time. Many folks are disillusioned. They want to keep the fruits of their labor for their own families. They feel their efforts benefit the layabouts who don't work at all. It didn't succeed in Missouri forty years ago and it's not going to work here. Young men are leaving the settlements for the silver mines at Pioche or Silver Reef. They're of the age when they want more for their labor than a few dollars a month in credit at the Church storehouse," Father said.

Before we unloaded, the wind picked up; towering dark-bottomed, white-topped clouds raced toward us. The men and boys rushed to secure the animals. I gathered the little ones and handed them to Mother in the wagon. Father, Lester, Reuben and I climbed into the other wagon where we joined a crate of four hens and a rooster. They clucked and scolded as the wagon rocked. We hunkered down and prayed for the best as hailstones danced on the billowing fabric wagon covering. Thunder and lightening skipped and played around us sounding like echoes of mountain avalanches.

Mother is like this skittish storm. One minute she's sunny, the next angry and lashing out, then she'll weep buckets of tears. Her moods rise like a towering white thundercloud while her under self darkens and drenches us. Most women aren't like her. Aunt Jane is calm and loving. Sister Taylor and others laugh off their discomforts and disappointments. Why is Mother the way she is?

The storm moved on. We climbed from the wagons, fearful of storm damage. Instead we saw a beautiful double rainbow. It was late afternoon, and the sun coming from behind the racing clouds shone from the west. The colors in the front bow were sharp and strong, while its echo was soft and pale. It was God's sign that he was with us and our journey would continue with ease and end in success.

The men strung a wide fishing net across the river. Boys went upstream and with sticks beat on the water to drive trout into the net. All the whooping, hollering, and splashing made me want to leave the laundry and jump into the river. When the net was hauled in, we gathered to see what had been caught. The rainbow trout flipped and flapped, gasping in the unexpected air. I felt sorry for the pink and silvery creatures as their wet bodies shone in the sun. They had gleaming white bellies, dark green backs and crimson gills. Their backs and upper sides were sprinkled with black spots like glossy polka dots on a pretty dress. They thrashed about until the men put them out of their misery with fish knockers. Their colors faded and they lay still.

The rainbow after the storm fed our souls and lifted our spirits and the rainbow trout provided food for our bodies. The fried fish were delicious and I thanked the Lord for his bounty. I also said a quick "Thank you, God" prayer because that morning I'd seen Mother rinse out the special cloths she used for her monthly.

"Father, Father," Lester hollered the next morning as he ran toward the men at the fish drying racks. "Come quick. One of the goats wandered into quick sand. Reuben tried to rescue the kid and now he's sinking too." We raced toward Reuben's shouts and the goat's bleating. The men carried the wood planks we use for tables and benches to the edge of the river.

"Lay them planks in a double line aimed to where Reuben is thrashin' round," Captain Jack ordered. "Push 'em out side by side. Then push the next two. That'll reach. I'll ease out on my belly and grab him afore he goes under."

We cheered when Captain Jack grabbed Reuben by the hand, tugged mightily and pulled him onto the boards. Reuben crawled to safety. The Captain squirmed farther out and caught the kid by a limp fore leg. The mucky, sandy, ungrateful goat kicked and bleated while they scooted back to solid ground.

I was glad Reuben hadn't been sucked under. He didn't tease and torment me like Lester did.

That evening Captain Jack lectured. "It's easy to pertect you'ns, yer chillern and yer animules from quicksand if'n you know what to look for. So you'all won't get the heebie-jeebies next time you come across this siteation I'm gona tell how to handle quicksand."

He was a tall, weathered, ex-trapper mountain man. His light brown scraggly beard was stained dark brown from the tobacco juice he spat out of the side of his mouth. There was more hair on his face than his head. A fringe of shoulder length, gray-brown hair hung below his big floppy brimmed leather hat. We saw his shiny pate when he took his hat off to go to sleep. It was whispered he had an Indian wife and children in Idaho.

"Quicksand happens when water seeps into sand just below the top. The sand looks dry but is slippery and boggy as hell when you, a critter or a wagon move onter it."

My friends and I giggled at his rough, profane language. He was the first gentile I'd met. We were not to curse or take the name of the Lord in vain, but we excused him because we needed him. Besides, he told astonishing stories around the campfire after prayers.

"If'n you specalate you've come to a batch a'quicksand, take a pole and test out the area afore you go trompin out onto it. Don't be a God damned fool and think it'll never happen to you. Push the pole down into the sand and get the feel of the siteation. If the pole slips lickey split down inter the sand and water seeps out round the pole it's mighty dangerus an stupid as hell for you to cross. If you or your critters get trapped keep movin as fast as a fox chasin' a chicken. When you stop and gawp round you commence to sink. A critter'll freeze up, start sinkin', begin to struggle, which makes em sink faster'n a rock in a rain barrel. If you need to rescue a person or animule frum quicksand, do as you saw me do today. If you can, tie a line onto the person or animule it'll help to haul'em out'a the trap."

When Mother came to say goodnight, she said, "I'm anxious to see Ionia, but even more I look forward to sitting in a real chair at a real table. Maybe I'm not cut out to be a pioneer woman!"

Was Mother trying to tell me she knows how difficult she can be?

Chapter Three

Orderville, Utah Territory, July 1885

Three days later we came to our first river crossing. Deep wheel ruts, campfire remains and rock shelters along the banks were signs of others who'd crossed.

"Should we camp here and cross in the morning?" Uncle Bill asked Captain Jack.

"No si-ree, Mr. Bill! We're goin' over today. If we stop now, it'd be our luck that there'd be a storm on them peaks tonight. The water'd flow down, raise the river over its banks an we'd be stuck as tight as a ring on a fat widders finger for days."

Captain Jack walked into the shallows and tested the sandy bottom with a long pole while we lightened the wagons by unloading Mother's two burner iron cook stove, pots and pans, tools and guns onto the rocky beach. I, with others, stayed behind while the wagons crossed. They took the elderly, the sick and women with babies and toddlers on the first trip.

The hard-working mules pulled the big wagons into the river. Water reached the tops of the wheels and swirled round the wagons. When the herders drove the animals into the water, the noise was deafening. The cows mooed, the goats bleated and the horses pranced with pleasure. The cattle and goats were frightened, but I found it as exciting as the frolicking horses did.

Eight wagons returned for us and our belongings. By the time we crossed and got everything stowed away, the sun was behind the mountain and a welcome cool breeze brushed my hot face. The women had cooked supper and we were hungry. All were pleased the crossing had gone well.

The next morning before we rolled out, I stood and listened to the river singing its glad gurgling song as it rushed over its rocky bed.

Goodbye, good friend river. I enjoyed camping beside you, eating your fish, bathing in and drinking your cool mountain water. Will I ever see you again?

The farther south we traveled, the hotter and drier it got. Rock formations along the trail confirmed we'd left the mountains and meadows of Cache County and Long Valley behind. Great heaps of sandstone boulders lay on the hills as if giants had tossed huge red, pink, orange, tan, and black striped rock candy around while playing a game.

One evening Uncle Bill announced, "Day after tomorrow we'll reach Orderville. Those with relatives may stay in the compound with them. Across the trail from the main gate is a meadow for our use and corrals for the animals. Our women and girls will help prepare and serve meals in the communal kitchen and do laundry in the washhouse. We'll be eating, worshipping and visiting with our fellow Saints for three or four days—a nice break in our journey."

As we approached Orderville, the trail wound through fields of corn, beans, carrots and other vegetables. Orchards were heavy with fragrant ripe peaches. Laden trees showed the promise of a bountiful harvest of apples and pears. There was a small vineyard with bunches of ripening grapes hanging from the vines supported by frames. The valley was akin to Eden before the fall.

I spotted a field of green striped watermelon. My mouth watered and I nearly keeled over with yearning. A melon had broken open and a flock of ravens pecked away with rapturous abandon. Their yellow eyes gleamed with pleasure. I wanted to run into the field and join them.

In contrast with the dull muddy colored desert, the fertile green fields and orchards were luminous under the searing mid-summer sun.

"Mother's going to enjoy her visit with Ionia. I've seen her laughing and chatting with Father as her anticipation grows," I said to William as he trudged beside me.

A line of tall Mormon trees planted for windbreak grew around the village. The slim, soaring poplars with their fluttering, dancing leaves marked most Mormon settlements. When we rounded a bend in the trail and saw

Orderville, it was a disappointment after the beauty we'd passed through. A high weather-beaten, brown, plank fence surrounded the compound. The gate was open and a crowd waited for us. Captain Jack led the way to the wagon park and corrals.

"Dag nab it, don't everbody get flummoxed and stop in the middle of the road. Keep movin' 'till the wagons are where I direct them to stop. Boys, get the animals into the corrals. Make sure the troughs are full of water. Stop gawkin' round and snap to it! Your friends and relatives ain't goin nowhere. Nowhere to go to round here anyway!"

The people of Orderville were as excited to have company as we were to arrive. Mother spotted a familiar face, stood, waved her hanky and called out, "Jeb, Jeb, where's Ionia?"

The wagon moved. Father grabbed her arm, "Sit down, Elizabeth. Don't fall. Be patient a bit longer."

By the time we settled the animals and secured our wagons Mother was beside herself with anticipation. "I wonder why Ionia didn't come to wave us in. Maybe she's feeling poorly or was busy cooking supper."

We crossed the trail and went through the gate into the unique place. Family quarters lined three sides of the compound. The back wall of each unit was part of the outside fence. Each family had its own sitting room, bedrooms and storage but none had their own kitchen, outhouse or laundry. In the center of the green lawn was a large building with a flagpole in front. Two flags, the Beehive flag of Zion and a United States flag, fluttered in the breeze. Mulberry trees shaded the walkways to the family quarters and central dining hall.

Mother saw Jeb Reid in his doorway with a baby in his arms. "Oh my, that must be why Ionia didn't come to meet us," Mother said as she ran across the grass. "Another fine child, Jeb. A boy or a girl? Where's Ionia?"

Father stopped short and held us back when he saw Jeb's expression. Tears rolled down Jeb's face as he told Mother of Ionia's death after childbirth.

"Stay here, children." He walked toward Mother with Parley on his hip.

Mother put her hands over her face and lowered her head. "Oh, no," she moaned.

Father put his arm around her, but she shrugged it away. She sobbed for a minute, wiped her eyes with her hanky and raised her tear-streaked face. She clenched her fists, narrowed her eyes and glared at Father.

"Ionia is dead. Childbirth is dangerous enough without being out here in the middle of nowhere. Men! All they think about is their posterity and what's in their pants."

Father turned to Jeb. "Don't listen to Elizabeth. She's sorry about your loss. It's her grief and frustration talking. She's apprehensive about going to Arizona. Let's take a look at the little one. Boy or girl?"

" Ionia wanted to name her after herself," Jeb replied as he placed baby Ionia into Mother's open arms.

"How're you managing, Jeb? How're you feeding her?" Mother asked. smiling at the bundle in her arms. Her anger had evaporated as quickly as it had erupted, but the glint in her eyes told me there was more to come.

"Last year I took a second wife, Melly, who gave birth to our first child a month ago. She has more than enough milk for two. My five older ones are good helpers, so we're doing well."

Many Orderville families were polygamous. I'd heard the grownups talk about plural families. I didn't like being a secret listener, but grownups never talked to me about important things such as why some men have more than one wife, so I kept still and listened.

Some men with plural wives were arrested and others went into hiding. I was glad Father had only one wife and didn't have to run away to keep from being sent to prison.

"How does any man contend with more than one wife? Some have three or four. Elizabeth and our brood are enough for me. The Church must change this teaching. I feel sorry for the women and children who're left without the support and comfort of a husband and father when a man goes into hiding. Some plural families have fled to Mexico," Father said, while shaking his head in bewilderment.

A bell rang. The adults moved toward the dining hall. Two young women approached my parents. The one in a brown dress took Parley from Father and asked us to go with them. I couldn't believe my eyes. They both looked the same, with long silver blonde braids, pale blue eyes and freckled noses. Their dresses were identical except for their color—brown and blue. I'd heard of identical twins but had never seen any.

"Hello, I'm Ollie and this is my twin sister Allie," the one in blue said. "We're assigned to show you around, tell you about supper and take you to the children's center."

I was apprehensive about Mother and wanted to stay with her. She'd been excited and happy for the last week. How would she react to Jeb's sad news? Would she crash down like a boulder in a landslide?

Father gestured to me to leave. Ollie took Richard and Roy by the hand, Allie carried Parley, the rest of us followed. They led us to a building with a sign above the door that said CHILDREN'S CENTER. Next to the center was a playground where four, five and six year olds ran, played and chased each other. There were two swings, a teeter-totter and a climbing set covered with lively, noisy children. William and Roy skipped over to join the fun while the two little ones and we older ones went into the center. A woman took Parley from Allie and scooped Richard up from the floor where he'd plopped down. His two-year-old legs could toddle only so far. They went through the door at the back of the room.

"This is the school room during the day," Ollie told us. "We'll sit and enjoy a story while we wait 'till time for us to eat. The toddlers and babies will be fed, washed and put to bed in the nursery, so don't worry about them."

I spotted an empty desk in the corner. A real school desk! Not benches like the others sat on. I made a beeline for it. I'd never sat at a desk. Wouldn't it be great if there was a school with desks in St. Johns? My, it felt good. I wondered what the big rolled up thing at the front of the room was. Sarah and Roxie sat by the window.

"Before we start, will some of you tell us about yourselves, your names, where you're from and where you're headed?" Allie pulled something down out of the roll hooked to the blackboard. I gaped in astonishment. A map of the United States rolled down right before my eyes. With a pointer Allie showed us Utah and Orderville and asked if one of us would come to the front. Daniel Richards introduced himself, traced our route, and asked, "How come we don't eat with our parents?"

"I know you're hungry," Ollie answered. "There's not room in the dining hall for everybody at the same time. Teenagers and children eat after the grownups finish even when we don't have company. You'll hear the bell ring when it's time for us. Don't worry, there's plenty of food. Any one else want to introduce themselves?"

I stood and said, "I'm Mary George from Mendon, near Logan. This is the first time I've been in a real classroom and sat at a real desk. Thank you for having us." Mother had taught us to mind our manners.

At the teacher's desk Allie commenced to read aloud from a book about a man and his servant, Friday, stranded on a desert island. The sound of her soft steady voice, the warm room and the excitement of the day made me sleepy. I put my head down on the desk and dozed off.

The next thing I knew the second bell was ringing. As we walked to the dining hall, I caught up with Sarah and Roxie.

We found a place on a bench beside a table. Ollie, Allie and several others shepherded the younger ones to child-sized tables at the side of the room. A tall man with red-hair and beard said grace. Girls, who were kitchen helpers for the day, brought large bowls and plates of food to the tables. The tables were smooth polished wood decorated with vases of red Indian Paintbrush and blue Lupine wildflowers. Salt and pepper shakers, a plate of butter, and jars of jelly and preserves stood next to the flowers. Each place was set with a shallow bowl, a cup and utensils.

Food bowls were passed around family style. The stew, light bread and cherry pie were as delicious as they had smelled. The cool fresh milk tasted wonderfully good. Our milk cow, Susie, had almost stopped giving milk and the little we got from her was for the toddlers and babies. We were thankful to God for his bounty and for the Saints who were treating us like honored guests. I enjoyed the meal even though I had a niggle of worry about Mother.

After supper everyone gathered on the lawn. I hadn't seen Captain Jack since we left the wagon park. Where had he eaten his supper? Their Bishop (the man with red hair) welcomed us, told of the plans for work and play the next four days and led us in prayer. After hymn singing, we were dismissed.

Father collected us while Mother went to the children's center to get Parley and Richard. "We've decided to bed down by the wagons. Jeb's place is full with his five children, Mellie and the two babies. We'll be better guests if we don't crowd in."

I dreamed Father and Mother were talking in strained urgent voices. They seemed to be far away and I could barely hear. I gradually woke and realized they were talking near the embers of the campfire. I kept my eyes shut and listened to their troubled voices.

"I want Ionia's baby. Jeb and Mellie have enough on their plate without another infant to care for. Mellie's only nineteen and has a baby of her own. They don't need another girl. I want that baby girl," Mother said with a peculiar pitch to her voice.

She sounded like a five-year-old begging for a doll. Why did she think Jeb would give away his daughter? Her voice shook and grated like a windmill needing some grease.

"Elizabeth, stop and think what you're saying. I'm sure our next will be a sister for Mary," Father said as he reached to touch Mother's shoulder.

"Don't touch me! I will never go through childbirth again. Look what happened to Ionia. We're going into the wilderness where there's no medical help for hundreds of miles. I lie awake dreading the rest of this foolish trip. Men! You know nothing of women's fears and anguish," Mother said as she stood and paced around the clearing. Her quiet sharp voice displayed her deep fear and anger.

"Jeb told me that in August he's moving his family to St. George. Mellie's parents are there and will help them get settled. The child is loved and well cared for. We can't always have what we want, Elizabeth. You know that." He stood and tried to bring Mother back to the dying fire.

"I told you don't touch me, Henry. Why can't we stay here and then go to St. George with Jeb and Mellie? There's a Temple, it's a growing town that can use carpenters, and the children could go to the Church academy all the way through high school. Henry, I beg you to abandon this crazy Arizona scheme."

"My mind is set. I've prayed. I've given my word. We will continue as planned. I'll hear no more of your foolish chatter. Go to bed, woman, compose yourself and thank God for your blessings. Morning comes early and you and Mary are scheduled to do laundry tomorrow."

Mother was hurting. Why couldn't Father see how splintered she was—like a brittle old broom handle that'll break the next time it's used? What could I do? I was young but I saw what was happening to Mother. I thought adults knew what to do. If they didn't know how to live and do things right, then who was in charge? They told me to go to God and tell my problems to him but I never got any answers—none from God and none from grownups.

I awoke to hear roosters encouraging the sun to rise and saw the first blush of day in the sky. Aunt Jane was shaking me, saying, "Mary, time to rise and shine. Where's your mother?"

"Isn't she in the wagon with Parley?"

"No, your father can't find her. I thought maybe she told you last evening that she was going on one of her walks or start the laundry early. Don't worry, she'll turn up soon."

No telling what Mother's doing or where she's gone. Should I tell Aunt Jane what I overheard last night? Maybe it'd be better to keep quiet and let the adults handle it. Father might be dismayed if he learned I heard their talk and then blabbed about it.

Aunt Jane came and helped my little brothers dress and wash the sleep out of their eyes. I took them to the outhouse for their morning visit and then we walked to the compound for breakfast.

Ollie and Allie were at the door to take the little ones to their tables; Aunt Jane took Parley and Richard to the children's center, and I found a place at a table beside my friends.

"Tomorrow we're scheduled to help serve and clean up, so we'll have to get up extra early in order to be here by five," Roxie told me.

"They sure are organized around here," Rhoda said. "My father says the way they schedule every little thing it's like being in the Army."

While my friends giggled about the cute boy sitting at the end of our table, I fretted about Mother. We were served pancakes and fresh eggs, which were favorites of mine, but they didn't sit well in my belly. I felt a cannonball rolling around in my stomach

When I returned to the wagons, Aunt Jane was waiting for me. We gathered both families' dirty clothes and linens. "Let's go to the laundry room, Mary, and get this load started. We should get it washed and hung to dry by early afternoon and then you can have free time."

"I'm worried about Mother. Are any of her things missing?"

"Mary, I know you're concerned. You're a good child and a blessing to your parents. I'm sorry you have to take on so much at your age. We have no news yet. Put down that sack of clothes so I can give you a hug."

The laundry room, on the outside of the west wall of the compound, was a marvel and I welcomed the distraction. There was a tall round metal boiler with a wood-burning heater at the bottom. Cold water was brought to the top of the cylinder by a set of hand pumps at the windmill powered well. Along each wall were shallow slanted narrow tubs—one for hot wash water and one for cold rinse water. We put our dirty things in the washtub, added soap slivers and opened the valve that carried hot water into the tub through a pipe. There were four hand-turned cranks along the length of the tub. Each handle was attached to a paddle in the tub that flipped and flopped our things over and under. We cranked and cranked until our things were clean, then Aunt Jane pulled the plug at the lower end of the tub. The dirty water rushed out through another pipe into a ditch that took the waste water to one of the irrigation ditches.

We picked up the clean clothes and dumped them into the rinse tub that was filled from the cold-water tank. At the end of the rinse tub was a strange contraption with two wooden rollers. "How does this work?" Aunt Jane asked a woman who came to start her laundry.

"That's Brother Crosby's contraption to help wring out your wet clothes. He also rigged up the water system. I'll show you how it works," she said as she picked up the end of a wet sheet with one hand and started turning the rollers with the other. She fed the sheet in between the rollers the excess water squeezed out and dropped back into the tub. "Be sure to keep your fingers back from the rollers unless you want flat fingers!" she joked.

"My goodness that looks like fun! Mary, turn the handle while I feed the clothes through. When we get a basketful we'll hang them on the lines, then come back and get the rest," she told me. "They'll dry fast on a sunny day like this."

When we finished and my mind wasn't occupied with laundry, I thought about Mother and didn't feel sunny. *Where was Mother? Where had Captain Jack and Brownie gone? People kept disappearing.*

The bell rang calling adults to dinner. "Mary, go to the children's center until your bell rings. We'll collect the dry clothes later," Aunt Jane said.

I didn't want to go to the center and be around a bunch of noisy kids. I was on the edge of tears and needed to be alone. I went to Mother's wagon.

I had to settle my thoughts. Everything was skitty wampus and I was angry. I felt both guilty and ashamed about being mad.

I closed the canvas cover and lay down on Mother's blankets. I smelled the fragrance of her lavender soap, picked up one of her books of poetry and held it against my cheek. She had marked "Evangeline" with a slip of paper and the tattered book fell open at that place. I began reading—

"This is the forest primeval. The murmuring pines and the hemlocks,
Bearded with moss, and in garments green, indistinct in the twilight."

My eyes misted and I couldn't see the words. *It was stupid. Big girls didn't cry. I was almost nine and should be able to handle whatever the day brought. Before nightfall Mother would wander in from wherever she'd been and wonder what all the fuss and feathers was about. Other times she left she came home before dark.*

I wiped my eyes on my sleeve and idly leafed through the pages of the leather-bound book. I found a section she'd underlined.

"Fair was she and young; but, alas! Before her extended,
Dreary and vast and silent, the desert of life, with its pathway
Marked by the graves of those who had sorrowed and suffered before her,
Passions long extinguished and hopes long dead and abandoned,
As the emigrant's way o'er the Western desert is marked by
Camp-fires long consumed, and bones that bleach in the sunshine.
Something there was in her life incomplete, imperfect, unfinished;
As if a morning of June, with all its music and sunshine,
Suddenly paused in the sky, and, fading, slowly descended.

How did Mr. Longfellow know how Mother felt?

The bell rang calling me to dinner, but I wasn't hungry. I dozed and woke when my cousin, Amy, the one who's sweet on Josh Blake, banged on the wagon. "Mary, Mary, are you in there? Mother sent me to find you. She needs help with the clothes."

I opened the canvas, climbed down and walked to the clotheslines with her. "Look at your eyes. They're all red and swollen and you have tear streaks on your cheeks. Here, I'll dip my hanky into this bucket of water so you can wipe your face. My mother's upset enough about her sister without having you blubbering around."

"Have you heard where Captain Jack is?" I asked, trying to change the subject.

"Yesterday, after we got the wagons and stock settled, I overheard him talking to my father. He asked if he could go off by himself since we don't need him right now. The way he talks makes me laugh."

He said "You don't need me right now and there's too much civilizin' goin on round here. I'd like to head up the canyon and check out some of the lakes and cricks up yonder. See if any beavers are paddlin' in a pond."

In spite of my worries, her imitation of Captain Jack made me smile.

"Father told him go ahead, but to be back by tomorrow so he could help us prepare to move on."

"At least he's accounted for. I miss having Brownie snuffling around. He has a nose that sucks up smells like a pancake sucks up syrup. Any word about my mother?" I asked dispiritedly.

"Nothing yet." She put her arm around me.

"Don't do that. I'll start to cry again," I said, and shoved her arm away. "Leave me alone and let's get on with the clothes."

The afternoon waned, dusk settled into the valley, night fell and there was no sign of Mother. The search parties returned and after supper went quietly to bed. There were no words to describe our feelings, so we didn't try.

I lay in my bedroll under the night sky and watched meadows of stars shift and move in their summertime pattern. Sleep didn't come until I started reciting the beginning of "Evangeline" and felt Mother's presence hover over me. *I couldn't bear the thought of life without her. I promised to be a better helper, a more cheerful daughter and never complain about doing the laundry again. Please, God, bring her back to us.*

In the morning, search parties prepared to go out again. "Wish we had Brownie to guide us," Father said. "Mary, you help Aunt Jane with your brothers, keep up your hopes and remember I'm counting on you to hold together. This is no time for hysterics, tears or despair."

I was glad it was my day to help in the kitchen and dining hall. I wouldn't have time to brood. While setting the tables for supper, I heard a commotion outside. Aunt Jane rushed in, grabbed my hand and said, "Mary, come quick. Josh Blake's just come from the sawmill with news of your mother."

I ran out of the compound and found Josh standing next to his lathered horse. His arm around Amy's shoulder. A crowd gathered to hear the news. "I went with a logging crew to fell trees. We were gone two nights. This morning the mill foreman told me a woman stopped in yesterday noon and asked for a glass of water. He said she acted strangely. She said she wasn't lost and didn't want any help. After she left, they found a blue flowered sunbonnet on the bench where she'd rested.

"Before we got back to the sawmill, a mountain man on an Appaloosa with a bloodhound dog stopped by. The dog sniffed the bonnet. The man thought it looked like one worn by a woman in the train he's guiding. He tied the bonnet to his saddle horn and headed down the trail to Orderville. When I caught up with Captain Jack he was leading Buster by the reins while Sister George rode astride and Brownie ambled behind.

"The Captain told me to ride ahead and tell you folks she's all right. She's got a sprained ankle, some scratches and bruises from a fall and seems dazed. They'll be here shortly."

"Wherever has she been and why did she go off by herself?" Aunt Jane asked.

"You'll have to ask her and Captain Jack. I came as quick as I could to ease your minds. Now I've got to cool off my horse and get him some water. Come on, Amy, it'll give us time to talk and make plans."

What are Amy and Josh planning? Things are happening so fast I feel I'm caught inside one of my brothers spinning tops. The important thing is that mother's safe. Too bad Father isn't here to get the good news. He'll be surprised, relieved and pleased to learn his wife was back in the fold. Will he be just a bit angry?

When the sun edged toward the peaks west of the valley we saw Captain Jack, Mother and Brownie coming down the trail. Mother was sitting astride the horse with her skirts hiked up to her knees. A stick splint was tied on her right ankle with Captain Jack's red neckerchief. Her braids were undone and

35

her hair was full of sticks and twigs. Her face and arms were dirty, and deep scratches showed through her bloody torn dress.

"Now, now the best thing to do is get Mrs. George off Buster, give her a hot bath an' put her to bed," Captain Jack said to Aunt Jane. "Here you go, ma'am, seein's how you're her sister you take over. Me, Buster an Brownie've done our part. No questions now. The three of us are gonna go to the creek and take a bath. Later, after everyone's gathered, I'll tell my story. Don't want to say it more than once."

"Take her to my place," Jeb said. "Jane and Mellie can tend to her."

Aunt Jane told me, "Mary, go to the dining hall and ask for a bowl of hot broth, bread and butter. Bring it to Jeb's quarters."

Why hadn't she said anything? Her eyes were blank and her face was as empty as a food cellar in May. What was wrong with her?

Chapter Four

Orderville, Utah Territory, July 1885

I brought the broth and bread. Aunt Jane poured a dark syrup into the broth from a medicine bottle. "What's that syrup?" I asked.

"It'll make her sleep and ease the pain from her cuts, bruises and wrenched ankle. She hasn't said anything, but I know she's tired and hurting. We've bathed her, put her into a clean nightie and doctored her cuts. She'll be better by tomorrow but, for a time, will need help walking. Go to supper and be ready for a surprise at gathering time this evening."

What surprise? Did it have something to do with Josh and Amy? What will father do about the trip? Will he and mother make up? He might be mad at her for the time she's wasted while they searched for her. He'll be happy she's back, but I'm beginning to learn you can have two different feelings at once. Will we stay longer? Will our group leave without us?

My mind hopped around like a drop of water on a hot skillet. I couldn't settle or solve one thing before it jumped to another.

Supper went by in a blur of talk, smells, hustle and bustle which took my mind off my troubles. Father returned to good news, but I didn't get a chance to talk to him.

After our gathering prayer, the bishop invited Josh, Amy, Aunt Jane and Uncle Bill to come forward. My cousin smiled sweetly as she came to the front wearing her nicest pink calico dress, a wreath of red and white summer flowers on her head and a small bouquet in her hands. Aunt Jane's eyes were red and she sniffled into her hanky as she and Uncle Bill walked behind Amy. Josh's hair was slicked back, his jeans were clean and his face looked solemn while his eyes sparkled. He'd asked Captain Jack to stand with him. The old mountain man was spiffed up in a clean red shirt, soft knee high beaded boots with a new eagle feather in the band of his sweat stained leather hat. He stood stiffly and self-consciously beside Josh.

I felt a wet nose nudge my hand, looked down and found Brownie beside me. I whispered into his floppy ear as I scratched his dark brown, loose skinned back, "What's going on, old feller? Thanks for helping bring Mother back to us. Is Captain Jack going to tell us the story of how you found her? Land Sakes! Josh and Amy are getting married. Never know what's going to happen next."

After the Bishop performed the short ceremony, he said they would stay in one of the vacant quarters for a short time and would go to St. George with Jeb's family. They'd be sealed for eternity in the Temple to complete their marriage vows, as all Mormon marriages should be.

I'm losing Amy. She won't be coming with us to Arizona. She's a big tease and calls me a tag along, but I love and depend on her. Losing, losing, losing. First Marmalade and my home, mother for two days and now Amy forever.

As if he sensed my sadness, Brownie laid his head in my lap, raised his droopy eyes to mine and groaned deep in his throat. "At least I still have you for a while," I murmured.

The Bishop asked Captain Jack to come forward and tell us how he and Brownie found Mother. "Wa'll, me'n Buster'n Brownie was a comin' down the trail frum the mill. I had Miz George's bonnet tied to ma saddlehorn and we just moseyed long enjoyin' the day. Brownie kept a snufflin' frum side to side along the trail and then ever onct in a while he come back to take a sniff of the bonnet.

"What are you after there, dawg? Have you picked up the smell of a bar or a mountain lion? You be sure to let me know iffen' you do so I can get ma rifle ready, I sez to Brownie.

"When he gets on the trail a some critter he'll set and howl first and then take off after it. That dawg ain't got the sense God give a goose and he ain't afeared a no critter. He's saved me many a time. Anyways, all of a sudden he sets down and commences to howl. He runs over to the top of the bank of the crik and back to me'un Buster. Does that about three er four times.

"Whut er you hollerin about? Thar ain't no animules down thar. He'd be runnin' through the briars 'n bramble on the other side by now and I don't hear a thang ceptin yore howlin'.

"Anyways, I cided I'd better take a look cause something shore had him pitchin' a conniption. I got off Buster and walked to the steep bank. I seed some broken bushes and a scrap a red cloth caught on a thorn. It was about ten feet down to the crick and a rocky ledge nex to the water. Afore I knew it Brownie scrambled down the bank and commenced to howlin' agin. I slid down to see whut the dawg'd come acrosst. Thar, on the rocks, was Miz George. She was plumb scratched up, her dress torn and her right ankle swoll up like a melon. She was a layin' on her side and looked like she was sound asleep, so I tried to rouse her. She groaned an opened her eyes fer just a minute as I turned her onto her back, but she wasn't really woke up. She was as limp as them flags up thar on the pole when thar's no wind."

Captain Jack walked to the small side table and took a long drink of water from the dipper in the water bucket before he continued. The group was quiet, listening intently. In addition to his scouting and trail skills he was a good storyteller.

"I'm not used to talkin' fer so long at one time. Alla these words are'a makin me thirsty. I need a couple a deep breaths afore I get on with it.

"Now I know ya'all don't believe in strong spirits, but I knew I had to try and get her awake an up on at least one foot or I'd never be able to get er back up that bank. Ma wife in Idaho makes the best blackberry brandy ya'd ever care to put yer tongue to an I always have a little bottle in ma jacket, only fer medicinal purposes, a course. I held her head up, put the bottle to her lips an got her to take a couple a sips. She commenced to coughin' and woke up perty good.

"Miz George an I scrabbled up the bank. I tole her she'd hafta get up onto Buster as I couldn't carry her an she sure as H couldn't walk that fur. Wall, at first she wouldn't get up on the horse, just stood an shook her head. I know she's a lady an ladies don't ride straddle a the horse but atter she tried a coupla steps on her melon ankle, she let me heft her into the saddle. While she set up thar, I took off her shoe, made a splint with a branch and bound up her ankle. She said nary a word.

"Pertty soon I heard Josh gallopin 'long, told him to get on into Orderville an let you know we was comin'. That's all I'm a gonna say as you all know the rest. Brownie, Buster an me are happy to be hepful. Now I'd like to meet with the young'uns, who'er learnin that special song fer the farewell evenin'. I'll be by the wagons under that big oak as quick as a beaver can dive down into his lodge."

I'd hoped to talk to Father about Mother, but it would have to wait. Captain Jack was teaching five of us a song to sing on our last evening in Orderville. It was the custom for visiting groups to put on an entertainment for the good people as a thank you. I liked our song and thought it'd be fun to show off, but I worried that some might think it was naughty. Captain Jack knew lots of verses that he said were too "grown up" for us and the ones he was teaching us weren't terrible. Brownie liked to join in the chorus as Captain Jack accompanied us on his mouth organ.

Some boys were reciting a poem, the women were singing two church hymns, and the men planned to give readings from the Book of Mormon. Captain Jack said we needed to lighten things up, so he taught us an old 'on the trail' song.

By the time we finished practice, it was time for bed. Aunt Jane sent Hattie to help put the boys down for the night. Hattie was Amy's younger sister and four years older than me. She had inherited Amy's job of helping. She wasn't as nice as Amy. She made no bones about not liking the extra chores.

"Mary, don't you ever get tired of all this work? I'd rather go walking with my friends or sit under a tree reading a book than always taking care of children. When I'm married I'm not going to have any children. I've cared for enough already," Hattie said grumpily as she helped Richard into his nightclothes.

That's one of the most surprising things I've ever heard! Not have children? I can't imagine a married lady choosing not to have children. I didn't know women had a choice. Some can't have children, but to say you don't want any! How can that be? Life gets more and more perplexing.

When I crawled into my bedroll I saw Father, Aunt Jane and Uncle Bill hunkered down by the campfire. I listened carefully to find out what was going on.

"Henry, I don't know if Elizabeth will be ready to travel day after tomorrow. How do the others feel about staying here longer? She still hasn't said a word. Did she respond to you when you went to see her?" Aunt Jane asked.

Father turned to his brother, "Bill, what do the others say?"

"Well, to tell it straight, they're getting restless. It will be August next week and we have at least a month of traveling to do. We've got to get to St. Johns before the end of September. Captain Jack wants to head south over the White Mountains before the first snow. He's meeting some trapper friends on the Gila and Salt rivers where beavers are still found. All are anxious to get the

Colorado River crossing under our belts and get this trip over and done with."

"Lord, I don't know what to do. When I saw her, she was awake but she turned her face to the wall and wouldn't speak. I know this move isn't what she wants, but I thought she'd come around. I can't hold up the train and I can't leave her here. Guess the only thing to do is bundle her up, put her in the wagon, watch her real close and pray for the best," Father said as he put his elbows on his knees and held his bowed head in his hands.

Aunt Jane said, "You need to talk to Mary. Poor child is having to grow up so quickly and take on a woman's tasks before she's ready. She's a sturdy child and has deep thoughts and worries, but remember, she's not yet nine years old. She needs to be told of our plans and tell her that we're willing to help. Most of all, you must tell her that you love her and none of this is her fault."

I drifted off to sleep feeling things would be okay. Maybe the grownups were in charge.

The next morning Father said, "Let's go for a walk, Mary."

We walked by the creek while Father told me the plans for the rest of the trip. While Mother rode in the wagon, Hattie and I would take turns riding with her. Aunt Jane planned to give Mother the syrup when she needed it. Jeb's son, Andy, was joining the train as wagon driver, replacing Josh.

"This isn't easy for any of us, Mary. I love and depend on you so much. Don't get discouraged and think you've done something to cause Mother's distress. It'll all work out and we'll be happily settled in our new home before you know it. Is there anything special I can do for you?" Father asked as he gave me a big hug.

"More than anything I'd like to go to school. I know Mother needs me at home, but I wish that I could go regularly. There's so much I don't know. Why are those striped boulders piled on the hills and how did they get striped to begin with? Why do some plants make us sick and others help us get well? How does a mother cow know which calf is hers?"

"I'll see what I can do. I didn't know it meant so much to you. Maybe we can hire a helper to come in a few days a week. I'll do my best. It's time for me to go to breakfast," he said as he patted my shoulder.

After breakfast we went with Captain Jack for one last practice. The boys planned to recite "The Pioneer." Sister Selkirk would be our schoolteacher in St. Johns, so she'd brought a lot of books along. Lester chose the poem from one of her books. They said it reminded them of Captain Jack and the many trails he's blazed for pioneers.

The rest of the day we did laundry, cleaned and re-packed the wagons, restocked our staples and filled the water barrels as we prepared our minds and hearts to leave that place of refreshment and refuge.

We gathered on the lawn after supper. The grownups sat on benches while we children sat on the grass. Father carried Mother, wrapped in a blanket, from Jeb's place and sat her on a chair to one side. He sat beside her and put a stool under her swollen right foot.

The program commenced with a talk by Uncle Bill. He thanked the community for all they had done to help us on our way and for the gracious way they've treated us. "The love of God shines forth from each of you and falls upon all who come your way. You are true disciples of Jesus Christ and Latter Day Saints who make Joseph Smith, in Heaven, beam upon you and your efforts."

First the women sang two songs, accompanied by Father on his fiddle and cousin Amos on the banjo. Next came six boys reciting "The Pioneers."

Long years ago I blazed a trail
Through lovely woods unknown till then
And marked with cairns of splintered shale
A mountain way for other men;

I watched Mother to see if she showed any reaction. She sat stony still, looking straight ahead. My attention returned as the boys said the last verse.

Another's name my trail may bear,
But still I keep, in waste and wood,
My joy because the trail is there,
My peace because the trail is good.

The audience applauded. They sniffled and wiped their eyes. Tears ran down the furrows on Captain Jack's face as he wiped his nose with his red bandana.

Father read passages from *The Book of Mormon* and then it was our turn.

My heart was hammering and my hands were cold and sweaty. I gripped Sarah's hand and we smiled apprehensively at each other. Each of us wore our best dress and a sunbonnet.

Maybe this wasn't such a great idea. Would Sarah, Rhoda, Roxie, Hattie and I be in trouble by the end of our song?

Captain Jack tried to reassure us, "Ever-one'll enjoy yer song. We all need some fun now'n then. Cain't be as solemn as a hangin' judge all of the time."

He introduced us. "These young divas are a gonna finish our program tonight by singin' a favorite song of the trail. It has many verses cause it's been round fer many a year and been added to by many a traveler. We've chosen four of the verses to perform fer you. I'll play along with the chorus on my mouth harp and Brownie'll chime in when the urge hits him. You all join in on the chorus while the girls do a little two step in the Irish style. I now present the 'Pike County Quintet.'"

The audience clapped while our older brother's who were glad their part was over, stood in the back and made faces to try and make us laugh. We went to the front, Captain Jack sounded a chord on his mouth organ, and we began——

Oh do you remember sweet Betsy from Pike,
Who crossed the big mountains with her lover Ike,
With two yoke of oxen, a big yellow dog,
A tall Shanghai rooster, and one spotted hog?

During the chorus the audience sang, Brownie pointed his nose skyward and howled, accompanied by Captain Jack while we girls did a hop, skip, jump dance with our arms held straight to our sides.

Singing dang fol dee dido,
Singing dang foldee day.'
They stopped at Salt Lake to inquire of the way,
Where Brigham declared that sweet Betsy should stay
But Betsy got frightened and ran like a deer
While Brigham stood pawing the ground like a steer.

I had worried about that verse, but most everyone laughed. My father frowned as he sat with his arms crossed over his chest and his hands held tightly in his armpits. That time, during the chorus, we heard "song dogs" joining in from the surrounding hills. Brownie's howling had stirred up the coyotes.

They swam wild rivers and climbed the tall peaks,
And camped on the prairies for weeks upon weeks,
Starvation and cholera, hard work and slaughter,
They reached Californy, spite of hell and high water.

During the next chorus I looked at Mother and saw her mouth moving as though she was singing along.

Good! She's aware of what's around her. Maybe she's on the mend. Only one more verse, but this is the one I'm really worried about. I've never done any thing like it.

Twas out on the prairie one bright starry night,
They broke out the whiskey and Betsy got tight,
She sang and she howled and danced o'er the plain,
And showed her bare arse to the whole wagon train.

When singing the last line we turned our backs to the group, bent forward from the waist and wiggled our bottoms. Laughter and applause erupted. They laughed so hard they could hardly sing the last chorus. We turned and joined them, Brownie howled, the 'song dogs' yipped, Captain Jack finished with a flourish and I peeked over at Mother. She had a big smile on her face and was clapping.

Thank goodness, everyone had a sense of humor. Even Father was clapping. The only dour face I noticed was the red-haired Bishop who had his hand in front of his mouth and a scowl on his brow while his eyes tried not to laugh.

The next morning Father took me aside, and said, "Mary, don't ever leave your mother alone. If you have chores to do, call someone to come be with her. We don't know if she'll try to run off again."

"What's wrong with her, Father? Why won't she talk? Her cuts are healing, her ankle looks better but there's something about her that's not right."

"If I knew the answer to your question, I'd be as wise as Solomon. We hope she'll soon come around. Maybe she hit her head when she fell or perchance she's being stubborn. She's furious with me for making this move. I pray about her every night."

How could someone look so normal and be so strange in the head? It took us away from our chores to watch her all the time. I needed my mother back. I wanted to hear her laugh.

As we prepared to leave Orderville, Ollie and Allie hugged me. "Mary, you're a smart girl and I hope you get to go to school in Arizona. If you can't go to classes, read every book you can get your hands on," Ollie said as tears glimmered in her eyes.

Amy and Josh waved and called, "Don't forget to write. You have Josh's folks box number in St. George, but we won't know yours in St Johns if you don't send it."

Father carried mother to the wagon. I got in with her and Parley and waited for our turn to pull into the line of wagons headed for Kanab. It was the first time I'd been alone with Mother since her fall.

Will she talk to me? No one's heard her talk since she came back. I want to know her side of the story. How did she end up in the creek bed? Had a wild animal scared her or did she fall while trying to cross the creek? Why did she run away in the first place? What's in the syrup Aunt Jane gives her? Makes her groggy all the time.

"Mother, I'm here to keep you company and care for Parley. Father's put a chamber pot in the corner. Ask if there's anything you need."

She made no response, lay back on the blankets, closed her eyes and dozed off. Parley was excited by the noise, movement and dust the train made as we pulled out. I thought he'd like to ride next to Andy, so we went through the canvas flap and sat on the splintery, wooden driver's seat. The wheels creaked, the wagons groaned, the drivers whipped the air over the mules' rumps and we were on our way. The older boys herded the livestock in a dusty cloud behind the train.

On the first day back on the trail, we traveled only eight miles before Captain Jack called a halt. "First day's allus a hard un an we need to get back into our routines," he said as he directed the wagons to a wide level meadow at the base of towering red rock cliffs. "Thar's a crick on the other side of the trail. You boys lead them animuls over thar to drink an then bring them back to be penned or hobbled nearby the wagons."

After the wagon stopped Mother sat up and looked more alert than she had all day. She still wasn't talking, but signaled she wanted to get out of the wagon. Following Father's instructions, I stayed right with her. She cautiously put her foot on the ground for the first time since her fall. With my help she limped to a boulder, sat down and watched us set up camp.

After supper the men in the priesthood carried Mother to a secluded hollow at the base of the cliffs.

"What're they doing?" I asked Aunt Jane as she helped me get the boys ready for bed.

"They're going to do a laying on of hands healing and a Priesthood Blessing for Elizabeth. I've seen it work many times, so I pray it helps my sister back to wholeness. You know, Mary, we aren't just a body or a mind or a soul. All three parts of us have to work together so we can be a whole person. Elizabeth's anger has taken over her soul and she needs to be brought into balance."

"Why do you keep giving her that syrup? It makes her sleep too much. What's that stuff called and since she's not hurting anymore, can we stop giving it to her?"

"We worry that she might run away again. We'll be in the desert soon and if she wanders off she'll die. This syrup is laudanum," Aunt Jane said as she showed me the amber colored medicine bottle. "If I felt she wouldn't try anything I'd stop giving it to her. It has opium in it and is a powerful sedative. Some people get addicted to it."

"What does addicted mean?"

"Well, it's like when some men always have to have whiskey or other strong spirits. Somehow your body and mind set up a craving for the stuff and you want it all the time. I'd hate to see Elizabeth have that difficulty on top of everything else. We could try giving it to her only at night and see how she does in the daytime. You'll have to be very vigilant for the next couple of days."

"I'm willing to do anything to help her," I answered, while I hugged my aunt. *I don't know what I'd do without Aunt Jane. I hope nothing ever takes her from us.*

Chapter Five

Lee's Ferry, Arizona Territory, August 1885

The burning August sun beat down as we made our way to Kanab. The wagon wheels churned up red dust that coated us like cinnamon on sticky bread dough. My lips were dry and chapped, my eyes itched and I commenced to sneeze. We longed for a summer rain, but nary a cloud was in sight.

Mother was better. She gestured for her book of poetry. After dinner she almost smiled as she settled back and dozed off. Hattie relieved me and I was free to walk. It felt good to stretch my legs and visit with Rhoda and Roxie.

"Kanab is where the trail splits," Rhoda said. "We take the left fork toward Lee's Ferry. The right fork goes west to St. George. They call the trail from Arizona to St. George the 'Honeymoon Trail,' 'cause so many newly-weds travel it to be sealed at the Temple."

"Someday one of us will travel the Honeymoon Trail with her new husband." Roxie laughed as she pointed to Andy. She was sweet on him even though she was ten and he was sixteen.

North of Kanab we climbed through pink sand hills. It was the hardest going we'd experienced. The hooves of the hardworking mules sank into the sand with each straining step. We were thankful to see the green Mormon trees when we rounded the last bend in the red cliffs.

Kanab was a Mormon settlement, but not of the United Order. Each family owned its own house in the midst of gardens and small orchards. Things were not organized as at Orderville but there was a camping area on the outskirts of town. While we started supper, Saints came from town to sell fresh fruits and vegetables. Sweet corn and red ripe tomatoes made our dried fish stew almost fit to eat.

After supper and prayers, Uncle Bill told us, "After such a strenuous day we need to remind ourselves why we're on this pilgrimage of faith. The cattle companies are trying to chase Mormon settlers out of St. Johns. The company says they are squatters and have threatened violence. Bishop Udall sent word to Salt Lake asking for a group of Saints to reinforce those who're doing the work of the Lord on the upper Little Colorado River.

"We're helping stabilize and expand the outer edges of Zion. If we persevere, have patience with the hardships of the journey and keep love in our hearts, the Lord will reward us with a piece of his kingdom here on earth. Captain Jack will tell details concerning the trail from Kanab to Lee's Ferry."

"If'n we don't have any breakdowns or mergencies, we should make Lee's Ferry in four er five days. We'll head due east and camp the first night at the base of the Kaibab Plateau. Thar's water there at Navajo Wells. The nex day'll be a hard 'un. We'll climb to travel across the edge of the plateau, but it'll be a mite cooler and there's lots a wood fer gatherin. We'll get over the plateau and down to House Rock Springs by nightfall. It'll be a long day.

"The rest a the way we'll be headen east with Vermillion Cliffs to the left and the gorge a the mighty Colorado River to the southeast. There's a couple a camps with water along the way. It's been only twelve yars since the fust wagons come this way, so while the trail's well marked it's mighty rough in places.

"Steer clear of getting water fer yerself er the animules at Soap Crik. Thar's somethin in the water that makes it taste awfull. Animules are generlly smart enough to shun it. I heerd a story about an early explorer lookin round with some Indian guides. They warned him not to use the water but he went right on and put his beans and fatback to boilin in a pot. Afore he knew it he had a pot a soap. Went hungry that night but had a good bath.

"The ferry's near where the Paria River runs into the Colorado. There's a nice open place whar it's possible to get to the river. Mr. Johnson's ferry operates frum thar. The climb on the other side is sumthin' else. We'll see how high the river's runnin', how long we have to prepare fer the crossin when we get thar. You've been a fine bunch to guide this fur. Mind what Mister Bill tells ya about bein patient. Keep yer final goal in mind and we'll come thru fine 'n dandy."

After getting the little ones and mother settled, I lay in my bedroll and looked up at the sparkling, star covered sky. Now that we were in the desert the night sky was a shining tapestry, a show, a spectacle I'd never seen before. Someone told me all those stars had names and moved in the heavens in regular pathways. I picked out the brightest ones that seemed to outline pictures then shift and form something else.

Is there a book that would teach me about the stars?

Parley said two or three new words every day. The next morning when I came from the spring with a bucket of water for Mother to wash in, I heard him prattling away and heard Mother answer. She didn't know I was standing beside the wagon. I was so happy to hear her speak that I didn't want to interrupt, but it was getting time to leave and I still had to clean up after breakfast and get our stuff stowed in the wagon.

Should I tell her I had heard her talking or pretend I didn't hear? Had she talked to Father or Aunt Jane and they hadn't told me? Questions! Questions! What to do?

I decided to keep quiet.

When the trail climbed into the pines, we smelled the scented air, listened to the song of the breeze blown trees and watch the scolding, bushy tailed squirrels run up and down, around and around the ponderosa. Mother decided to walk alongside the wagon. I helped her down as she gingerly put her right foot to the ground. She took my arm and we walked together. Parley was sleeping and Father had William, Roy and Richard with him in the other wagon. The world was bright and clean and happiness seemed possible again.

"Look at the flowers, Mother. They look like little fairy hats I saw in a picture book. I wonder what they're named?"

I waited for an answer, but she only shook her head. We walked for a while and then she signaled Andy to stop so she could get on the seat beside him.

I tried. Maybe she'll be willing to talk by evening.

When we began the descent from the plateau, everyone got out of the wagons. Going down a mountain is harder than climbing one and the drivers' worries showed on their puckered brows. They chained special brakes of heavy logs to the backs of the wagons. The wagon brakes were checked to make sure they'd work. A runaway wagon and team was disaster for animals and wagons alike. The drivers watched for pull outs in case they began to lose control.

The drivers and teams inched their way down the boulder-strewn stair stepped slope. We slowly hiked downhill. Parley was in his sling and I held onto Mothers arm as she limped beside me. The wagons sounded as if they might break apart as they were yanked first one way then another.

Captain Jack rode beside the train calling out, "That's good, nice and slow, jest be patient. No need to hurry. Better to get there later in one piece than get thar sooner in a pile a splinters."

We were walking faster than the wagons so when I saw a shady place with a rock to sit upon, I guided Mother to the side for a rest. We watched the teams and wagons pass and saw the drivers straining to hold back the mules. The muscles in the men's arms bulged with effort as sweat traced lines down their dust-coated faces and they called to the teams to settle them down.

Our walk off the plateau took all afternoon. Mother's ankle was swollen and she limped, leaning on me more as the day wore on. The wagons got down safely, but two mules and three goats, thinking they smelled water ran off and tumbled down a cliff before the boys could catch them. The sun had gone down behind the mountains and there was welcome shade by the time we reached the flats.

Everyone got back in their wagons and rolled on another mile to House Rock Springs at the base of sheer sandstone cliffs. It was pitch dark by the time we made camp, watered the animals, and ate supper. Lester had found a dripping honeycomb in an oak tree and we enjoyed a taste of sweetness on a trail cracker.

Father stored the rest of the honeycomb in a covered water bucket at the back of the wagon. One of the boys shot a deer which was quickly dressed and hung in a tree.

"Tomarra won't be so long and hard. Y'all can actally sleep in fer an hour er so in the mornin'," Captain Jack told us.

Uncle Bill was so tuckered out he didn't have a gathering, offer prayers or call for hymn singing. All went right off to sleep, except me. I kept hearing that sweet honey calling me. "Mary, Mary, come and have just a bit more." I had a sweet tooth and it had been a long time since I'd had any sweets. I tiptoed to the back of the wagon, dipped my greedy hand into the bucket and gorged on heavenly honey.

I ate too much. I woke during the night and knew I was going to throw up. I stumbled through the dark to some bushes and heaved so hard I was sure I was turned inside out.

Serves you right, Mary George. The wages of sin are upon you. Stealing and sneaking around are bad acts. You know better.

I groaned and wobbled back to my bed, covered my face in shame and finally went to sleep.

Sun shining in my face woke me. I hadn't slept this late for years. I smelled breakfast cooking and felt like throwing up again. The muscles across my shoulders and in the front of my legs were as sore as those on my belly. Between yesterdays walk and my transgressions, I hurt all over. I couldn't enjoy the beauty that surrounded us. It was as if God had put us through a rough time and then rewarded us with a gift when we overcame our hardships. I felt too awful to appreciate it. I didn't want to let on that I was sick so I got up, put a smile on my face and got on with the day.

The Vermillion Cliffs glowing with layers of gold, pink, orange and red with strips of dark brown and black stood like sentries to the north of the plain.

What makes rocks seem like layers of a cake? Where do those shining colors come from?

I didn't see Aunt Jane give mother the syrup last night. Had she forgotten or did she figure mother was too tired to run off? Was mother still in the wagon? About that time she poked her head out the front canvas and beckoned for me to help her.

"Good morning. Are you and Parley ready for a bite to eat before we roll out?" I asked.

She didn't answer, but gestured that she'd like to take care of her morning needs. We walked to an area behind some juniper trees set aside for women and girls, came back to camp, got Parley and quickly washed our hands and faces. They ate breakfast while I shook out and folded bedding. I couldn't even watch them eat.

I heard Father ask, "What happened to all the honey? Just a little bit left in the bucket. Some critter must have gotten to it."

Before we left, Uncle Bill said, "At the base of the cliffs is an area where earlier pioneers scratched their names, the date they passed this way, where they were from and where they're headed. Captain Jack says since we'll be having a shorter travel day, there's time to go, read the names and if you wish, to inscribe your names on the sandstone."

My friends and I saw names and dates of the earliest Saints to pass this way. 1873, 1876, 1880 were marked. It seemed we were latecomers. I hurriedly scratched "MARY GEORGE, nine yrs old, 1885."

You should add, SINNER, in great big letters after your name. Will anyone ever read my name and speculate who I was? I wasn't quite nine but I was closer to nine than eight. Sometimes I felt really old—maybe twenty something.

We hadn't seen the Colorado yet, but when the wagons stopped and the breeze blew from the southeast we heard low rumbling sounds like thunder over the far mountains. After dinner we came to Soap Creek. Some of the smart aleck boys had to try it for themselves.

"Yuck, phooey, awful," Lester, spat and stuck his tongue out. "I should've listened to Captain Jack."

"The animules're smartern you boys. Allus got to test and find out the hard way." Captain Jack laughed as one of the boys doubled over and puked into the creek. "Little bit a sperience is the best teacher. No way round it."

We stopped at Jacob's Pools named for a famous Mormon explorer and missionary to the Indians, Jacob Hamblin. There was green pasture for the stock, several springs and abandoned rock buildings. Everyone enjoyed fried venison steaks for supper and from the leftovers we cut strips to dry for jerky.

Uncle Bill, Father and Captain Jack invited us to walk with them to a place where we could look down at the river. Mother decided to try and she let Father take her arm.

I was happy to see them together. I think it was the first time mother had willingly let father touch her since their argument at Orderville. Father talked and pointed out things of interest, but Mother remained quiet and solemn.

After a half-hour's walk we arrived at the rim of the gorge. We looked down and saw and heard our challenger roaring wildly between its rock walls. A chill went up the back of my neck as I watched the legendary, muddy, red river.

We have to cross that torrent? Now I know why some call it the Devil River.

"At Lee's Ferry the river's wider, not so squashed tween the cliffs and we'll get acrosst with no trouble. The Johnsons took over at the behest of the Church when John Lee wuz arrested, tried and executed in 1877. He wuz accused of bein in charge of the 1857 Mountain Meadows Massacre. Some say he wuz a scapegoat jest to get the Feds offa the church's back. Since I'm a gentile, I hev no opinion, but I got my spicions."

Uncle Bill decided it was a good place for prayers and song. Our voices drifted across the great canyon and were blown back to us on the cool evening breeze. Some pretty little bushes with shiny three pointed green leaves grew next to the path. I picked some, sniffed and tossed them aside because they smelled unpleasantly oily.

Our excitement and apprehension grew as we approached the crossing. The river was the divide between civilization and the unknown desert wilderness. We found an isolated compound surrounded by fields and orchards. The Johnson's had a two-story home big enough to house their family of nine children and still have room to take in travelers. They also made a living by selling or trading for the products of their fields and operating the ferry. Sister Johnson was famous for her fresh baked bread and rolls.

There were corrals and barns for the animals and a camping area, with a row of trees alongside to break the ceaseless wind. The grandness of the place was awe inspiring yet threatening. The Johnson's were glad to see us.

"Emma Lee, John Lee's seventeenth wife, named this place Lonely Dell," Sister Johnson told us. "It's better now than formerly but it gets mighty lonely. We're glad to have a chance to visit and catch up on what's going on in the world."

"What's the level of the river? Will we be able to get acrosst right away er will we be waitin' a while?" Captain Jack asked.

Brother Johnson, wiping sweat from his face with a red bandana, came from the blacksmith shop, "We'll know better tomorrow. A Navajo came by and said there was a big rain up the Paria yesterday. It'll take a few hours to see if the river rises too high to make the crossing tomorrow. Make yourselves to home, rest and enjoy the scenery. I'll know in the morning whether we can get you started tomorrow or if you'll have to wait longer. How many wagons and animals have you?"

"Ten wagons and teams, fifteen extra horses and mules, two cows and twenty goats. Each team has four mules. There's seventy-five Saints including babies and toddlers," Uncle Bill answered.

"With that large a group it'll take two days to cross. The charges are three dollars for each wagon and team and twenty-five cents for each extra animal. We don't charge for travelers," Brother Johnson said. "Tonight, I'll meet with the men and boys in your party to explain how the ferry works and answer questions. Good to see you again, Jack. It's been a time since you've been this way. Is Brownie with you? The last time he came he ended up with a snootful of porcupine quills. Never heard a dog howl so loud."

"Yup, he shore larnt a lesson that time. He's around, probly with Mary George. He's taken a powerful likin' to that little gal," Captain Jack replied, slapping his dusty hat against his leg.

After we made camp, Mother waved at me with the back of her hand, letting me know I had some free time. I walked to the sandy beach and put my hands in the river. The water was icy and clear in the pools along the edge. With my cupped hands, I brought a cooling drink to my mouth, rinsed my face and let the breeze dry my skin. Trailing green willows, yellow daisy wildflowers and the oily smelling shrub I picked at Jacobs Pools grew beside the water. I wouldn't pick the oily leaves, but chose a bouquet of yellow flowers for Mother and Aunt Jane.

It's nice to have time to myself. Living in a wagon train is like living in a big city. Lots of people around all the time. I like to be by myself now and then. It's peaceful and gives me time to think. I hope I never have to live in a city.

I saw some pretty blue lupine that would go with the daisies. I pushed my way through the stinky bushes but I didn't pick their shiny leaves.

Sister Johnson sent two daughters to our campsite with four loaves of fresh baked bread. Such a treat! It had been awhile since we'd had anything in the bread line except "trail crackers." The girls said they had fresh eggs for sale as well as watermelons, peaches and some nice vegetables.

"Mary, you and Hattie get Rhoda and Roxie and go with these girls. Here, take some coins and get whatever you can for the next few days. We can use some variety. I'm sick of dried trout," Aunt Jane said.

After supper, the men and older boys went to meet with Brother Johnson. We cleaned up and enjoyed sitting around the flickering fire, visiting and sharing our concerns about the crossing. Mother listened quietly but didn't add to the conversation. I wasn't feeling good—hot like I was blushing all over—so after Parley, Richard and Roy were settled, I asked Aunt Jane to make sure Mother got to bed. I crawled into my bedroll and was asleep as soon as my head hit the pillow.

At the time when the sky turns pearly pink but not light yet, I woke to find my eyes swollen almost shut. I tried to pry them open but could see only a sliver of the sky.

This is scary. What's wrong? I'm itchy and hot. My head aches something fierce. My mouth is dry and my tongue is a ball of cotton. I can't be sick now. Mother and Father need me to be well and strong. I felt disgraced and ashamed. *What have I done to find myself in this pickle? Am I being punished for stealing the honey?*

I groaned and tried to sit up. I really needed a cup of water. I stood and walked dizzily to the water barrel. I felt like I was standing on a bouncing ball and couldn't keep my balance. My arms and legs were itchy and bumpily.

What should I do? If I have smallpox, I'll infect my brothers and that would be a crime. Oh, Lord, what have I done to bring this on myself?

Tears ran down my face as I wobbled to the base of a tree and collapsed. Brownie came and snuffled his way onto my lap. "What will I do, Brownie? I'm sick and won't be good for anything," I cried as he tried to lick my face. "No, don't do that. I'll make you sick too and Captain Jack will hate me."

Last evening I heard a woman talking about the family that lost their children to smallpox. She said it was very contagious. "Smallpox killed ten children from one family here at Lonely Dell. Their graves are on the hill."

I will go to Hell if I knew I had smallpox and didn't let others know. If they all get sick and die it'd be my fault.

I decided to sit with Brownie for a few minutes before I ran away. All my dreams were smashed on the rocky shore of this awful disease.

The next thing I felt was Hattie shaking me. "Mary, wake up. Why are you sleeping on the ground with Brownie's head on your lap?"

"Hattie, get away from me. I've got smallpox and have to go off by myself to die. I'm never going to get to Arizona."

"You stay right there. I'm going for my mother."

Father and Aunt Jane came. Father carried me to the Johnson's front porch and called to Sister Johnson to come out and look at me. About then, I must have passed out because when I got my wits about me again, I was in a bed with clean white sheets and Hattie was washing my face with a cool cloth.

"Hattie, I told you to stay away from me or you'll sicken and die. Please leave me. Where am I?" I asked.

"You silly goose! You're not dying. You're not going to infect anyone. You've got a walloping case of poison ivy," Hattie said as she dabbed stinky lotion on my arms. "These blisters, the swelling and the itch are caused by those smelly green leafed bushes by the river. Mother told me to tell you you're in Arizona and have been for four days."

"I'm glad I'm not going to Hell and I've at least made it to this part of Arizona," I murmured and fell asleep with a sigh of relief.

Later, as I wakened, I heard Mother and Aunt Jane whispering.

"Elizabeth, it's time you stopped being so angry and stubborn. I don't care if you never speak to Henry again, but Mary needs you. The rest of your children and all on the mission need you to take up your tasks and pull your share of the load. We've stepped in and done your chores, but a weak mule in a team drags the whole train down. I know you can talk. I've heard you responding to Parley and your ankle is as good as healed. Put your feelings aside and come back to reality. Mary won't be herself for a week," Aunt Jane spoke firmly to my mother.

I held my breath and kept my eyes shut. Tears of self-pity dribbled down my cheeks.

Will Mother say anything? Oh, God, Please make her answer.

Mother walked to my bedside and put her hand on my hot, blistered forehead. "Mary, I know I've been difficult and I know I have to take up the reins of my responsibilities. I love you, my daughter. Your task is to get well."

Tears spilled onto my face and I sniffled into the hanky Mother put in my hand.

Mother turned to Aunt Jane. "When will we be crossing?"

"Brother Johnson says we have to wait until tomorrow. The water is rough and high today from yesterday's cloudburst up on the Paria. Six wagons and teams will cross tomorrow and four the next day. The ferry can take two wagons and teams at a time. They plan for our families' four wagons to go day after tomorrow," Aunt Jane said.

"Good, that'll give Mary time to recuperate. I need to dab this lotion on her blisters. If she gets to scratching it'll make it worse and scars will mark her for the rest of her life," Mother said as she shook a bottle of brown colored stinky liquid. "Okay, Mary, this might sting a little, but it'll keep you from itching and scratching. How do your eyes feel? They don't look quite as swollen as earlier."

I thought I had died and gone to Heaven. I felt great. Mother was talking again and all my misery was worth every word she said. I lay there and let her dab away and felt loved and cared for.

That evening Hattie woke me. "Mary, here's supper. I've brought chicken in gravy, fresh biscuits, a piece of watermelon and a big glass of milk that's cold from being stored down in the well. Can you sit up and eat something?"

I smiled as I sat up and leaned against the headboard. People were treating me like a princess! Hattie put the tray across my lap and sat down to visit while I ate.

The next day passed in much the same way, except I didn't sleep as much and I heard lots of noise down by the river. I went to the window and watched what was going on. The crossing had begun and seemed to be going on schedule. Tomorrow it would be our turn. Father came to see me and told me I'd ride in a wagon while every one else stands on the deck.

"The hardest part'll be when we climb up the other side. There're plans to build a dug-way slanting up the south side of the river, but so far it's all on paper. We'll climb a steep trail to the top of Lee's Backbone. You can see it from the window. It's that long, sharp, jagged ridge that runs east and west on the other side. To lessen the wagon's load all the folks have to walk and carry as much as they can."

"Where will we catch up with the train? They won't go on without us, will they?" I asked.

"No. We've stuck together this far and there'll be no separating this close to our goal. They'll camp at Navajo Springs, eight miles beyond the river and wait for us. The next part of the trip to Tuba City, then to the settlements along the Little Colorado River will be hot and rough going.

The next morning, Father carried me to a wagon. I saw the other wagons lined up ready to get on the ferry that looked like a gigantic raft. It was wide enough for two wagons and teams to ride side by side. Wooden fences along each side kept people and animals from falling off. There was a hinged ramp at each end. Ropes and U hooks tied the wagons to the ferry.

The river was wide and ominous as it rushed past. "How will we keep from being washed downstream? How many people have drowned at this crossing?" I asked.

"Get in, lie down and don't fear the crossing. Only one man was lost when the ferry slanted sideways some years ago. They've increased its size and have had no problems since," Father said.

"Where's Andy? Who's controlling the team?" I asked.

"He'll stand on deck holding the reins and lead the team onto the ferry. He'll control and calm them as we cross. See you on the other side," Father said as he headed to the other team and wagon.

Without a problem, excepting a skittery mule that Andy calmed by scratching between his eyes and whispering into his ear, the wagons rolled onto the big, flat ferry. Father said it's twenty feet wide and forty feet long. When the wagons were tied, the folks walked on and stood along the railings. When we got to the other side the barge would return for the rest of the animals and the herders.

I heard my friends calling and waving to the Johnson family as we pushed off. It was a holiday and everyone was in high spirits. I was missing all the fun, but I was so happy about Mother's recovery that I didn't care. I looked ugly with blisters, swollen face and brown lotion spots all over me so I was glad to be by myself.

The men on the shore pushed the barge into the river using long poles. Along the sides men with poles pushed on the river bottom and guided us across. The current carried us downstream and we came to the west side south of the place we put in.

I haven't seen Captain Jack and Brownie. They must've gone with the group yesterday. What was that thump? Oh, it must have been the barge bumping the shore.

"Okay, you fellers, don't just stand thar with yer fingers up yer nose. Hop to it and grab those tie up ropes. Hitch em up tight to those stakes on the beach. As soon as we're snugged up you drovers, lead them teams and wagons onta dry land," I heard Captain Jack directing.

"Good, he came back to help us get to Navajo Springs!" I felt safer when he was around. "Come on, Brownie, come and ride with me," I called. Roxie and Rhoda lifted my big brown friend up into the wagon. Brownie didn't care if I was spotted and pure ugly.

As Captain Jack directed, our mule team was taken off and hitched to the front of the other wagon so they had eight mules to haul it up the steep rocky trail.

"Dubble teamin's the only way to get over Lee's Backbone. We found that out yestaday, so I come back to help you'all make the trip. When they get to the top all the mules'll come down and haul this last wagon up. Don't nobody git into the wagons. Just hitch up yer git along and hike up."

The climb was rough, bouncy and hot. It was nearly noon when we were up over the ridge and down the other side. The herders brought up the rear with the livestock and we rolled across the flat, desolate, treeless land on the way to Navajo Springs.

Chapter Six

Little Colorado River Valley, Arizona Territory, August 1885
We rejoined the company at Navajo Springs. At breakfast I noticed although Mother was talking, she wasn't speaking to Father. "Mary, tell your father he needs to watch Roy and Richard. Last night, I found them sleeping with Lester, Reuben and the animals. I fear they could be trampled."

Father was close by. I began repeating what Mother said, he nodded showing me he heard, shook his head and walked away.

Grownups play silly games.

After morning prayers, Captain Jack said, "Today we'll travel twelve miles up Roundy Creek and stop at Bitter Springs. It's a gradule slope, but the trail is over slick rock and hard packed sand so we won't git bogged down. Thar won't be water in the crik, less thar's been a rainstorm at the divide. Don't count on gettin' any water out of Bitter Springs. If thar is water it'll taste terrible, but it won't make you sick,"

The sun was barely over the red cliffs and it was already hot. There were no green trees, shrubs or weeds to ease the eye. Everything in sight was either red rock, red sand or clear blue sky. The sun shone down on us with the focus of a magnifying glass.

The day dragged on, the heat grew intense and Mother wet a cloth to wipe and cool myself with as I lay in the wagon. She wore a dripping wet cloth under her sunbonnet as she walked beside the wagon. We longed for night.

While setting up camp at Bitter Springs we heard thunder rumbling and saw tall, white, puffy clouds with dark gray bottoms gathered in the west.

"Looks like we may get a storm," Uncle Bill said. "Get supper quickly so we can shelter in the wagons."

After a hasty supper, eaten as we watched the ominous storm approach, Captain Jack told the boys, "You'll take them animuls over aginst them cliffs to the west. Don't cross the crik, go over thar to them eroded caves on this side, at the base of the cliffs. They'll give you shelter. Thar's goin to be thunder, lightning, hail an rain. The animules'll get scairt an try to bolt. Do the best you can. The rest of you put anything that might blow away, includin' small chillern, in the wagons, climb in an hold tight. If we're lucky we'll get coolin' rain along with the big blow."

Mother, Parley, Richard and I, along with the crate of chickens, hunkered down in one wagon. Father took William, John, Roy and Andy, our driver, into the other wagon. A sharp gust of wind shook the wagon and made the fabric cover billow and wave. I peeked through the back flap and saw a ghostly landscape. Sunlight filtered through the roiling clouds and colored the air a murky yellow green. The red hills and cliffs were dark and sinister as they loomed over us. Sand filled air hid then revealed the creek, cliffs and other wagons. Huge thorny balls of tumbleweeds rolled across the ground. Dust drifted through our canvas shelter powdering our hair and clothes. Parley cried with fright. I huddled down and buried my face between my snugged up knees.

We were going to get blown into the next state. The shrieking wind carried the sounds of the animals' terror filled cries. Could they keep the animals from stampeding? I smelled rain, but didn't hear anything but howling wind, flapping canvas, sand scouring the wagon and Parley's whimpering.

Plop, splat, plunk! Giant, fat drops hit the canvas. We prayed for more to fall, settle the dust, fill the creek and cool the air. The wind died, the plopping stopped. The howling ended. We were disappointed that so few drops had fallen.

"Mary, take Parley outside and check on the other wagons," Mother said. "I must shake the bedding so we won't sleep on sand tonight. See if you can find out how the herders and animals fared."

Parley and I left the wagon as others were climbing from theirs. We shook like wet dogs to get the sand off and laughed at the grime around our eyes and mouths that made us look like clowns.

Father came. "Are you all right? The Smith's wagon blew over and one of the little ones has a broken arm. I've sent Andy to help the boys bring the animals back. Sure wish we'd gotten a good rain out of all the bluster."

"Wall, Mary, did you injoy that six inch Arizony rain?" Captain Jack teased.

"What are you talking about? That wasn't any six inches. Barely a few drops fell," I answer peevishly.

"You don't know whut ter look fer. Look yonder on that slab of sandstone. Thar's a wet spot and six inches over thataway's another, an six inches in the other direcshun is another! That's a six inch Arizony rain! You'll see lots of them in these parts."

We were busy setting things to right when a thunderous sound made us freeze. We heard a grinding, tearing roar. A wall of water, at least eight feet high barrelled down Roundy Creek. Uprooted trees, bushes and boulders as big as a horse trough tumbled downstream. I'd never heard a train, but thought it must sound like that.

"Must've been a real gully washer up on the divide," Captain Jack declared. "It'll pass in a half hour an then we'll have a gentle stream to water the horses, wash the sand out of our hair and fill the water barrels. Do you feel how much cooler it is?"

I wished I could take a bath. I still itched from the poison ivy. Scabs had formed so I knew I was getting better, but Lordy, how I did itch. Putting wet sand on the worst spots helped to ease it a bit. When it dried, I looked and felt dirty.

That evening Captain Jack announced, "Tamarra we'll be riden along some limestone cliffs. With this good rain to the south of here ther's goin to be plenty of water in the basins at the foot of the cliffs. It'll be a good stoppin' place, nine miles up the road, and you wimmen can do laundry, we'll fill the water barrels again and whoever wants can take a coolin' bath."

Limestone Tanks were as refreshing as we'd hoped. For the first time since we left Orderville, Mother and I were alone. She seemed her old playful self as we splashed and frolicked in the rock basin full to its brim with cool clear rainwater.

"Why aren't you talking to Father?' I asked.

"Mary, there are things you won't understand until you're a married woman. Let's just leave it at this: your father and I've been together for many years and I don't intend to change that. We have a basic disagreement about where to live out our days. I need things your father doesn't understand.

Sometimes a dark fog descends upon my mind and I change to another person. It's scary, but there's nothing I can do about it. Try to be patient with me and always remember that I love you."

The gradual climb grew steeper as we traveled uphill to the divide. Behind us, the creeks ran toward the Colorado River while those to the south ran into the Little Colorado. Cedar and piñon pine trees were loaded with cones full of nuts. The air was cooler and the piney scent refreshing.

"Bring a blanket," Captain Jack told us after evening meeting. "You're a gonna injoy yer first tree whackin, nut gatherin, piñon injoyin party!"

After we gathered under a stand of pines, Captain Jack told us about pi on pines and their little hard shelled nuts. "These scrubby lookin', wide spreadin' pines grow some of the bes tastin' nuts you'll ever crack between your teeth. No sense in lettin the squirrels eat em all. The Injuns hereabouts, Hopi and Navajo, been gatherin' and eatin' em fer more years than the white man's been on these shores. This is the season of ripenin', so there's plenty for us, the squirrels an our Injun friends.

"See how these cones are openin up so the nuts can drop out," he said as he reached up, picked a cone and gave it a good shake. "Them little brown nuts come droppen out all ready fer you to injoy. Spread your blankets under these trees. You boys grab a stick er a broken limb and commence to knockin' them cones off the branches.

"The nuts'll fall and you can gather em in your blankets. After the boys knock down the cones, you set on the blankets and pry out the nuts that haven't fallen out."

The boys liked bashing and whapping the trees, the women enjoyed a few minutes to sit and watch the men trying to crack the shells with their teeth, without smashing the nut meat.

Finally Father asked, "Captain Jack, how do you get the meat out of the shell? We need a demonstration."

"Oh, you greenhorns! Everbody watch as I'm gonna show you this only once. Take the nut, put it tween your fust molars, then ease down gently. You'll hear it crack, then roll it over and crack it on the other side, then spit out the shell and enjoy. Yer really good at it when you can put em in one side of your mouth and spit the shells outten the other side!"

We practiced cracking, spitting and enjoying the creamy little nuts. The women sacked some for another time. When we started back to camp, I saw Brownie loping toward me. As he got closer I smelled something awful.

"Brownie, you stinky hound, come here! Mary, don't touch him er he'll get you skunky. Gol durn it. Dawg, when will you learn? Them little black 'n white critters don't run fast er have big sharp teeth. They have a special defense. This isn't the first time you've tangled with a loaded polecat, and as stupid as you are it won't be the last."

I watched Captain Jack drag Brownie to a tree, loop a rope around his neck and front legs in a harness and tie him up. "Now, dagnabit, you set thar and smell yourself fer a while until I can figure out whut to do. At least yer down wind of the camp," he said as he stomped down the hill. "If you was a pair of skunk sprayed overalls, I'd dig a hole and bury you."

Poor Brownie. He comforted me when I was sick, now what could I do for him? Maybe Mother would let me have the cold dishwater to wash his face. He moaned and scratched his eyes and snout with his paws. He'd howl and keep us awake all night.

Mother gave me the basin and a rag saying, "Don't think it'll do much good, but you'll feel better for trying."

"Whewh-eee! Brownie you are the stinkiest dog ever. I should've put a clothespin on my nose. Here, let's try to clean that stuff out of your eyes and off your face," I said as Brownie whimpered and slithered to me on his belly. "Skunks are like dill pickles. You never know which way they'll squirt so you have to watch out in all directions. Tomorrow I'll take you to the creek bed for a sand bath. Right now you have to bear with your stink and humiliation. Don't howl and keep us up all night."

I patted my friend's nose and walked back to camp. He whimpered for awhile, then gave up and went to sleep. The next morning I took Brownie to the creek and rubbed him with wet sand. Then I dumped two buckets of creek water over him. Starting with his tail and ending with his floppy ears, he shook his body, giving me a good spraying in the process. With nary a thank you nuzzle he ambled off to find Captain Jack.

We planned to go as far as Willow Springs and stay there for two days. The Saints had a mission to the Hopi people at nearby Tuba City. At Willow Springs we found wonderful, clear, and good tasting water flowing from the base of the cliffs. If you've never had to ration water, you wouldn't know how precious good water is.

Pillars of red sandstone encircled our camp. They looked like blanket wrapped hunched giants and I felt they watched us set up camp. I told Lester, "You'd better watch the animals closely tonight. Those stone giants look mighty hungry."

"Mary, you have an imagination like nobody else. If I gave you a pony you'd turn it into a unicorn. Must come from those books you like to read."

"Well, might do you good to learn something new once in a while. There's more to life than watching the back end of a jackass all day long."

"Mary, come and look," Rhoda called.

Cousin Hattie was helping Mother, so I went with her. On the face of the cliff above the spring were hundreds of carved names, dates and sayings. "Arizona ain't no place fer amatures, Experience is another word fer mistakes," and others that didn't make sense to me. The men and boys understood them though, because they laughed like they were reading a joke book. The cliff was a newspaper written on rocks.

Later Uncle Bill spoke about Tuba City. " The Moqui, or as we call them, the Hopi, whom we'll visit at Tuba City and Moenkopi, are different from other tribes in Zion. When Jacob Hamblin came as a missionary to them in 1858 he was impressed by their stone villages, fields of crops, the men's weavings, and respect for women. Their underground kiva rituals reminded him of our own temple ceremonies. There are some who believe these light-skinned Lamanites are descended from early Welsh explorers who came to the southwest hundreds of years before Columbus discovered America.

"We'll treat them with the respect of brothers. Those who wish may visit Tuba City, where the new woolen mill is located and Moenkopi, the Hopi's mesa top village. The church is in good standing with these people and we will not behave in such a way as to change that."

How exciting! Some men and boys would stay and tend the animals. Mothers with small children and the old folks who might not be able to make the climb, stayed in camp.

I am on the verge of discovering something really new. I feel it in my bones! Will Mother want to go? She's been more herself lately and Aunt Jane has stopped giving her the syrup. She seems resigned to the trip. I wish she would talk to Father. I hate being the go-between.

The next morning Captain Jack rode by on Buster. "Mary, yer pa says you can come with me up to Tuba and Moenkopi iff'en you want. He's gonna take your mother on his horse. Maybe if the two of them have a little time tagether they can come to a meetin' of the minds. Yer aunt'll stay and watch the younguns. Give me yer hand and I'll heist you up."

"You bet I want to come. Thanks, Captain Jack. Where's Brownie? Isn't he coming?"

"Nah, I'm afeard he might get curious about the underground kivas an disappear fer days 'n days. Better he stay here and help the boys mind the stock."

I put my arms around his waist, grinned like a cat with a bowl of cream and off we went. The trail was rocky and steep so we didn't go fast, which gave me time to look around and enjoy the view of standing rocks, sand hills and desert that looked like it'd been painted with watercolors. To the southwest were mountains with clouds caught on their peaks.

"What are those mountains called?" I asked.

"Them's the sacred peaks of the Hopi. The Rain gods live thar and when all's right the clouds swell, drift this way and bring blessed rain. The men perform dances and ceremonies to make the rain gods happy so they'll bring the rain. They've built rock walled tanks and basins to catch the run off. They use every drop."

When we arrived at Tuba City, Mother called to me. Father went to the main building to meet with the missionaries who lived at the mission.

Mother and I walked to Moenkopi, the old Hopi village . The sun was high and the rock walls radiated heat. We kept to the shady side as we walked along the footpaths between the ancient buildings.

"Tuba City is a strange name for an Indian mission, isn't it?" I asked.

Mother answered, "It's named for the Hopi chief who befriended Jacob Hamblin. Chief Tuba knew his people would never give up their own beliefs, but he was willing to let the missionaries teach his people modern ways of weaving and irrigation. The Chief wanted his people to learn to speak, read and write English.

"We're told they are one of the lost tribes of Israel. The only ones I know of who've converted are Chief Tuba and his wife. I think they look upon it as the sociable thing to do and haven't really changed their inner beliefs."

We turned the corner and found ourselves in the town square. Women and children had laid out their pottery, weavings and fruits and vegetables to sell or trade.

"Mary, look at the set of dishes. These mothers make play dishes for their daughters, just like we make dolls and toys for our children. These are lovely. Four saucers, bowls and cups all made of clay and painted soft blue, yellow and gray. I'd like to get them for you. I don't have any coins but let me dig around in my bag and see what might interest her."

While Mother looked in her pocketbook, I smiled at the girl who stood behind the seated potter. I wanted to be friendly and waved my hand in greeting. The brown skinned girl, with straight, short black hair cut in bangs across her forehead and sparkly dark eyes, smiled in return. Her loose fitting knee-length tunic was made of coarsely woven white cotton. A bright red, white and black sash was tied around her waist and she wore soft leather boots. She looked cooler than I felt in my long sleeved, high necked, ankle length skirt and petticoats.

"Maybe she'll trade for this," Mother said and held out a round hand mirror framed in ornately carved silver.

"That's your special gift from your mother. You can't give it away."

"That's for me to decide. I want to get you a gift and the mirror is the only thing I have that might interest her."

The potter and the girl, who I guessed was her daughter, spoke in soft singing words while they held the mirror in front of their faces. They tilted it this way and that to reflect the sunlight and giggled delightedly when they saw themselves in the silvery mirror.

"I think they like my offer," Mother said as she touched a bowl. She waved her hand over the set and indicated she wanted to take it with her. I held my breath until the potter nodded her head, reached for a small wooden box and put the pieces in it, padding each piece with dry straw.

I've never had such a lovely present. Mother must love me very much to trade the mirror her mother gave her. I'll treasure them and someday pass them on to my daughter.

"Mary, these dishes are works of art. We'll count them as your Happy Ninth Birthday Present. Who knows what we'll find in St. Johns when your birthday comes. Can you carry them, or would you like me to hold the box?"

"Oh, Mother, thank you. Don't worry. I'll hold it carefully."

Mother bent and kissed my cheek. Tears glittered and she sniffed into her hanky. "We'd better get back to the mission and see if it's time to return to camp."

At the mission the men were coming out of the woolen mill. Father smiled and said, "Ahh, there you are, Elizabeth. We'll be going to camp after we enjoy a picnic the women have prepared. You and Mary join us."

"Father, Mother traded her mirror for a set of doll sized pottery dishes for me as an early birthday present! I have them in this box. May I put them in your saddlebag while we eat? I must be very gentle with them."

After our picnic, eaten on tables and benches set in the shade of cottonwood trees, we started back to camp.

"So, how wuz yer fust visit to an Indian village, Mary?" Captain Jack asked as Buster picked his way down the rocky trail.

"Mother traded for a set of pottery dishes for me. I don't know if I'll play with them because they're so pretty. I might break a piece. When I have a home, I'll put them on a shelf to admire and remind me of today. I wish I could have talked to the girl I met. Do all Indian people talk the same or in different languages?"

"Wall, some of em are kinda the same, but you ken usully make yerself understood if you start with a smile. Some understand more Spanish than English. You should start with Spanish."

"Could you teach me some? For instance how do you say 'Hello' and 'Goodbye?'" For the rest of the ride I listened and repeated my first Spanish words.

It was a wonderful day—as full of discoveries as I'd hoped. My first Indian pottery, my first Indian friend and my first Spanish lesson. If Mother had talked to Father, my world would have been perfect.

The clouds blown by the west wind, hovered over Willow Springs. We scurried to be ready for the storm. This one was more than a six-inch rain, but it lasted for less than an hour. After the rain the desert bloomed with fragrance.

I wrapped the box of dishes in an old blanket and threatened dire consequences to any brother who touched the bundle. I put it carefully in the corner of the wagon with my doll and my book. "I'll show it to you on my birthday in St. Johns," I promised Rueben.

On our second day at Willow Springs we did housekeeping, laundry and baking. In the afternoon, I saw a group of Hopi children sitting on the hill. They were as curious about us as we were about them.

The girl I'd met ventured down the hill, waving her hand to catch my attention. To practice the Spanish greeting Captain Jack taught me I said, "Buenos Tardes." She didn't reply, but grabbed my hand and led me to our wagon. She was curious about how we lived in our houses on wheels.

I climbed into the wagon seat and she followed. She peeked into the crowded, dark wagon bed and looked surprised. She gestured to the hills and sky and I understood she was telling me she would rather live in her village than in a wagon. We laughed as I pointed to myself and nodded in agreement.

We climbed down from the wagon, she smiled, took a small cloth wrapped parcel from her pocket and handed it to me. Before I unwrapped it she was gone, scampering up the hill like a nimble goat. I watched her climb, saw her wave from the top of the cliff, waved in return and then she was gone. I unrolled the cloth and found a carved wooden figure painted with bright colors. The face had a bird's beak and arms carved like feathers.

"Captain Jack, what kind of doll is this?"

"I saw yer Hopi friend bring you something. Let me take a look."

He hefted it as if weighing it, looked at it from all angles and said, "Mary, you've got a special doll here. I ken tell it's carved from cottonwood root cause it's so light. It's the image of a Thunderbird. You member I told you about those gods that live on the mountains west of here? This doll ain't no god, but is a copy of the Thunderbird god that brings the rain. See, here in this hand it holds a lighnin' bolt. The Hopi's use these dolls to teach youngens about their beliefs. They call em Katsina or Katchina Dolls. That girl done give you a real special gift. Take good care of it and don't let any one talk you outta it."

That night I slept with the Katsina beside my pillow and dreamt of Hopi gods who live on high mountains. I awoke to hear thunder rolling in the distance and knew the gods were at work.

We began our trek southwestward toward the Little Colorado River with trepidation. Last evening Uncle Bill told us, "The next portion of the trail is the longest, driest and most barren that we'll traverse. It's only twenty-five miles down Moenkopi Wash to its junction with the river, but it's the hot time of year, waterholes and springs are few and may be dry. We'll carry as much water as we're able, use only what we must and expect to suffer distress along the way. We hope thunderstorms will cool us off and allow us to replenish our water supplies.

"You'll see cattle carcasses and bones along the trail. A herd of cattle perished on this part of the trail. The cowboys weren't experienced with handling large herds under these harsh conditions. The stock, maddened by thirst, stampeded. Most died in the river bed while trying to dig to water that wasn't there."

The sun blazed in the Arizona sky. By noon we were exhausted and the animals were stumbling. The babies cried and fretted, begging for wa-wa. My eyes burned; my nose and throat were dry. Each breath felt like a metal file scraping across a dull saw. Mother tried to calm the little ones in the wagon. I plodded along listening to the wooden wheels screeching and screaming in the heat and dryness.

Captain Jack halted the train. "We'll take a noon break here whar you'uns ken walk to them cliffs and get a little shade. Take yer dinner and a blanket to rest on. By three the sun'll be a bit lower and we'll start agin."

For the next two days we left before first light, rested at noon and traveled until it was dark. Our water was running low, but the animals on which our lives depended, had to be given enough water to keep them moving. We suffered from thirst. Yesterday we came to Five Mile Wash that had a few water holes left but the green stinking water was tainted by dead rotting fish. On the third day from Tuba City, we hoped to get to the river. Maybe we'd find water on the surface or seepage at the bottom of holes.

Before we started that morning the men dug two graves. Brother Smith and baby Sadie Richards died during the night. Sadie was four months old. She was a pioneer, but never got to write her name on a newspaper rock. Their bodies were wrapped in sheets, dirt and sand thrown over them and as many rocks as we could gather were placed on top. There was no time or materials to make a marker. Only God would know where they lay.

Mother is making a valiant effort to do her share, but she's strange and distant. Is the fog creeping and closing in? I pray she won't disappear. She'd never survive this desolate country on her own.

When we arrived at the junction of Moenkopi Wash and the river, there was no water in sight. The men dug seep holes in hopes water would trickle into them and we'd have water for drinking by morning. The herders took the stock to the base of the cliffs to a stagnant pool. The animals were so thirsty they drank the foul wormy water.

Uncle Bill said, "As we continue up river there'll be vegetation and water will be easier to find. If we get water in the seep holes by morning we'll stay for a day or so for wagon repairs and rest. The heat and sand rubbing the wheels is causing near breakdowns that must be fixed before we push on. You've earned the right to call yourselves true pioneers. The worst is about over, so hold true to the faith, trust in God and continue in praise."

What was there to praise? I was dirty, hot, worn out and worried about Mother. She wouldn't get out of the wagon and help with supper. Her eyes looked as empty as our water barrels.

You're being tested. Are you a weak kneed ninny? Buck up! Do one chore after another and soon we'll be in St. Johns and all hardships will be over.

During the night two teams of mules ran off. The herders went looking for them, while others worked on the wagon wheels. The water that seeped into the holes was salty, thick and barely drinkable, but we scooped it into buckets to let the sand settle.

"Why, this here water's not bad," said Captain Jack. "You just hev to git used to bitin it off and chewin it afore you swallow. Be careful of quicksand along the river. I took a scoutin ride earlier and found some bogged down cattle carcasses upriver. Watch yer little ones. Tie ropes round their middles so they can't wander."

The long hot day passed. The herders straggled in about three o'clock with the runaways, the wagon wheels were mended and greased and we would continue south along the river the next day.

Chapter Seven

Sunset Crossing & Holbrook, Arizona Territory, August, 1885
We left before dawn, rested at noon and traveled til dark. Everyone was tuckered out. The animals had to be urged along with whip flicks. We were about out of the oats and dried corn we'd brought for their emergency feed. Would they eat trail crackers? Days passed in a haze of endurance.

One night Captain Jack said, "We've been doing twelve miles a day. Have to go twenty miles each day 'til we cover the eighty five miles to Sunset Crossin. The weather will cool as we go upriver, so we'll cease restin at noon. There're sand dunes ahead. The first wagons to come here in 1873 give up at the dunes and backtracked to Lee's Ferry. We'll get through in fine shape if we don't get a sandstorm.

"We'll pass Black Falls. If it's rained in the mountains we'll see the falls in action. When there's water in the river it's a sight to see it rushin over the black rocks and fallen twelve feet. Expect grazin' on the hills around the falls. Mebe you'uns could do some heavy prayin' tonight. The mules are so hungry, thirsty and balky they might lay down and not get up."

After bedding down, I heard Father, Uncle Bill and Aunt Jane. "Henry, I'm worried about Elizabeth. Has she spoken to you yet? We need to watch her," Aunt Jane said.

"No, she's smiled and gestured, but hasn't said a word. I thought she was all right. What's the problem, now?" Father asked impatiently. "What we really need to talk about is our dwindling food supply. What do you have, Bill?"

"If we come to grazing for the animals, we can use the corn and oats we've saved for them, for ourselves. There's not much, but it would get us through three or four days. There are trail crackers, a few jars of fruit, a little flour and sugar and a quantity of deer jerky. It's tough to chew, but soaked in water, mixed with boiled corn or oats it makes a nourishing mush."

"We might be all right. With what we both have left, and if we get some grazing, we'll make it to Sunset Crossing or St. Joseph. Jane, why are you concerned about Elizabeth?"

"Last night, I got up to go behind the women's bushes. On my way back I saw Elizabeth on the riverbank. She was muttering and shaking her fist at the sky while pacing in a frenzied way. I took her arm. 'What's wrong? Who are you talking to?' She turned and looked at me with such rage that it frightened me."

"'I'm talking to God. I'm furious with him. I'm as mad at God as I am at Henry. This entire venture is foolish and I'm the only one who knows it. You think I'm the crazy one, but I think I'm the only sane one in the lot.'

"I led her to the wagon, got her settled and went to bed. This morning I asked about her nighttime stroll, but she says she doesn't remember anything. I've watched her today and she's moody, but doing her share. You must pay attention to what's happening."

Good, I'm not the only one worried about Mother. Things had better be as nice in St. Johns as Father's pictured or Mother will be madder than a nest of riled hornets. Why don't grownups pay heed to each other? Father acts like Mother's being contrary and could change the way she feels if she had a mind to. She has deep problems and can't change the way she is. The only good thing about this, except for the exciting new things I've learned, is that my parents aren't sleeping in the same bed. It's been almost a year since Parley was born and there's no baby on the way. If Mother stays mad, maybe Parley will be the last baby.

I drifted off with the Thunderbird doll next to my pillow and prayed to God for rain and green grazing. I didn't pray for my mother because it didn't do any good.

The hills along the trail looked like a baby's head when it begins to grow a fuzz of hair except this fuzz was green. A strong stream flowed in the river channel. We passed the falls, enjoyed the sound, sight and cooling spray. The air was cooler, the green hills and trees eased my sun-scorched eyes. The herders took the animals to the stream, then into the hills for their first taste of fresh grass in two weeks. We sighed with relief.

Our clothes were sandy and smelled of sweat. We were a band of rag tag gypsies. My hair was dirty, my feet hurt and I itched from sand flea bites. At least the poison ivy rash was gone.

Rhoda and I asked Captain Jack, "Can't we stay a day at this nice place so we can get cleaned up?"

He answered, "Well, we could stay here an injoy the scenery and git spiffed up or we can get to whar we want to go. It's like chasin' two rabbits. You end up losin' em both. You gotta choose one or the other. We're movin' on tomorra."

Captain Jack was cantankerous. Was he tired of us and our different ways? Last evening I saw him shake an empty blackberry brandy bottle while looking at it in disgust.

I bet he can hardly wait to deliver us to St. Johns and meet his friends on the Gila River. I'll miss him and Brownie.

That afternoon we saw Indian ruins on the other side of the river. After we set up camp in a grove of cottonwood trees, the herders took the animals into the riverbed. A narrow creek in mid channel was all that was left of yesterday's torrent.

"Mary, walk with us to the ruins," Father said. "Hattie and Aunt Jane will stay here. You can do your work after supper."

The rock ruins were golden in the late afternoon sun. They were in such good condition I expected to see children playing, women cooking and hear dogs barking. The wind blowing through the empty rooms made the sound you hear when you blow across the top of an empty bottle. The timber and brush roofs had fallen into the rooms and some walls had caved in. We walked through the brittle late summer bushes and weeds, watching for snakes and potholes. As we came closer, the ruins loomed larger. Some buildings were high and round like towers.

Where had everybody gone? Why had they taken everything and moved away?

"Someday someone will come and discover what happened to these people. They spent much time and labor on this place. Look at the irrigation ditches by the river," Uncle Bill pointed out to us. "See that cone shaped volcano to the south? Maybe the people fled an eruption. We'd better get back. Captain Jack has the hurries, so we have only an overnight stopover. I'd like to come back when I have time to explore."

While my uncle talked, I poked around a room at the back of a ruin. Just enough light came through the short T-shaped door to let me spot something shiny and smooth. I tapped the round shape and heard a hollow sound, like when you thump a ripe melon.

"Brownie, come and sniff. I don't want to find I've scared a rattlesnake," I said. After he did a few snuffles, I reached down and pulled a clay pot out of the dirt and weeds. I brushed the dirt off a white, brown and black pot. It was as big around as a ten-pound sack of flour and had few cracks. The neck was decorated with a scalloped edge and I could see marks made by the potter's fingernails. Something rattled and when I turned it over tiny ears of dried corn fell out.

"Mary, we're going back," Father called. "What have you found? My word, looks like a storage jar. You're the lucky one!"

At the bottom of the hill I stopped, turned in a circle and looked at the pleasing country. The slanting sun cloaked the land in the colors of God's rainbow. When I held the pot I felt a connection to the potter. I was nearly out of room to store my treasures. It was a good thing we were almost to our destination.

At camp, supper was ready and all seemed well. Mother was unflustered and enjoyed the cool evening breeze from the mountains where the Hopi gods lived. After supper and prayers, she asked me to walk with her. She was quiet, so I kept still and waited. She started to speak, then stopped, furrowed her brow and was silent.

Finally, she began, "I've made a decision. Some families are talking about going back to Utah if this winter in St. Johns doesn't prove successful. If the weather, the people and the mission don't go well, they're prepared to return to Utah next summer.

"I want you to know I shall not return. Henry persisted, against my wishes, in bringing us on this journey and he will live with the results of his pigheadedness if things go badly. I know we're to have faith and trust this is what the Lord wishes for us, but I have nightmares of foreboding. I pray I'll be proven wrong. For better or worse we will not return to Utah."

Why is she telling me this? What will I do if Uncle Bill and his family leave? It's going to be bad enough when Captain Jack and Brownie go. Will there be new friends to help? I hugged the promise Father had made that I'd go to school. Each day I found new things to learn about, and his promise allowed me hope.

"Mother, things will be fine. We'll be with other Saints, the weather is said to be warm enough to grow citrus trees and we're all healthy. You told me not to invite trouble in before it knocks on the door." I answered with false cheerfulness. A lump of fear and confusion grew in my stomach.

Our wagons rolled on, the hills were green with grass, and on the third day we passed Grand Falls. They were wider and deeper than Black Falls but there wasn't water in the river so they weren't as impressive. We neared Sunset Crossing, the northernmost Little Colorado Mission settlement. Remembering the oasis of Orderville, we anticipated seeing friends and enjoying fresh food and a bath.

We found an almost deserted ruin. Such a disappointment! If I'd been a baby I would have cried and stamped my feet.

While we set up camp, Father and Uncle Bill went to see if any Saints were still there. Cattle and horses grazed and chickens pecked along the river. A windmill sounding like it needed greasing turned noisily in the wind. The place was so deserted looking that the cemetery on the hill was lively by comparison.

After our supper of oatmeal mush spiced with dried apples and chunks of deer jerky, they told us, "The only ones here are Lot Smith and his families. The villages disbanded several years ago," Father began. "The river flows bank to bank or is as dry as an empty well. The settlers, starting in '76, built dams to hold the water for farming. Every spring the banks eroded and the dams washed away. Water carved new channels around each end. If the water didn't tear out the sides of the dam it went under the sandy riverbed. After years of hard labor and much expense, they gave up.

"Personal difficulties developed between the colonists and Lot Smith, who's in charge. Brother Smith has a reputation as being a hard man. Especially upsetting was the practice of plowing profits back into the company in the form of more livestock and the lack of proper bookkeeping.

"Brother Smith didn't allow the members anything beyond food and clothing. When a family leaves the Order they're supposed to take the property they brought in and any share of the profits due them, but since there was no system to keep track of profits, many families left with less than they came with.

"He is known to have a fierce temper and a short fuse. Once, one of his wives went to the corral where they were branding calves to call the crew to dinner. He reacted with rage at being interrupted and turned the hot branding iron on her arm. She'll carry that Circle—S mark for the rest of her days. Two years ago he sent ten families east into New Mexico, to Ramah."

Uncle Bill picked up the story, "Those who remained have gradually moved to St. Johns, Ramah, Snowflake, Heber, Pinedale or south to Mesa, in southern Arizona. Conditions here are harsh."

Mother's blue eyes bored right through father as if to say, "See, I told you so. Not even the most devoted United Order members could make anything out of this Godforsaken land. This is just the beginning."

Sunset Crossing, Brigham City, Obed and Taylor, had been disbanded. St. Joseph, managed to build a dam that held. Their Captain was more amenable to dissent and discussion than was Lot Smith, so St. Joseph survived.

Captain Jack described the next leg of our trip. "We'll roll upriver to St. Joseph startin' tamarra. It's twenty-eight miles, so should take only a full day an part of another. On the way you'll see the ruins of Brigham City, Obed and Taylor. Frum St. Joseph we'll angle east, still followin' the river, to Horsehead Crossin'. You might hear and see a locomotive huffin' and chuffin' as it climbs the grade toward Flagstaff. In some places the trail's next to the tracks. Drivers, be ready to hold the teams steady. Horsehead Crossin' may have its new name by now. They wuz gonna change it to honor some railroad bigwig by the name a Holbrook."

We made such good time that we arrived at St. Joseph by evening. Saints came from the settlement to sell fresh vegetables, plump chickens and wonder of wonders—three green and white striped watermelons. Supper was a joyful celebration. After weeks of mush, jerky and trail crackers (which even the mules and Brownie wouldn't eat) we laughed, sang and acted like prisoners set free.

We bedded down with satisfied stomachs and happiness in our hearts. The end of our journey was just a hop, skip and a jump down the trail. Our only sadness was the death of a mule. Old Black sank to his knees under a cottonwood tree and died.

This morning Captain Jack said, "Before we get to Horsehead, there's things you need to know. You'll be tradin' and buyin' there, but remember it's not a Mormon town. Thar's bars, saloons and other stablishments which I won't mention cause there's ladies present. These places are fer the use of the cowboys who come in offa the big ranches hereabouts. Wimmen an girls, don't go wanderin' round by yerselves. Most of the cowboys are respectful of wimmen folk, but when they git a snoot full of rotgut whiskey you never know whut they'll try. Thar's a saloon name of Bucket of Blood, that's known fer its rowdiness. Don't wander south acrosst the tracks.

"After we get settled, I plan to mosey that way an ask about my buddies who er sposed to meet me in a few weeks on the Gila River or at Fort Apache. Jake, the bartender at the Bucket, usually knows the whereabouts of any who travel through. Mebe he'll have a letter fer me frum my wife in Idaho. I'll be back day after tomorrow in time to start the last part of the journey to St Johns."

Uncle Bill started our travel to Horsehead Crossing, "Lord keep us in the palm of your hand as we come in contact with gentiles. Thank you for your care of us in the wilderness. Help us stay mindful of the precepts of our faith and allow us to move through the next days untouched by the temptations of the flesh."

Temptations of the flesh! Whatever does he mean? Will I see more Indians? Will there be a store where I can buy new shoes?

The papers I'd lined my shoes with scrunched up and my feet chafed on the ground. The tops flapped and my toes were open to the sunlight. My stomach fluttered with butterflies of excitement.

Mother was in high spirits as she rode on the wagon seat with Richard and Andy. Maybe thinking of being in a town again had chased the fog away. She loved stores, libraries and crowds of people. I wondered how big Horsehead Crossing was. Compared to where we'd been, a town of more than a hundred people would be a city.

As we moved east, low red rock hills and bluffs were on our left. On the right, across the willow-lined Little Colorado River was a view that went on forever. I saw herds of red and white cattle grazing on lush green grass. From out of nowhere came a flock of small, bouncing, tan and white animals. I stood and watched them play tag as they jumped and pranced on dainty feet. They were playing! As quickly as they had come, they turned and flowed, like water poured from a bucket, down into a wash and were gone.

My feet hurt. The trail was smooth and sandy so I took my shoes and stockings off.

If I leave them here Father will have to buy me a new pair. Mother says a lady is never seen in public without shoes. Is that what Uncle Bill meant as a temptation of the flesh?

I put them in the back of the wagon. The warm dust puffed between my toes and my feet felt fine when they could spread out. I walked toward Horsehead Crossing, feeling daring and unladylike.

We reached Horsehead Crossing early in the afternoon. Captain Jack led us to the campground northwest of town. The herders corralled the animals, filled the troughs with water and the feeding tubs with the last of the oats. I handed Parley to Mother and went to the back of the wagon to get my shoes.

The men gathered to make plans. It must have rained that morning because there were puddles and mud on the ground. The air was fresh and the cool breeze from the west brought a hint of autumn in this third week of August. We couldn't see much from the camping area as there were cottonwood and poplar trees and low hills in the way but we heard a train's whistle and the engine's huffing as it pulled into the station.

Father finally came and said. "Captain Jack rode ahead this morning and returned with new information. The name of the town is now Holbrook. It's the major shipping point for supplies going south. There are lots of freight wagons and teams in town. Those heavy outfits can't stop on a penny. They won't watch for you—you look out for them.

"There are three dry goods stores, a grocery, a barber shop, a newspaper print shop, a bakery and five saloons. The saloons have billiard parlors on the premises and are near the tracks and depot. The Bucket of Blood has a history of unsavoryness, so avoid it. You might get caught in the crossfire between trigger-happy cowboys. There are two respectable hotels with Ladies Lobbies where you can sit and rest. Mrs. B. F. Frank has an up-to-date millinery and dressmaking establishment. If any of you children have a few pennies saved that are burning holes in your pockets, look for the Breed Bros. Cheap Cash Store. We'll leave day after tomorrow for the three-day trip to St. Johns.

"Bill and I are going to the barber shop, the newspaper office and the post office. There may be letters in General Delivery that have been held for us," Father finished and went to meet Uncle Bill. They acted like two horses that could hardly wait to start the race.

Mother, Aunt Jane and Hattie put their heads together to plan our schedule. We couldn't all go at once since someone needed to watch the little ones. Our trips to town would be more enjoyable without toddlers. Lester and Reuben would take turns watching the animals. Mother would take Hattie, William and me with her while Aunt Jane stayed with her two and our three little ones. After we returned, Aunt Jane and Sister Selkirk would be free to go.

On our walk to town I asked Mother, "Did Father say anything about a new pair of shoes? These are as holy as the Bishop on Sunday and they hurt my feet."

"Mary, you're getting reckless in your speech. Captain Jack has not been a good influence. We all, especially the Bishop, strive to be holy every day, not just on Sunday. Father said to look for shoes, but you must choose the sturdiest and roomiest ones. You can stuff the toes with rags or paper until you grow into them. Is there anything special you are looking for, Hattie?" Mother asked.

"Mother told me to find the druggist. Sammy has a terrible cough and is listless. We're worried about him and Mother wants to talk to a druggist or a doctor and see what he recommends," Hattie answered, worry in her voice.

The train we heard earlier was at the depot. Dust hovered over the town. Rough bearded men hustled back and forth from the open boxcars to the waiting freight wagons. Some outfits were two and three wagons long with eight to ten mules each. The noise was deafening, the activity frenzied and the dusty air smelled of horse droppings.

"Mary, Hattie, William! Come this way. Don't stand there gawking like you just combed the hay out of your hair! The stores and shops are north of here. Let's find the Sheriff's Office and ask for directions to the stores we need," Mother said.

She spoke to a well-dressed man, "Sir, please direct us to the Sheriff's Office."

The man removed his wide brimmed, cream-colored hat and replied, "Madam, it would be my pleasure to do so if we had a sheriff. There are no lawmen in Apache County and we don't have a jail. Anyone who gets out of line or needs to sleep off a drunk is locked up in the back of Sing Lee's Laundry. Sometimes those who've been offended take care of it with their rifle or pistol. The dispatched offender is then taken to Boot Hill for eternal rest. Can I help you?"

"We need to know the whereabouts of a mercantile, a grocery, a druggist or doctor and the Cheap Store," Mother answered with all the dignity she could muster after the startling story of Boot Hill.

While they talked, I took a good look at the gentleman. He was the spiciest man I'd ever smelled. He was clean-shaven except for an amazing rusty mustache that extended a couple of inches from each side of his upper lip. His coppery hair was slicked back by something that wasn't bear grease. His face was unlined except for some crinkles around his clear green eyes. He was as tall as Father, and dressed in fancy Sunday go to meeting clothes, but it wasn't Sunday. His white shirt under a green satin vest and a gray striped coat was as white as the feathers in a bald eagle's tail. His walking stick had a snarling wolf, brass head. All the men and boys I'd known had hands that were scarred, calloused and dirtied by hard work. What work did he do in order to have clean soft hands and be dressed in such a fine way on Tuesday? My, he did smell good, like cinnamon and lemon extract mixed together.

"Mama, I want to go watch the train," William pleaded.

"Not now, William. Maybe later. Come along; let's get started. Thank you, sir, for your help." Mother smiled.

He bowed, replaced his hat and strode off in the direction of a building with a sign above the ornately carved door saying Lafferty's Palace. I saw him knock, wait to be invited in, and enter as a young woman in white apron and cap closed the door behind him. Windows, covered with red velvet curtains edged in white lace faced the street.

Why did they keep their curtains closed in the afternoon?

We walked on wood plank walkways until we came to the grocer's. Next door was the Cheap Store, and Mother said, "Mary, you and William go next door. He has two bits to spend. Hattie and I will look in the grocers for fresh fruit and vegetables. Don't leave until I come. Watch William. You know he fancies wandering."

The Breed Brothers Cheap Cash Store was a ramshackle building with rooms opening off of rooms. "Now, what can I do for you, little lady?" a short, round, cigar smoking man asked as he popped up from behind a counter.

"My brother wants to buy a toy. He has twenty-five cents. Which room should we look in?"

"Well, young feller, what kind'a things do you favor?" the clerk asked as he took the smelly cigar out of his mouth and tapped the ash into a dish on the counter. The dish was shaped like a train engine that had A &P written on the side.

"I like trains. Can I buy one of those dishes that look like an engine?"

"Sorry, young'n, that ash tray was give out by the A & P as a souvenir when they first come to Holbrook two years ago. There're train things on the last counter in the next room. Maybe you'd like a cap er a bandanna like the engineers wear. There're some metal models but they're more than two bits. I'll be here to collect the cash."

William and I walked past a maze of counters, through a door and into the next room. Across the room some dolls caught my eye. I'd never seen dolls like those. I was drawn, like iron filings to a magnet, by those elegant dolls. Three were propped on the counter by wire stands. They all had long curls, one's hair was as yellow as an August sunflower, another's was black as midnight and the third's was reddish brown like the color of our newborn colt. Their satin dresses were trimmed with lace and ruffles and each held an elegant beaded purse in her prettily posed hand. Each tiny fingernail was a rosy pearl. On their feet were shiny, black, dainty dancing slippers. Their eyes weren't real but I felt them looking at me and thinking, "Who is this raggedy girl with plain brown braids, sunburned nose and grubby hands with broken nails? Her shoes are shabby high tops that could never be worn for dancing."

Even though I imagined they looked down on me, I was in love. Minutes passed while I gazed and daydreamed about owning such beauty.

"Mary George, where is your brother?" Mother's voice cut through my dreams like lightening through a cloud. "Why can't you do what you're told?"

"Sir, where did the little boy go?" she asked the clerk.

"He bought a toy engine which I sold him for half price, said his mother was at the grocer's and off he went," he replied from inside a cloud of smoke.

"He knew exactly where he was going," Mother said sternly as she coughed and tried to wave away the smoke. "Mary and Hattie, go to the depot and ask about William. Hattie, give me your parcels. I don't like to send you two out by yourselves, but I have no choice. I'm going across the street to the post office inside the druggists. Dr. Robinson is both postmaster and doctor so I'll ask about medicine for Sammy. Henry may have been there or possibly, I'll find him there and let him know what's happened. This is as good a time as any to start speaking to him. When you find William, or any word of him, come to the post office. I'll deal with you later."

"Oh, boy, am I going to get it! Darn William. He's as hard to keep track of as a calf that knows it's about to be branded. Father'll be so mad that I'll never get a pair of new shoes. I love my brothers, but there are so many of them and I'm the one who's always in trouble. I hope he gets a good licking for running off," I grumped.

"What color is William's shirt?" Hattie asked. "Easier to spot someone if you have a color to look for."

"He's wearing a blue checked shirt, overalls and no hat," I said. As we neared the depot, the noise, dust and commotion snowballed. The wagons were loaded, the teams hitched and in line to leave. The locomotive huffed and breathed steam while it prepared to leave. The whistle blew, HOOT, HOOT, HOOOOOT!

"What if that rascal has hidden on a wagon or the train?" I said. Tears clouded my eyes and a lump grew in my throat.

"Look Mary, there he is!" Hattie cried over the din and pointed to the door of the depot.

The fine gentleman we had met earlier held William while he waved to the train engineer as the train pulled out. William was wearing an engineer's cap and beaming like he'd just won first prize in a three-legged sack race.

I was in trouble and he was having a grand time. He'd get it from me after Father paddled him. Here he came, walking beside the man like nothing was wrong, beaming to beat the band. "Mary! Mary! Look at the hat the engineer gave me. Took it right off a his head and give it to me. I asked him to give me a ride, but he said it was against the rules. I have to wait to grow up before I can go on the train by myself."

"Hello, Mary. I'm Mr. Winthrop. We met earlier. I'm glad I found this young whippersnapper before he got into serious trouble. Let's find your mother and relieve her worries. Are you with the families in the wagon train that came in today? We've been getting more and more folks coming into the territory. Pretty soon it'll be downright crowded around here. There's already one-hundred full time folks in our fair city."

I glared at William. Hattie answered because I was so mad I couldn't talk, "Yes, we've been traveling from Northern Utah for three months. We're headed for St. Johns to convert the Indians and start citrus groves. Aunt Elizabeth said to meet her at the post office."

Mr. Winthrop looked startled, "Citrus groves! Never heard of citrus growing in this climate. Here's the post office and I see your aunt talking to Dr. Robinson."

Father and Uncle Bill arrived at the same time from the opposite direction. Father smelled good, his beard and hair were trimmed, but he wore a questioning frown. I know he wondered what we three were doing in the company of a stranger, why my eyes were red and where did William get that hat? He'd be in for another surprise if Mother spoke to him to explain it all.

We crowded through the door; Mother tucked a bottle into her purse and said to Father, "Good, you've arrived just in time. I must go to the campground and relieve Jane. Mary, you've found William. I'll deal with both of you this evening. Hattie, come with William and me. Henry, take Mary to the A & B Schuster Mercantile and find her a pair of suitable shoes. Bill, I don't care what you do," she ordered as she marched out the door, parcels under her left arm, pulling squalling William by his left ear.

I sank down on a bench by the back wall while the men introduced themselves and talked. My knees were wobbly, my hanky was soaked and I was thirsty.

Was wanting that doll and forgetting about William one of the temptations of the flesh?

Dr. Robinson, noticing my distress brought me a cup of water, which I gulped like a thirsty puppy. Big city life was too much for me.

"I hear you gentlemen are from Utah, headed to St. Johns. What do you know about your destination?" Mr. Winthrop asked.

"We've been sent to reinforce the Mormon community at St. Johns. I'm in charge of starting citrus groves in the sheltered areas along the river," Uncle Bill replied. "I'm William George and this is my brother Henry. What business are you in, mister?"

"I'm Bertram Winthrop. I hope you're well versed on the climate and conditions at St. Johns. Winters are harsh. Not all of Arizona is hot and sunny throughout the year. I'm sure two astute gentlemen like yourselves know what you're getting into. I own the finest gambling house, billiard parlor and barber shop this side of Albuquerque. You look like you have just come from my tonsorial shop. The billiards and gambling rooms are behind and upstairs. We also sell the finest spirits available in this part of the territory. I call it Winthrop's, For Men."

"Thanks for finding my son," Father said. He looked taken aback when he learned of Mr. Winthrop's business. "We'd better find Mary some shoes. I'd like to take my wife out to supper tonight. I need time alone with her to mend fences. Is there a respectable dining establishment here?"

"Mr. Fred Harvey has opened a dining hall next to the depot. Doesn't look like much on the outside—four rusty, dented boxcars joined together—but the interior, service and food will surprise you. He will soon build a permanent place for the many passengers expected to come on the train who will need a pleasant, prompt dining place. Mr. Harvey has plans for a chain of dining rooms at all major stops on the railroad. Each one will be a Harvey House. I plan to be there this evening with a lady friend of mine, Miss Bridget Lafferty, who operates another men only establishment, Lafferty's Palace, where appetites of another kind can be satisfied. Good day," he said as he tipped his hat and left.

"Well, Bill, looks like our contact with the Gentiles is off to a rousing start. I must check General Delivery for mail. I also have letters to send to let our families in Utah know how we're faring. What are your plans?" Father asked.

"I'll go to the depot to see if any of the seeds and tree cuttings I ordered have come. I asked for delivery the last of August. I want to go by the *Holbrook Times* newspaper. We've been out of touch for three months and I wonder what's happening between the church and the Federals about polygamy. See you later," Uncle Bill said.

Father received letters from Utah and mailed the ones from us. "Elizabeth will be happy to hear from her mother. Here's a letter from Amy and Josh in St. George. Bill and Jane will be glad to hear from her. I'll save these for your mother to open. Hope there's no bad news, as your mother isn't very sturdy these days. Let's go shoe shopping," Father said as he held his hand out to me.

Father's hands were callused, rough and big. My hand disappeared inside of his. I felt safe when he held my hand. "Schuster's Mercantile is in the next block, beyond the Apache House Hotel. Would you like a glass of cold lemonade before we tackle the shoe shopping? The sign in the window of the hotel says they have ice and lemons on hand and are serving lemonade at tables in the lobby."

"Yes. I haven't had any since last summer in Mendon when a peddler came through with fruit from California. Thank you, Father."

I felt grown up sitting alone with Father. He always let me know I was special, after all, I was his only daughter. He loved my six brothers, but maybe there is a different feeling for daughters.

"Okay, Mary, tell me what kind of shoes do you have your heart set on?"

"I need some sturdy, high top, heavy soled shoes. Mother says to get them big enough to give my feet room to grow and to last through the winter. Someday I'd like to have a pair of shiny black low-topped shoes that would be special for Sunday School and dances. That's just a dream."

A girl wearing a clean white ruffled apron over a dark blue long skirt and a white blouse brought two frosty glasses of lemonade. A red cherry, stem attached, sat on chunks of ice in each glass. I'd never seen a drink done up like this and waited to see what Father did with his cherry. He picked the cherry up by its stem and dropped it into my glass.

"You've been a good trouper on this trip. You deserve an extra cherry. It won't be many years before you won't want to go for lemonade with me. You'll be more interested in the young fellows who'll be flocking around."

My ears burned and I turned red with embarrassment and pleasure. Did he really think I was pretty enough to have boys come a courting? "Boys will never flock around me. I'm plain and awkward. Boys are partial to girls with blonde curly hair, giggly high voices and dainty hands. My hands and arms are as strong as a boys, my hair is straight, plain brown and my voice is matter of fact, no nonsense," I answered with a sigh. "I bother people by asking too many questions."

"Giggles and frills don't hold up. Good sense, sturdy bodies and curious minds wear well. Some young lad will be lucky to find favor with you and I'm sure you'll choose wisely," he said as he drained his glass. "Ready to go shoe shopping?"

Chapter Eight

Holbrook, Arizona Territory, August 1885

The mercantile was dark after the bright sunshine. It smelled of leather, soap, pickles and hay. "Kindly direct us to the shoes," Father said to the clerk.

"Are you needing shoes for yourself or for the little lady? We have sections for both men and ladies," the young man replied.

"My daughter needs sturdy work and walking shoes. Do you have something in the ladies section?"

"Follow me. While we pride ourselves on our selection, we don't always have what the customer needs and must order from Albuquerque. Will you be in Holbrook for a while?"

"No, we need them today. Next week we expect to be in St. Johns. She's in dire need of shoes. Even if we buy from the boys department we'll buy today."

Buy from the boy's department? Such an embarrassment. Not only am I homely, but I may have to wear boy's shoes.

I wanted to shrink and fall through a knothole in the squeaky wood floor.

"Let's look at the ladies counter and see if there's anything suitable. Mary, we'll get you fixed up for the winter," Father said.

There was nothing in ladies shoes that would do unless all the lady did was walk no farther than three blocks or go to dances every night. I glumly followed them to the boy's counter.

I'm going to end up with big clunky things that'll make the kids in St. Johns tease and ask if I'm a boy. My brothers will be the worst. I want to make a good impression on my first day at school, but how can that happen if I'm wearing boy's clodhoppers?

"Have a seat, young lady, and I'll measure your foot. Take off your shoes and put your foot on this device. You've walked many a mile in those shoes." The clerk's blue eyes smiled as he tried to cheer me up.

He went to the shelves and returned with four pair. "Take a look at these beauties. Choose what you like, then try them on."

Each pair was equally unappealing and my heart sank. "They all look about the same. I'll try them on and choose the pair that feels best."

I made my choice, Father stuffed wadded newspaper into the toes, paid the bill and I clumped out of the store in my new, brown shoes. The soles were hard and thick. I felt I was walking on stilts. The stiff leather high tops rubbed and chafed my ankles but they would soften with wear. I choked back my disappointment, smiled and said, "Thank you, Father. My feet will be warm and snug all winter."

I needed to accept what was instead of wishing for pie in the sky, fancy, dainty black dress shoes. I'd wear clodhopper shoes, patched and mended clothes, eat bread and milk for supper and work for the neighbors to earn extra money. I would not surrender my dream of going to school.

We found Mother at Aunt Jane's. Sammy didn't look good. He was pale, sweating and having a hard time breathing. They wiped him with damp cloths and gave him more of the doctor's syrup. Both were happy to hear from family, but while reading they glanced worriedly at Sammy.

"Jane, we can talk about the news later. It would do you good to go into town for a while. Take Hattie with you. She didn't get much of an outing earlier. Sister Selkirk left with her daughters and you can't go alone," Mother urged her sister. "Mary, those shoes are just what I had in mind."

"There weren't many to choose from, but these are good and sturdy. Jane, after you return I'd like to take Elizabeth to supper. We'll be marking our twelfth wedding anniversary come November fourth and there may not be a place in St. Johns that's as nice as the Harvey House. Elizabeth, will you step out with me this evening?" Father stood with a hopeful smile on his lips as he waited, hat in hand, for Mother to speak.

"We do have things to discuss. Will that be all right with you, Jane? Mary and I'll get supper for the boys and the little ones and there'll be something hot for you and Hattie when you get back. I bought sweet corn from a Snowflake farmer who was selling from the back of his wagon and a piece of beef to make stew. Don't worry about Sammy. We'll take care of him. The medicine should start helping him to breathe easier in a spell."

As Aunt Jane and Hattie left, Uncle Bill came from town. He struggled with two big sacks of dry rootstock and a sack of seeds. Father went to help and they huddled and talked about what had arrived.

Mother and I began preparations for supper; the older boys returned from caring for the animals and started washing up. The little ones played stickball or chased each other around and over the red sandstone boulders back of the campground. Mother checked on Sammy and said his breathing had eased and he was sleeping.

Sister Richards came by. "Elizabeth, we've become close on this trip. I couldn't love you more if you were my blood kin. Mary and Roxie are true friends. With a heavy heart, I've come to tell you we won't be going to St. Johns. Marriner has decided to go to Snowflake where his cousin lives. We got a letter from Ammon and his wife, Sariah, and they beg us to settle near them. Since we aren't on an assigned mission, we're free to change our plans."

Tears came to Mother's eyes, her lip trembled and she and Sister Richards hugged. "Janet, I surely will miss you. You like to read and talking with you about books and life has kept me going when I felt like giving up. Mary will miss Roxie more than you can imagine."

The two of them walked away from the wagons for a private talk. I was left stirring the pot of stew, shucking the fresh corn while carefully saving the husks and silk in a burlap bag. The earth had dropped out from under me.

What a day! Holbrook, Mr. Winthrop, the dolls, losing then finding William, hearing Mother speak to Father again, having lemonade with Father and buying the clunkiest pair of shoes I've ever seen and now this. My tears dripped into the stew.

Oh, well, it probably needs salt anyway. Too many comings and goings all at once make me skittywampus.

Brownie smelled the stew bubbling in the pot, or maybe he knew I needed comforting because he ambled over and nudged my knee. "Brownie, you'll be the next to go. Why does everything change all of a sudden?" I wiped my tears on my apron, scratched Brownie behind his floppy ears and checked the kettle of water to see if it was hot enough to put the corn in.

Lester came from the washstand at the back of the wagon. He was wiping his head and neck with a flour sack towel when he spotted my shoes. "Golly

Gee, Mary, didn't they have any uglier ones? They'll be good in the fields for stepping over cow pies. Better be careful not to step on your partner's foot at the church dances or you'll put him in a cast for months. Reuben, come and take a look at Mary's dainty dancing shoes!"

He laughed and pointed to my feet. Reuben had always been kind to me, but as he got older and spent more time with Lester and the other boys, he joined in their jokes and pranks. He was just a year older than me but he'd moved into a different world on this trip.

"If you two don't stop teasing me I won't give you supper. You can eat hay with the horses and goats. I'm tired of being the butt of your teasing and joking. Girls are important and both of you stink. Get away from me! Leave me alone! I've had all I can take for one day," I yelled at the top of my lungs.

I dropped three large rocks into the burlap bag of corn husks, grabbed the bag and started swinging it with all my might. I knocked Lester on the side of his head, smacked Reuben in the gut and chased both of them halfway into town.

They were laughing and running while I was swinging the bag and crying. Blood trickled down Lester's face from a cut on his forehead. I didn't care. I tried to smack him again. "You're bullies," I shrieked through my tears. They kept laughing and running. Brownie was enjoying the chase and added to the noise by howling in his best bear-chasing yodel.

We ran around a bend in the path and almost collided with Aunt Jane and Hattie. My aunt dropped her parcels, dodged the swinging bag and grabbed my arm. She hollered at Lester and Reuben. "Whoa, boys, what's this ruckus about? Pick up my things and help Hattie carry them to camp."

Sweating, red faced and bloody, but still chortling, they followed Hattie.

"Mary, what happened? I've never seen you lose your temper like this. Your brothers are big teases. Aren't you used to it by now?" Aunt Jane asked.

She put her arms around me and I dropped the burlap sack, leaned against her and cried. After a few minutes I told her all that had gone wrong on a day that was supposed to be such a fine one. While I told my tale of woe I realized either she'd gained weight in her belly or she was in the family way. Since we'd not had an abundance of food, I bet she was carrying another child.

She wiped my face with her hanky, smoothed my flyaway hair, and said, "Mary, some nice days go sour ever so swiftly. That's why we need to appreciate every day that God gives us. Store up the good times to remember when things go topsy turvey. Now, let's get to camp so your folks can leave for their special evening. How's Sammy?"

I shrugged my shoulders in reply. When we arrived Mother was doctoring Lester's cut. Aunt Jane told her my tale and Mother barked at my brothers, "For your unkindness to Mary, you two will clean up after supper tonight and tomorrow. Teasing is not a joke, and both of you know better. Mary, go spend time with Roxie since they're leaving at first light tomorrow."

"Come on, Brownie, let's go see people who love us," I said over my shoulder as I walked away. I stuck out my tongue and glared at Reuben. He looked sheepish and moved his toe around in the dust. I was glad he was ashamed! He used to be my special brother.

Roxie and I hugged and cried. We promised to write and visit. I think she was also crying because of her crush on Andy, who was going to St. Johns with us. I couldn't stand to drag out our goodbye, so I didn't stay long. As Brownie and I walked back to our wagons, his ears drooped, my heart was heavy and my new shoes hurt. I wished I'd kept my old ones to wear until these got broken in. Old shoes are as comfortable as old friends.

Mother had changed into her white cotton dress with small flowers printed on it. Father had slicked back his hair and combed his newly trimmed beard. They looked happy and young as they left.

I pray they will have a good talk and come to a meeting of the minds. I hope Father will listen to her worries. Really listen—not just hear her words.

I helped Aunt Jane and Hattie feed the little ones supper. The older boys and some of the wagon drivers helped themselves to the beef and vegetable stew, fresh corn and some light bread Aunt Jane bought in town. After we got everyone else taken care of, the three of us settled down to enjoy our meal. The corn was the best I'd ever had.

"How come they grow such good corn in Snowflake?" I asked as I reached for another ear.

"Surefire tasty," said Hattie. "Maybe it's the good water from Silver Creek or something special in the dirt."

"Probably has something to do with the weather," Aunt Jane added. "I hope we'll be able to grow good vegetables in St. Johns."

We munched in a silence broken only by the crunching of the corn between our teeth. I noticed the different ways people eat corn off the cob. I started at one end, took three rows at a time and went clear to the other end. Then I went back and mowed down the next three rows. Hattie went around and around until she got to the other end. Aunt Jane went from one end to the other, back and forth back and forth. The little ones ate chunks from the cob in no order at all.

After supper, I enjoyed reading while sitting with my back against a boulder. Sister Selkirk kept me well supplied. "Mary, if you keep this up you won't have anything new to read this winter. I'll put you to work teaching the younger ones to read," she said a few days ago when I asked for a new book.

Lester and Reuben threw grumpy looks at me as they washed, dried and cleaned up the supper mess. Served them right. I waved happily to them and continued reading.

Uncle Bill called us together for evening worship and announcements. We were a small group because many were in town. Captain Jack wasn't expected back until the next day, Mother and Father were on their outing and three of the wagon drivers hadn't been seen since morning.

He announced the Richards were leaving us for Snowflake. "We will miss our companions with whom we've shared this long summer's trek. Let us remember them in our prayers and wish them God speed to their new home. We also give thanks to the Lord for our safety on the long and arduous journey, which is nearing its end. We pray for the healing of our son, Sammy. We'll spend one more day here then leave for St. Johns on Thursday morning. Spend tomorrow wisely and prepare your wagons and your souls for the last three days of travel."

After singing, "All is Well" we scattered to our wagons and beds. The sunset blazed pink, gold, and orange. The sky darkened, stars appeared and we were at peace under God's heavens.

I lay in my bedroll and drifted into dreams of school, a pretty white house with an orchard and friends to play with. I was jerked awake by the sound of men singing, laughing and stumbling. I sat up and wiped my sleep blurred eyes in time to see Captain Jack riding Buster, herding our three missing drivers into the wagon circle. Andy, Kayle and Will were staggering around like an old cow who'd eaten loco weed. Uncle Bill, barefooted and pulling up his suspenders shushed the group. "Shut up, you stupid boys. Stop that caterwauling. You are a disgrace. Where did you find this lot of fine young men, Captain Jack?"

"I wuz walkin from the Bucket over to McDonald's stable to check on Buster when I passed the Perkins & Taylor Billiard Parlor & Saloon. I heard a ruckus so stuck ma head in to see whut wuz happenin'. These three good Mormon lads wuz putting on a show for a gang of ranch hands. The cowboys wuz shootin' at the floor as close to our friends feet as they could to see Andy, Kayle and Will dance. Never havin' had any likker in their guts before, they were powerful affected by the whiskey they'd partook of."

Uncle Bill stood with arms folded across his chest and a thundercloud on his face. Andy crumpled and lay flat out on the ground. Kayle and Will wobbled and wove like pine trees in a high wind.

Captain Jack continued, "I went in, corralled the three dancers, walked to the stables, climbed on Brownie, and herded these country bumpkins here for you to care for. I magine they won't need much chastising frum you as they're already as sick as a dog that ate a frog."

By this time the adults had gathered round. The Richards were relieved to have Will show up as he was their driver. Brother Selkirk led Kayle to their wagon and gave him a swift kick in the butt and left him where he fell, to sleep it off. Andy crawled to the edge of camp and threw up.

Another temptation of the flesh! I've never seen the effects of alcohol before now. No wonder the church teaches against it. Why are there so many saloons in the world if this is what strong spirits do to you?

"I've got a few more people to see and business to tend to," Captain Jack said. "I'll be back tomorrow and ready to leave on Thursday mornin."

Andy's heaving slowed and I took him a cup of water. He had a few sips and started urping all over again, so I decided to leave him be. I had dozed again when I heard Mother's laugh as she and Father returned. I was glad they were safely back and hadn't succumbed to any temptations. I was weary of city life. I covered my head, closed my eyes and slept.

The next morning Mother entertained us with an account of their supper at the Harvey House. "You wouldn't believe a place that looks so decrepit and rundown on the outside could be so gracious on the inside. It was a joy to be waited on by clean courteous young women, each wearing a long black dress covered with a ruffled white apron. The tableware sparkled on snowy cloths, the water had ice in it and the menu was surprising. I felt like the Queen of England to be treated so royally. I chose braised lamb chops, while Henry ordered a roast of beef. We enjoyed mashed potatoes with gravy, fresh green beans, hot rolls and butter. I had lettuce and tomato salad while Henry ordered clam chowder. Dessert came with the meal so we each had a piece of chocolate cake with vanilla ice cream. The meal cost us only one dollar each! What a treat. Did anything interesting happen while we were gone? I notice Andy doesn't seem to be enjoying his oatmeal this morning."

We heard the Richards calling their goodbyes. We went to their wagons, hugged and kissed, promised to write and waved them on their way.

"How will they know the way since Captain Jack is staying with us?" I asked Father.

"Brother Richards' cousin, Ammon, came into town yesterday to peddle corn. You had some for supper. He'll meet them in Holbrook and lead the way."

"Does it snow a lot in Snowflake? Is that why they named their settlement such a pretty name?" I asked.

Father laughed, "No, it's named for the two founders, Brother Snow and Brother Flake. They get that question all the time."

After the Richards left, we returned to our wagons and the grownups decided how to spend the day. Father and Uncle Bill had business in town, Mother and Aunt Jane needed to do laundry and wagon cleaning, the herders would take the animals to the hills beyond the campground. Hattie wanted to go to town and do more shopping. I wanted to stay away from the big city. I volunteered to take the young ones to the creek that ran beside our camp to let them play. William had to help with the laundry as punishment for wandering yesterday.

I gathered up Roy, Richard, Aunt Jane's Rachel and Alma. Sammy was too sick to go with us. We borrowed some buckets, spoons and spades to have a quiet morning at the creek. The warm sun, gentle breeze and trickling stream of water were soothing to me after my hectic day in Holbrook. We took off our shoes and stockings and frolicked like spring lambs.

When the late August sun signaled noon, we collected our toys, put our shoes on and trooped, wet, sandy and in high spirits to camp. There was a shiny, black two-seater buggy parked under a cottonwood.

Mother called, "Mary, we have visitors who want to say 'Hello' to you."

Mr. Winthrop stood by a woman with a frilly white parasol shading her long black hair. She wore a lacy straw hat and creamy pink dress. The woman and Mother were chatting.

Who in the world is she? I look like a dirty orphan and Mother wants me to come and meet this fancy woman. She's dressed like the dolls I saw in the store. Where on earth did Mother meet her?

"Hello, Mary. Good to see you again. Looks like you've had a good time," Mr. Winthrop said. "My friend, Miss Lafferty, and I met your parents at the Harvey House and they invited us to ride out and visit."

I brushed my messy hair back from my face with a grubby hand and gave Miss Lafferty a small curtsey as Mother had taught me to do when meeting adults. I glanced up and met Miss Lafferty's kind blue eyes. She seemed to be looking me over, from my new clodhoppers to the top of my head.

"Hello, Mary, pleased to meet you. Mr. Winthrop told me how brave you were to roam around Holbrook in search of your brother. How old are you?"

"I'll be nine on the twenty-first of October, Miss Lafferty. You're dressed like a doll I saw at the Cheap Store yesterday," I said. "I hope when I grow up I'll have fancy clothes like yours. Especially the shoes."

"Thank you, Mary, you'll get your wish one of these days. Are you excited about going to St. Johns and starting a new life? What do you hope to do there?"

"I want to go to school and learn about the world. I like to look at rocks, clouds and Indian pots and learn about stars and far off places I've read about. Where are you from, Miss Lafferty?"

Mother put her hand on my shoulder and said, "That's enough, Mary. Get cleaned up for dinner and wash all that sand off the children."

"Goodbye, Mr. Winthrop, Miss Lafferty. I enjoyed meeting you. Maybe I'll see you again if I ever come back to Holbrook."

They talked with Mother while I collected my charges. We splashed and rinsed in the tin basin on the washstand. I felt like I did when the dolls were judging me. Miss Lafferty was so dainty and clean and pretty.

Will I ever get the dirt from under my fingernails, my hair shiny and curly and my clothes and shoes fine and fancy? Pie-in-the-sky Mary. You're plain, sturdy and curious. No use yearning after the impossible. My parents love me, God loves me and my brothers tolerate me. What more can I ask for?

After dinner, Mother asked me to walk with her. It'd been a long time since we'd talked and I had many questions. "Mother, you've never explained what happened to you in Orderville. Will it happen again? I couldn't stand it if anything bad happened to you. Did you know what you were doing? How did you end up in the streambed? Is Aunt Jane going to have another baby? Are you feeling better about being a pioneer? People say it gets real cold in St. Johns in the winter, so how can Uncle Bill grow citrus trees there? What did your mail have to say about our folks in Mendon? Is Grandma Mary all right?"

"Mary, stop! You overwhelm me. One thing at a time. Today isn't the time to talk about my mishap in Orderville. Your father and I have discussed it and will tell you someday. I'm not happy about our move and I wasn't cut out to be a pioneer. I believe Henry finally realizes that. We've agreed I'll never have to make another long wagon trip. I may make short ones but never again will I set out for three months into the wilderness in a wagon. Yes, Aunt Jane will have a child next spring. She's not well and I pray things will be easier in St. Johns. She is worried about Sammy. Her usual sunny disposition has gone behind a cloud.

"Uncle Bill's heard about the cold winters in northern Arizona and has doubts about his mission. I don't think the church authorities studied the matter well and jumped to the conclusion this climate is like St. George where the winters are mild. If oranges won't grow, maybe apples will.

"The news from Mendon is that all are well and they're anxious to get news of us. My mother, Mary, is living with my sister Rhoda and her husband Peter Hansen, so she's well cared for. You can read their letters later. Any more questions?"

"No, except why did Mr. Winthrop bring Miss Lafferty to see us?"

"Here's a shady spot under this cottonwood. Let's sit and enjoy the view. I met Miss Lafferty last evening. We chatted about things in general and then she started asking questions about you. Mr. Winthrop had described you to her and he was impressed with your 'spunk.'"

"Miss Lafferty is a successful businesswoman. While I don't approve of her type of 'social service'—don't ask me what it is because I won't discuss it with you—I give her credit for turning her misfortune around and becoming independent. She was abandoned by her fiancé in Gallup and found herself penniless with only her wits to provide for her needs. Shortly thereafter she gave birth to a girl. She brought her daughter to Holbrook when the railroad reached here. Last year there was an epidemic of typhoid fever and the eight-year-old died. Her name was Christine and her mother loved her very much. Shortly before Christine died, Miss Lafferty met Mr. Winthrop and they became friends. They aren't married but they look after and care for each other. Our church doesn't approve of that sort of relationship, but then I don't always agree with the church."

"How sad. I guess you can't tell much about a person just by the way they look or dress. She seems sunny and happy and is so pretty. Maybe someday she'll have another baby to make her happy again," I said

"She wanted to meet you and see what size you are. Seems she has some of Christine's dresses, hats and shoes she's ready to part with. She asked me if it would be all right to give them to you. Mr. Winthrop will bring a parcel for you later. I don't know how appropriate the items will be or if they will fit, but we'll be grateful and I'll help you write a thank you note when we get settled again."

What luck. I hope they'll fit. Whatever they are, they'll be better than my worn out things and maybe there'll be a pair of black shiny shoes to wear to Sunday School and church dances. I won't say that to Mother. She might think I'm complaining and I don't want to hurt her feelings.

"Well, aren't you going to say anything? I've never seen you at a loss for words before," Mother said as she hugged me. "You deserve a treat like this. We love you, appreciate you and know this trip has been hard for you. Have to get the clothes off the line, start supper and pack in preparation for leaving."

That evening, Mr. Winthrop came with a grocery carton tied with brown string. "Mary, your mother says it's all right for you to accept this. Miss Lafferty wants you to have her daughter's things instead of letting them rot away in a dark closet. Enjoy, have fun, learn all you can and come back and see us someday."

I took the carton from him and put it on the ground. He stayed on his horse as I said, "Give my thanks to Miss Lafferty. I'm sure I'll enjoy Christine's things and will always be grateful to her. Tell her I'll write soon."

He tipped his hat, turned his horse and was gone. I saw a tear in his eye.

I took the box to Mother. She helped me open it. "My word, Mary, there's a lot of stuff crammed into this box. Three dresses—a fancy one of sky blue silk with lace around the collar and cuffs, two cotton school dresses with ruffled pinafores and lots of petticoats and stockings. Two pairs of shoes that have barely been worn. Hope they fit. And look at this, a frilly bonnet made of the same blue silk as the dress."

I held the dresses up and looked at them with wonder. I'd never had a store bought dress before. I was anxious to try on the shoes so I sat on a tree stump, took off my clodhoppers and slipped into the most beautiful pair of black, low top, soft leather shoes I'd ever seen. They were a little big, which meant I'd be able to wear them longer. I walked around Mother swishing my worn skirt above the princess shoes, parading like a peacock in the park. I'd never seen a peacock parading but had read about how they strutted around.

"Mary, don't go getting above yourself. Pride goeth before the fall. Pretty is as pretty does. You're most fortunate to inherit this, but wear them humbly and thank God for your blessings. Don't go bragging and strutting around in front of Hattie and the other girls. You'll make them feel bad and you'd end up with fancy clothes and no friends. What is the other pair of shoes like?"

I pulled a shiny brown pair of low top tie up oxfords out of a paper bag. "These will be perfect for school when the weather is good. I can use the clodhoppers for traveling and wearing in mud and snow. I know you and Father bought me what I really needed, but these others are for special times. Isn't this fun? Just like Christmas!"

Mother replied thoughtfully, "Let's put these things back in the carton. Let me have time to think how best to handle this situation. I didn't realize there would be so many things and of such high quality. "

Captain Jack and Brownie returned as it was getting dark. Brownie came and slept beside me. I fell asleep hugging the thought of my new clothes and imagining all the places where I would wear them.

What had Christine been like? Did she read, look at rocks, make pictures out of clouds and watch the stars dance across the sky at night? I'm sorry you got sick and died and I hope you're having fun in Heaven. Thank you, my friend, whom I'll never know.

When we left Holbrook it was sunny, breezy and there was a touch of fall. The next day would be the first of September and I noticed the sun was farther to the south and its light seemed softer. We crossed the Little Colorado River as we left town, then crossed again as we turned east and headed for St. Johns. We planned to stop at Cottonwood Wash for the night.

After gathering time Uncle Bill asked Captain Jack to tell us about the next two days. "Afore we head out tomorrow I'd like to take who ever's interested, to see one of the wonders of the west. Tomorrow'll be a short travel day so we'll have time for a side trip to see the Petrified Forest. In this country you'll find rocks that ain't rocks. Seems as tho this part of the west was once covered by an ocean. Some parts were swampy places where huge, tall trees and ferns and strange animules lived. The weather dried out, the swamps and ocean disappeared and the trees and animules died. Now we see whut's left in the form of gigantic rock tree trunks. A friend measured a trunk that's two-hunnert-ten feet long and five feet across the butt. Don't spect to see any trees standin up, but watch for the fallen trunks. There's pieces of many colored petrified wood layin' on the ground. Some folks build houses out of the chunks. Iffe'n you want to take a look, be ready right after the sun comes up and I'll lead you to some interesting sights.

"Tamarra night we'll stop at where the Zuni River runs inta the Little Colorado. The day atter that we'll arrive at St. Johns."

We cheered and clapped. The end was in sight. I could hardly remember living in a real house with rooms, furniture, a roof and a kitchen with a stove.

Our early morning walk into the Petrified Forest was fun. I wanted to know what changed wood into stone and why it had so many pretty colors. I picked up some small pieces to put with my other treasures to remember this day by.

I watched Mother and Father walk arm in arm. Mother was laughing excitedly as they viewed the strange country. Sandy hills that look painted, large fallen logs, and no living trees or bushes made it seem like we were on a different planet.

We left late in the morning and made the Zuni River in time for supper. All were in a high state of expectation and excitement, yet there was a feeling of loss.

Captain Jack and Brownie would leave us soon. We'd meet new people, find places to live, learn new ways of getting what we needed and hoped that our long held dreams wouldn't prove false.

Chapter Nine

St. Johns, Arizona Territory, Autumn 1885

It was September 6, 1885. Captain Jack rode ahead to find a place to camp. We followed the river and approached St. Johns from the north. We passed through sandy, many-colored layered hills—gray, pink, orange or black. Near town tall Mormon trees, cottonwoods and willows grew along the river. Flocks of sheep grazed on knee high golden, end of summer grass. It must not have rained for a time because between the rolling wagon wheels and the roving sheep we arrived at St. Johns in a cloud of gritty dust.

"Found yer Bishop Udall and he said to direck you to the tithing lot north and west from town in a spot called the Meadows. The river's close and there's a corral for the animules. The Bishop'll be out to greet you after a while. Follow me and we'll be set up in a jiffy."

When we arrived, Father said, "This is truly the land of milk and honey; grazing land, water in the river and forested mountains to the south."

In mid afternoon a tall, sandy haired, bearded man, followed by two women and a group of young people appeared. The women and children carried loaves of bread, pots full of stew, bottles of milk, water and sacks of cookies.

"Welcome to St. Johns! We've been praying for your safety and have looked forward to your arrival," the tall man said. "I'm Bishop David Udall, this is my wife Rachel and her sister Sarah. Greetings and blessings from the Saints in St. Johns. We've brought gifts to make your first day easier. Let us pray together, giving thanks for your safe trip and place our trust in God for a good beginning to your mission in this outpost of Zion."

After a long prayer, the men shook hands, introduced themselves and walked to the shade of the cottonwoods. Rachel and Sarah gave the food to our mothers while we children stood and gawked at each other.

Finally I approached a girl who looked my age, and said, "Hello, I'm Mary George from Mendon. We're glad to get here. We've been traveling since June. Have you always lived here or did you come in a wagon?"

The blonde girl with brown eyes and freckles said, "I'm LaVerle Merrill. Glad to make your acquaintance. I was born here. The farthest I've ever been is Holbrook. Do you have any books I can borrow?"

"I have some of Sister Selkirk's. She's a school teacher and will be happy to lend you books. Do you have a real school with maps that roll down from the wall and blackboards to write on?"

"Not yet. We have classes at the church. It'll be nice to have a lady teacher. Brother Reynolds is mean. Maybe he'll teach boys and Sister Selkirk will teach girls."

Mother called, "Mary, come take care of Parley. We must unload the wagons so we can take the wagon beds off the wheels."

"Why on earth do they want to do that?" I asked LaVerle.

"Most new settlers live in their wagon boxes until the men get a house built. There aren't any empty houses in St. Johns. There are two dugouts by the river that some people lived in last winter, but they're awful. I hope you won't have to live in one," LaVerle said while making a face as if she smelled a rotten potato.

"Why take the boxes off the wheels?"

"So they can use the frame and wheels to go to the saw mill at Amity to get logs and boards and carry other big things," LaVerle answered.

I took Parley from Mother and watched the women and older boys haul our things out of the wagons. I watched to make sure no one treated my treasures roughly. It took four husky men to get Mother's cook stove out of our extra wagon.

"Carry it over under the trees, close to the river," Mother ordered. "I'll set up my kitchen under a canvas cover close to the water. It'll be good to cook on a stove again instead of a campfire."

Father and Captain Jack were talking. "What are your plans, Captain? I know you're itching to be on your way south. My brother will pay the rest of your fee as soon as he's set up. We're going to miss you and your animal companions. Thanks to you we've had a good trip."

"Wall, Mr. George, thanks for your preciation. We was plumb lucky to have such a smooth journey. I'm rarin' to go off on my own for a while but first Buster needs some new shoes, I need a shave, a hot bath, a good hotel meal and a comftable off the ground bed. The Bishop can tell me whar to go for them things. I leave day after tomorrow."

Bishop Udall approached Captain Jack and asked, "Did I hear you say you plan to leave shortly? Which way are you headed?"

"I'm planning to meet some trappin' buddies at Fort Apache. They left a message in Holbrook to the effect that they'd wait for me. Times wastin' and I got to get on my way over them mountains to the White River and foller it to the fort."

"I ask because you may be in danger traveling in that direction by yourself. We've had reports of roaming bands of Apache renegades looking for whatever they can steal. The young men get restless when winter's coming. The Whitings had a close call last week while moving cattle down from the mountains. Lost three of their beeves, but no horses. They were well armed and had their four sharpshooter sons along. One of our freighters is loading three wagons of hay to take to the fort. He'll be ready to go in four days. Why don't you wait and ride with them?"

"Have to get movin' sooner'n that. Besides, a freight outfit'll take at least a week to get there. I've been in Indian country all my life and got along just fine. Have a Shoshone wife up in Idaho," Captain Jack answered. "Whar can I git Buster shod, git me a sprucing up, a good meal and a clean bed?"

The Bishop remarked to Father, "That sure is a good-looking Appaloosa. Don't see many of them around here. He'd be a prize for an Apache brave."

The next day the Taylor family told us they'd decided to go up river to Alpine. "There're too many Gentiles in St. Johns," Brother Taylor told Uncle Bill. "Have you been into town? I counted six saloons, two houses of ill repute and one Catholic Church. We Saints are outnumbered at least eight to one. Me and mine prefer a less civilized place where we'll be left alone and not have to learn Spanish to conduct business at the mercantile."

Rhoda's family was leaving. Of the ones we started with, only the Selkirks and we two George families were left. Would any of us be left by the end of winter?"

"Aren't you on a mission?" Uncle Bill asked sternly. "How can you ignore the orders of the church?"

Brother Taylor said, "I figure the powers that be in Utah didn't know what kind of country this is. I hear you'll never grow citrus in this climate. The people don't want us moving in and I can't say as I blame them. We have our ways and they have theirs. We Saints do better when we move into empty lands and start from scratch. Spanish sheep-herders and cattlemen have been in this valley for two-hundred years. Upriver there're several Mormon settlements, Springerville, Amity and Alpine to name a few. It's higher, colder in the winter, but there are more trees, grass and water. Most important is that we'll be with our own kind."

"I will not ignore the instructions of my mission. We'll stick it out here and with God's help do what we've been sent to do," Uncle Bill replied solemnly.

When the Taylors left for Alpine, Rhoda and I hugged, cried and vowed to write. I helped Mother cook and clean up after breakfast, then walked to the river. I just sat. All I felt like doing was sitting.

We had arrived in the land of milk and honey. Now what? I felt like crying.

Mary, you are a crybaby. If you aren't careful Aunt Jane will cut out your cry bag. That's what she told the toddlers she would do when they whined and cried. Is my cry bag bigger than normal? Where is it anyway? I don't want anyone cutting anything out of me so I best stop boo-hooing.

Mother was calling, "Where have you been? Parley's fussing, I need water hauled from the river and put in the washtub. Jane says Sammy's taken a turn for the worse. You're never around when I need you. Stop wandering off and tend to your chores." Mother's eyes were red, they sparked with anger, her face was blotchy and her voice tight.

"I'm sorry. I needed to be alone for a few minutes."

"Well, this is no time to be la-di-da. When you grow up and live in a fine white house and have servants waiting on you, you'll have time to be Miss Priss. Take the bucket and start filling the tub. Put Parley in his sling so you can keep track of him. I'm going to stay with Sammy while Jane and Hattie go find a doctor."

"Where are Father and Uncle Bill?"

"Never you mind about them. They're going about their business and we'll tend to ours," she snapped and stomped away.

What in the world set her off? Maybe traveling wasn't so bad after all. Just got up, dressed, ate breakfast and rolled on. Now that we're here, there's a whole huddle of new things to decide and fret about. The wagons look strange without their wheels. They hunker down on the ground like a herd of fat white cows with no legs.

"Come with sister," I said to Parley while lifting him into his sling. I picked up the water bucket and headed for the river.

By noon Aunt Jane and Hattie returned with a Navajo woman. Her face was nut brown and wrinkly. Her gray hair hung over her shoulders in two long braids tied with yellow yarn. She wore soft leather boots, a three-tiered gathered red skirt and a long sleeved green top. Strands of turquoise and silver beads hung around her neck and in her right hand she carried a tattered black doctor's bag.

"Elizabeth, this is Grandma Burntwater. She is the only medical help in the area right now. The doctor's in Springerville repairing cowboys who got into a knife fight with Mexican herders. He won't be back for days. Sammy needs help now. How is his breathing? Has he eaten anything or been able sleep?" Aunt Jane asked.

"Do you trust your son to an Indian? How do we know she knows what she's doing? Does she speak English?"

"I am a healer to my Navajo people and speak English. Before I came to live with my son, I worked with an American doctor at Fort Wingate, in New Mexico. Maybe I can help him breathe more easily."

Aunt Jane and the woman went into the wagon. Mother called, "Mary, get some water boiling and bring it as soon as you can. Sammy is struggling."

I did as told. Hattie and I stood and watched the pot, which took forever to boil. "What was town like?" I asked. "Is it a nice place? Did you see our church? How many stores are there?"

"Well—I didn't see much except for Main Street. Most buildings are built of mud bricks and have tin roofs. It's smaller than Holbrook and there are few trees. The town looks dirty. I saw Captain Jack at the blacksmith's getting Buster shod. He said he'd be out this evening before he leaves for Fort Apache."

"Did you see our fathers? Wonder what business they're taking care of."

"Mother said they're looking for a place to live. Because Sister Selkirk is a teacher, her family will live in the back room of the church. Brother Selkirk got a job with the freighting company that takes hay and other goods to Fort Apache. Andy is working with him. I saw the Catholic Church. It has a high bell tower. It's the tallest building."

When the pot finally boiled I took it to the wagon. Soon I smelled a spicy odor and heard Sammy coughing. I peeked in and saw Grandma Burntwater holding a towel over Sammy's head while he breathed the fumes in the steam. He coughed up some goop and breathed easier.

"Use these dried herbs. Every two hours put a half cup of them in boiling water and have him breathe deeply to get the fumes into his lungs. If it's going to help, he'll be better in two days. He may be too weak for it to do any good. Some things are beyond medical help," the woman said as she left the wagon.

"What can I pay you?" Aunt Jane asked.

"Let's see if he gets well. That would be pay enough. I'll return tomorrow."

After dinner, we busied ourselves with laundry and were finished when the men returned. The older boys had taken the animals to the hills to graze. They took food and water to last a couple of days.

Captain Jack came at suppertime. Buster was loaded with saddle packs and a bedroll. He pranced with excitement as if he knew he was off on a new adventure. Brownie nuzzled my leg. I dropped to my knees, lifted a floppy ear and whispered, "You be a good watch dog and keep Captain Jack and Buster safe. You know you're the most important one. You can hear and smell things before the others can, so you have a big job."

He growled softly in his throat as if to tell me he knew his responsibilities. "I'm missing you already. Maybe someday I'll have a Brownie. I'll call him Brownie, Jr."

While I washed the dishes, Captain Jack mounted Buster, whistled for Brownie and they headed toward the foothills. I stood with my hands in the hot soapy water as tears ran down my cheeks and dripped into the dishwater.

Later I lay awake and listened to the grownups confer around the campfire.

"What does the housing situation look like, Henry? Are we going to spend the winter huddled around the stove here on the river's edge? Did you find the snug warm cabin you promised?" Mother was angry in her polite way. This place wasn't what we'd been led to expect.

"We saw two dugouts near the river. They were used last winter so most of the work has been done. The back walls are dug into the hill and are lined with upright cedar posts. Our kitchen stove will keep it warm."

Uncle Bill continued, "They're close to the river north of town. We will stay there while we get lumber from the mill and build our houses. We inquired about work. We need cash since we've arrived at the end of the growing season and won't be able to grow what we need."

Mother and Aunt Jane looked at each other. Neither said a word. They stood and went to Sammy who was coughing worse than ever.

The cold autumn wind whispered through the cottonwoods. Dry yellow leaves fell. I skooched as far down in my bedding as I could, shut my eyes, fell asleep and dreamed of our snug house in Mendon.

The next morning, yellow and brown leaves covered my bedroll and were stuck in my hair. Sammy was worse. Aunt Jane couldn't wake him; he breathed in short shallow puffs and his skin was waxy. Uncle Bill went for Bishop Udall. The men would lay their hands on Sammy and give him a priesthood blessing.

I prepared breakfast, cleaned up and kept the little ones busy while Mother and Aunt Jane stayed with Sammy. While I entertained the children, Grandma Burntwater walked into camp.

"How is the boy? I thought about him all night."

"He's not good. His mother is afraid he will die today."

"Some have a short time on this earth while others live many years. It is not for us to understand. We can only try to get along and help when we can. Death comes in many ways and sometimes is a blessing. I'll go to the wagon to see what I can do."

Grandma Burntwater intrigued me. She smelled and looked like an Indian, but talked and acted like a white person. It wasn't an unpleasant odor. Smoke, sheep fleece, sand and sun.

How old is she and why does she live with her son? Why does her son live here instead of on the reservation, where most Navajos live?

My thoughts were interrupted by the return of Uncle Bill and the Bishop. Father joined them and they went to Sammy. Aunt Jane, Mother and Grandma Burntwater stood outside and waited.

"He's gone," Uncle Bill said sorrowfully as he put his arms around his wife. "We've lost our baby. God will have a place for him in Heaven."

"We have our own cemetery," Bishop Udall said. "I'll have a coffin built, a grave dug and set a time for services. I'm sorry for your loss, especially at the beginning of your stay with us. We'll do all we can to help, but your greatest solace will come from your faith that someday you'll be reunited with Sammy. Your memories will keep him alive in your hearts. I'll return later with the coffin and tell you of the arrangements. Brother George, come with me while your brother stays with his wife and child."

Uncle Bill kept his arm around Aunt Jane as they walked the riverbank. Mother and Grandma Burntwater went into the wagon to wash and dress Sammy for his last earthly journey.

Later I learned that most Navajos are afraid of the dead and won't go near a body except to bury it as soon as possible. If a Navajo dies in his hogan, it is abandoned and a new one built. They fear the spirit stays near by and will make the living sick. Grandma Burntwater had learned some Christian ideas at a mission school and held a curious mixture of Anglo and Navajo beliefs.

Hattie and I prepared and served dinner for our saddened families, put the little ones down for a nap in the other three wagon beds. Then we shed our tears.

When Grandma Burntwater left, I ran to catch her. "Could I visit you someday? I have questions about the Navajos and how you came to be here. I'd like to learn how to be a healer."

"Child, you have a mind that yearns to be filled. There is a sparkle about you that will attract all kinds of love and trouble. I live on the way to Concho. My son is a herder on one of the Spanish sheep ranches. Look for three hogans on top of a hill. Do you know what a hogan is?"

"Yes, I saw some when we arrived. They're round little houses with smoke coming out of a hole in the roof."

"Come and sit by my fire and we will talk."

Lester and Reuben returned to camp that evening. Uncle Bill told them the sad news, "Sammy has passed away. Services and burial will be tomorrow."

After supper we hauled water to wash the dishes and fill the washtubs. The men started fires in the stone rings. The women and girls bathed first because we don't get as dirty as the men and boys.

After baths, Reuben whispered, "Mary, I need to talk to you. Lester and I found something very strange in the foothills."

"Is this some kind of a joke? It's no time to be jollying around."

"No, this is something you'll like. We found an Indian cave. There were broken pots and spear points in the dirt at the mouth of the cave. We didn't go in because we didn't have a lantern and the tunnel bent so it got dark real quick."

"Tell me more tomorrow. We need to sleep and get up early for the funeral."

After I got into my bedroll I thought about Brownie. I wished I had him to snuggle against to keep me warm. I wouldn't even mind if he snored in my ear. I wondered where they were bedded down on this sad night.

The next morning the men and older boys carried the coffin to the church while the rest of us followed. After the service and burial the women of the church planned a dinner. I wanted to wear the Sunday dress and bonnet from Miss Lafferty but Mother thought it was too fancy.

"Mary, wear one of the cotton gingham frocks with a pinafore. The brown low top oxfords will be good as we have to walk into town to the cemetery and back to the church for dinner."

I was excited to be going to town for the first time and hoped to see LaVerle. Since Roxie and Rhoda had gone, I didn't have a friend my age. Hattie was okay but she was a cousin and four years older.

The church was crowded. The day had turned hot, the windows and doors were open and flies and bees joined the service. While we sang the closing hymn I opened my mouth too wide and a fly buzzed in. Because I didn't know what else to do, I swallowed it and hoped it wouldn't make me sick. I was glad it wasn't a bee.

Most of the Saints stayed behind to set up tables and benches for the dinner while our family followed Sammy's coffin to the cemetery.

LaVerle grabbed my arm as I walked out, and whispered, "I'll save you a place next to me at dinner. That's a nice dress you're wearing. See you later."

With heavy hearts we buried Sammy. He lived through the hardships of the journey to St. Johns only to die before we were settled. Aunt Jane and Uncle Bill wept as the men shoveled clumpy clay riddled earth into the open grave. I was startled to hear a sharp cry—scree, scree. I looked up and saw two bald eagles soaring high across the blue sky. They were ships sailing the ocean of sky.

Father carried Parley and walked beside Mother. Her stony face gave no hint of what she was thinking. I was sad, yet excited and looked forward to going back to the church to visit with LaVerle and meet other girls my age. I wanted to ask Sister Selkirk when school would be starting.

As we left the cemetery I saw Grandma Burntwater motion to me from under a cottonwood. "The eagles came to carry the child's soul to Heaven," she told me. "I found this eagle feather on the road as I walked this morning. It told me all is well with the child. Keep the feather to remind you of him and know he is with you in your heart."

Before I could stammer "Thank you" she turned and was gone.

That night before I slept I thought of things I'd heard and seen.

Aunt Jane is starting to show she's with child. She isn't the same cheerful person as a few months ago. She spends more time by herself and depends more and more on Hattie. I wish Amy were here. Amy's expecting her first child soon after Aunt Jane expects her eighth.

LaVerle introduced me to the girls from town. Some were friendly, some were shy and one was too uppity to bother with a newcomer. They liked my dress and pinafore and I received compliments. I followed Mother's instructions to be modest and say "Thank you." "You don't make friends by trying to impress people but by being friendly, asking their opinion and finding out what they like to do,'" Mother had said.

School would begin in two weeks. We'd be in the dugout by then and I hoped Mother would keep her promise to let me go. My heart's desire was within reach.

Lester and Reuben didn't want to go to school. They wanted to help Father and Uncle Bill build furniture, herd the animals and get a real job to earn money of their own. I didn't understand them. They were only eleven and ten but they'd turned into independent ruffians. I guessed their brains weren't set up for book learning like mine was.

One night I dreamed Brownie was snuffling in my ear and snuggling against my bedroll. I reached out from under the covers, scratched behind his ear and went on sleeping.

"Mary, wake up," Father said. I didn't want to wake and lose Brownie again. "What's Brownie doing here? How long has he been here?"

That woke me in a hurry. "I thought I was dreaming," I answered fuzzily as I sat up. "Brownie, where did you come from?" He had a deep scratch and dried blood on his left back leg. He limped when he walked to the river to get a drink.

"Bill, wake the boys. Something's wrong. Lester, go tell Bishop Udall we need someone who knows this country to help search for Captain Jack. We'll get breakfast, pack food for the trail, saddle the horses and be ready to leave in an hour," Father ordered. "Mary, wash Brownie's leg, poultice it, and get him something to eat. His nose will guide us."

What in the world has happened? Brownie would never run away without cause. My heart pounded with panic. Calm down, Mary, you always think the worst.

The men, a guide from town and three older boys rode off on the trail to Fort Apache with Brownie loping behind. Lester and Reuben were left in charge of the animals and were mad they didn't get to go. "Gosh darn it, I'm too old to be left behind with women and babies," Lester snarled. He kicked a dirt clod at me. "Be a crybaby and tell Mother what a bad boy I am."

"Mary, Jane and I are going to look at the dugouts." Mother said. "You and Hattie are in charge here. Keep the little ones occupied, give them dinner and try to get those winter squash peeled and boiled for supper."

Hattie was quiet and answered my questions with yes or no. What was the matter with her? Maybe she was turning into a teenager and getting moody.

"Hattie, are you all right? You seem different today."

"You're a busybody. Always wanting to know what's going on. Maybe I don't feel like telling anything to a little girl like you," she answered.

"I'm not such a little girl. I'll be nine next week. Sorry you think I'm a snoop, but that's the only way I learn anything. Sometimes I feel folks think I'm a block of wood with no feelings and no brain. As soon as I can I'm going to find Grandma Burntwater's hogan. She said she'd talk to me."

I stuck my nose in the air, gathered the little ones and took them on a treasure hunt along the river. I told them to look for certain things and the first one to find it got a point. The one with the most points won a piece of horehound candy. They scurried ahead looking for a white rock, a red leaf, a blue bird feather or a twig shaped like a Y.

On our way back to camp, Hattie came to meet us. "I'm sorry to be a crank," she said. "You're the best friend I have, but I don't feel good. My gut's crampy, I have a headache and am out of sorts. Mother says maybe it's my time to become a woman. I'm not ready for that. It's such a mess with bleeding every month and having to wash out the special cloth pads. Boys have it easy. I wish I'd been born a boy."

"I wondered what was wrong, but that never came to mind. After we give the little ones their dinner and put them down for naps, why don't you take a rest? I'll peel the squash and get them cooking."

She hugged me saying, "What would we do without you?"

The rest of the day was quiet. Mother and Aunt Jane returned while everyone was resting. "Come and walk with me, Mary," Mother said. "We haven't had time together for a long spell. How do you like St. Johns?"

"I've only been away from camp for Sammy's funeral. What's the town like? Did you find the dugouts? How is Aunt Jane? She looks pale and weak. I hope this baby is going to be all right."

"The dugouts are caves in the side of a hill near the river. They are dark, damp, and dirty. They'll protect us from the weather and our stove will keep us warm. I never dreamed I'd be a cave dweller."

"Is there a wooden floor or will we be right on the dirt?"

"The floor is hard packed dirt. I hope I hold up better than the woman who lived there last winter. She lost her mind and threw her newborn child down the outhouse. They took her to Holbrook, then by train to an asylum in

Kansas which takes care of pioneer women who break down. This is not an easy life.

"Aunt Jane is grieving for Sammy, worried about the new baby and discouraged with their mission. Uncle Bill is a farmer. He doesn't have another trade like blacksmith or carpenter. Your father should get work since he's a good carpenter."

"When will we move? The days are getting short and the wind has a wintery feel," I said.

"We hope to move before the weather changes. I pray the fall storms wait another week. The dugouts are little more than caves but they will give us more protection than the wagon beds. I can't cook outdoors in rain or snow. I know you're eager to start school and Sister Selkirk is planning to begin next week but I'll need you with me until after we move."

"What do you think has happened to Captain Jack?"

"Mary, one thing I've learned in my twenty-seven years is that the things you worry about often don't happen. It's the things you never think about that sneak up and surprise you. Maybe Captain Jack is hurt and sent Brownie for help. Try not to think the worst. I do that too often. The trouble is that I'm often right."

"What about Aunt Jane? Hattie isn't herself either."

"Jane will be all right. She's worn out and needs time to recover from Sammy's death. She's not happy about having another child right now and she's disappointed with the conditions here in St. Johns. It's going to be a hard winter. You and Hattie will have to grow up sooner than you would have in Mendon, but we have no choice. Someday you'll look back on this as one of the events that shaped your life."

"What about Hattie? Why is she so weepy one minute, grumpy the next and then all of a sudden making fun of me and calling me a baby?"

"She's becoming a woman. You know about the monthlies. It'll happen to you one of these years and you'll find yourself living in a body that seems like a stranger. Be patient with her. We'd better get back and see what we can find to have with the squash for supper. Maybe the men will bring fresh meat when they return. Our larder is getting mighty bare."

After supper, made from the last of the jerky, boiled squash and a loaf of fresh bread Mother had brought from town, we went to bed. I didn't sleep. All night I kept an ear open to catch the sound of the men returning from their search.

Bishop Udall and his wife came to see if we'd had any news and to let us know that a storm was brewing. We must move. Mother asked for their help to get our things from camp to the dugouts.

"I'll send some men and boys from town to get you into shelter. They can bring my big wagon and move your things in two or three trips. They'll be back before noon with the wagon and their strong backs. That stove is going to take some heavy lifting."

Mother said, "We hope our men return sometime today and they can help with the move. Jane and I appreciate your concern. What should the herders do with the animals?"

"There's an old barn and corral north of the dugouts. Rachel, stay here and help while I ride to the pasture and tell the herders to move the stock."

We spent the morning packing, watching the sky as long wispy white clouds thickened and turned gray. We listened for sounds of horses returning from the mountains. The only horses we heard were the workhorses pulling the large flat wagon into camp to move us.

Mother and Aunt Jane took the little ones with them on the first trip. Hattie and I stayed to watch our things and be there in case the searchers returned. We wrapped up in a blanket and huddled together behind some bundles of bedding trying to stay out of the increasing wind.

"Mother says that someday we'll look back on all this and see that it is important to our lives," I said to Hattie through my chattering teeth.

"I'd rather be in front of our fireplace in Mendon with a cup of hot cider in my hand, instead of here in this Godforsaken, freezing, windy, dirty place," Hattie grumped.

"Do you hear that?"

"What? I don't hear anything but the wind whistling down the mountain."

"There it is again. I think I hear Brownie howling."

We huddled and listened, but heard only the team with the wagon coming back for the next load. We were loaded and ready to go when I was sure I heard horses and Brownie. The sound blew in on the wind from the west. "Wait, just a few minutes," I told the driver. "I hear the search party returning."

We saw Brownie first, running through the dead leaves and dust whirled up by the wind. His ears flapped and he barked in greeting as he loped along. I jumped down from the wagon and hugged him. He groaned deep in his throat and gave me a slobbery kiss on my cheek before he ran to the river to get a drink.

Next came Father and Uncle Bill followed by the rest of the searchers.

Where was Captain Jack? Had they found him or learned where he was or what had happened to him? There was a blanket wrapped bundle tied to Father's horse. The men looked gloomy and grave. Something awful had happened. My fears had come true.

Father and the men driving the moving wagon, talked then he came to me as I sat hugging Brownie. "Mary, Captain Jack was ambushed and killed by Apaches. They stole Buster, but Brownie got away. According to the movers we need to go into town, leave Jack's body at the undertakers, and finish shifting into the dugouts before this storm starts dropping snow."

We buried Captain Jack in the Catholic cemetery. The Mormons wouldn't let him rest next to Sammy, but the Catholic priest said he could be buried in a plot behind their church. It was a cold, clear, still day. Light snow covered the ground excepting for the freshly dug grave. The White Mountains were snow covered and sparkled under the bright October sun that gave light but no warmth. Only a few people came to the grave to hear Father say a prayer and a blessing.

I wore last year's coat that was too short in the arms and barely came to my knees. I didn't realize I'd grown so much. My hands were cold because I didn't have any mittens, but my feet were warm in my Holbrook clodhoppers. Brownie leaned against my legs and whimpered. He knew his master was gone. I rubbed him behind his ear and whispered, "I'm sorry Captain Jack is dead, but I'm going to take good care of you."

When the men found Captain Jack lying on the ground with four bullets in him they couldn't find his hat with the eagle feather. I'd watch for that hat whenever I saw Apaches in town.

Chapter Ten

St Johns, Arizona Territory, Autumn 1885

I turned nine two weeks after we moved into the cave. Mother wrapped the Hopi dishes in one of Christine's pinafores and tied it with red yarn. I remembered that happy summer day at Moenkopi.

Mother fried a chicken in the black iron skillet and baked a chocolate cake. There was nothing to make frosting with so there was none. She stuck one of our precious candles into the top. Everyone sang "Happy Birthday" to Parley, whose birthday was a week before mine, and to me. I made a wish and we blew out the flame.

There were only Mother, William, Roy, Richard, Parley and I. Father, Lester and Reuben were working in the shingle mill at Eager. Mother tried to make my birthday special but it was dreary.

I hated the dugout. With each passing day I hated it more. We were warm but it was dark, damp and dirty. The absolute worst thing about St Johns was that it was infested with bed bugs. Our dugout was the capital city of the bedbug nation.

We weren't bothered at first but when the wood posts and mud walls warmed up, out they came like soldiers following a bugle call to attack. One morning we woke to find our bodies covered with little red bumps. The bites itched dreadfully. Mother dabbed us with the lotion she'd used for my poison ivy. Everyone in St. Johns suffered from the infestation and what to do about it was a major topic of conversation among the women.

If the weather was nice, we hung our bedding in the sun, wiped the bed frames with coal oil and caught as many of the crevice dwellers as we could. The little beasts hid in the cracks and joints of the wooden bed frames. One day William and I caught and squished three-hundred and seventy-one of those vicious, blood-sucking bugs. We saved them in a jar to show Father.

After my birthday supper, when the boys were down for the night, I said to Mother. "I'm nine years old and haven't been baptized. That bothers me. I've read and studied my catechism book so many times that I have it memorized. When do you think we'll be settled enough for me to start school?"

"I know you're eager to be baptized. You were eight before we left Mendon and it should have been done there. I'd hoped it could be done this month but the weather has turned cold, there's not enough water in the river for you to be immersed and Bishop Udall told me we'd have to wait until spring. There will be a group of children ready for baptism in May," Mother said.

"What about school? Father made me a bench, Sister Selkirk is saving me a slate board to do my sums on and I have clothes to wear. I really need to get out of this cave and go to school. If I don't start soon, I'll fall behind the other students."

"I know it's important. Hattie's helping Sister Selkirk teach the younger girls their lessons. She likes it and says she'd like to be a teacher. Right now, with Henry gone, I can't manage without you. If tomorrow is a nice day why don't you go into town? I need some things from the mercantile. I know you need to get away."

I was disappointed and annoyed. My dream was slipping away. Aunt Jane and Uncle Bill were having a hard time too, so I shouldn't be selfish and think only of my own woes. The only work Uncle Bill found was at the stable. He felt the job was beneath him but it brought in a little cash. He also took care of the few animals we had left. After we got here, three mules died, two goats were killed for meat and one milk cow was traded to Mr. Sol Barth, who ran the mercantile. He gave us credit to draw on so we could get a supply of flour, sugar, salt, baking soda, and other staples before winter set in. During December, January and February the trail to and from Holbrook was regularly impassable and Mr. Barth ran out of supplies. People stocked up for the winter.

Aunt Jane and Uncle Bill's two older boys hired out to a sheep outfit in Concho, so they were making their own way. The boys stayed in a bunkhouse, had their meals in a dining hall and were happy. When they visited, I overheard them telling Lester and Reuben what a great way of life it was and why didn't my brothers go to Concho also? There were about two-hundred people and over 100,000 sheep. They kept the sheep there in the winters and took them into the mountains in summer.

After the flocks settled for the night the boys walked around the sheep swinging a lighted lantern to keep the wolves away. There were wolves here too. I'd heard them howling and singing to each other. I wouldn't go to the privy at night because I didn't want to be a snack for a hungry wolf.

The next day was cool and breezy but not stormy. Mother gave me a list and some coins and told me to go to town. "Take your time, Mary. Just try to be home by noon."

My first trip to town by myself. At least I'll walk past the school, see if I can find Grandma Burntwater's hogan and find someone to help me learn more Spanish.

"Come, Brownie, let's go," I said to my friend.

Brownie still watched for Captain Jack. He'd lay by the road, with his chin on his paws and his ears spread out on the dirt. Whenever he heard the sound of a horse he sat up and looked expectantly down the road. It broke my heart to see him so sad and grieving. He missed the Captain more than anyone.

On the way I detoured off the main street to pass by the school. Sister Selkirk taught the girls, while Brother Reynolds tried to teach the boys. He had a hard time keeping order and the boys were not nice to him. I thought it must be hard to teach children of all ages at the same time, especially when most of the older boys didn't want to be there at all.

Hattie told me about a poem one of the students snuck in and wrote on the blackboard in Brother Reynolds room.

"Oh Lord of love from up above,
Look down on us poor scholars
They have hired a fool
To teach the school
And are paying him forty dollars!"

Willard Ashcroft confessed and said his father, Brother Ashcroft, told him about writing that poem on the blackboard when he was a student back in Illinois. Willard got a good thrashing for his trick and had to go early for a month to start the fires in both rooms.

When I walked by the school, I saw the door to the girls' classroom was ajar. I heard the older girls, with Hattie's help, reciting their sums. I peeked through the opening and saw Sister Selkirk reading a story to the younger students who gathered around her on their benches. I smelled the waxed floors, chalk dust, black ink and dusty books. Tears ran down my face. I yearned to be inside, not peeking in. I turned and ran to Main Street before my sinful feet walked me right through that door.

Brownie thought it was a great game as he ran ahead. All of a sudden he stopped, sniffed the air and his tail stood straight up. The hairs on the back of his neck rose and he commenced to quiver.

"What's the matter, Brownie?" Two doors down the street was Coronado's Cantina. Even this early in the day, a gang of cowboys and Apaches sat on the porch or leaned against the wall. They laughed, joked and tossed pennies into the dusty street while drinking from tin cups.

Brownie growled deep in his throat, his ears laid back and he had a wild gleam in his eyes. I had to corral him before he attacked. I grabbed him by the loose skin on his neck and steered him across the street to the livery stables.

"What are you doing here, Mary?' Uncle Bill asked as I dragged Brownie into the dim stable.

"Tie Brownie up so he can't attack that Apache on Coronado's porch. Put him in a stall and tie him up or we'll have a real ruckus on our hands."

"What's going on that's got both of you so flustered?" Uncle Bill asked as he looped a rope around Brownie's neck and chest. He made a harness Brownie couldn't slip out of, dragged him to a stall and closed the gate.

"Look across the street. See that tall Apache standing just off the steps, the one wearing the leather hat? There's an eagle feather sticking up on the side. That's Captain Jack's hat," I whispered.

"By golly, you're right. Wonder if he rode in on Buster? Was he one of the gang that killed Captain Jack? That one's name is Bah Nubah. Stay here while I hunt up Brother Merrill. He's the closest thing around here to a lawman and he'll know where to look for Buster. There's probably a place where the Apaches tie their horses when they come to town."

Because there were no lawmen in St. Johns the Mormon settlers formed the United Forces of St. Johns. They invited all male citizens, Mexicans, Mormons, sheep men and ranchers to join in a united front against the lawlessness that plagued Apache County. When the Texas Rangers ran the rustlers and outlaws out of Texas, it seemed they landed in Arizona Territory around Holbrook, St. Johns and south into the White Mountains.

They often joined forces with off reservation Apaches and caused grief and disruption in the lives of ranchers and settlers. Children were kidnapped, horses and cattle stolen, sheep slaughtered. Saturday nights the bars and cantinas were full of drunken men. On those nights, citizens made their beds on the floor so as not to be caught in the crossfire of feuding gangs.

From inside the stable, I watched the bunch across the street. I wanted to tell the men, when they returned, whether the Indian wearing the hat had left and if so, which direction he'd gone.

Brownie didn't like being cooped up and howled but soon he quieted down. He whimpered just enough to tell me his feelings were hurt.

Uncle Bill returned, "Brother Merrill has gone to get help. They know places in the river thickets where the Apaches tie their horses."

"Do they know what Buster looks like? What will happen if they find him?"

"They'll let us know. We'll put our heads together and devise a plan. Have to be careful not to stir up a hornet's nest of Apaches. Go get Bishop Udall. Just act natural. Walk over to his place and tell him we need his advice."

"Be sure to keep Brownie penned," I said as I left.

Sister Udall invited me in, gave me a cool drink of water and went to the barn to get her husband. "You're surely getting a taste of the frontier, aren't you, Mary? It isn't for the faint of heart. I hope we can bring this to a bloodless conclusion," he said.

When Brother Udall and I returned to the stables, Brother Merrill and two other men were there. "Mary, Brother Wilhelm will walk you home and keep a tight hold on Brownie. It will be better if you two are out of the way. Take Brownie inside and don't let him out until I tell you all's clear," Uncle Bill said.

"But I haven't been to the store, I haven't found Grandma Burntwater's hogan and I want to stay here and see what's going on," I protested. "What are you going to do if you find Buster? Did you already find Buster? I want to see him."

"Leave, now. This is no time for questions. Do what you are told."

Brother Wilhelm delivered Brownie and me to the dugout, gave Mother a brief account of what was happening and told her to keep us indoors for the rest of the day. He then went to the school and told the teachers to keep the students in until further notice.

Another day that began with such promise turned slow and tiresome. I read to my brothers, drew pictures in the dirt floor, and made sure Brownie didn't nudge the door open as he had learned to do.

After dinner, Mother walked to Aunt Jane's dugout and left me in charge while the youngest ones napped. I was surprised when William came home." I thought you were supposed to stay in the school," I said.

"Brother Reynolds couldn't stand being cooped up with us, so he told the big boys to walk the little boys home and then go home themselves."

"Did you have dinner yet?"

Parents took turns providing the noon meal for students. It was soup or stew, beans and cornbread, or whatever the women could scrape together. The families supplied all of the schools needs, including the buildings and the teachers' pay.

"Yes, we had bean soup, even had a little ham in it."

"Well, whatever you do, be quiet. Roy, Richard and Parley are sleeping on their bunk. Sit down and read a book or something," I said grumpily. I resented that he got to go to school and I didn't. I sat in Mother's chair near the stove and picked up the socks I was knitting.

Uncle Bill returned after dark. He stopped and asked us to come to their dugout to hear how the Defense League outsmarted the Apaches. He began, "I know it's crowded but settle down and listen. We discovered Buster and four other horses tethered amongst the willow thickets south of town. Brother Udall sent one of his boys to the bartender at Coronado's to ask if he'd help. Jesus Baca is a good family man, even if he is a bartender and he agreed to assist us. Cowboys and Apaches love to gamble as much as they like to drink, so Señor Baca called the porch loungers inside to take part in a poker tournament. The players would get free drinks during the event in exchange for part of any money they might have won at game's end.

"By noon the cowboys and the Apaches were snockered. The Defense League owes Señor Baca a goodly sum for the liquor. By two o'clock the Indians were snoozing peacefully on the floor. Some cowboys left town but we weren't interested in them.

"Señor Baca locked both doors to his place, waved a red bandanna at the window and we proceeded to the next part of the plan. Brothers Wilhelm and Merrill, Bishop Udall and I ran to the thicket to get two horses. We had to take more than Buster in order to confuse the situation. We didn't want Bah Nubah to think town people had stolen the horses. Better to let him think a thieving cowpoke or Indian had made off with them.

"I think Buster recognized me. He whinnied in greeting but I didn't have time to visit. We took the horses to Udall's barn."

I couldn't hold it any longer, "Was Captain Jack's saddle and any of his gear on Buster? How are you going to keep Bah Nubah from finding Buster and the other horse?"

"Captain Jack's saddle and some of his gear were on Buster along with the Apache's things. We left Bah Nubah's belongings on the ground but kept the saddles and Captain Jack's possessions

"Bishop Udall's cousin in Ramah has been wanting to buy a couple of good mounts. Within the hour, while Bah Nubah and his buddies are still incapacitated, Brother Wilhelm and his sons will take Buster and the black and white filly through the Zuni Reservation to Ramah. Zuni's dislike Apaches, so Bah Nubah probably won't risk looking there.

"When Brother Wilhelm returns with the money, we'll divide it. Henry told me that when the search party discovered Captain Jack's body, he found a paper in the Captain's pocket with the name and address of his wife in Idaho. We'll write a letter telling her of her husband's death. Most of the money from the sale of the horses will go to her. Some will be used to pay Señor Baca for the liquor."

Mother spoke up, "Mary has a nice hand and she spells well. It will be a good task for her."

I asked, "Can I see Buster before he goes to New Mexico? Brownie would like to see him too. Can we, Uncle Bill?"

"Sorry Mary, it's too risky. Brownie's apt to start howling and alert the whole county. I have something of Captain Jack's that Señor Baca gave me," Uncle Bill said as he took an old floppy, wide brimmed leather hat out of a burlap bag.

"I'd like to have the eagle feather from the hat," I said. "What will you do with the hat?"

"I think we should send it to his wife. His son might like to have it. I guess it's all right for Mary to have the feather. They can always get another one in Idaho. Who has that paper?" Aunt Jane asked.

I wanted the eagle feather as a memento of Captain Jack to help me keep him in my heart. Even though I hadn't seen the eagles soaring at his funeral, I knew he had gone to Heaven. Maybe the birds were busy on that day guiding some other soul. Captain Jack was a good man and he had opened my mind to the outside world in a gentle, funny, brave way.

I held the feather in my hands and heard him say, "Mary, we can't be as solemn as a hanging judge all of the time." Tears of sadness and joy came to my eyes.

There it is again. Having opposite feelings at the same time.

"Captain Jack's note is under the bed in Henry's letter box," Mother said. "I'll look for it in the morning. When Henry returns with cash we can buy writing paper, then Mary can get started."

We sat quietly waiting for Uncle Bill to dismiss us with his blessing before going to our dugout. Into the silence came the sound of five horses galloping away from St. Johns, splashing across the shallow Little Colorado River and then fading away. We sensed an important part of our lives was over and our pioneer journey was irrevocably part of the past.

I'd begun writing the letter to Mrs. Silver Moon Morgan in my head as soon as Mother volunteered me for the task. I had no paper, so no matter how hard the letter clamored to get out of my mind, it had to wait for Father's return.

Two days later they returned from Eager with cash in their pockets and a load of lumber on the wagon. I was anxious to tell Father about Mother's spells of strange behavior. He was home for three days before I got up the gumption to tell him. We had walked to town to do some errands and were on the way home.

"Mother is acting peculiar again. One day I found her at the edge of the river, barefooted and with no coat. The bottom of her dress was dripping wet, so I knew she'd been wading in the icy water.

"She said, in a little girl voice, 'Isn't it a lovely warm day, Mary? I think we should have a picnic on the back lawn, under the arbor with the lilac blossoms blooming all around.' I took her hand, led her to the dugout, sat her down by the stove and dried her feet. I was terrified. She dozed in her chair. When she wakened she was her normal self. I didn't tell Aunt Jane because she's not well and has enough problems of her own."

He shrugged off my worry, "All we need to do is get out of the cave. Those dugouts aren't fit for man nor beast, much less women and children. She'll be fine then."

I gathered my courage and persisted, "Father, you don't see her as I do. I told you on the trail, there is something not right with Mother and you didn't want to hear about it then either."

"Mary, there's nothing wrong. All women have bad times now and then. I have good news,"

While I'd been in Barth's Mercantile, choosing some paper and envelopes, Father was busy talking to the owner of the livery stable and Uncle Bill. I watched the three men as they talked jovially and shook hands as if they agreed on something. As soon as we got home Father and Mother went for a walk while I put away our purchases and prepared dinner.

Now that Father and the boys were back, we had to eat in shifts. In order for all of us to be together at the same time, some had to sit on the bunks and the rest had to be careful to not step on the little ones. Brownie's tail had been hurt one too many times and he retreated to the farthest wall under one of the beds whenever he was inside.

Ever since Lester and Reuben came home, they'd been ornerier than ever. Father tried to keep them busy out of doors, but sometimes the weather was so cold, windy and wet that there was no other place for them to be but underfoot.

"I'm going to Concho and signing up with the sheep ranch," Lester said one evening. "At least over there when I'm not working I don't have to put up with a bunch of crying babies and there's room in the bunkhouse to move around. Reuben, are you going to come with me?"

After supper that night Father told us, "Today when Mary and I were in town, I saw an empty store on Main Street. It used to be Fancher's Feed Store. I asked Mr. Crosby, who is taking care of the place, if it was for rent. It's a two-story building with a nice garden plot and a small corral and a barn out back.

"Bill and I think if we do some remodeling there will be room for both our families. We'll stay upstairs and Bill and Jane will use the backrooms on the first floor. We'll share a common room at the front, as our kitchen and eating area. It's affordable, and by building some partitions, we'll have a cheerful roomy place to live."

"I'll do anything to get out of this dank, dark cave," Mother said. "Last Sunday at church, I heard that one morning last spring, the family that was staying here woke one morning to find rattlesnakes all over the floor. When the weather warmed, the snakes crawled out of the rocks behind the cedar posts and commenced to breed right here where we sit. I've had nightmares since I heard the story."

"Lester, I know you've been talking about going to Concho, but we need you and Reuben to help with the remodeling. We'll be in our new home before Thanksgiving if all goes well," Father said.

The next week went by in a blur. The heaviest job was moving the stove. It was transported and hooked to the existing stovepipe one morning and we moved into our partially remodeled home that afternoon.

"Mary," Mother called to me from downstairs, "come and help hang this front curtain."

I was upstairs sitting on a crate, gazing out the window in a tiny room at the back of the building. My room! The first room that was mine alone. For the rest of my life I would have only one other. I had big plans. I imagined bookshelves, clothes pegs, white ruffled curtains, a single bed with a blue and white quilt and colorful pictures on the rough plank walls. I'd have a rag rug on the floor for Brownie to sleep on and a low cupboard with a washbasin on the top and shelves below to put my folded clothes on.

I went downstairs, climbed up a rickety old ladder and fastened the curtains in place with a hammer and short nails across the top of the big front window. "Now we won't feel like we are living in a fishbowl," I said.

Mother had found the bolt of red and yellow plaid, cotton fabric on markdown at Barth's Mercantile. After she and Aunt Jane made the curtains on Sister Udall's treadle machine, there was enough left to make a tablecloth and a small curtain for the front door window. The bright colors made the place cheerful.

The next day Aunt Jane and Uncle Bill moved their family into our Main Street home. Although we had always been a close family, we had never actually lived together. I resented Hattie's strutting around like a queen bee. She put on airs and lorded it over me because she not only got to go to school, she was Sister Selkirk's assistant.

She told me, "Mary, there is more to life than taking the nightjars to the privy, washing and ironing clothes or scrubbing floors and washing dishes."

"Well, Miss Hoity-toity! Somebody has to do it. Your mother isn't well, my mother can't do it all, so I end up doing your share of the work," I replied as I flounced off to the washtubs in the back yard. It was a long time before we were friends again.

Brother Becker, from Springerville, came looking for a crew to come to work cutting ice blocks out of his lake. Lester was as antsy as ever and he signed up for a dollar and a half a day. The Beckers had built a big icehouse and stored ice packed in sawdust all winter. They sold it in the summer to the cantinas, bars and anyone who could afford it

One day, Father took me aside and told me, "I think we've got things worked out so Mother can spare you most days so you can attend school. I'll be doing carpentry work for Fred Colter at his Cross-Bar Ranch. He needs a bigger bunkhouse and another stable. The job should last through the winter. With 12,000 head of cattle he keeps lots of horses and cowboys.

"Aunt Jane and Mother will help each other with the little ones so now you get your wish. Work hard and enjoy yourself. Reuben has decided he's not ready to strike out on his own and is staying in town. He'll be attending school with you and William. I worry about Lester. He's getting too big for his britches. I hope he doesn't fall into bad company. Lester is easily swayed by others and is trying to grow up too fast."

I was in Heaven. I had my own room, no bigger than a large chicken coop, but all mine. I loved maps and geography lessons. I made friends and had fun at recess. I enjoyed the hot lunches, and best of all I learned how to recite poems and sayings written by famous people.

Each week Sister Selkirk assigned a piece for each of us to memorize and recite on Friday afternoons when the parents were invited to visit. I reveled in it and found I had a talent for performing in front of an audience. One of the first poems I ever learned is still fresh in my mind.

Where we walk to school each day
Indian children used to play—
All about our native land,
Where the shops and houses stand.

It went on to tell that there had been no streets, no houses, no people except Indians and was written by a lady named Annette Wynne. I wondered if she had been a pioneer and lived in a place like St. Johns. A place that was nothing like we had expected. No white houses with picket fences, everything built of mud bricks called adobe. Few stores, but lots of bars and cantinas. Both the Spanish and the Apaches resented us and neither showed any inclination of converting to our church. The weather was wretched. Ever since we arrived it had been cold and windy.

I asked Bess Hale, a girl at school, "How long have you lived here?"

"I was born here after my parents came from Mesa. They thought it was too hot there, so they decided to move to St. George. They stopped here to see my mother's sister for a few days and when they were ready to leave, the wind was blowing so hard that they decided to wait until it died down. That was nine years ago. It never stopped and we're still here."

"You mean it blows like this all year, not just in the winter?"

"Well, one day a couple of summers ago it stopped for a day and we had a picnic. The wind in the summer is hot and dries your skin. In the winter it's cold and freezes your nose. Once in a while it stops and you really notice it. My brother was walking to the pasture one day when all of a sudden the wind stopped. He fell down because he was so used to leaning into the wind!"

At least we were out of the dugout, Father had a steady job, Lester was happily on his own and I was in school.

I was uneasy at how well everything was going.

Chapter Eleven

St. Johns, Arizona Territory, November & December, 1885

Thanksgiving Day was cold and gloomy. School was out for two days and most students were thankful. I would rather have been in the classroom. Aunt Jane spent the day in bed, Hattie went to the Selkirk's for dinner, Parley, Richard and my cousins Rachel and Alma had the croup. Mother and I put a nice meal on the table, but there was no festivity.

My cousin John came home from Concho. He said chasing wolves was too scary for him. He was a good hunter and brought us a fat deer so we had venison roast. He reminded me of Captain Jack in the way he'd disappear into the boondocks for weeks.

While we were out of school I wrote a letter to Captain Jack's family.

Dear Silver Moon Morgan and family,

My name is Mary George. Captain Jack was our guide on our wagon train trip from Utah to Arizona. We came to like him very much. We also liked his horse, Buster and his bloodhound dog, Brownie.

I am sorry to send you news that your husband and father was ambushed and killed by some White Mountain Apaches. He was on his way to meet friends at Fort

Apache. Brownie ran away and came back to our camp in St. Johns to let us know what had happened. The men rode out, found his body and brought it here where we held a service and buried him.

Some weeks later Buster was found in the possession of an Apache and our men were able to take him back. He has been sold to a good owner in New Mexico.

First the men paid the bartender at the cantina for the liquor it took to make the Indians drunk so they could slip away with the horses. I enclose Captain Jack's hat and a postal money order for $85.37, which is the amount left from the sale of Buster and another horse. The second horse was taken from the Apaches because they deserved it.

We are sad about the death of your husband. He was a good man and a fine friend. I am keeping Brownie and promise to take good care of him.

I remain,
Yours Truly,
Mary George,
St. Johns, Arizona Territory

I sent the package to Mrs. Silver Moon Morgan, in care of the Indian agent, Fort Hall, Idaho.

Aunt Jane and Uncle Bill put their stove in the bedroom on the first floor to provide the baby with a warm place to begin its life. Aunt Jane was weary and spent much time in bed. Her feet and ankles swelled and she kept them raised as much as possible. She wasn't having an easy pregnancy. She grieved for Sammy and missed Amy very much.

"I wish I'd never heard of St. Johns," I heard her say to Mother. "I don't believe it will get better. Citrus can't grow in this climate. The bare rootstock has died, several of our animals have died and Sammy and Captain Jack have died. Something is wrong with the child I carry. I am discouraged and disillusioned."

It scared me to hear her talk like that.

What if she starts acting strange like Mother? Until then, I had talked to her when Mother drifted off. From that time on, I tried to keep my own counsel and not worry so about things beyond me.

Uncle Bill still worked at the stables and was able to be home every night, which made us feel safer. Autumn turned to winter. The weather was cold and stormy. Sometimes Father couldn't come home for weeks at a stretch.

There was always a lot of commotion on Friday and Saturday nights when the cowboys from the sheep camps and cattle ranches came into town to have a high time. Since we lived right in the middle of town on Main Street, we heard the yelling, shooting and horseracing ruckus.

Mother and Aunt Jane scared and teased us about Pat Traynor. They used him like a Boogey Man who came to take away bad or mischievous children by saying "If you don't mind your manners and be good we'll call Pat Traynor to come and teach you a thing or two."

Stories about Pat Traynor were exciting and thrilling in a forbidden way. From the stories I'd heard, he was different from any man I'd ever met. It was said he lived near Springerville with his Spanish wife, who had married him without her family's permission. His horse, Diablo, was a beautiful black Arabian with a white patch on his forehead. His black saddle was decorated with silver and the bridle was black with silver tips. Pat always wore a black beaver cowboy hat, silk shirt, black leather vest, pants and chaps.

He was an Irishman with black hair and green eyes, and we heard he'd come here after a set-to in Dodge City or Abilene, Kansas. He had many notches cut into the butts of his black guns, but no one knew how many men he had killed. When he disappeared for two or three months, everyone speculated as to where he was. All we knew for sure was that he had a herd of fat cattle with him when he returned.

Whenever he came to St. Johns, he stayed at the Barth Hotel and put his horse in Crosby's stables and that's where Uncle Bill met him. He said Pat Traynor was pleasant and polite, but never friendly.

One Saturday, the cowboys gathered in front of Coronado's began to follow and tease four Mormon men who were returning from work at the dam and canal construction site. The troublemakers shot at their feet to make them dance. One cowboy shouted, "Let's see if it's true that a bullet won't kill a Mormon!"

We rushed to the front window and watched the drama unfold right before our eyes. We'd heard the story that Mormons thought they were so special to God that even a bullet wouldn't kill them. Some Gentiles said it to make fun of us.

Just as the cowboy aimed his six-shooter at Brother Whilhelm, Pat Traynor galloped up, and with his black lasso whacked the drunken gunman on his right arm. The troublemakers ran like cockroaches when you light a lamp.

"That was like a story from a book," I said. "Maybe someday I'll write these things down so I can share them with my children. If I don't, I may forget it all," I said to Mother.

"You should start a journal," Mother answered. "You have a way with words."

One evening, a week before Christmas, there was a knock at the door. Father was stranded at the ranch by a snowstorm so Uncle Bill answered it. A snow-dusted man tipped his hat and said, "Sorry to bother you. I've come from up Springerville way with a young man named Lester. He has a broken leg. He says his folks live here."

"How bad is he? I'm Lester's uncle, Bill George. Elizabeth, something's happened to Lester," Uncle Bill called to Mother.

The man said, "I tried to make him comfortable under a canvas in my wagon, but I'm afraid it was a mighty rough ride. I need help to get him into the house. My name is Jim Pipken, most folks call me 'Pip.' Get a hat and coat as it's down right wretched out here and we'll bring him in."

They brought Lester in and put him on a cot in the front room. There was a splint on his left leg and some flour sacks wrapped around his foot. He was pale and groaned as Mother and Aunt Jane took off his wet cap and coat and unwrapped his foot.

Uncle Bill asked Mr. Pipken, "Can you stay the night? Take your horses to the barn. I'll come and help you get them settled."

"That's mighty kind of you, Mr. George. I'll take you up on your offer. After we get Red and Blue out of this storm I'll tell you what happened."

Red and Blue are unusual names for horses. Wonder how that came about?

"Mary, fill the kettle and heat some water, then go upstairs and get my medicine bag. Lester's in terrible pain. We may need to make him unconscious in order to set his leg. I wonder if Doctor Pulsipher's home or if he's at the cantina getting drunk," Mother said.

Aunt Jane responded, "I'll send John to fetch the doctor. The storm is getting worse so he should take Brownie to keep from getting lost."

Dr. Pulsipher had been a doctor in the War Between the States. After that he had never been able to settle for long in any one place. He'd lived in Ramah, but said it was too tame for him. "Ramah's all Mormon and too sober and serious for me," I heard him say one day at the stables.

"St. John's gets real lively on the weekends and there's always someone around willing to bend an elbow with me."

John went to hunt for the doctor around the time Uncle Bill and Mr. Pipken walked in the back door.

"Are you hungry?" Uncle Bill asked as they shed their snow dusted coats and hats.

"Sure could use something hot to take the chill out of my bones. Do you have any coffee?"

"We're Mormons, so we don't have coffee. How about a bowl of soup and some sassafras tea?"

"Sounds good to me. I'm from a Mormon family, but fell away years ago. Did some stupid things and was excommunicated while I lived at Ramah. Don't think I'll ever be one of the flock again. Too much time has passed and I haven't mended my ways. Thanks," he said as I handed him a cup of tea and went to dish up the soup.

The men sat in front of the stove while I took the little ones to their rooms and put them to bed. Mother and Aunt Jane did what they could to comfort Lester.

"If John can't find Dr. Pulsipher, maybe Grandma Burntwater will help us set this leg," Mother said.

"I'm not much help," Aunt Jane replied. "I don't have any strength in my arms these days. One of the men can hold him down while another strong person yanks that bone back into place."

I sat at the table and listened to Uncle Bill and Mr. Pipken visit. They didn't have much to say of interest until I heard Uncle Bill ask about Red and Blue.

"Well, I got Blue a couple of summers ago. I helped him into this world at Fort Wingate. I was banished from the church at Ramah where I'd been the postmaster. I knew the postmaster at the fort. It's over the Zuni Mountains northeast of Ramah. I went hoping I could get work helping with the mail or wrangling horses for the cavalry. I'd been fired from the post office, charged with embezzling money. My friend had heard about it, so he couldn't let me work with him. The Captain in charge of horses at the fort hired me for a pittance plus board and room.

"Anyway, one of the gray mares was foaling and was having a terrible time. I offered to try a trick I'd learned from a Navajo. I put my arm into the mare, turned the colt which was trying to come out backwards and pulled him out by his forelegs.

"He was a scrawny little thing and a strange color—a blue gray. The mare wasn't able to nurse him so I took on the task and soon Blue thought I was his mother. I made a thin mix of canned milk, corn syrup and corn meal. I poured the mixture into a whiskey bottle. Cut a finger off a leather glove, poked a hole in it and tied it to the bottle.

"After a while the Captain said I could keep him. Later, I doctored a colt that had tangled with some barbwire. I called her Red not because of her natural reddish color but 'cause she was covered with blood. I saved my pay and bought her. I'm real fond of them. They're the only friends I have," Mr. Pipken said.

"What happened to Lester?" I asked.

Just then, John ushered Doctor Pulsipher into the room. The doctor had a head of bushy, wiry, white hair. I'd heard him tell how it turned white overnight after he was in a big battle. He said he'd worked in the hospital tent for two days and nights with no let up and when he next looked in a mirror his short straight brown hair had turned white. When it grew longer it was not only white, but was wild and stuck straight out. "The consequence of all the horror I saw at Gettysburg," he told everyone.

"Well young man, let's take a look at your leg. The first thing is to cut these trousers so I can see the problem. Bring me a pair of shears to cut the side of your pants leg. That way your Ma can sew them back together. No use to waste a good pair of pants.

"What happened to you, boy? Looks like you got on the wrong end of an angry mule. Shinbone's broken clean in half and pulled out of place. Lots of swelling around your ankle and circulations poor in your foot. How old is Lester?" he asked.

"He turned eleven last week," Mother replied.

"Good looking husky boy. Would have thought he was at least fourteen. Do you have whiskey in the house? That's the best thing to make him pass out. Don't want any of that watered stuff they sell to the Indians. It's going to hurt like hell when I jerk that bone into place. If I don't get it right, he'll have one leg shorter than the other and walk with a gimp the rest of his life."

"I'll go to Coronado's and get whiskey," Uncle Bill said as he pulled on his coat. "Come on, Brownie, I'll need your help in getting home in this blizzard."

The wind howled and blew as loud as the freight train in Holbrook. John and I had to push with all our might to close the door behind Uncle Bill and Brownie.

While we waited, Mr.Pipken told us about Lester's accident. "I drive the team and wagon for Becker's. I haul block ice from the lake to the icehouse. Yesterday, when this storm threatened we wanted to get as much ice in as we could. Sometimes there's a hard freeze, followed by a thaw and the ice turns to slush.

"Lester and others were cutting ice out of the lake, loading the blocks onto a sled and pulling the sled to the bank. The wind was howling, everyone was tired and the wagon was about full. We were on the last load of the day when two of the blocks slid off. He heard the noise, tried to jump out of the way, but slipped and fell. One of the blocks caught his right leg. I heard the bone snap."

"We're grateful to you for bringing him home," Mother said as she stroked Lester's forehead. "Boys try to grow up so fast and sometimes get hurt doing things that are too much for them."

Dr. Pulsipher said, "I saw that in the war. Young men who should have been home or in school were pressed into service in jobs that would have been difficult even for grown men."

Uncle Bill and Brownie returned with a quart jar of whiskey. He handed it to the doctor and took me into the cramped room under the stairs where Hattie and her two little sisters slept. Hattie was staying over at a friend's house so we sat on her bed.

Uncle Bill whispered, "I shouldn't have taken Brownie to the cantina without his leash and muzzle. Bah Nubah was there. He didn't pay any attention to us until Brownie started growling. Then Bah Nubah and his buddies huddled together and started talking Apache real fast and waving their arms around while they looked over their shoulders at Brownie. I dragged him into the back room and we left out the back door before the Indians could determine who we were.

"I'm sure Bah Nubah killed Captain Jack or had a hand in it. Don't let Brownie out of the yard and when you take him anywhere, keep him under control. We don't need Brownie attacking that Indian. We have enough trouble on our plate right now."

The doctor added some water to a cup and mixed in progressively larger parts of whiskey. Lester was barely able to swallow it. After hacking, coughing and teary eyes it got easier. It didn't take long before Lester was out like an empty lantern. I saw the doctor take a couple of sips but he didn't cough and sputter. Feeling faint, Aunt Jane went to her room.

I wanted to watch but Mother sent me to my room. I listened from the top of the stairs but heard only the doctor's quiet voice telling Mother and Uncle Bill what to do. Then there was a SNAP! Lester's shinbone was yanked into place. Then, I went to bed.

Someday I'll be old enough to watch all the really interesting things that only grownups get to see.

The storm blew out during the night leaving the ground covered with six inches of snow and the sky a freshly washed blue blanket. Mr. Pipken took Red and Blue and struck out for Becker's Lake. Lester had a terrible headache and was green about the gills. Mother tried to ease the pain in his leg by giving him laudanum every four hours.

Lester had never been a pleasant person but now he was even worse. I was told to entertain him, so I didn't get to go to school for three days. I read to him from my schoolbooks, but he said they were boring. He liked to draw, so I devised a game.

"Draw a picture on my slate of something you saw at Becker's and I'll tell you a story about your picture," I said. Because of the medicine, he'd doze off in the middle of my stories but I didn't mind. It was better than his bossiness and grouchy complaints.

Father came home on the third day and Mother said I could go back to school. For weeks we'd been practicing the Christmas Eve program. I was one of the narrators, reading Bible verses while others acted the story of Jesus' birth. Hattie thought she was Queen of the World because she was Mary. Luther Rothlisberger was Joseph. Hattie was sweet on Luther and imagined herself already married to him, but he couldn't have cared less about her.

Father was home for three weeks. The work at the ranch had stopped because of bad weather and with Christmas and New Years almost upon us, the owner sent the workmen home.

Mother needed his help with Lester and she wasn't so strange when Father was around. I could handle it when she stopped what she was doing and stared vacantly into space. It looked like she was listening to someone or something. At least she wasn't wandering around outside like a lost soul.

When I asked, "Mother what have you been hearing?"

She'd reply, "Why do you ask that? I haven't heard a thing except the wind blowing."

Aunt Jane spent her days in bed. She liked me to read to her from the Bible and the Book of Mormon. She had never been to school and could read very little and wrote only her name.

"When is the baby due?" I asked. "Do you want a boy or a girl?"

"I think I'm seven months along. Should be about the first of March when he or she, I don't care which, makes its appearance. I've been poorly this time. A strong healthy child is all I hope for."

Our only Christmas celebration was on Christmas Eve at the church. We didn't have a tree or decorations at home. Mother agreed I should wear the blue silk dress, bonnet and black shoes Miss Lafferty had given me.

When my turn came to recite, I was nervous but quickly got into the spirit. I stood on a platform at the side of the stage and said:

"And lo, the angel of the Lord came upon them, and the glory of the Lord shone round about them: and they were sore afraid."

I loved my piece and especially the section when I got to speak for the angel.

"And the angel said unto them, "Fear not: for, behold, I bring you good tidings of great joy, which shall be to all people."

I really got in to it and acted when I spoke the angel's words. I spread my arms wide to include all the people in the room and ended splendidly with:

"Glory to God in the highest, and on earth peace, good will toward men."

As I finished my grand performance I heard gasps and giggles from the audience. I glanced over my shoulder to the stage and saw that the Angel was losing his wings. His white robe was hiked up in back and tucked into the waistband of his holey long johns. A slice of pink butt cheek peeked out. He'd made a trip to the privy before his glorious entrance and hadn't put himself back together properly.

His back was to the audience as he proclaimed to Mary, Joseph and the shepherds. Reuben, a shepherd, eased behind him and yanked the white costume out of his long johns and we continued.

I had a flash of anger but smiled right through it. How dare that Angel butt into my part of the program?

I went to my chair and the next speaker read the rest of the story. While we sang Christmas Carols, the embarrassed angel slipped out the back door and we saw no more of him for several days.

It was a Christmas tradition for Brother Whiting to make popcorn balls for every child. He grew the corn, popped it, his wife made the syrup and his family made the balls in a washtub. The Whitings set store by their contribution to Christmas and we appreciated their generosity. He took two big bags of his treat to the Catholic priest to give to their children after Christmas Eve services.

Saint Nick stood at the door dressed in red long johns, red knit long hat with a white wool tassel on the end and a fake wool beard. A pillow was stuffed into his johns to make him fat and the end of his nose was painted red. He was a good Saint Nick with a jolly Ho! Ho! Ho! The odd thing was that his pillow middle was the only part of him that was fat. He was unusually tall and so skinny he looked like a stick man drawn by a five-year-old. He was a cousin of Bishop Udall's, visiting from Ramah.

Our parents had ordered two crates of oranges from California. They'd been brought to Holbrook on the train and then by wagon to St. Johns. As we left the church each child under the age of sixteen received a cloth bag tied with a red ribbon that held a popcorn ball and an orange from Saint Nick. It was our only Christmas gift and we were as happy as we could be.

It had been snowing for two days but that night was clear and cold. The wind ceased for several hours, the stars glittered, and when we stopped to gaze at the wonders in the sky I heard for the first time, the high silvery song of the universe. If you've ever walked out under an icy clear sky on a frosty night you know what I mean. My heart swelled with love, my eyes watered and I was reassured that somehow all would be well.

Aunt Jane had stayed at home. She had a pot of hot-spiced apple juice ready when we returned. Later when I prepared for bed, I folded my beautiful dress in tissue paper and put it back into its box, pulled on my flannel night dress, crawled under the quilts, warmed where Brownie had been lying and said my prayers. My orange smelled of sunshine, sand and warm winters with gentle breezes. I put it on my pillow so I could enjoy it in my sleep. I thought it was the best Christmas ever. I was drifting off to sleep when the clear sound of the Catholic Church bell rang out over St. Johns announcing the day of Jesus birth.

On Christmas Day Mother roasted a wild turkey John had shot. We sang Christmas songs and listened to our parents talk about the holidays in "Merry Old England." Aunt Jane missed Amy in St. George, James, in Concho on the sheep ranch and Sammy. She cried and went to bed early.

Five days after Christmas, Bishop Udall visited. "Brother George, I have visitors from Ramah who need a place to stay for a few nights. Bishop James McNeill and his nephew Tom and a friend of theirs, Andy Merrill are here to pick up freight Sol Barth is bringing from Holbrook. The rest of us are full with family who've come for the holidays. Can you put their horses in your barn and provide a piece of floor to sleep on?"

"Always room for our brothers," Father said.

The Bishop made introductions, took his leave and Father and Reuben led our guests to the barn to care for their horses.

Hattie was home that day and she was immediately all a twitter over Andy Merrill, "Have you ever seen such blue eyes?" she gushed.

Hattie would have fallen in love with any male between the ages of fourteen and twenty who didn't look at her cross eyed.

"What's the matter with you? All you think about is boys. One of these days you're going to gush over the wrong man and get yourself in trouble," I grumbled to her.

When they came from the barn, Mother and I had the table ready and offered them each a steaming bowl of turkey soup and cornbread. We had already eaten, but Father and Uncle Bill pulled chairs to the table to visit.

"Tell us about Ramah, Brother McNeill. Before Christmas we had a visitor who said he used to live there. Maybe you know Mr. Pipken," Father said.

"Pip Pipken was here?" Brother McNeill asked with surprise. "We haven't seen him for several years. He absconded with large amounts of post office and church money. He should be arrested and thrown into jail."

He'd told us he was in trouble but we hadn't realized it was serious. We were stunned to think we had sheltered and fed a crook. He brought Lester home, so we had to think he had some good in him.

You sure can't tell a book by its cover or a man by his looks. Now, Tom McNeill, the Bishop's nephew looks like a nice boy to me. Hasn't said a word yet, just been listening and enjoying the soup. Looks about Lester's age, which would make him twelve or thirteen. Maybe I'll get a few words out of him later. Wonder if he likes to read?

Chapter Twelve

St. Johns, Arizona Territory, January, 1886

The day dawned cold and breezy. Snow covered hills glittered under the winter-soft southern sun, wearing their finest to say goodbye to 1885. Reuben and I asked Tom to ride to the foothills on an outing. Tom said I could ride behind him on his horse, Baldy, and Reuben rode Father's horse, Coaley.

As we prepared to leave, I spoke to Tom, "Last fall, Reuben and Lester discovered a cave. They saw arrowheads and broken pieces of pottery just inside the mouth of the cave. Do you like to learn about Indian things? Here's a bag of leftovers for our lunch. Will you put them in a saddlebag?" I was talking too fast and asking too many questions. I watched Tom saddle Baldy while I caught my breath.

He was rough around the edges with straight, shaggy, reddish brown hair. His trousers ended midway between ankle and knee as if he'd hiked them up to wade a creek. The arms of his jacket left a good two inches of wrists exposed. A pair of scuffed boots with the toes curled up made his feet look twelve inches long. His callused hands were large, but gentle as he handled Baldy.

He spoke slowly while a small smile played around his lips. His fair Scot skin sunburned easily and his nose and cheeks were ruddy in contrast with his gold flecked green eyes.

How long it will take him to grow into his hands and feet? He's going to be a tall man.

"You can't ride astride in that dress," he said. "See if Reuben has a pair of overalls, a shirt and jacket you can wear."

"Oh, shucks," I muttered. I'd wanted to impress Tom with my feminine beauty, but he hadn't noticed. He was right about riding astride in a dress. I'd have to impress him another time.

Thank goodness Mother's ideas of being a lady had changed since we'd been here. I'd learned you could be a lady no matter what you wore. Milking cows, struggling through knee high snow to get to school or slopping through mud to gather the animals from the pasture weren't chores easily done while dressed for a tea party. I had inherited a pair of work clothes from Reuben and ran to my room to change.

Why care about impressing him? He's a gangly scruffy boy I'll never see again. I don't know if he likes any of the things I do and, besides, I'm too young to be concerned with boys.

We rode into the brilliant December day. It was cold, but warming quickly. Crystal icicles that hung from buildings and trees were dripping. Rabbits and ground squirrels ventured out from their burrows and scampered across the crusty snow. Fox and deer tracks criss-crossed as if the animals were out for a stroll. All of God's creatures enjoyed this respite from winter.

Tom said, "Earlier you asked if I liked to learn about Indians. I go into the hills around Ramah and hunt for ruins and things the Indians left behind. More people lived here hundreds of years ago than there are now. When I was little, I lived at Sunset Crossing and there was a big Indian ruin across the river. We took our animals there to graze. I liked to sit and look out over the valley and think about who lived in that big ruin. Have you heard of Sunset Crossing?"

I was surprised to learn he'd lived there. I managed to sputter out, "Yes! I was there last summer. I spent an hour at the ruin and wanted to stay longer but we had to keep moving. When did you move from there to Ramah?"

"We'll talk later. Reuben is waiting at the top of that hill. We must be close to the cave. Don't want to get separated," Tom said as he spurred Baldy into a slow gallop.

I hung on with my arms around Tom's waist and rested my head against his back. He handled a horse well and I felt safe with him.

When we caught up with Reuben, he gestured and said, "We'll follow this ridge until we get to that rock outcrop. The cave entrance is on the other side of the rocks. Everything looks different than it did last fall but I'm sure I'm on the right track."

The horses picked their way around the point of rocks and we saw the mouth of the cave partly hidden by a Juniper. "It sure looks dark in there," I said. "Did you bring a lantern?"

Reuben answered, "Look what I found in the lean-to by the barn. Here's a half dozen long candles and I took some lucifers from the can on the stove."

Tom tethered Baldy and helped me down. I was surprised at how easily he did it. I wasn't a skinny little thing. People called me sturdy. He made me feel as light as a feather.

"Do you want a snack before we go exploring?" I asked.

"Do you happen to have any of those delicious trail crackers?" Reuben asked with a grin.

"I tell you," Tom said, "there were times at Sunset Crossing when I'd of been happy to have a trail cracker and a clear glass of water. I would've felt like I was a king at a banquet!"

"I made turkey sandwiches, brought popcorn and I have my orange. It smells so good that I haven't been able to eat it," I said.

"I've got piñon nuts," Tom added. "Have you ever had any? Do you know how to eat them? There are lots of trees near Ramah and last September the whole town went on a day long picnic and picking party."

"Captain Jack, our Gentile guide taught us about them," Reuben answered. He challenged Tom, "I bet I can spit the shells farther than you."

With a lot of cracking and spitting, Tom and Reuben held their contest. I was a lady and carefully removed the shells with my fingers. Tom won with a six foot spit.

The entrance to the cave was high enough so we could stand. Reuben gave Tom and I each a candle and put the extras in his jacket pocket.

"You have the matches?" I asked.

Reuben answered, "Yes, Miss Worry Wart. What good are candles without matches? They're in my other pocket."

As our eyes adjusted to the dimness inside the cave, we saw it quickly narrowed to a low tunnel. It got dark very quickly so Reuben lit his candle and led the way.

"Put your hand on my shoulder, Mary, Tom put yours on Mary's. Hope we're out of this tunnel soon. When Lester and I came here last fall, we only got this far," Reuben said.

By the time he finished talking, we were in a much larger area. We stood and gazed around.

Tom said, "Reuben light my candle so I can see the far wall. There's another tunnel to the right. I've been in caves where you could easily get lost and never be seen again. We must stay together."

Reuben lit my candle and I followed Tom across the center of the cave to cubbyholes dug into the far wall. We passed a fire ring in the center of the cave floor. Surrounding the ring were flat rocks placed in a manner resembling seats. I looked up when I felt a cool breeze coming from above. I couldn't see any light but there had to be a fire draft hole up there somewhere. Powdery dirt covered the floor and every time we stepped, it puffed up from under our feet.

I asked, "Tom, do you hear the sound of water?"

He stopped and listened. "Yes, sounds like an underground stream. Reuben, stay with us. Don't go down that tunnel by yourself. There's water here somewhere."

I said, "Look at all these bones. Looks like they had a feast and tossed the bones into this corner. All kinds of bones—cow, deer, squirrels and even some fish bones. Where do you think they found fish around here?"

Tom reached into the cubbyholes to see if any thing interesting had been stored there. He pulled something out and stuck it into his pocket but I didn't see what it was. When Reuben joined us he asked if we would go down the other tunnel with him.

Tom said, "Since there's running water close by we'll need to pick up some pebbles to throw ahead of us. If there's a stream or a pond we'll hear the plop as they hit water. Come on Mary, stay close."

"I want to look at the pots piled up over there," I said. "Some of them are real big and most are unbroken."

"We'll look at them on the way back," Tom said. "Reuben's about to have a fit to get into whatever's beyond this tunnel. We have to stay together."

"Oh, all right, boys are always the bosses," I grumbled but went along.

I was in the middle, with my brother in front and Tom behind. Our candles flickered from faint whispers of air. They had burned halfway down. The sound of running water became louder and I smelled moisture in the dank musty air. We had to get down on our hands and knees because the ceiling sloped downward and the floor angled upward. It was hard to hold on to my candle and crawl at the same time.

Tom called out, "Reuben are you tossing rocks ahead of you? I don't hear them hitting the ground."

Reuben started to yell back to us, "Yes!" But it turned into, "Yeeaahh!" and we heard SPLASH and then "HELP, HELP, blub, glub——I can't swim!"

Tom and I scurried toward the sound of thrashing arms and splashing water. When we came to the end of the tunnel Tom stood and held his candle high. He handed it to me saying, "Hold both candles up so I can see what I'm doing."

He unhooked his trousers and pulled them off, tied the bottoms of both legs and cinched the belt tightly. Reuben was three or four yards from the edge of a round pool of black still water. Still, except, where he was flailing around.

I averted my eyes so I wouldn't see Tom in his long johns. The pool was in a large round room lined with smooth polished stone. The wall was a rainbow of colors like the petrified wood I'd seen at the Petrified Forest. Was this a holy place?

I was yanked back to our crisis by Tom saying, "Mary, I'm going to lie on the edge and toss my trousers to Reuben. Hold on to my leg so I don't fall in."

I put the candles on the ground propped between two rocks. Then I grabbed Tom's right leg with both hands and held on for dear life. He was too busy to be embarrassed about my seeing him in his underwear, so I figured I shouldn't be embarrassed either.

He flung his trousers out to Reuben who was able to grab one leg and Tom pulled him to the bank.

Our candles were sputtering and about to go out. Tom said, "Give me another candle, so I can light it from these before we're left in the dark."

Reuben shivered and dripped as he reached into his pocket and looked at us with panic in his eyes. He said with a wet croak, "They're gone and the matches are sopping wet."

"Mary go to the mouth of the tunnel so we can find it before we're in the dark," Tom said as he untied his trousers and wrung them out. "Take Reuben's hand and Reuben, grab hold of my trouser leg. We have to get back to the main cave before our candles are gone."

So it was that I was in the lead, crawling along, holding both candles dripping hot wax in one hand, and praying for all I was worth. One candle sputtered out halfway through, but the other lasted until we reached the main room and were able to stand.

From the far side of the cave I was barely able to see a dull grayness in the pitch-black space. I said, "I see the entrance to the outside tunnel. Hang on and follow me."

I stumbled into the rocks around the fire pit and barked my shins. I almost fell into the ancient ashes, but Reuben held me up.

We hunched through the tunnel and reached the bright sparkling day. I started to cry. Tom struggled into his soaked trousers. Reuben's lips were blue with cold and his teeth chattered.

"Wh-a-ts the m-ma-tt-er, M-M-ary?" my brother asked. "Thanks to you and T-T-Tom, I'm okay."

"I'm crying in relief that we got out of this place in one piece and alive. I'll never go in there again," I said while blowing my nose and wiping my eyes on my hanky. "What do we do now?"

Tom answered, "I think I'd better take Reuben home as fast as I can. I need to get him inside and out of his wet things before he gets the croup. Mary, you'll have to ride Coaly and come by yourself. Think you can manage it?"

"Of course," I said.

Tom took off his warm sheepskin jacket and gave it to Reuben. He was cold, but Reuben was wet and chilled to his bones. It was one of the kindest things I'd ever seen.

"See you at your house, Mary," Tom called as they galloped away.

I climbed on Coaley, opened the bag of food I'd taken out of the saddlebag and ate while taking my time riding to town. I had a lot to think about—the cave and its pile of pots, the pond in the rainbow lined room and Tom.

I've met a boy I admire and he'll be leaving in a couple of days. Perhaps I'll never see him again. He probably has a girlfriend in Ramah.

I turned my thoughts to the cave and what I'd seen. I swore I'd never go in again with out a grownup and a kerosene lantern.

By the time I got home and put Coaley in the barn, Tom had given Reuben into Mother's care and was taking the saddle off Baldy and brushing him.

He said, "Mary, Reuben and I told your mother that Reuben tripped and fell into an iced over pond. He didn't want to get into trouble for going into the cave. He and Lester want to keep the cave a secret. Can you go along with that?"

"It's a sin to lie. I'll just not say anything about it," I answered. "I don't want to get anyone in trouble. You were brave to rescue Reuben. My brothers are big teases and sometimes aren't nice to me but Reuben is the best one I have. Thank you."

Two days later the load of freight arrived from Holbrook. Brother McNeill, Andy and Tom loaded their wagon and headed home. I was sorry to see them go but I had other things to think about. School was about to start again, Aunt Jane's baby was due in a couple of months and Father had gone back to the ranch.

When I went to bed that night, I found a small newspaper wrapped parcel on my pillow. I unwrapped it and realized what Tom had found in the niche in the cave.

It was very heavy, carved from dark green, almost black stone. By the light of my kerosene lamp I looked at it from all angles and finally saw that it was a perfect small buffalo carved a long time ago. The carving had short legs, a humped back and two small horns. I loved it! I'd never seen anything like it and Tom had given it to me. Even if I never saw him again I would keep the buffalo in my treasure box, take it out now and then and think of him.

A week later Mother said, "I found this ledger in a cupboard and thought you could write your stories in it. The cover and edges are raggedy but we'll cover it with fabric and make it like new. Most pages are blank so there's lots of room to write."

We found a scrap of the plaid she'd used to make curtains and after stitching a new cover on the book, it was mine. I hugged the empty book and vowed to write something every day. Each blank page was full of promise and possibility. At the top of the first page I wrote the same thing as in my catechism book. "Mary George, Her Book."

I resolve to keep it hidden under the cornhusk pallet on my cot so my snoopy brothers can't get their hands on it. My feelings for Tom, my worries about Mother and Aunt Jane are personal. If they read about Tom my brothers will tease me forever.

School began. I was happy to be away from Lester. He could get around on the pair of crutches Father made. One of his tricks was to stick a crutch out and try to trip any child who walked by. I walked around him so he couldn't reach me. To tease Brownie, he'd hold up a scrap of meat or bread, call Brownie, dangle the treat above the dog's nose then pop it into his own mouth. Brownie caught on real fast and refused to play Lester's game.

Lester whined, "I'm tired of being cooped up. I'm about to go out of my mind. When is Dr. Pulsipher going to cut this cast off and free me from my prison?"

Mother answered, "Another week, Lester, and don't think you'll be the only one happy to see you out and about. You're not a good patient. I pity the woman who marries you and has to put up with Henry Lester George!"

I was surprised to hear Mother speak so sharply. As a rule she kept her feelings to herself, but Lester was getting under her skin. Aunt Jane required more and more care, Lester was constantly cantankerous and Father was gone most of the time. Hattie, Reuben, William and I were in school all day so

Mother had all the laundry, cooking and cleaning to do. Alma, Roy, Richard and Parley were too young for school so were underfoot.

One day when I came home, I was surprised to find Grandma Burntwater sitting beside the stove having a cup of tea with Mother. She said, "Good to see you, Mary. You never came for a visit. I stopped in to see how things were going with your family. I find your mother needs help so I'll be staying for a while. My son and his family have gone to Concho to work at the sheep ranch and I'm alone on the hill."

"I'm sorry I never got to your place. I thought about you and still have questions. I'd like to know about the people who lived here long ago. I have my own room now. We can visit there."

Mother spoke up, "Mary, that's a change we need to make. Grandma Burntwater will be sleeping in your room. You're the younger so we'll make a bed for you on the floor."

Grandma Burntwater said, "No, no, I'm used to sleeping on the floor and can't sleep any other way. I'll bring my bedroll and other things from the hogan tomorrow, when I come to stay."

I was a taken aback but realized it was the only place for her. Maybe it would be fun to have her in my room. Mother would have her help during the day and Grandma Burntwater and I could talk privately.

Was she going to be paid for her help? The grownups never talked about money with us kids but I knew we didn't have an overabundance. There are times when our cupboard gets pretty bare. It's a good thing John goes hunting. They'd paid Dr. Pulsipher with a deer John had shot.

Uncle Bill was worried he was going to lose his job at the stable due to lack of business. "I can go work on the dam to keep myself busy, but that's volunteer labor and won't bring in cash," he said one evening. "If things don't get better after Jane has this baby we're going to consider asking to be released from our mission. This place isn't what we were led to believe."

My heart rose into my throat and my stomach flip-flopped. I was frightened at the thought of their leaving.

What will we do? What will I do without Aunt Jane?

When Dr. Pulsipher took the cast off Lester's leg and said he could go, he went. Aunt Jane's oldest boy, James, came home from Concho for a visit and when he left, Lester went with him. Mother was glad to see him go.

One evening I smelled something rotten in my room. The odor drifted from my bed so I looked under my pillow, then at the foot of the cot under the quilts. There it was, a furry green ball that had been my orange. By saving it I lost it. I never had a taste. I'd wanted to share it with Tom on our outing but Reuben's swim had sidetracked me. I'd forgotten all about sharing and had stuffed it under the covers that afternoon. The moldy orange taught me you have to enjoy things in the moment and keep them only in your memory, not under a quilt.

One night, Grandma Burntwater said, "Ask me some questions, Mary. I'll answer as many as I can."

"Why do Indians call themselves different names like Apache, Hopi, Ute and Navajo?"

"Navajo is a Spanish word. When the men in metal jackets came from Mexico they heard the Pueblo people call us Navahu. In Pueblo language it means those who live in a place of great planted fields or place of large flat land. They thought the Apache and we were the same. Our legends say both tribes came from the far northland centuries ago.

"It was so long ago it is remembered only in legend and song. My people stopped and stayed on the flat lands and mesas, while the Apaches wandered south into the mountains and east into New Mexico. Some went far south to Mexico. The Apache spread out farther than the Navajo.

"We call ourselves diné, which means the people. Each tribe calls itself 'The People' and we tell our own stories and sing our own songs. Some tribes say they came from the south, some from the north and some from the east or west. Each tribe had its own places and we knew where we belonged until the white man came and moved us around. Things have not been the same since the Spanish came from Mexico and the Anglos from the east," Grandma Burntwater said.

"Tell me more stories another night," I yawned, turned over and went to sleep.

One time when Father was home, I overheard him and Uncle Bill talking.

Father said, "I think there's only going to be another month's work at the ranch. We're worse off here than in Mendon. At least there we owned our house and land. Did you hear Brother McNeill speak of Ramah?"

"From what he said I gather Ramah is a settlement of Saints. It would be a friendlier place but the weather isn't any better. Moneywise things are worse for us than you. My job at the stables ends this week. The little bit I've earned has been just enough to pay our part of the rent," Uncle Bill said with heavy sadness.

I was doing the dishes while I pretended I wasn't listening. Mother was in Aunt Jane's room. In the corner by the kerosene lamp, Hattie helped Reuben with his arithmetic. William sat on the stairs with the little ones, in their nightclothes, around him while he read them a story. Everything looked normal and happy but I knew that again, things were about to change.

Chapter Thirteen

St. Johns, Arizona Territory, February, 1886

No, no, no. I'm just getting used to living here. I have my own room, I've made friends, Mother has Grandma Burntwater to help and you promised I would be baptized this spring. Now you're thinking of leaving?

Mother went to the table. "Are you talking about finances?" she asked. "Sister Udall is going to teach me how to make yeast from wild hops. I'll trade the yeast to Mr. Barth for needed supplies. There's a demand for bread yeast at this time of the year because the freight wagons can't get through. The cooks at the ranches make lots of bread to feed their hungry crews. Mary can stay home from school and help. It'll be good for her to learn how to do it. When she has a family she may need to make her own yeast."

"I hate to take Mary from school, but that's a good idea. Grandma Burntwater's here to care for Jane and the toddlers. What do you need besides the hops? Will Mr. Barth let you have supplies on credit until the yeast is ready?"

Uncle Bill said, "I'd tell Hattie to help you but she's earning a dollar a week helping at school and she'll be the only one of my bunch, except for James, who's working. I'll have to sell my mare's foal as soon as he's old enough to leave his mother. I don't know what else to do. Soon I'll run out of things to sell."

Mother said, "Mary, find a piece of paper to write on. I'm going to Sister Udall's to get the recipe. Will you come with me?"

"Can we bring Brownie? He's been so confined that he's got cabin fever," I asked.

"Guess it'll be all right. Haven't seen Bah Nubah and his gang for several weeks. Get your coat and let's stretch our legs," she replied.

Mother and I walked along the road, careful not to slip on the puddles that froze up as soon as the sun set. Brownie loped ahead, sniffing and marking the brittle weeds. Spring was a far away fairy tale. I didn't remember what it was like to be out without a heavy coat and to walk without watching for ice on the road. January dragged.

"Mother, I overheard Father and Uncle Bill. Do you think we'll stay?"

"Mary, you do have good hearing. Let's not worry right now. Even if Jane and Bill leave we aren't going anywhere. Do you remember what I said while we were camped near Sunset Crossing?"

"Well, not really. What did you say?"

"I will never again go on a long wagon trip. Your Father ignored my wishes when he demanded that we come here. With or without Jane and Bill I will not take a trip like that again. I refuse to be yanked from place to place like a gypsy. I need to know where home is," Mother told me in a firm, angry tone.

Sister Udall's girl answered our knock and invited us in. She called her mother who came from the kitchen and invited us to sit at the table. Mother took the piece of brown wrapping paper and a pencil from her coat pocket and they talked about gathering hops, boiling and mixing them with rye flour and the long process it took to make yeast.

Gathering the wild hops in the cold windy outdoors was fun. We took the little ones and they enjoyed the outing. They carried the bags while Mother and I clipped the dried pods. We cleaned and crushed the hops, put them in a large kettle and added water. The mixture boiled for an hour and then we strained out the husks. We added a measure of rye flour to the warm water, stirred it well and when the mixture cooled to room temperature Mother added chunks of active yeast. We moved the pot away from the stove. If it were too hot the yeast would die but if it was too cold it couldn't grow. By the next morning the house smelled like a saloon.

We divided the fermented mix, added enough barley flour to make dough. Using the biscuit cutter, we cut each rolled piece of dough into flat, thin circles. We laid the circles out on planks set on sawhorses in the backyard, to dry. I was put on sentry duty to keep the birds and other curious critters away.

146

By that evening the yeast was hard and dry. We kept some for our use and took the rest to Mr. Barth.

Each disk would make many loaves of bread. The baker only had to break off a small piece, soak it in warm water overnight and use it for mixing and baking the next morning.

We repaid Mr. Barth for the rye and barley flour, paid off other supplies we had received on account and had enough credit to get staples like flour, sugar, dried beans and rice. For a special treat Mother brought home three glowing jars of home canned peaches.

The next week I was jubilant to be back in the classroom. I didn't understand children who hated school. I'd been out of school for a week and the day I returned was as refreshing to my mind as a cool drink of water to my throat on a hot summer day.

What's the matter with me? I like to read and learn things that no one else cares about. My curiosity even aggravates my teacher.

"Mary, I don't know everything. I don't think Chinese people walk upside down. I don't know why volcanoes erupt or why most birds scoot down a tree trunk backwards. I don't even wonder about things like that. Your mind is too busy. Go sit down and read your book," she impatiently said one day.

It was early February, cold, wet and blustery but the days grew longer, the sun moved to the north and a few brave green leaves poked through the snow along the south facing section of the back fence. Would they would be crocus or daffodils as we had grown in Mendon?

One Tuesday, just before supper, Aunt Jane began to have labor pains. Mother and Grandma Burntwater did what they could but they needed Dr. Pulsipher. I was the only one around so Mother told me, "Grab your coat, take Brownie and run fetch the doctor. Tell him it's an emergency. It's too soon for Jane to go into labor."

The sun had set and day light was fading. The doctor lived only four blocks away, but we had to run down Main Street, past the stables and Coronado's Cantina. I didn't have Brownie on a leash and he ran ahead, glancing back over his shoulder to keep track of where I was. His floppy ears waved as he ran and I knew he was happy to be out of the yard. Bloodhounds love to run and to roam. As he ran past the far corner of Coronado's, he skidded to a stop, turned and growled. The hair down his spine stood straight up. I yelled, "Brownie! Come! Now!"

He ignored me and stalked toward the cantina. It was then that I saw, lounging in the evening shadows, two blanket wrapped Apaches. Brownie ran up the steps and lunged at the taller of the two men. I heard a shot at the same moment I saw the gleam of a silver pistol in Bah Nubah's hand.

I screamed, "You've shot him! Help! Help!" I turned and looked down the deserted street. Brownie lay at the bottom of the steps. I ran to help him and almost reached him when one of the Apaches threw a blanket over my head, picked me up, threw me over his shoulder and ran toward the river. It was almost full dark and there was no one to help me. I was being stolen and was so shocked that my brain stopped working.

I heard the men talking but didn't understand a word. Through the heavy blanket the stench of liquor on their breath was strong. I knew when we reached the river because I heard water flowing and bumping onto the boulders and ice along the banks.

Were they going to drown me?

The Apache threw me face down over the back of his horse. I felt him tie my legs and hands to his stirrups. He kicked his horse and we raced away. It was dark, cold and I was terrified.

Will anyone come looking for me? Is Brownie dead? Mother is counting on me to fetch the doctor, but the doctor won't know he's needed.

Tears ran down my face and I could only snuff up the snot.

Will they find my body? I'm going to die. I hope the eagles will come and take my soul to Heaven so I can be with Captain Jack.

I fainted. As I regained consciousness I realized the horses had stopped and I smelled meat cooking. Someone untied and lifted me off the horse. When I was put on the ground, I couldn't stand. My legs folded like wet noodles. An Apache woman helped me to stand and led me to the campfire. She murmured words that held no meaning but her tone sounded as if she was trying to soothe my terror. I desperately needed to pee. She pointed to a clump of bushes beyond the camp and beckoned a girl who looked my age to take me there. I could tell we were in the mountains because I saw, gleaming in the firelight, banks of snow and leafless white barked trees we called "Quakies." The air was cold and very thin. Walking to the bushes and back left me breathless.

Spaced around the large campfire were tent-like shelters made of hides stretched over poles. The girl smiled shyly at me but I was too scared to respond. The woman offered me a tin cup of hot broth. It warmed my stomach and my hands as I drank thirstily from the cup. I was very hungry. I hadn't eaten since noon and it must have been midnight by then. I wasn't offered food, but was led into a shelter where they signaled I was to lie down. The girl lay beside me and the woman covered us both with a wool blanket. I didn't think I could sleep but I did and awoke to the sounds of the Indians breaking camp.

The girl who had the job of taking care of me handed me a piece of bread. It was the size of a small plate, puffy and crispy like it had been fried. It was delicious.

The woman called the girl Dahtiyé. I touched her shoulder, because I'd heard it wasn't polite to point at an Apache, and asked, "Dahtiyé?"

She nodded and touched me as she looked at me with questioning eyes. I said, "Mary," and put my hand on my chest.

"May-ree," she replied and touched my shoulder again.

We both smiled and giggled. Dahtiyé covered her mouth with her hand when she laughed.

I looked up as a shadow fell over us. Bah Nubah grabbed me by my left arm and pulled me to where the women were loading camp gear into a wagon. He forced me onto the wagon, made me lie down and tied my hands together and my feet and legs to the stakes in the side of the wagon. A man tied a rope over my chest so I couldn't sit up. I lay flat on my back, on robes and blankets and was covered with another heavy robe. The men fastened a canvas cover over the bed of the wagon so I couldn't see out. I heard the hiss of steam as water was thrown onto the campfire, heard children's shouts, the jingling of horses being readied and then with a jolt the wagon moved.

What is to become of me? What is happening in St. Johns? Surely they are looking for me by now.

Tears flowed and puddled in my ears. I took three deep breaths and tried to think of what to do about the pickle I was in. I gave up and said a quick "Lord Help Me" prayer. In time the jostling of the wagon and the steady rhythm of the horses lulled me to sleep.

When I awoke I felt the wagon going downhill. The air was warmer than it had been earlier. I tried to remember what I'd heard about the geography of the land south of St. Johns. I'd seen the mountains but didn't know how far south they went or what was on the other side.

Sometime in late afternoon, the band stopped for the night. A woman uncovered me, helped me down and gestured for Dahtiyé to come. I was glad to be out of the wagon but felt lightheaded from lying down so long and I was hungry.

It was still light. I could see things I hadn't seen the night before. I counted eight men, ten women and twelve children setting up camp. Some of the women had babies on their backs or hung on tree branches in a wooden cradle. None of the babies cried or fussed as they watched the group with their almond shaped, shining, dark eyes.

The babies reminded me of Aunt Jane. I hoped she was all right and if the baby had been born, I prayed it was a nice strong child. I was angry and suffered from my helplessness. Handling things was what I did. My family depended on me and here I was in the wilderness with a band of Apaches, who scared me out of my wits. I started crying and reached for my tear-soaked hanky to blow my nose.

Dahtiyé took my hand and led me to a nearby stream and let me know I could wash the grime from my face and hands in the icy water. I rinsed out my hanky and flapped it in the sunlight to dry before I put it in my pocket. I cupped my hands and thirstily gulped down the water.

I bet I look a mess. My braids are starting to come undone, my dress is dirty and I smell of smoke and Indians. Do they ever take a bath?

My blue checked dress and white pinafore was my favorite of the ones Miss Lafferty had given me. Now it was grimy gray. Thank goodness I had on my Holbrook clodhoppers because the ground was muddy when it wasn't frozen. I shivered in my old blue coat and walked to the fire.

I looked beyond camp and saw that we were at the edge of a large flat meadow. The mountains were behind us and I could see a far distance to the south. Dahtiyé took me to a flat rock and gestured for me to sit. She went to the fire and returned with two clay bowls of stew with flat bread sitting on top. She showed me how to scoop the stew with the bread.

After we ate, the women and older girls put up the shelters while the men gathered a short distance away.

Were they discussing me? They keep looking at me.

Several raised their voices and they quarreled.

Maybe they don't know what to do with me. Are they mad at Bah Nubah? Did he think it was a big joke on the white man to steal one of their children? Does he know our men took Buster and the other horse? Does he think we know who killed Captain Jack?

My mind whirled like a top.

The next morning was worse. I hadn't slept. My mind was tormented with thoughts of what the day might bring.

Had they decided what to do with me?

After breakfast some boys circled around and poked at me with sticks. They yelled and laughed as I twisted and turned to keep from being jabbed.

They tried to lift my skirt and look under it to see what I had on. I batted their sticks away and looked frantically around for the woman or Dahtiyé.

I couldn't see them and no one paid any attention to my predicament. A stick scratched my wrist and blood dripped down my hand and onto my dress. I tore off a piece of petticoat and tried to tie it around my wrist to stop the blood.

Had they decided to torment me and try to make me run away? I'll be a goner for sure if I'm abandoned.

I watched the women loading the wagons, but no one came for me. The boys kept circling and taunting me. I put my hands over my ears to shut out their wild sounds and sat on the ground before my knees could fold and I fell. I put my head down between my knees and sobbed.

All of a sudden the boys stopped tormenting me and ran to get on their horses or into a wagon. I looked up as Dahtiyé took me by the arm and pulled me to the last wagon in line.

They had planned to leave me behind! My friend shoved me into the wagon bed and I crawled under the canvas cover. My sobs slowed and I decided I must be as quiet as I could so none of the men would know I was still with them.

Since I wasn't tied down, I could peek out the side of the wagon through the gaps between the wooden slats. We'd been traveling for several hours when over the sounds of the wagons and horses, I heard the bawling of cattle. I saw a huge cloud of dust coming from the west.

The wagon stopped as the cattle came closer. Through the dust I thought I saw a man riding a black horse leading the herd. Soon I heard hoofs galloping nearer and nearer. I could see the man more clearly now and saw he was dressed all in black.

How can I get his attention? What can he do if the Apaches want to keep me? Maybe they will trade me for ransom. Mary, this is a chance. Do something—anything, to draw his attention.

I squinted my eyes and peered through the crack. The Apaches were snaking around a bend in the trail and then everyone stopped. I watched the man in black ride to the Apaches who waited astride their horses.

Will he come my way? Oh please, come over here! You're my last chance. I'm at my wit's end. God only knows what they'll do to me if I'm not rescued soon.

Time was a tortoise that crept as I lay under the canvas fretting and worrying. I remembered something Father once said. "Worry is like a rockin' horse. It's something to do that doesn't get you anywhere."

What's happening up there? What were they talking about? What can I do to catch the horseman's attention without alerting the Indians?

I decided to hang something out between the slats. I tore the sash from my dress and prayed he would notice it.

With a lurch, the wagon moved. My hopes shattered, but I dangled the sash through the crack and prayed. The wheels creaked, the weak February sun on the canvas cover warmed my hiding place. I began having trouble breathing in the hot, stuffy confined space. I'd almost decided to start screaming when I heard a horse approaching. The wagon slowed and stopped. Dahtiyé's mother drove the wagon with Dahtiyé beside her.

Do they hope the man will rescue me?

I painfully forced my hand through the crack and fluttered the sash like a fisherman jiggling a worm in front of a fish. The horse stopped. I squinted through another crack and to my joy, recognized the man in black. It was Pat Traynor.

I'd cut my hand when I pushed it through the narrow crack. He grabbed the bloody sash and hid it in his pocket. He whispered, "Be quiet! Be patient! I need to get help."

My heart pounded in rhythm with his horse's hooves. I was dizzy with fright. My breath came in shallow gasps. The wagon moved slowly. Above the creaking wheels, I heard the Apache men arguing and yelling. In time they quieted—the wagon stopped and all was still.

The men dismounted and stood as if they were waiting for something. An eternity passed before I heard cattle bellowing and hoofbeats. Two cowboys led three cows, while another cowboy and Pat Traynor brought up the rear. He veered off and headed toward me while his cowboys guided the cattle toward the Apaches.

When he yanked off the canvas, sunlight blinded me. He grasped me around the waist, sat me behind him on Diablo and said, "Hang on tight, no sense in staying around for the tea party."

Diablo flew across the flats and we soon began climbing. We moved so fast the juniper and oak trees blurred as we rode past. When Mr. Traynor felt it was safe to stop, we paused beside a stream.

Diablo snorted and plunged his muzzle into the cold water. I cupped my hands, brought the water to my mouth and drank deeply. Mr. Traynor rinsed his face and dried it with a bandana. He asked, "How in the hell did you end up with them? Who are you and where do you belong? Snatching you cost me three head of cattle. I think the woman and girl driving your wagon knew and wanted me to take you off their hands. It would be big trouble for them if the Army learned they had kidnaped a white girl. I don't think the men knew what I planned. They demanded the cattle in payment for allowing me to cross their land with the herd. My men created a diversion so I could grab you and get away. If you hadn't been there, I would have given them only one old cow but I wanted them to be very happy for a few minutes. Hope my men and the herd will get to my ranch with no more trouble."

I took a deep belly breath and began to cry.

"Now, now, no time for blubbering. We need to keep moving. Up you go," he said as he hoisted me onto Diablo "I need to know which direction to ride in order to take you to your people."

"I live in St. Johns," I stammered.

"That'll take two days. Let's not dawdle and draw flies. Hang on and we'll be at one of my line shacks in time for supper. Old Barney'll be mighty surprised to have company drop by."

We arrived at the shack in late afternoon. A wisp of smoke rose from a stovepipe that poked through the tar paper roof. The smoke promised a warm place to spend the night.

My legs and my behind were weary from the long ride and I needed to visit the bushes behind the shack. While I tended to my needs, Mr. Traynor cared for Diablo. He unsaddled and put him in a corral that was sheltered on one side. I'd learned that a well cared for horse could mean the difference between life and death. That's why they lynched horse thieves.

Chapter Fourteen

Apache County, Arizona Territory, February, 1886
A stooped man with wild, white hair and beard came from the shack. "Well, well, if it isn't the boss man! Glad to see you. Gets mighty lonesome out here with only the wolves and coyotes to sing along with my harmonica. Didn't expect you. What's happenin'?"

"I brought a herd from Mexico and ran into a band of Apaches by the Blue River. Found something I didn't expect. Here she is. Barney, meet our guest."

Barney put out both hands and said, "My, my! I bet you're a real purty girl when you're cleaned up. What's your name?"

When he held my hands, I felt the calluses caused from years of hard work and rough outdoor living. His quiet shy smile and a twinkle in his deep blue eyes, almost hidden beneath bushy white eyebrows, told me I was welcome.

"I'm Mary George, from St. Johns."

"Let's go inside and see what I can rustle up for supper," he said.

While Barney rummaged in the wooden chuck box, Mr. Traynor and I sat on stools near the pot bellied stove. "So, you're Mary George. Are you related to Bill George who works at the stables in St. Johns? I talked with him last fall. Nice fellow."

"He's my uncle. My father is Henry George and my mother is Elizabeth. My father and Bill are brothers. We live together in the old feed store on Main Street."

"How long had you been with the Apaches and how did you come to be with them?"

Barney held up two cans of beans and a sack of cornmeal. "Just the thing for a cold February evening. Beans and cornbread. I have a piece of bacon somewhere. Let me look in the cold safe." He went to a burlap-covered box that hung on the side of the shack and pulled out a piece of something green. "A little moldy, but I'll trim it, chop it and put it in the pot with the beans. Let me get supper started before you tell your tale. I'm hankerin' for a good yarn and don't want to miss a word."

"Mr. Traynor, may I lie down for awhile?" I asked. "I'm tired."

Barney waved toward the cot in the corner, "Go right ahead. Me and the boss'll talk business whilst I cook." The bedding was grimy and I hoped there were no bedbugs. It was warm and I was so tired I slept as soon as my head hit the soiled lumpy pillow.

An hour later Mr. Traynor woke me and invited me to the table for the best beans I ever tasted. Outside, the wind picked up, rattled the window and gusted under the door. I was safe and warm in the old line shack with two new friends.

After we cleaned up the supper pots and dishes, I shared my account. "Your family is sure to be worried sick," Mr. Traynor said when I finished. "How are your cuts? Let's see if they need cleaning and new bandages." He washed and wrapped my right wrist and hand and said, "Stop calling me Mr. Traynor. Surely, after all we've been through, we're friends. I know you've been taught to call grownups Mr. or Mrs. but I'd rather you call me Pat. Barney and I'll sleep on the floor; you take the cot."

During the night a light dusting of snow blew in on the wind. We had cold cornbread and hot black coffee for breakfast. I'd never tasted coffee because Mormons shun it. I found it bitter, but it was hot so I drank while asking God's forgiveness for polluting my body.

Pat said, "I've decided to ride to my ranch instead of heading straight to St. Johns. I'll send a man to tell your family you're safe and we'll be in St. Johns tomorrow. Diablo has had a hard trip and with the two of us on his back he needs to take it slower. I'd like to see my wife and let her know I'm back from Mexico"

Now that I was safe and my parents would soon learn of my whereabouts, I was excited to be going to his ranch. I looked forward to meeting his wife. Many stories floated around about Pat Traynor and I would get to see which were true.

The morning was much colder than the day before and I wished I had my overalls to keep my legs warm. When I was mounted, Barney brought a blanket and tucked it over my lap and down my legs. "There, you go. Knew I was a savin' that old blanket for someone special," Barney said as he patted my knee. "Enjoyed your visit. Come again."

When the sun was high, we rode under the log pole arch and through a gate which marked the Rocking T Ranch. There was a flurry of activity at the door of the main house. Pat jumped off Diablo, ran to the porch and whirled a woman in his arms. Excited children, clapping adults and yipping dogs surrounded them.

A man lifted me off the horse. "Well, well, Pat usually brings back cattle. Where did he come by you?"

"Mary, come and meet Celina," Pat called. "Celina, this is Mary George from St. Johns. She's the reason I'm home early."

The striking dark haired, brown-eyed woman smiled and extended her hand. Her hands were so clean and soft that I was ashamed to offer my grubby, scratched and bandaged hand. She gave no indication of concern about my messy appearance. After shaking hands, she put her arm around my shoulder and guided me to the porch. "It looks as if you could use a hot bath and hair wash. Juan, tell Angelina to prepare a bath for our guest and to lay out some of Maria's clothes. They look to be the same size."

I answered, "Thank you. I'm ashamed to meet such a lovely lady while I look like a rag tag gypsy. A bath and a hair wash sound nice."

The group moved noisily into an airy high ceilinged entryway. "Papa, Papa, what did you bring us?" two small boys asked as they clung to Pat's legs. The dogs barked and jumped around and Celina tried to calm things down.

"Everything in good time. Be patient. I'm sure Papa has brought something for each of us, but first he and I need time to talk."

Juan returned, "Angelina said to send Mary to the bathroom and she will take care of her."

Celina spoke to a quiet girl with long black braids who stood to one side watching the hubbub, "Maria, take Mary to Angelina and these two noisy boys into the kitchen to Anna. Tell her to give them a treat and keep them busy while Papa and I talk in the library."

Maria took her little brothers in hand and smiled at me. "Follow us. We'll leave Diego and Armando in the kitchen and then I'll take you to the bathroom."

I had never seen a separate room for bathing. All my baths had been in the washtub on the kitchen floor. The tub was a big white oval standing on eagle claw feet. On the opposite wall was a throne I soon learned was a commode. This was a different world than the one I'd just come from or the one I'd lived in for nine years.

Angelina was a rosy cheeked, gray haired middle aged woman. She spoke in accented English and I tried out my broken Spanish on her. I undressed, loosened my matted braids and she took the dirty torn bandages from my hand then invited me to step into the tub's hot lilac scented water.

"Ahhh," I sighed. "Is this what Heaven feels like?"

She handed me a washcloth and a bar of smooth white soap and I washed my sore aching body. At first my cuts and scratches stung and burned, but then felt soothed.

"Put su cabeza back," Angelina told me. "We wash your hair."

I lay back in the tub. Angelina gently untangled my hair. She scrubbed my scalp and hair with soap that smelled like vanilla and lemon and cinnamon all together. She poured warm water from a porcelain pitcher to rinse my hair and then rubbed cream into it. I wished I could stay longer but she held up a big white towel and said, "You out now."

After I was dry she wrapped me in a pink flowered, flannel robe and gave me slippers for my feet. She gently rubbed yellow salve into my wounds and wrapped my hand and wrist with a roll of soft bandage. With a heavy silver comb she untangled my hair and brushed it with a stiff bristled brush.

"Vamanos," she said and gestured for me to follow. We climbed to the second floor and she opened the door to a small cheerful room. A set of clothes lay on the bed. There was a blue cotton dress, underwear and a petticoat, stockings and shoes that showed some wear but fit perfectly. The dress had a white lace collar and cuffs that matched.

Maria came as I finished dressing and said to Angelina, "Anna needs you in the kitchen to help put dinner on the table. I'll help Mary with her hair and bring her down."

"Your hair is still damp, so let's tie it back with a ribbon," Maria said. "Dinner will be ready in fifteen minutes. Would you like to see the house before we go to dinner?"

"I'd like to look around. Thank you for letting me wear your clothes. Do you know what's happened to my things?"

"They're being washed, dried and ironed and will be ready by the time you leave tomorrow."

Maria took my arm and guided me to the end of the hall where a set of wide stairs descended to the first floor. "The six bedrooms are here on the second floor," Maria said. "Look out this window and you will see where the maids and ranch hands live. Over there is the barn and two of the corrals." Two large log cabins and the barn were built of the same materials as the main house. Everything was neat and clean.

"Let's go down and I'll show you where Juan and I have our lessons. There isn't a school close by so Mama teaches us. She was educated at a Catholic school in Santa Fe. When Juan turns fourteen, he will be sent to Santa Fe to go to school. I will miss him. I wish I could go to a school with other students. Do you go to such a school?"

"Yes, I go to classes in St. Johns at the Mormon Church. There are two rooms, one for boys and one for girls. I can't go all the time because my mother needs me at home. She is not always well. I love to read and have been helping the younger girls learn."

At the bottom of the stairs we turned right, passed along a hall with two doors opening into it, and came to a room with book lined walls. From three big windows I saw a pond. A trout rose to a mayfly and mallards paddled in the water. Bare willow trees draped over the water and I imagined how lovely it would be when the willows leafed out and mother ducks led their peeping ducklings in a line behind her.

"This is the library and classroom. You said you liked to read. We have books in both Spanish and English. Mama insists we know how to speak and read her language as well as Papa's. You can choose a book after dinner."

A bell sounded. Maria took my arm and guided me to the dining room. I had never been in such a house and if Maria hadn't led the way, I would have needed a map.

The dining room was at the opposite side of the house and had a wall of windows that looked out onto a view of the snow covered mountains. Inside, small trees in large pots made me feel like we were in a garden. The dark green leafed trees were citrus of all kinds. There were lemons, oranges and some large yellow fruit that I'd never seen before hiding amongst the leaves. My mouth watered at the thought of a juicy orange. I wanted to ask if I could pick one, but then I might seem greedy. The next time I got an orange, I would eat it right away.

Celina sat at one end of the table and her husband at the other. She said, "Sit here beside me Mary so we can talk."

There were ten of us seated around the ample lace covered table. I noticed the chairs matched, and in the center of the table was a decoration made of glass that looked like a bouquet of lilies. Each place was set with matching large and small plates and glasses that sparkled from the candles flickering beside the glass lilies. The heavy knives, forks and spoons gleamed.

Pat asked another guest, a tall, dark bearded man to say the blessing and the food was brought from the kitchen. I don't remember what we ate, but I know I appreciated it.

I was overwhelmed to be eating in such a splendid place, and to top it all off the food was served by three young women in white caps and aprons over dark blue dresses.

Surely, I am having a fairytale dream from which I will shortly awake. I will find myself with the Indians, fearing for my life.

When the meal was cleared away, a basket of fresh fruit was passed. I chose a fragrant round, thick skinned orange and after caressing its dimpled, yet smooth surface, cut away the rind and ate it segment by segment. Each little sac of juice burst in my mouth with an explosion of summer and sun.

Celina tried to engage me in conversation by asking "Tell me about your family, Mary. How many brothers and sisters do you have? Are you happy to be going home tomorrow?"

"Seven brothers——no sisters. I'm worried about my mother and my aunt and I think I've caused them lots of worry by getting kidnapped by the Apaches. I fear I might be punished when I get home."

"Mary, I'm sure they will be overjoyed to hear you are safe and on your way home. My husband sent Angelina's son, Faustino, to St. Johns."

Pat, who had been in deep conversation with the tall man, looked my way and said, "I have business to tend to and need to take some things to St. Johns. Can you handle a horse? It'll be easier if you can ride by yourself while I lead the pack horses."

"If the horse isn't a bucker and we don't go too fast I'll do fine," I answered.

"Good, I have just the mare for you. Now, if you ladies and boys will excuse, us Mr. Westbrook and I have some differences to settle. We'll be in my office and don't wish to be disturbed."

Westbrook! I'd heard that name around the stove in the evenings when Father and Uncle Bill talked about the outlaws who lurked in the canyons and mountains around St. Johns. A Mormon man was murdered by a 'Westbrook' in Springerville. The only reason given was that, "He wanted to see if a bullet would go through a Mormon." The posse never caught him.

I remembered rumors that Pat Traynor was an expert at sneaking across the border into Mexico and bringing back large herds of cattle. My fairytale had turned into a nest of lawlessness and cattle rustling. I could hardly wait to get home. I did what I always did when I needed to calm myself. I went for a walk with Maria and then looked for a book in the library.

"Here's one about the early Spanish explorers who came through this valley over three-hundred years ago," Maria said as she held out a heavy leather bound book. "It has lots of drawings. Here's a picture of the mountains near here. The peaks are the same."

I lost myself in tales of the Spanish conquistadors led by a man named Coronado. I learned that those who came north from Mexico City searching for gold, named St. Johns, El Vadito, meaning "Little Crossing." They crossed the Little Colorado River there and went east to Zuni. The explorers continued east until they came to a big river they called The Rio Grande. The afternoon flew and soon I heard the bell calling us to supper.

It was a simple meal and Pat and Mr. Westbrook did not join us. Soup and cornbread, followed by custard pudding with sweet butterscotch syrup on the bottom were served. Afterward we went to the parlor with Celina. She read to the little boys until they nodded off, while Maria, Juan and I played checkers and dominoes. At eight o'clock we were excused to go to our rooms for the night.

The high metal framed bed with goose down mattress and cover invited me to snuggle down and go right to sleep. I dreamed of Brownie running through a mountain meadow full of summer sunflowers with Captain Jack and Buster. I woke with a start. My cheeks were wet with tears. Did my dream mean that Brownie was dead? I had a hard time going back to sleep and tossed and turned for the rest of the night.

It was barely light when Angelina shook me awake. "Mary, time to get up, dress and eat and be ready when Sen or Traynor is ready to ride."

My clothes were on the chair beside the bed. There was also a pair of boys' trousers. The bloody sash had been washed and sewn back on the side of the dress. There was only a slight stain to show where I'd bled all over it. My Holbrook clodhoppers were mud free and polished. After I dressed, Celina brushed and braided my hair.

Her hands moved smoothly and quickly. "Don't be afraid to go home. Your family is lucky to have such a plucky, pretty girl. We've enjoyed your visit. Maria would like to hear from you so write now and then. Anna has some hot mush for you in the kitchen. Go and eat quickly. My husband is almost ready to ride and he doesn't like to be kept waiting."

The household slept as I hurried down the stairs to the warm kitchen. The dogs slumbered quietly near the big wood burning range. Anna had prepared food for me to take. I was happy to feel an orange in the bottom of the bag.

Celina came for me and we went through the silent, dim house to the front porch. She held out my now clean outgrown coat and I put my arms through the too short sleeves and buttoned it up. Pat waited for me, holding the reins of a light brown young mare.

"This is Bayou. Her mother came from Louisiana. Up you go," he said as he hoisted me into the saddle. He adjusted the stirrups to fit my legs, checked the straps holding the saddle and patted Bayou on her rump.

He hugged Celina, mounted his horse and took the reins of two packhorses. With a wave and a soft "Let's go!" we trotted down the drive, through the gate and onto the trail beside the river.

Bayou was obedient and gentle. She followed Pat and the pack horses as if she knew what was expected of her. I had time to look over the countryside, admire the snow-covered peaks as they turned pink in the dawn and think about going home.

Chapter Fifteen

St. Johns, Arizona Territory, February & March 1886
On our way to St. Johns, we followed the Little Colorado River. There was ice in the shallows along its banks and neither the cottonwoods nor willows had leafed. It was cold and clear but I was warm in my coat and Juan's trousers. Dark clouds in the west foretold a late winter storm.

Pat was grumpy so I didn't try to visit when we halted to stretch our legs and let the horses drink. Once I offered a cold biscuit and ham sandwich. "No, thanks. Not hungry. Have problems on my mind. Feel like taking off over the mountains to be free like I was when I left home at fourteen. My life is bogged down with too many people and things. Perchance, I've got too much tumbleweed in my blood to settle down. I underestimated Mr. Westbrook. I didn't think he was smart enough to be a crooked cattle rustler or was sly enough to betray me. Forget what I just said. Let's move on."

I'll never understand grownups. Looks to me like Pat has everything a body could want but he's not happy.

We neared Eager and Springerville. I wanted to ride down the main street so I could see the sights, but we kept to the trail along the river. Didn't Pat want to be seen?

North of Springerville he slowed for me to catch up. "Look across the river, Mary. There's a prehistoric Indian ruin against those cliffs. The settlers go there to collect pots, arrows and spear points."

At first I didn't see it, then, "There it is. It's built of the same rock as the cliffs and blends right in. What do folks do with the things they find?"

"This country's been inhabited for thousands of years, but no one knows who those people were. Folks from back east are interested in old Indian things. Museums send buyers to collect. Other buyers are traders who sell to travelers or who have started their own collections. Did you see my things in the library?"

"Yes. How much do people pay for those things?" I asked thinking of the pots in the cave.

"Depends on the buyer, the condition of the relics and how hungry the seller is. Each deal is different. Let's move on. Should be in St. Johns in three hours."

Hmmm. Glad I've kept my mouth shut about the cave. Maybe I'll be able to help my family.

We followed the river downstream and passed the dam south of St. Johns. The men of the town had been laboring for over a year to get it finished by spring in order to catch and hold the spring run off. More and more settlers were arriving and in order for them to make a go of it, they needed irrigation water.

Last fall, the Bishop gave Uncle Bill seed for winter wheat and he planted fifteen acres of grain on land owned by the church. Most of it sprouted but then died for lack of water. Others had planted potatoes, oats and lucerne. Alfalfa was called lucerne in England, so that's what my folks called it. No crops had flourished. If we had money or something to barter, we bought what we needed from Mr. Barth's store or ordered from Holbrook. As a last resort, we'd go to the Bishop and ask for help from the storehouse. It held donated goods the church set aside to help needy church members.

We stopped while Pat looked at the dam. "Hope it holds up under the spring run off. Real heavy snow pack in the mountains this year. It's always good to get rain, but when the rains come at the same time as the melt, it's trouble."

My mind was not on the weather or the dam. My heart pounded, I felt like I had just run a race and my hands were cold and clammy. As we drew near town both anticipation and dread washed over me. We stopped in front of my home. As Pat helped me dismount, Father came out.

"Mary, oh my Mary! I feared I'd never see you again. Our prayers have been answered. My lamb is back in the fold," Father exclaimed as he swept me off my feet in a bear hug.

I was speechless and shed tears of joy as I buried my face in Father's neck and held on tight. I was safe again. Even though home was an old feed store, I was jubilant.

Father put me down and extended his hand, "Mr. Traynor, we are forever in your debt. If there is ever anything we can do for you, just ask. Your man came last evening with the good news, but he couldn't stay and relate the circumstances. Can you visit so we can serve you refreshment while you tell us how you rescued Mary?"

"Glad I found her. You have a spunky, smart girl. It'd be better if she tells you about it. I have some business to see to. It's imperative that I return to my ranch as soon as possible. I'm expecting trouble with a herd I acquired in Mexico. Maybe another time. Mary, no matter what you hear, I hope you'll always have friendship in your heart for me and Diablo. The older you get, the more you'll see that people have many sides," Pat said as he extended his hand to me. "Have to git." He gathered the reins of the pack horses and was on his horse and gone. Father would come to regret the debt he owed Pat Traynor.

"Is everyone inside?" I asked.

Why hadn't any body else come to greet me?

Father led me to a bench beside the door. "I have things to tell you before we go in. We've just come from the cemetery. Eleanor was born the night you were kidnapped and lived only a few hours. Jane and Bill are grievously saddened by her death, especially so soon after Sammy's passing. Jane is up and about but the light has gone out of her. It's as if she's died inside. Bill grieves the loss of his children but he is even more saddened by the change in his wife."

"I hoped the new baby would comfort Aunt Jane. Did Bah Nubah kill Brownie?" I asked.

"Elizabeth first suspected something was wrong when she heard Brownie howling. He was bleeding from a gunshot wound to his right hip. She brought him in, left him with Grandma Burntwater and went looking for you while Bill went for the doctor. She couldn't locate you, so came home. Doctor Pulsipher finally arrived and said he hadn't seen you. She sent John out to look.

"He came back with the news of your kidnapping. Some cowboys at Coronado's heard the shot that injured Brownie but paid it no attention. Bill then went to Coronado's to get more information. He learned one of the customers saw Bah Nubah throw a blanket over someone and carry them away. Bah Nubah and friend took off in the direction of their horses. No one knew which way the Apache's had gone. By that time it was pitch dark so the men decided to wait until morning before forming a posse to rescue you. I didn't hear of your disappearance until the next day when they came to the ranch to get me. We didn't have Brownie to help us and by dark we gave up and returned to town. We feared you were gone for good."

"Is Brownie dead?" I asked again.

"No, and you have Grandma Burntwater to thank for that. When I arrived I figured he was a goner and wanted to put him out of his misery. He howled all the time and kept the children stirred up. Grandma Burntwater wouldn't let me shoot him. She asked if she could take him to her hogan and try to heal him. She also took Parley, Roy, Alma and Rachel just to get them out of the way. They loaded Brownie into the wagon and off they went. I don't know how Brownie is, but I know he's alive."

"Where's Hattie? Is she here to help Mother with Aunt Jane?"

"I don't know where she is. She came for a couple of days and then went back to work. She stays with the Selkirk's most of the time. A little high and mighty if you ask me. I think she needs a good kick in the pants and a reminder of who her family is, but she's not mine to correct."

"How's Mother? I worry about her more than anyone. I know I failed to fetch the doctor and then Aunt Jane's baby died and all these awful things happened because of me!"

"Now, now, don't forget you're only nine. We grownups have fault in all this and there are always things over which no one has control. In fact, I'm thinking we don't have much control over anything. I need to tell you about Mother, then we'll go in."

"Do you have a hanky? I lost mine and I need to wipe my face and blow my nose," I said as I tried to prepare myself for what Father was going to say. He handed me his handkerchief, put his arm around my shoulder and said, "Elizabeth blames herself for what happened to you. She says she should never have allowed you to take Brownie.

"Even though the doctor was here he couldn't do anything. She was a sickly little thing and couldn't nurse. There were other things wrong and she never would have been normal.

"At first Elizabeth was all right, but after things quieted down she sat in the rocker and went into a fog. Her eyes were empty and she responded to no one. After I returned from the search, I carried her upstairs and gave her some laudanum. She slept for twenty-four hours."

"Did she go to the services today? What is she doing now?" I asked.

"She went to services, but came back and sat in the rocker. She moans, cries and wrings her hands. Jane cares for herself and the four little ones are at the hogan. Bill and I have been doing the cooking and washing. We are trying to decide what to do about our predicament. When we go in, approach your mother quietly, touch her on the shoulder and tell her who you are. Having you home may snap her out of it."

I did as Father directed. Mother turned her empty eyes to me and said, "I had a daughter named Mary. I sent her on an errand and the Indians kidnapped her. It's my fault. I'm sure she's dead and suffered greatly before she was released to God. I will surely go to Hell for my carelessness."

"Mother, it's truly me, Mary, your daughter. I was rescued and I'm here with you."

She covered her face with her hands and wept. "I don't want to live anymore. God has deserted us in this awful place where babies die, children are kidnapped and we nearly starve to death. You look like Mary, but I think they are trying to fool me. I want to go to bed and never get up."

Father helped Mother up the stairs, put her to bed and dosed her with the syrup. When he came down his broad shoulders were slumped, his step was slow and his eyes were red.

Reuben went to the hogan to tell Grandma Burntwater I was home and that she, the children and Brownie could return. When they came, I put my arms around Brownie's neck and buried my face in his loose skin. I cried tears of joy. He howled and put his front paw on my shoulder.

"Thank you, thank you, Grandma Burntwater. Father told me what you did and I will be forever grateful. Will he walk again?"

"He'll always limp and won't be able to run very fast. His days tracking and hunting are over. He's only a pet now."

The children cried, "Mary, Mary! We're so glad you're home. Were you scared? Did the Apaches hurt you? Were they mean? Did you meet any good Indians?"

"Let's go in and I'll tell everyone at once." Aunt Jane fixed popcorn, we drank the remainder of the apple cider from last fall and I told my tale. The little ones fell asleep halfway through and by the time I finished I also was ready for bed.

During the night the storm blew in from the west and we awoke to a wet, late winter snow. Tree limbs bent to the ground. The snow melted and roared down from roofs.

By March, the wind was warmer and came from the south. Spring had come again and our spirits rose with the temperatures. I returned to school, where I told my story again. I also wrote it in my journal as not to forget.

Grandma Burntwater told me, "Dahtiyé means 'Hummingbird' in Apache. It is a nice name. Whenever you see a hummingbird you will think of her and say 'Thank you.'"

Mother gradually came out of her fog and spent more time downstairs in her rocker. One day she asked, "Mary, is it really you? When did you come home? I don't remember anything since the day of Jane's baby's funeral. Will you tell me what happened?"

"I'm tired of telling it. I wrote it in my journal. Would you read it instead?"

So Mother read my journal and continued to recover. Aunt Jane and Uncle Bill were quiet and sad. Uncle Bill was working at the stables again as business picked up.

He came home one evening with a story of his own. After supper we gathered to hear about the cattle rustling in Yavapai County, south of Prescott, which was the capital of Arizona Territory.

"Early pioneers came from Illinois through Arizona on their way to California to the gold rush. They found gold mining was a rich man's business. It takes a lot of money for machinery to dredge the creeks and to dig underground for gold. Some took up farming in California and some returned to Arizona.

"Since the end of the Civil War, the United States has been building and operating frontier forts to protect us from the Indians. The Army needs lots of beef so the cattle business is booming. One family that returned from California was the Cartwrights. They have a sizeable operation south of Prescott. A month ago they went on their spring roundup and discovered a herd of their CC cattle was missing. Jackson Cartwright and his five sons were madder'n hornets whose nest has been whacked.

"Seems as though someone saw a man dressed in black riding a black horse in the area. He had six cowboys with him. No one saw them do anything wrong, but it was said that they didn't look like they were up to any good.

"Cartwright has organized a posse to look for his cattle. They plan to come this way and should arrive next week," Uncle Bill said.

My heart jumped into my throat. I thought about Pat Traynor and his herd of "Mexican" cattle.

Was he a rustler? What did Mr. Westbrook have to do with it?

Father said, "If those rustlers are smart they'll change that CC brand to

OO and if they're still around here they should keep moving east into New Mexico."

"It's none of our concern. Let the posse and the authorities handle it. We have enough problems of our own," Uncle Bill said. "I went to the dam today with Bishop Udall and some of the other men. They're worried about the dam holding. That spell of warm south wind last week melted a lot of snow and the reservoir is filling fast."

"Hope we don't get heavy rains in the next couple of weeks," Father said.

I woke during the night to the sound of rain pounding on the tin roof. There was a leak and I had to move my cot to keep dry. I went to the kitchen and got a bucket to catch the drip. The drip, drip, drip kept me awake. It finally slacked off and by morning the sky was clear. The road was muddy with puddles in the ruts.

While walking to school, I stopped and watched a large puddle. Something was swimming around in it. I'd heard of Arizona polliwogs, but didn't believe it until that morning. Frogs lay eggs that stay dormant all winter until rain fills the puddles and the polliwogs hatch overnight.

That afternoon I took a large jar and caught some. I took my prize into the house to show to my little brothers. Aunt Jane was in the kitchen and I showed them to her. "Mary George, take those slimy things right back to where you got them. I won't have polliwogs and frogs in my house."

"But I want to watch them grow into frogs. Don't you think it would be interesting?"

"I have more important things to think about than polliwogs turning into frogs. Get them out of here. Go dump them. Now!"

I took them to the yard, but I didn't dump them. I wanted to take them to school.

I bet Sister Selkirk will enjoy having them in the classroom.

Later that evening it rained again. It rained all night and we had buckets and kitchen pots on the upstairs floor in every room. I lay awake and listened to the song the drops sang as they hit the containers. "Plink! Plank! Plop! Drip! Drop! Splash! Splatter! Spatter!" Each container made a different sound as the water hit. I could tell by the sound when a bucket was almost full and then I'd open the window and dump the water outside. In the morning it was still raining. Father and Uncle Bill ate a hurried breakfast, took some tools and rushed out of the house.

"Where are they going?" I asked Mother.

"The men have been called to the dam. Some cracks have developed on the west side and they are going to reinforce it with rocks. The impounded water is almost to the top of the dam."

"Should I go to school?" I asked.

"I need you here. There may not be classes today. Only a duck would be happy to go out in this downpour," Mother said.

I went to the yard and dumped the polliwogs. Water in the ditch was high and running fast. The yard was covered with water and I stepped on rocks or patches of weeds to keep my shoes out of the mud. It was a gloomy dark day. The little ones were fussy. Mother and Aunt Jane rolled up the rugs, piled chairs on top of the table and carried foodstuffs to the upper floor. Their mood was ominous. The rain continued.

After dinner, eaten while we sat on the stairs, Grandma Burntwater came from her hogan. She'd gone to tend her animals. She dried off and said, "I put the animals inside the hogan. I see you've prepared for the worst. What do you hear from the dam?"

Aunt Jane replied, "John came and got some soup to take to the men. He said the dam looks like it'll hold if the rain slacks off but we should prepare for the worst. We're far enough from the river so we won't have to evacuate. We may have to stay upstairs."

Grandma Burntwater said, "Give me some soup. I'm chilled. When I've eaten I'll stay with the children and see if they'll nap. Mary, go up and get them settled on your parent's bed."

When she came into the room, I had put the children down. "Tell us a story," Alma said.

"Do you know an Indian story about why it is raining so much?" Rachel asked.

"I know the story about how Snail Girl brought water to the land. Would that one do?" She and I sat on a blanket on the floor.

While the rain drummed on the roof, the leaks plinked into buckets and Brownie snored with his head in my lap, Grandma Burntwater told us a Navajo story.

"When the people first came to this land from their old land far below because they were fleeing a flood, no one thought to bring fresh water. All the water they found was salty and no one could drink it. First Woman sent members of Water Clan, beaver, otter, turtle and frog beneath the salty ocean to find the place where freshwater bubbled up from the other world. Every one of them got sidetracked and brought back things like water lilies, sea shells and the empty water jar with its coral stopper. Finally, Snail Girl asked to be sent. They knew she was very slow, but no one else would go. She took the jar, found the bubbling spring and returned with freshwater. She had been gone so long that the people had left and scattered across the land.

"As Snail Girl moved slowly up a hill looking for the people, the water jar bounced on her back, cracked and the water leaked out leaving a wet trail behind her. She fell into an exhausted sleep and was awakened by First Woman who had followed the water trail. First Woman sang a song of thanksgiving and the small wet trail turned into a wide deep river of fresh water that ran down to meet the salty ocean. Snail Girl was blessed with a little water jar that she carries on her back all the time and she leaves a wet trail everywhere she goes. From that time on, the people knew how precious freshwater was and how careful they must be with it."

By the time she finished, the children were asleep. I whispered, "Do you know any way to stop all this freshwater from falling?"

"No, but I know when people interfere with rivers and build too close to them they have troubles. I am just an old Navajo who watches. I know of no way to stop what people, white or Indian, do."

Father, Uncle Bill and John came home in time for supper. They were wet, exhausted and muddy, but hopeful. "We've done all we can. It's in the hands of the Lord," Father said.

"How will we know if the dam breaks?" Mother asked.

Uncle Bill answered, "They've set a schedule of men to keep watch. If they see the dam start to go there will be an alarm sounded by the Catholic Church bell. Men will ride through town to warn those in danger to get to higher ground. I tried to find Daisy, our one remaining cow, and bring her into the barn. No sign of her."

"Sounds like all we can do is go to bed and pray," Mother said as she and Aunt Jane cleaned up and put pots, pans and dishes on top of the cupboards. All of us slept on the upper floor that night. The children thought it was great fun to sleep on the floor. The rest of us were weary with worry and didn't sleep soundly.

The clanging of the church bell, pounding hooves and shouts from the street awakened us. It was dawn and the rain continued. "The dam has washed out! Head for high ground or stay on the upper floors of your homes," One sentinel cried as he rode past.

Father and Uncle Bill ran down the stairs to put rags, rugs or anything else they could find under the doors to try and keep water out.

170

I heard the roar of the flood and looked out the window to watch. Whole trees, roots and all, floated down Main Street. Outhouses glided by as horses swam across the torrent trying to reach the hill behind our barn. I found Father and Uncle Bill sitting on the stairs, helplessly watching muddy water ooze under the front door. By 8:00 a.m. the rain stopped, the water began to recede and sun shone brightly down from a blue sky onto a soggy St. Johns.

We were lucky. We had a second floor to go to, all of our animals, except for Daisy, were accounted for and we still had an outhouse. Some lost their homes, two Apaches drowned as they lay drunk by the river and many farmer's early planted crops were destroyed.

Two weeks after the flood, as I walked to school, I heard a team of horses behind me. I looked over my shoulder and saw a large black coach pulled by six black horses stop in front of the stables.

"Mary, Mary George! Is that you? It's me, Maria Traynor. Come here so we can talk."

I hurried across the street and found Maria, Juan, Angelina and Celina in the coach. "What a surprise. I feared I'd never see you again. Where are you going?"

Celina Traynor turned her head away and wiped her eyes with a hanky. Maria answered, "We're going to live in Santa Fe with Mother's family. Two wagons with all our possessions are following us to Holbrook where we'll catch the train. I'll get to go to a real school!"

I wanted to ask about Pat, why were they leaving their beautiful ranch and did it have something to do with Mr. Westbrook and a herd of cattle. With great effort, I bit my tongue and thanked them again for their kindness to me. When the horses were watered the coach left and Maria waved happily from the coach window.

I was puzzled and thought of the Traynors all day. I'd ask Uncle Bill if he'd heard anything about them. Instead he handed me a letter he'd written. He asked me to copy it and correct his spelling and grammar. After I read it I forgot about the Traynors. I felt I'd sat down on a chair that wasn't there.

Chapter Sixteen

St. Johns, Arizona Territory, April & May 1886

Uncle Bill spoke well, but he couldn't write well. He'd never been to school. "Will you read and correct my letter to the President of the Church? I'll copy your version and send it to Salt Lake City."

I took writing paper from my school folder and by the light of a kerosene lantern, did as he asked. Tears splashed onto the sheet and blurred the ink. I folded the original and slid it into a pocket in the cover of my journal. Someday someone would want to know why Uncle Bill and Aunt Jane returned to Utah.

His letter read:

St. Johns, AT, March 30, 1886

President Taylor

Dear Brother:

It is with Regret that I am Compelled to Write To you, To ask you would Be so kind as to send me my Releice From this place. I Desire a Honorable Releice and I now give you my Reasons For asking you for it.

I was called to Come to St. Johns one year ago last March, and I sold my place in Mendon, Cachie County for Fifteen-hundred Dollars, which I have Consumed all But three small ponies, hardly sufficient to move with. I am a good farmer and was cent here to grow citrus trees. But this is a Cold place and not suted to citrus or much uf anything else.

Our Bishop as Been kind to me in Letting me have seed Grain. I put in Fifteen acers of grain and I don't think that I shall raise Fifteen Bushels. All Died Want of water, have Drawn From the Relief Fund till I Cannot sume up Corriage to ask for any more my Wife is now gone to Ask the Bishop For Some Flour as we have none in the house at this time. My brother has been of grate help to us but he has meny problems of his own. This is Rather tuff to have to go to the Church For Your support When I am ampley able to earn our Living if I Could Get Good paying Work to Do to earn it.

I have buried two of my children Since I Came here Last year and some of my horses have Died and the Last Cow I had got Drounded about two weeks ago this is the reason I am so hard run for means: it looks utterly Impossible For me to support my Family, my children have Cried once for bread Since I have Been Here in this place. But I had something to sell then to Buy Something, But now I have nothing to sell to get anything with.

Dear Brother I Desire my Releice So that I can Get Back time enofe to earn Some Breadstuff For the Winter For I Can not get it here, only from the Flour that Was sent here From Utah.

Dear Brother Please sen me an Honorable Releice For I do not Wish the Church to Support me When I am able to work For my living if I culd get the Work to Do. I have a Wife and Six living children. Our daughter is now situated in St. George and we would go to be with her in a warmer place where I culd grow trees. Please Do not Delay Answering and your Well Wishes and Brother in the Gospel of Peace

William George Jr

Plese send answer to William George at St. Johns; Apache County Arizona Territory

After I finished, I cried even more.

How can we survive here without them? Mother has never been without her sister. Father looks to his brother for guidance and advice. None of us has ever lived without family near by. This is a calamity we will never get over.

The next morning, I handed Uncle Bill the corrected letter. My eyes were red and my heart was heavy. Aunt Jane hugged me and said, "It is time for us to go. I don't know what your folks plan, but they will take care of you and your brothers. We can't leave until we are released and that will take months. Your father isn't on a mission so he can go whenever and wherever he wants. Maybe you will go with us."

Mother didn't leave her room that day. I was in no mood to go to school. After dinner Brownie and I went with Grandma Burntwater to the hogan to check on her animals. The fresh spring air raised my spirits. I had never been inside her six-sided hogan. She showed me her favorite things that hung on or were stacked against five of the walls.

In the sixth wall was the east-facing door. In all hogans, the door faces the rising sun. Colorful Navajo rugs she and her mother had woven hung on the walls or lay on the hard packed dirt floor. Her floor loom leaned against a wall with an unfinished rug on it. Strands of turquoise beads and silver sand cast squash blossom necklaces hung on wooden pegs.

"The white people say we wear our wealth around our necks," she laughed. "Our jewelry is not worn to show off, but to honor our Gods. Turquoise is a holy stone and keeps us well. It reminds us of the blue summer sky. We don't have banks to keep our money in so we keep it in jewelry. A trader will pawn a piece and keep it until he is repaid. A silver and turquoise bracelet is a work of art and the man who makes it enjoys creating just as the Gods enjoyed creating the world. Some white people are buying our rugs and jewelry. It gives our young ones a way to earn white man's money."

We fed and milked her goats, gathered eggs from her chickens and swept the floor. I didn't have to talk, entertain anyone or explain why I was sad.

"Mary, silence is healing. Not all feelings or questions have to be spoken about. Let the breeze, the warm sunshine, the animals distract you from your troubles. Don't spoil today by fretting about the future. Let's sit in the doorway and enjoy the day."

Because the sun had moved to the west, we sat in the shade and looked out over the strange painted hills that, according to my teacher, had once been covered by an ancient sea. I was startled when a small pile of gravel started crawling.

"What's that?"

Grandma Burntwater reached down and picked up a gray pebbly lizard shaped like a pancake. "Brother Horned Toad has come for a visit," she said as she gently flipped him over. His belly was smooth and creamy yellow.

"You rub his tummy gently and he calms down. You try it." She put the little creature into the palm of my hand.

While I rubbed, she sang a Navajo song. The "Horny" Toad seemed hypnotized by my gentle rubbing and the sound of her voice. We sat under the wide, wide sky, felt a gentle breeze and shared the day with the lizard. Grandma's song soothed me. I put the horny toad down; it scurried into dry leaves at the base of a nearby juniper.

"What does your song mean in English?"

"I have it written down. My son translated it to teach to his children. I'll go look for it." She returned shortly. "Make a copy for yourself. You won't be able to sing it, but you can learn the words and say it."

Father returned to the ranch. Uncle Bill worked part time at the stables and Aunt Jane gradually took over Mother's chores. Grandma Burntwater moved back to her hogan, but several times a week she came to drink sweet tea with Mother and Aunt Jane.

The joy had gone out of school. I held my breath when the post office rider stopped at Barth's. The grownups weren't talking about the coming changes. I tried to keep my mind on my coming baptism. I studied my catechism book in preparation for my baptism and confirmation. Mother made me a white robe from an old bedspread to wear during the ceremony.

On Saturday, April 7, we went to the river. The men had dug a round pond near the edge and lay some large rocks for us to walk on as we went into the water. Brother William Gibbons would perform the ceremony.

Father came from the ranch with two cowboys he'd converted. Mother was not herself yet, but she gave me last minute instructions. "The water will be cold, but don't yelp. Brother Gibbons will hold you under the water for a few seconds while he prays. Keep your eyes and mouth closed, don't breath and for Heaven's sake don't thrash around. If any part of you pokes out of the water he will do it again."

The eight year olds would be first, and then it would be my turn. The cowboys were last. They stood to one side wearing their winter long johns and looked more nervous than any of us kids. Mothers held blankets to warm their wet children. Father had blankets for the cowboys.

Each of us in turn were dunked and prayed for and were wrapped to keep the cool spring breeze from chilling us. Sam Ashcroft, an eight-year-old, struggled and made a fuss and had to be dunked again.

When all had been baptized, we stood beside the river and sang "The Beautiful River" and "Gathering in Zion." Solemn Mexican children watched the proceedings. I'd heard they were baptized when they were babies, their priest sprinkling Holy Water on their heads. Our ways were as strange to them as theirs were to us. Now that I had Catholic friends like Maria Traynor and her family, I didn't think they were bad. Just different.

The next day, a Sunday, the newly baptized were confirmed and officially named as members of the church. Mother let me wear the blue silk dress and matching hat. My brothers, Lester, who'd come from Concho for the occasion, and Reuben stood in the back of the church. They made faces at me to try and make me laugh. Would they never give up?

One day during the week after my baptism, I was walking home from school and noticed a crowd of men and horses at the stables. My uncle called, "Mary, come and talk to Mr. Cartwright."

Uncle Bill took my hand and said, "Mr. Cartwright's here looking for a herd of missing cattle. Do you remember me talking about it?"

"I remember," I answered as my uncle led me into the office and bunkroom of the stable master.

"Mr. Cartwright, this is my niece, Mary George. Maybe she can help."

"Young lady, take a seat whilst you and me have a confab. I'm Jackson Cartwright, owner of the Cartwright Cattle Company. I hear you had an adventure a few weeks back. I have questions about what you saw or heard."

I looked at Mr. Cartwright and nodded. He wore a wide brimmed cowboy hat with a band of leather decorated with silver buttons. He took his hat off to wipe his face and forehead with a red bandana. He had thinning red hair. His pale blue eyes looked kindly, but his manner was brusque. I knew he wasn't one to put up with any nonsense. His jaw, under week old red stubble, was square and his lips were thin and straight with no hint of a smile. He was chunky, solid and tough looking. I could tell he'd worked hard all his life, mostly out of doors and didn't take kindly to any one stealing from him.

He intimidated me and I stammered, "I, I'll t-t-try to help. I don't know wh-wh-at you w-want to know. C-could I have a drink of water?" My mouth went dry when I realized I'd have to tell about Pat Traynor and his herd of Mexican cattle. Uncle Bill went to the pump in the stable yard and returned with a tin cup of water.

"It'd be best if you start at the beginning and tell me about your time with the Indians, where you think you were, when you first saw Pat Traynor, etc. When I want to know something special I'll ask," Mr. Cartwright said.

"Can my uncle stay here?"

"No harm in that," he replied. "Mr. George, pull up a stool. My boys can take care of their horses. Won't be long afore most of them hit the cantinas for a bit of refreshment. It's been a long ride and they've heard about the recreation offered in your fair city."

Uncle Bill could tell I was nervous. He patted me on the knee and said, "Go ahead, Mary, tell your story like you told us."

I did as he said. Mr. Cartwright interrupted to ask about which direction we went, which mountain shapes I remembered, how many Apaches were in the band and other similar questions.

When I got to my rescue, his eyes narrowed to slits. He wanted to know exactly what Mr. Westbrook looked like, what Pat Traynor said about him, how many cattle did they give to the Apaches, did I notice a brand on the cows rumps?

I was weary by the time I came to telling about the Traynor family's return to Santa Fe. With relief, I heard Mr. Cartwright say, "Thank you, Mary. You're an observant girl. If you were a boy I'd say you have a bright future ahead of you. Run on home and if you think of anything else you want to tell me, I'll be at Señora Borrego's establishment for the night. We'll ride early in the morning."

It wasn't until later, when I lay on my cot trying to go to sleep that I got mad at what Mr. Cartwright had said.

If I were a boy! That was an insult. Someday I'd show him and all the boys like my brothers who think I am only good enough for teasing. I'll show them that girls and women have as many brains, as much get up and go and as much ambition as any man.

I was so mad and riled up that it took me hours to get to sleep.

Early the next morning, I heard horses being saddled, men calling to one another about the great time they had last night and finally Mr. Cartwright's order to move out. I went to the window in the hall and watched as they headed south along the river.

I hope you never find your cattle. Do you good to ride all the way to Texas and never see hide nor hair of them.

Some days later, Brother Wilhelm returned from a freighting trip to Fort Apache and brought interesting news. I overheard him talking to a group of men after church services. "The upshot of the whole shebang is that we'll be bothered no more by Bah Nubah," Brother Wilhelm said.

After Sunday dinner, I asked Father to take a walk. I had to know what had happened to my kidnapper. I also had a lot of other questions. I'd been feeling as if I was living on quicksand. Not knowing what was coming drove me crazy.

What were his plans if Uncle Bill took his family to St.George? How did he think Mother was taking all these changes?

We walked to the river and found a shady spot under a newly leafed willow where we sat and talked. "This morning I overheard Brother Wilhelm say we would have no more trouble from Bah Nubah. What was he talking about?"

"To make a long story short, when the Cartwrights left here they went over the mountains and down the White River to Fort Apache. Jackson Cartwright wanted to make sure the Army knew his herd had been rustled and to ask them to keep an eye out for any cattle with the CC brand.

"A soldier who had just come off patrol mentioned he'd visited with a band of Apaches on Carrizo Creek between Cibecue and Grasshopper. Bah Nubah was with the band that had two cows with brands on their rumps that appeared to have been altered.

"Cartwright took three of his men and scouted over that way. He sent the rest east to the Blue River. When Cartwright and his men got to the Apache's camp he found they had one cow left. He knew it was one of his not only by the altered brand but by the notch in the cow's right ear.

"The men questioned the elders. They said they had found it wandering in the bush and had brought it along because it seemed lonely! About that time Bah Nubah and two of his friends came sneaking into camp. One of Cartwright's men spotted them in the bushes and ordered them to come out and show themselves. Bah Nubah came out of the bushes with his rifle pointed at Cartwright.

"Cartwright put his hands up in order to show he intended no violence and only wanted answers as to where they had gotten his cow. One of Cartwright's men had crept up behind the three. He stepped on a dead tree branch that broke sounding like a gun shot. Bah Nubah whirled and shot at the cowboy, wounding him in the shoulder. That gave Cartwright time to draw his pistol and shoot Bah Nubah. Killed him with one shot.

"The whole thing was about to turn into a massacre when some women ran between the two sides and calmed everyone down. The Cartwrights were outnumbered and they were lucky to get out alive. The ranchers took Bah Nubah's body to Fort Apache, told the story and rode east to join the rest of their posse. That's all I know about that. No one was sorry to see Bah Nubah go to his reward."

I asked, "Did Mr. Cartwright rescue his cow?"

"No, he left it for the band to enjoy. A peace offering. What else do you have on your mind?"

I asked about his plans if Uncle Bill left, how Mother was doing and told him how hard it was to have everything so uncertain.

"Don't you worry. Everything's going to work out. You are a worrywart. I have some ideas and have started making plans, but no sense in eating the pudding until it's set." I could get no further details.

None of the grownups thought we children felt as much tension as we did. When I grow up and have children, I'll talk to them, explain to them and take their questions seriously.

Gradually, my worries eased. Brownie could wander and I no longer had nightmares about Bah Nubah. Uncle Bill and Aunt Jane seemed to have given up hearing from President Taylor any time soon. Maybe they had changed their minds and would stay even if they were released. Mother slowly regained her balance and was pleasant, though vague.

On a day in mid May I skipped to school. The robins and mountain bluebirds had returned from the south, lambs and calves ran and played in the pastures and the apple trees were in fragrant, full bloom. The bees were busily buzzing in each blossom. If we didn't get a late frost there would be a good crop of apples come fall. At school we were preparing for the end of school program and I chose to recite the Navajo poem Grandma Burntwater had sung to the lizard. I'd made a copy of "Little Horned Toad" and memorized it.

I said it to myself on that bright May morning.

Little horned toad
Living in the sand
Tell me a story
Tell me of the time
When you spoke like a man,
When you knew Mr. Coyote.
Tell me how you teased him
And how you ran away,
And how he cried with anger
All day, all day.

Little bluebird
Take me with you
Show me where you live,
Give me feathers from your coat
And to you I'll give

Many hairs from my white goat
To line your nest with.

That afternoon, the post rider stopped at Barth's. He swung a full mailbag from behind his saddle and went into the store. I was feeling so fine that I paid no special notice. It wasn't until the next day that the mail was sorted and available for pickup. When I came from school I found my aunt and uncle sitting at the round kitchen table with open envelopes.

I knew the answer had come and my heart sank to my toes.

"Here's a letter from Amy, Mary. You'll enjoy hearing about your new cousin. They've named her Georgia Jane and say she's a fine healthy baby. Here, take Amy's letter," Uncle Bill said.

I got a drink of water from the bucket and sat by the front window in Mother's rocker to read my cousin's letter. I kept peeking at my aunt and uncle as they read and re-read one of the other letters. I was happy to hear Amy's good news but a feeling of dread rose in my stomach and pushed up into my throat. I wanted to ask about the other letters but didn't want to be rude or snoopy.

Uncle Bill rose from the table and went to the back door. He called to John who was in the barn caring for the few horses we had left, "John, I have an errand for you. Saddle one of the horses and ride to the ranch to fetch Uncle Henry."

Aunt Jane started up the stairs saying, "I'll talk to Elizabeth and see if I can get her to agree to come to St. George with us."

After supper, John and my father rode into the back lot. Aunt Jane told me to take the young ones upstairs and prepare them for bed. "You stay upstairs also, Mary. We grownups need to talk seriously about important things."

I turned and saw my mother sitting in her chair by the window. Her jaw was clenched; her eyes shot lightening bolts at her sister and her knuckles were white. She twisted a hanky in her lap.

Chapter Seventeen

St. Johns, Arizona Territory, June 1886

I strained to hear the adults' voices while putting the noisy children to bed. Decisions that would twist and turn my life like a desert dust devil were being made.

I dressed for bed and lay on my cot. Brownie snored on the braided rug making it impossible to hear what was being said below. I tiptoed to the top of the stairs, sat and listened.

Uncle Bill said, "Jane and I are going to St. George. We will not stay here a moment longer than necessary. It will take time to gather the money to buy a wagon and team. Tomorrow I'll send word to James that he is to come from Concho as soon as he can collect his pay. Mr. Barth plans to make a delivery and will take my message. Hattie has earned and saved some money and we expect she will contribute."

"We wish you would come. We've always been together, I can't imagine living with out you," Aunt Jane added.

There was silence. The teakettle whistled and I heard water pouring into the teapot. Even though the church said we shouldn't drink black tea, my family loved tea. We usually drank herb tea, saving black tea for special or serious times. What kind of tea was in the pot tonight?

Father cleared his throat, "Ask Lester to return also. I want him close to home. There's work for him and Reuben at the sawmill. Elizabeth and I have talked about what to do, but nothing has been decided. She'll tell you her thoughts."

Mother began, "You believed it was only my illness speaking when I told you this trip would end in tragedy. I am extremely angry at the church for sending Bill on this futile mission. I am bitter, Henry, that you let your brother talk you into bringing your family to this den of thieves in a God-forsaken land. I get no comfort from being right. We are in a fine pickle. I have no suggestions."

Father asked, "Will you go to St. George?"

Mother replied icily, "This time I'm sticking to my guns. I will not cross that barren desert again. It is only by the grace of God we survived it the first time. Crossing the Colorado River once was enough. I would rather stay here than make that trip again."

Aunt Jane pleaded, "Elizabeth we may not get the money we need for several months. By then the weather will be pleasant. It will break my heart to leave you and your family here."

"Why can't you understand me? I will never take another long wagon trip to a place that I know nothing about. I refuse to discuss it further," Mother added with steel in her voice.

Uncle Bill said, "We accept your decision. It's between you and Henry as to what you will do. We need to discuss what we have that I can sell in order to get travel money."

"Since we've been living together, it's going to be hard to divide our goods. I'll get a piece of paper and pen so we can start a list," my ever-practical, common sense aunt volunteered

My head and stomach ached. I was weary and went to bed. The dividing of blankets, pots and furniture was of no interest to me. The next weeks were grim. The boys worked at the sawmill, Father continued at the ranch, Aunt Jane took in laundry and ironing. Uncle Bill continued at the stables and worked for Mr. Barth in the evenings cleaning the mercantile. Mother did nothing but rock in her chair by the window.

Hattie had a conniption when she learned she was not only expected to leave, but that she was asked to donate her earnings to the family purse. "I'm happy here! I have a job, I have someone to live with and Judd Udall, the Bishop's son, is courting me. The money I've saved is for my trousseau. We love each other and plan to marry as soon as I'm sixteen," Hattie yelled at her parents.

Uncle Bill tried to calm her, but she only became angrier. "I might as well have been born into a gypsy family. Back and forth, up and down, move here then there. I refuse to go. You let Amy marry Josh and do what she wanted. Now it's my turn. It's my life!" she shouted as she stormed out. Aunt Jane put her head on the table and wept. Mother sat in her chair and silently rocked back and forth.

My mind wandered to an idea that occupied me like a sore tooth. I couldn't leave it alone. I remembered the Indian pots in the cave. I loved Aunt Jane and Uncle Bill and my cousins and I dreaded their leaving. I wanted to prolong their departure but things were miserable. Father stayed at the ranch. Mother said very little and faded in and out of her fog. Some days I thought of running away.

One evening after school was out for the summer, I asked Reuben to take a walk with Brownie and me. "I've heard some people pay money for old Indian pots. Have you told anyone about the cave? I wonder if those pots are still there."

"Scared me so bad when I fell into the black pool that I don't want to think about it ever again," Reuben replied. "What are you getting at?"

"If we brought pots to town who would buy them? How could we bring them from the cave? We'd need a wagon of some sort," I said. "Would it be stealing from the Indians to take the pots?"

"I see Mr. Barth is still in the store. Let's go and ask him a question or two," Reuben said.

Mr. Barth was always ready to visit when there were no customers in the store. Reuben asked about some small Indian pots displayed in one window. He answered, "Once in a while an Indian comes in and wants to barter old things for canned goods or calico. I like to get them because I make a nice profit. Justin Bowlin, from Bluewater, New Mexico looks for artifacts. He sells them to collectors or tourists. The train stops at Bluewater and he quickly sells what he has on hand. Haven't seen him all winter, but reckon he'll come by before June is over."

I asked, "How much are those little pots worth?"

"Let's see what I've written on the bottom. This white one, with the black painted designs would go for fifteen dollars. That's what Mr. Bowlin could ask at his trading post. I'd sell it to him for eight. I'd make a profit of three dollars and he'd make almost double."

Shivers ran up my spine when I thought of the money we could get for the pots. Reuben started to say something about a big pot he'd seen. I kicked him in the ankle to make him stop talking.

"Ouch, Mary, why'd you do that?"

"Time for us to go. Thanks for the visit, Mr. Barth."

When we got outside, Reuben growled, "What's the matter with you?"

"We need to talk to Father. He'll be home in a day or so. He got a letter from Ramah, and Lester took it to him. Lester said that after Father read the letter, he said he would be here shortly. Father's the one to help us decide about the pots."

"You're right. Father's a good bargainer and he'll know how to get the pots to town if we decide to sell them."

Father, who was always up for adventure, was excited to learn our secret. "Let's not tell any of the others until we explore and find out what's still in the cave. No use to get hopes up before we know for sure. I have to get a letter off to the postmaster at Ramah. There may be a good job for me there. That would solve a lot of problems."

Two days later, I packed a picnic, Father and Reuben hitched two horses to the wagon and we rode to the foothills. We took old blankets and boxes just in case.

Aunt Jane had asked, "Where are you three off to? You act like you're going to a country fair."

Mother didn't say anything, just sat and rocked with a far off smile on her lips. It seemed she had left her body and lived in a place that none of us knew about.

We had rehearsed this part. I said, "Father wants to show us the new bunkhouses at the ranch. They're finished and they said Father could have the wood scraps to make furniture. We're going to help him load the wagon."

Father waved and said, "See you this afternoon, Jane."

The sky was bright blue that June morning. White puffy clouds played tag with the breeze and we sang as we rode the rising trail. When the trail petered out, we tied the horses and wagon to a tree and did the last bit on Shank's mare. We were eager to show Father the cave so decided to go in before we ate.

At the entrance, Father lit a kerosene lantern. The air was damp and cool. Everything looked the same. When Father held the lantern high, we saw there were more pots than we remembered. I saw the cubbyhole where Tom McNeill had found the small, green stone buffalo.

"Where is the pool you fell into, Reuben?" Father asked.

"Over this way. See the tunnel entrance? I don't know if you'll be able to get through. You're so tall. You'd better crawl. Mary, carry the lantern. You're the smallest," Reuben said.

The pool and the decorated walls were as I remembered. We gazed with awe and were impressed with the work it took to make that beautiful place. Father scooped up some water. He smelled, and then tasted it. "Tastes metallic, like copper," he said. "Before it gets here the snow melt or spring that feeds this pool runs over veins of copper. When you find copper you frequently find turquoise."

He gestured to return to the big room. Reuben lit another lantern so we could look more closely at the pots and cubbyholes. Father said, "Let's go to the wagon and have our dinner while I think about this. I am overwhelmed. We want to do the right thing."

We unhitched the horses from the wagon. They would stay nearby, drink from the stream that tumbled down the rocky slope and graze on new spring grass.

I unpacked the bread, cold beef, canned peaches and cookies and put them on a blanket in the shade. No one spoke as we ate. The silence was broken by the blue jays scolding us for invading their home. I threw breadcrumbs to let them know we were friendly. They flew out of the juniper tree and eagerly gobbled up the crumbs. Then they looked at me with their glossy black eyes and cocked their heads as if to ask, "Is that all?"

Father was deep in thought. He stood and walked to the stream for a drink. He scratched the horses behind their ears, patted their necks and walked downstream. Reuben and I waited. He was praying. Finally he walked up the slope and said, "I have decided to take some pots to Mr. Barth and let him judge their worth. If he likes the designs and quality, we may negotiate for a sale. I don't like to take what doesn't belong to me, but we are in dire need."

Later, in town, Father brought Mr. Barth to the wagon and unwrapped several of the pots. Reuben and I stayed with the wagon while Father went inside with Mr. Barth.

After an eternity, Father returned. He got into the wagon and drove to the back of the store.

Father said, "We think it's wise to take the pots out of the wagon here rather than on Main Street. Help us carry them into the storeroom. The trader from Bluewater will be here next week and then we will learn their worth."

"Why are we taking the pots in the back door?" I asked. "Are you afraid of someone seeing them?"

"It's better to keep things under your hat until the deal is closed." Father replied. "I'm not ashamed of having taken them, but I don't anyone else to catch wind of it. Your discovery may be our way out of St. Johns"

Father wrote a letter to Ramah, but he didn't ask me to correct it. I think he told Uncle Bill about the pots because he and Aunt Jane became cheerful. Mother began to come out of her fog and spent time out of doors. She liked to walk by the river, often taking the little ones with her.

No one talked about the impending move or the approaching split of our families. I was on pins and needles and needed to talk to someone who would not "Shush" me. I decided to go see Grandma Burntwater, sit in her doorway and tell her of my worries.

"Mary, what did I tell you about spoiling today with worries about tomorrow? Not knowing is hard but it's better if we don't know what's in store for us. Would it make any difference if we knew the future?" she asked.

"I just want this to be over and for us to be settled in a nice house on a quiet street with lots of shade trees. I want to know Mother is going to get well. It's strange having a mother who is different. I want her to be like other mothers. A mother who's not angry all the time, who doesn't disappear into a far away place pretending she's someone else.

"Recently, I came in from gathering eggs and feeding the chickens and found her sitting in her rocker by the window. Everyone else was out. She had gone to my room, taken my blue silk dress, slit the dress up the back and put her arms into the sleeves. She had my dress on and the matching bonnet on her head.

"I'm the Queen of England and you are my maid," she said. "Bring me a cup of tea while I wait for Albert to return."

"I was astonished by what she'd done to my dress. I was afraid she had lost her senses for good and would never come back. After she drank the tea she rose from the chair, walked up the stairs and went to bed.

"When Aunt Jane returned from her errands I told her about Mother. She shook her head, 'Just when we think she's getting better, she gets worse. I'm sorry about your dress. Maybe I can mend it. I'm glad she isn't with child again. It would be best if she has no more children.'"

Grandma Burntwater listened and slowly shook her head. "The mind is a mysterious thing. We don't know what causes it to twist and turn like a whirlpool. Maybe she will be better when all this is settled. If she doesn't have her sister to depend on, she may pull herself together."

I left the hogan and walked home in a mood that wasn't much better than when I had arrived. When Mother no longer had her sister I knew who she would depend on and it wouldn't be Father. I didn't know if I was up to it but there was no choice. I would be ten in a few months and I supposed that was old enough to carry the load.

When I got home, I found Father and Reuben waiting. Father said, "We've good news from Mr. Bowlin. He arrived this morning, inspected the pots and sent word for me to meet him at Barth's. He will buy as many pots and other Indian articles as we can bring him. He'll be here for two days. We'll go to the cave in the morning and bring back as much as we can."

The news lifted my spirits. "How much did he say he would pay?" I asked.

"All depends on their condition, size, decoration and number. He was especially interested when I told him about the stone buffalo that Tom McNeill found. We didn't look in the niches. I'll search tomorrow."

We repeated our drive to the foothills. We had more blankets, old cartons and some straw. When we moved the pots from their jumbled piles, it stirred up lots of dust, so we tied bandannas over our mouths and noses. Some pots were plain reddish brown with no decoration. Others were painted white and decorated with symbols of lightening, clouds, rain, birds, lizards or deer. I found one with three horny toads painted as if they were chasing each other round the pot. One large pot had small ears of dried corn in it. Some were cracked; some were broken into many pieces while others were in two or three pieces. Perhaps those could be mended.

"I'm going to search the niches," Father said. "Reuben, come hold the lantern as high as you can. I'll poke a stick in first in case a snake or some other critter is holing up." It wasn't until he explored the third one that he found something. "Look at this! It's a carving of a bear. There's a shallow depression on its back as if it were meant to hold something."

The bear was only four inches long and a couple of inches high. He went through the other five niches and found two other items. One was a round piece of turquoise with a hole near one edge. Maybe it was meant to hang on a string for a necklace. The other was a sea shell with turquoise chips embedded in it.

It took many trips to carry our treasures to the wagon. We set them on the ground and stopped to have dinner before we packed them. Father counted seven large unbroken plain pots, ten broken or sharded plain pots, fifteen smaller painted, decorated pots, a bag of painted pieces and three carvings.

Going back, Father held the team to a slow pace. We eased across creeks, avoided boulders and rocky places in the trail and hoped our precious cargo wouldn't break. We were dusty and tired, but hopeful. The money would surely be enough to allow Uncle Bill and Aunt Jane to leave shortly. What would Father and Mother do with our share?

Their decision would decide the course of my life. Eventually I would no longer be a gypsy. I would have a husband and home of my own, but at the cost of estrangement from my family who would harden their hearts against me.

Chapter Eighteen

Ramah, New Mexico Territory, January 1889

Father wouldn't be home for at least two weeks. He left on his mail route over the Zuni Mountains to Fort Wingate on Friday and the blizzard hit on Sunday. Brother Bond came to tell us the trail was closed. We knew Father was safe, warm and well fed at the fort. That was more than I could say for us.

Our supply of flour was almost gone and there was no milk for baby Ezra. Mother had painful, gathered breasts and she refused to nurse him, even though she'd been told frequent nursing was a way to overcome the condition. She preferred to apply hot packs, but they were useless. Five shriveled apples were left in the barrel. That morning I used the last cornmeal for mush. The woodpile beside the back door was shrinking at an alarming rate. When Mother woke from her nap, I'd break a path through the waist deep snow and go to the Tietjens for help.

Lester was on the mountain at the sawmill. Reuben was in St. Johns boarding with the Udalls while attending the new Academy for high school students. I was in our snug stone and timber house with Mother and five little brothers. It was up to me to get help.

Our nearest neighbors, the Tietjen families, lived a half mile towards town. They lived in three separate houses as Brother Ernst Tietjen had three wives. They would help us.

I sat beside the stove and watched my brothers play a game with round pebbles and toy horses while Mother lay on her bed in the darkened bedroom. My mind wandered back to when we left St. Johns for Ramah. Father had been sure that, this time, we would find our patch of paradise.

It was the summer of 1886. We'd made $800.00 from the pots. Uncle Bill and Aunt Jane insisted we keep $500.00, since we'd discovered and sold the pots. With what they had saved, the added $300.00 allowed them to leave by the first of July.

When I stood in the street and waved goodbye, part of me died. It was as if someone had sliced a sliver off of my heart. I sensed, and it was to prove true, that I would never see them again.

We prayed for their safe journey. Then Father said, "I've been offered a job carrying the mail from Ramah to Bluewater, Fort Wingate, Gallup, St. Johns and back to Ramah. It will provide us with a small but steady income and we will live in a Community of Saints."

Mother stopped her relentless rocking, stood and faced Father with fire in her eyes. She made fists of her hands as she walked to him and pounded him on his chest.

She screamed, "I will not go on another wagon trip. I refuse to drag these children on another wild goose chase."

Father grabbed her hands and forced them down. My knees turned to soft clay, Parley and Richard cried, Lester and Reuben busily perused a Sears and Roebucks catalogue while William crawled under the table and put his thumb in his mouth. We had never seen our parents act that way.

"Elizabeth, come, sit in your chair," Father said as he led his sobbing wife to the rocker. "I've heard nice things about Ramah. The Burnhams, Tietjens and Merrills settled there ten years ago. Now there are fourteen families including some who were sent by Lot Smith in '82 from Sunset Crossing. Do you remember Brother James McNeill who visited last fall? He and his three families think highly of it."

Mother's only response was to continue crying. After taking her a clean hanky I coaxed her to drink a sip of water. We didn't know what to do. Father carried her to the bedroom that had been Uncle Bill's.

She screamed, "I will not go! I will kill myself before you force me to move again. You brought us to this hellish place, now I hope you suffer as I have suffered. I will throw myself into the river or slit my throat before I'll let you drag me into the unknown again."

"Hush, you're frightening the children. Take this to calm your nerves."

" Hush yourself! You and your pie in the sky ideas are enough to drive anyone crazy. We'll never have a secure life with you dragging us from place to place. We'll live on the edge of poverty never knowing where we'll get the money to provide for the children. You will reap what you sowed when you see your children grow up in this mud hole with little schooling, no family nearby and hear them cry for bread when there is none," Mother screamed. "Don't force that down my throat. It's easy for you to make me woozy so you don't have to deal with the real problems. Get out and leave me alone."

Father shut the door, soothed the little ones and tried to make us older ones believe things would work out. Lester and Reuben were red faced, embarrassed by Mother's fierce words. I was bewildered. My heart hardened toward Mother while a shiver of delight ran up my spine when Father said we were moving to Ramah. Tom lived in Ramah. I treasured my memories of Tom, our trip to the cave and the stone buffalo.

Don't count your chickens. He may not remember you and he may have a girlfriend. Having two different feelings at the same time perplexed me. I was impatient and angry with Mother but happy about moving to Ramah. Was it a sign of growing up? Was that why grownups often seemed confused?

Father bought two wagons, four mules and two more saddle horses. I was able to ride most of the way. Father and Lester drove the wagons. Reuben and William rode together while Parley or Roy rode with me. They also liked to ride in the wagon. The third horse was the spare. It was fun to be traveling. Mother, having been tied into one of the wagons, endured in silence.

We traveled to Ramah in late July 1886. The blue sky and warm breeze gave no hint of the wicked winter storms that often buried western New Mexico in deep snow. The journey took three days and the farther east we went, the prettier the country became. Pine and juniper covered hills soon gave way to layered, brightly colored bluffs and mesas. In the distance we saw the rounded tops of the heavily forested Zuni Mountains.

We followed the Zuni River to the Zuni Pueblo. On the second night we stopped near the ancient settlement and saw the pueblo style dwellings from our camp. I wished we could stay to explore but there was no time. I glimpsed sandstone walls and narrow winding streets full of mystery. The people were not friendly. None came to our camp to sell food, jewelry or pottery.

Father told us, "Centuries ago the Spaniards came this way on their way to the Rio Grande River. They were searching for gold and were so disappointed to find none that they killed many Zuni men, stole their women and children and left the people with hatred in their hearts. Ramah is twenty miles beyond the pueblo. East of Ramah is part of the Navajo reservation. Grandma Burntwater's daughter lives there at Pine Hill."

The next day we traveled beside the Rio Pescado. Irrigation ditches ran from the river into fields of alfalfa, corn and fruit orchards. Ramah was as different from St. Johns as night from day. There were no saloons, no drunken cowboys lounging on the streets and all the buildings were made of rosy colored sandstone or sturdy logs. The town was laid out in square one acre blocks with three or four homes to each block. Mormon trees grew along the streets shading the town. Each lot had a small barn, a garden plot and fruit trees. Hollyhocks and bushy peonies bordered the well-kept yards. Morning glories twined on log fences that enclosed the lots.

We passed a store with a sign over the door that read McNeill's Mercantile. My heart skipped. I saw a post office, church and schoolhouse. All streets were marked with name signs. We arrived on Tietjen Avenue, crossed Bond Street, Lewis Street and found Ashcroft's at the corner of McNeill and Tietjen.

We'd been invited to stay there until Father built a house. The Ashcrofts had an addition on the back of their house for new residents and travelers. I worried about how Mother would behave. I hoped she wouldn't make our new neighbors think badly of us with poor behavior.

We pulled into the lot behind the Ashcroft home. Brother James Ashcroft and his wife, Emaline, came to meet us. Father took them aside, talked to them at some length, and then went to the wagon to help Mother down. I held my breath.

Please, God, make Mother be her good self. This is a new start. I like this place. I want people to like us.

Mother was quietly pleasant as we made arrangements for the animals, unloaded the wagons and were shown where we'd stay until we had a place of our own.

We slept on cornhusk pallets on the floor of the one room guesthouse and took our meals with the Ashcroft family. Sister Ashcroft took pains to be friendly to Mother.

The next day Father rode north of town with Brother Tietjen and Brother Bond to scout out a piece of land for us to claim. While they were gone Sister Ashcroft invited Mother to a Relief Society Meeting at the church so she could meet other women in Ramah. Since many of the men had two or three wives, there were more married women in town than married men.

192

Father returned late in the afternoon. I heard him tell Mother, "Tomorrow I want you to ride with me to the land I've chosen. It will be a fine homestead, but I want you to see it before I finalize a claim. It's near the dam that creates Ramah Lake. The lake provides irrigation water. There's timber on the acreage, meadows and sandstone nearby with which to build a house." Mother nodded but didn't speak. She looked resigned to her fate.

The new house was exciting, but even more important to me was that it was only four days until Sunday. We'd go to Sunday School in the morning and Church services in the afternoon. I hoped to see Tom, but I also wanted to meet other young people.

Mother and Father agreed on the land and Father hired a crew of young men to help build the house. The area, two miles north of town, was called Dam Valley.

On Saturday we packed a picnic. Mother drove us to the site of our future home. When we arrived we found a group of Navajos who'd come looking for work. Under Father's supervision, it wouldn't take long to build our house. Father would pay the workers with money from the sale of the pots. Mother walked around the top of a rise. She made marks in the dirt to show us where the house would sit. It would have two large rooms and a sleeping loft.

We set our picnic on a blanket under the spreading branches of an old oak tree. Father came to eat with us. "Look at that view!" He swept his arm through the air pointing across the lake, the hills and down the valley to the rooftops of Ramah. "We'll live out our lives here in beauty and comfort."

That Sunday, I saw Tom with his family in the main hall before we divided to go to classes. Boys and men went to their room and women and girls to theirs. I tried to catch his eye, but he didn't see me. After we were dismissed, I spoke to him.

"Hello, Tom. Remember me? I'm newly arrived from St. Johns." His face got red, he coughed and blew his nose before he replied. "You look familiar, but I don't remember your name."

He was standing with some friends who laughed and poked him in his ribs. "What's the matter, Tom? Don't tell us you don't remember this cute little filly. She's all you've talked about all winter and spring," one of the Tietjen boys teased.

Without another word, Tom turned and left. I was mortified. I should have waited until he was alone. I hoped I'd have another chance after church services that evening. When they began, I saw the people he'd sat with that morning, but he wasn't there.

I saw him in town or at school, but he avoided me. Soon I stopped trying to talk to him. There were plenty of other boys to meet and lots of girls to have fun with. I was ten years old and had more fun with the girls. Some became lifelong friends, some, eventually relatives by marriage.

As soon as the house was finished, Father built a barn and corral for the animals. It was too late to start a brood of chickens so the hen house was put off until spring. The chickens had the run of the barn.

By November, when icy wind raged down from Mt. Sedgwick, we were in our own home with a barn and a corral for the animals. Mother made muslin curtains for the windows and braided a rag rug for the kitchen. She seemed content.

Father was gone on his mail route for a week every month. He enjoyed getting out into the world, visiting with soldiers at Fort Wingate, ranch men near Bluewater, Indian traders and railroaders in Gallup. He brought us the latest news from St. Johns regarding Jackson Cartwright's futile search for his cattle.

"I was told that Cartwright and his posse followed signs of the herd to Columbus, New Mexico, at the Mexico border. The townsfolk palavered about a dead man found hanging from tall saguaro cactus. He had been shot in the back of the head, his hat had been carefully placed on top of the eight-foot cactus, and all his outer clothes were laid carefully on the ground at the base of the saguaro. He, in his underwear, was tied spread eagled to the cactus arms.

"A note was found in his coat pocket along with his wallet and several thousand dollars in cash. The note said, 'This is what happens to sneaky, stupid, double crossing cattle rustlers with no loyalty to those who've taught them all they know.' The dead man was Mr. Westbrook. Didn't you mention him when you told about your kidnapping, Mary?"

I nodded. My mouth turned to dust—my hands turned clammy. Could Pat Traynor have been so cruel?

"The Sheriff took the cash, buried Mr. Westbrook and with what was left dug a new town well," Father said.

I went to school four days a week. Mondays, I helped Mother with the laundry. Reuben, William, Roy and I walked the two miles together, usually joined by some Tietjen children. I had a hard time figuring out who belonged to who in that family. Not only were there three wives, but two of them had the same name and were first cousins. To tell them apart they were called Emma O. and Emma C. His third wife, Amanda, was a converted Navajo.

Emma O. and Emma C. each had five or six children who all had straw blonde hair, blue eyes and freckles. Amanda's two children were easy to recognize because they had dark hair and eyes.

Their father spoke with a heavy Swedish accent. At first I had trouble understanding him. He was one of the first Mormon missionaries to come to New Mexico and had settled Ramah because he believed it had a prosperous future both for farming and converting the Indians.

We arrived too late in the summer to start a garden. Father earned enough to allow us to buy needed items at the store. By December the store was closed because the shelves were empty. We bought home canned fruit and vegetables from other families. Father purchased flour, sugar and other staples in Gallup. We realized we must prepare the meadow for planting as early in the spring as possible.

In April Father borrowed a plow from Brother Bond. Using our faithful mules, we cleared the meadow and prepared the soil for our garden. Rueben and I helped Father.

Mother gradually became herself. Our family was finally in the right place. I noticed she and Father were playful and affectionate. Each week, when I helped with the laundry, I watched for her monthly cloths and they appeared when they should. I hoped there would be no more babies, even if I never had a sister. A baby sister now would be too young to be a friend.

On a summer day, as I hoed the cornfield, Tom surprised me. "Hi, Mary. My mother is building a summer shack farther up in the canyon. It will be a place for her milk cows to graze and she can be on her own for part of the year. She wants to provide for herself and her children by selling milk, cheese and butter. We're going to be neighbors. I'm on my way with a load of lumber. Want to ride along to see where she's going to build? I'd like you to meet her."

I was dumbfounded. He had ignored me for a year, now he was friendly. Was it because he was alone? I went to the house, told Mother where I'd be, rinsed my hands and face and went with him.

"Can I bring my dog?" I asked. "Brownie doesn't get around very well since an Apache shot him and he's getting old. Is there room in the wagon?"

"I can lift him up here at the back. He can enjoy the scenery."

During the ride, Tom told me about his family. "Brother James McNeill is not my real father. He's my birth father's brother. When my father, Thomas Reid McNeill, died in Utah, Mother was left a widow with two children—my younger sister Jenny and me. A year later when Uncle James and his wife, Aunt Phoebe, were called on a mission to Sunset Crossing, they asked my

195

mother to marry James and be his second wife. She agreed and that's how we happen to be in Ramah. My brother Jamie was born at Sunset Crossing, Roxie was born in '84 here in Ramah. I don't get along with my stepfather and sometimes I don't think my mother does either."

When I met Mary Jane McNeill on that summer day in 1887, she put her arm around my shoulder, looked me in the eye and said, "Mary, I'm glad to meet you. I know we're going to be friends. Call me Aunt Mary Jane."

Tears came to my eyes as I looked into her sparkly green eyes. She was a little woman, hardly taller than I, with unruly dark red hair that struggled to get free from the bun at the back of her neck. I didn't realize until that moment how much I'd missed Aunt Jane.

That summer the gardens were bountiful. We had sweet corn to eat, corn to dry and grind for meal and for the animals' winter feed. In the fall, we pickled and bottled vegetables, fruits, pork, beef and chicken. Aunt Mary Jane sent her daughter Jennie to help out. In exchange for Jennie's help, we gave her bottled goods. We traded fresh produce for milk and butter.

Because of our hard work, fine weather and lack of insect pests, we were well provisioned for the winter. All went well until Mother became with child. She was sick, threw up for months and had swollen legs and hands.

The next summer we worked as hard as the summer before, but our luck changed. In addition to having to care for the house and Mother, I was in charge of the bug and worm picking parties in the garden. Both Father and Reuben, who was home for the summer, helped in the garden. I hated those crickets, potato bugs and big horned worms that multiplied five times faster than we could kill them. William, Roy, Richard and Parley thought it great fun to catch and squash bugs and worms. They had contests to see who could kill the most each day.

Then the hail came. One afternoon in late July, great white-topped clouds billowed and blew across the sky covering the sun. The wind stopped. Hail pounded. We ran for cover as the apricot sized ice balls attacked our precious garden. The storm lasted ten drumming minutes, but in that short time it wiped out our winter food supply.

After salvaging what we could, we replanted, hoping for a long warm autumn. It was not to be. Joseph Ezra was born on the twelfth of September; two weeks later winter roared down the mountain. The winter of '88-'89 was frightening and it was only January. Our neighbors had little more than we.

Parley's tugging at my arm dragged me back from my woolgathering memories. "Sister, it's cold. Put wood in the stove."

I stirred up the fire and added wood. Mother came from her room. I said, "I'm going to the Tietjens and ask for help. We're about out of firewood, the animals in the barn need tending and there's nothing but cornmeal mush left to eat."

I climbed the ladder to the loft, dressed in several layers of clothing, including an old pair of Reuben's overalls and two pairs of mittens. At the front door I pulled on a pair of Fathers boots over my shoes,

Mother said, "Be careful you don't get lost. I wish Brownie was here. He'd make sure you'd find the way."

"I wish so also but if wishes were fishes we'd all swim in the sea," I replied. "I'll get there, don't worry. I have no choice." I shut the front door, stood for a moment to orient myself, and headed toward the road. I watched for the big blue spruce tree. I would turn right just beyond it.

It was hard, slow going. The snow was 'up to my straddle' as Father often joked. It was crusty on the top but not hard enough to keep me from breaking through. I churned my way toward the faint outline of the spruce thinking of Brownie and his death.

Last November, I went out one morning to feed and check on the chickens. Brownie came, slowly but with persistence. Suddenly the hair on his back stood on end, he growled and snarled at a fast-moving blur that ran behind the hen house. He tried to chase whatever it was but couldn't move very fast. His barking cautioned me. I back stepped to the safety of the back porch. I heard a shriek and knew Brownie was in trouble. A golden tan mountain lion grabbed him by his throat and shook him so hard that it broke his neck. It was over so quickly. The lion dropped limp Brownie, picked up a dead chicken and streaked into the trees. We cried as we buried our friend in the not yet frozen earth at the base of the blue spruce tree.

I found the tree, turned right and knew that if I walked straight ahead I'd soon see the outline of the first of the Tietjen cabins. A sharp flurry of wind driven snow blinded me and I shut my eyes. When I opened them I was lost. I wasn't sure which way I should be headed and didn't know the direction from which I'd come. I stood alone in a whiteout feeling the cold seep through my layers of clothing. I had to keep moving. I took three cautious steps, stubbed my toe on a large rock and fell headfirst into a drift. My head hit a rock.

I must get up. My family depends on me. I will freeze to death out here. No one will find me until the snow melts in the spring.

I tried to get up. My arms and legs were heavy, my brain was fuzzy and I was very sleepy.

I'll rest for just a minute.

Chapter Nineteen

Ramah, New Mexico Territory, January, February & March 1889

A dog barked. I felt digging in the snow, and then a warm sloppy tongue slurped across my face.

It must be Brownie! Had I died and gone to Heaven? Was Brownie welcoming me? If I am dead, why am I so cold? I thought you didn't feel anything after you died.

"Mary, Mary, wake up. Lars, brush the snow off her legs while I wake her up," a voice said.

My eyes felt frozen shut and the only response I could muster was a moan. The dog continued barking and my bewildered, slow as molasses in January brain, finally told me I wasn't dead.

Strong arms pulled me onto my feet from the snow bank. My legs buckled, but someone caught me. "We have to get her inside. Sven, grab her on the other side. We'll carry her to the George cabin," another voice said. "Star, stop barking. Mary's alive, thanks to you, but no need to have a conniption."

"Can you hear us, Mary? We're taking you home. When Star smelled you under the snow she started barking and digging."

Warm tears thawed my eyelids. Sven and Lars Tietjen carried me in a cradle of crossed arms to our front door. The bright sunshine glinting off the snow hurt my eyes but told me the blizzard had moved on.

The German shepherd frolicked. She tunneled under drifts, jumped at heavy-laden fir branches and rolled in the snow like a child at play. She loved it, but she had her own fur coat. Mother answered their knock with a cry, "Mary, thank God you're all right. I've been pacing the floor. Take her to my room so I can get her out of those wet clothes."

"Our Mother, Emma O., was worried, so she sent us with a basket of food. Father told us to check on your animals and make sure you had firewood," Sven said.

I still couldn't talk as Mother removed the heavy wet layers of clothing from my shivering body. She covered me with a quilt and gently rubbed my feet and hands.

"Have to be careful about frostbite. Tell me when you feel pins and needles in your feet. William, get me a bucket of snow. Bring it here so I can rub your sister's feet and hands with it. I must bring her body temperature up slowly."

My hands and feet began to prickle and sting. I cried. "I'm sorry, Mother, I failed again. I fell, bumped my head and couldn't get up. Ohhh, my fingers and toes hurt. Can't I hold them up to the stove? My nose is stinging, too."

"Not yet, grit your teeth and bear it. It won't last long. You'll have less chance of losing fingers, toes and nose if we do this right."

I heard Sven bring in the basket of food then leave to help Lars. They were older boys whom we girls thought handsome. I was humiliated for them to find me so bedraggled, but thank goodness they found me. With a clear sky, it promised to be far below freezing by evening.

When I stopped shivering, Mother put a warm flannel gown over my head, wrapped me in the quilt and put me in her rocker by the fireplace.

Sister Tietjen had sent bread, jam, canned chicken and goat's milk for the baby. Everyone's cows had stopped giving milk. The Tietjens had a small herd of goats in their large barn which gave milk year round. Mother warmed some in a pan, poured it into Ezra's bottle, fitted with a deerskin nipple, and fed him. She had tried to feed him watered down cornmeal mush but he spat it out.

Sven and Lars stacked wood by the back door before they came in to ask what else we needed. "Mother says she'll come tomorrow and bring more food. Is there any thing special you need?" Lars asked.

"We owe Mary's life to you boys and Star. I have no words to express my gratitude. We'll appreciate anything you can spare. When my husband comes, he'll bring flour, sugar, corn meal and as many other foodstuffs as he can buy. Then we can share with you."

Sven leaned over, touched my shoulder and said, "Get well, Mary. I claim the first dance at the Valentine party and Lars gets the second. We want to see

200

those toes of yours skipping and tapping."

I'll be the Belle of the Ball!

The end of my nose remained numb for another day. I recovered with no permanent damage except for slight frostbite on both little toes. I didn't need to have them cut off, but for the rest of my life they hurt when my feet got cold.

Sister Tietjen came the next day. Mother was happy to have an adult to talk to. They went into the bedroom.

I looked forward to Father's return. Things were easier when he was here. I wished Reuben was home to help instead of attending the Academy. I was jealous of him. He went because he was forced to. Tom was there also. Two mothers taught the school in Ramah and they concentrated on teaching the young ones to read, write and do simple sums. I was the teacher's helper and didn't learn anything new. I missed Sister Selkirk and the school in St. Johns.

I'd turned eleven last October and saw changes in my body. I was growing up. It would soon be too late for me to get an education. It was expected of us girls to marry and start a family when we reached fifteen or sixteen.

I will not abide by that expectation.

Mother and Sister Tietjen finished their visit. Mother said, "Thank you, Emma, for showing me how to use my hands to break the block in my breasts. I feel better already."

"Nurse Ezra every two hours today to keep your breasts from getting congested again. Drink lots of water," Sister Tietjen replied, putting on her hat and coat.

What did they do in the bedroom that made such a difference? There's so much I don't know about being a woman and a mother. How can I find out about those things? I wish I had a book about caring for mother's and babies. Aunt Mary Jane, Tom's mother, has lots of books and likes to read. I'll ask her when she moves back up into the canyon in the spring. She's going to have a baby next summer.

In the winter she lived in town with Brother McNeill and his other two wives Phoebe and Lizzie.

Father came home with as much food as he could bring on the sway backed pack mule. We were able to share with our neighbors and still have enough to last us until spring.

One evening, Father said, "Elizabeth, this last trip about did me in. I'm too old for this job. Three years is enough. I've decided to tell the postmaster to look for a younger man."

"Henry, you're only thirty-seven. That's not old. Besides, what do you intend to do to make a living? You've always hated farming and you aren't good at it."

"While I was delayed at Fort Wingate I talked to the quartermaster. He said their biggest need is potatoes. They have plenty of beef and flour but fresh potatoes are hard to come by. Brother Bond told me the soil and climate here in the canyon is perfect for potatoes."

"Henry, I would be uneasy without a steady income. This might end up being another of your pie-in-the-sky ideas. You can't do all the work. Reuben will be home from school in April, but he's not a hard worker like Lester and Mary."

"I've been hearing talk about Lester and his friends at the sawmill. Maybe it's time to send for him to keep him out of trouble, as well as having his help at home."

Father had to make one more trip before he could quit. He was scheduled to be in St. Johns the middle of February. I remember because that was the week of the Valentine's Day Dance. Mother had sewn up the back of my nice dress; the one she cut when she believed she was the Queen of England.

"What happened to your lovely dress?" she asked when I requested her help to mend it.

"Don't you remember when you cut it up the back and put it on? You sat in your rocker saying you were a queen."

Mother lowered her head and covered her eyes with her hand. "No, I don't remember. I'm beginning to realize that I leave and someone else takes over. It scares me, but I don't know what to do. Will you forgive me?" she asked with tears in her voice.

My eyes clouded and I cleared my throat, "Can it be fixed so I can wear it to the dance?"

She mended the dress, but it was too tight in the bust. "My goodness, Mary, you're developing. Take the dress off and I'll add some gussets to make it fit better. Bring me the hat. I can take some matching fabric from the veil and insert it above the waist."

The dance was held late in the afternoon so the young people could be home by eight in the evening. Brother McNeill played his mouth organ, Brothers Lewis and Bloomfield the fiddle, while Sister Garn was on the piano. A light supper was served at six o'clock. The round and square dancing resumed after supper lasting until seven thirty when we were dismissed with a prayer.

Lars and Sven claimed several dances and I was the envy of the other girls as I twirled around the hall with them. While catching my breath I felt a tap on my shoulder.

"Tom McNeill! I thought you were in St. Johns!" Without thinking I threw my arms around him and gave him a hug.

"All right, I'm glad to see you too, but you're embarrassing me. Step into the coatroom so we can talk."

He took my hand and led me to the coatroom. Tom was fourteen now and much taller than last fall. Neither he nor Reuben had been home for Christmas because of bad weather. "How is Reuben? How come you're here? Are you sick? Do you ever see my cousin, Hattie?" I babbled to cover my feelings.

"Calm down, Mary," he said, holding my hands and looking down at me from his new height. "I'm fine. Mother wrote me to come home to enlarge and make the shack up the canyon into a year-round cabin. She wants to move before the baby is due and file a homestead in her own name."

"I didn't know women could do that. Isn't Brother McNeill going to file for her?"

"Women can file for themselves. It isn't done very often, but it's legal. She wants to make her own way, have her own land and be free of owing anybody anything. Gratitude becomes a burden when you are constantly reminded of it."

"Did you hear that Brownie was killed by a mountain lion and I almost died from freezing in a blizzard?"

"I heard about it from the Mormon telegraph. News travels fast from mouth to ear. I sometimes think that all some folks do is gossip. Can I call on you tomorrow morning? I have something for you. I'll stop on my way to Mother's place. She has a load of lumber ready for me to haul to the shack."

"You can tell me about Reuben, Hattie and school. What do you have for me? Give me a hint."

"It's time to get back to the dance. Don't want any gossip about us hiding in the coatroom. The stories about Hattie are enough," he whispered as he led me back to the dance.

I walked home with Lars, Sven and two of their sisters. Star had waited for us. We were glad to have her along because the two-mile walk into the canyon was spooky at night. We often heard wolves howling and mountain lions screeching. Lars carried a kerosene lantern. There had been a thaw and the road was muddy so I changed from my dancing shoes to a new pair of clodhoppers Father had brought from Gallup. After settling into bed, my mind returned to what Tom had whispered.

What's happened to Hattie? Father checked on her when he was in St. Johns. He said that she and the Bishop's son were planning a wedding next fall.

Hattie wasn't my favorite cousin, but I admired her spunk when she refused to go with her family to St. George.

I got up early to get my chores done before Tom came. On Saturday there was no school, but we still had regular chores. I gathered eggs, fed the chickens, set some bread to rise, emptied and scalded the chamber pots and cooked breakfast by nine o'clock.

Mother wasn't feeling well so I had extra tasks. She was able to care for Ezra and herself. Ezra, at five months, had started crawling. Father built a pen to keep him out of harm's way. He was happy to be with us in the kitchen and he couldn't crawl out the door, up the stairs or burn himself on the stove.

I repeatedly ran to the front window to gaze down the hill beyond the blue spruce. When I heard Tom's wagon approaching, I pulled on my coat and ran to meet him.

"Good morning, Mary, my friend. How are you on this fine February morning?" Tom sounded like a schoolmaster. I knew he was teasing me when I saw the grin on his face and the twinkle in his gold flecked, green eyes.

I replied, "Good morning, young man. This fine morning suits me finely. And how are you and your kith and kin?"

Tom grinned as he handed me a box with holes poked into the top. It was tied with twine. "For you, my pretty maid. Something you disclosed last summer made me think of you when I beheld this golden jewel."

We walked to a bench near the barn. I untied the box. An orange striped kitten, hardly as big as my hand, looked at me with robin's egg blue eyes and said "Mrreeooww?"

I carefully picked up the kitten, nuzzled her neck as she began to purr. "Oh, Tom, you've brought me a Marmalade!" Tom gently wiped away my tears of joy with his handkerchief.

We sat on the bench in the pale February sun stroking the kitten. I wanted to throw my arms around him, stroke his head and neck and kiss him. I didn't know how Tom felt, but I sensed we were using the kitten to express our feelings. Finally I remembered to ask about Hattie.

"Your father will be home soon, he'll know more than I do. All I know is that Hattie and Judd Udall aren't sweethearts anymore and Hattie is most unhappy. Rumors were floating around but I don't want to tell you any falsehoods."

"Can you come in to say 'Hello' to Mother? She would like to hear how your mother is."

"I have to deliver this lumber by noon. I'll speak to her tomorrow at church."

"Thank you for Marmalade. She's going to sleep in the house next to my bed. I'll not have her freezing in the barn. Is she weaned?"

"Yes. You can feed her anything she'll eat. Have to go. See you tomorrow."

I sat with Marmalade in my lap for a few minutes before I put her back into the box. I carried her into the house and up the stairs. We'd brought the plaid curtains from St. Johns and used them to make a drape to hang across one end of the sleeping loft to enclose a place for me. Four younger brothers shared the rest of the loft. Ezra slept in his crib in my parent's room. When Reuben and Lester were home in the summer they slept in the barn. Father built a cupboard for me with doors on the bottom and shelves across the top. On the shelves I displayed my treasures; the Hopi dishes, the eagle Katsina doll, the Sunset Crossing pot, the green stone buffalo and the horny toad pot from the cave. I also owned three books.

From the small window under the slanting eaves of the house I looked down the canyon, across the valley to the green trees and rooftops of Ramah. In winter, the sun helped warm my refuge and in summer I opened the window to catch the breeze.

Eventually, I'd tell Mother about Marmalade, but for now I wanted her to be my secret. I made a shallow tray out of an old fruit-packing box and filled it with sand from the stream bank. She knew what it was for so I never had a mess on my floor. A willow basket lined with fabric scraps was her bed. I fed her scraps from our table and goat's milk from the Tietjens.

When Father returned, everything was thrown into such an uproar that my fears about Mother discovering Marmalade faded. He arrived one afternoon in the first week of March. We had begun to worry, since he was a week overdue. He didn't come alone. Hattie was with him. Father stalked into the house, told Hattie to go upstairs, took Mother into their bedroom and firmly closed the door.

When I finished supper preparations, I ran up and found Hattie lying on my cot weeping her eyes out. "What in the world has happened?"

Hattie gulped, blew her nose and tried to talk. "I-I-I'm going to have a baby," she blurted.

"You? You said you'd never have children. Your life was planned and it didn't include children. You were the one who was going to get an education, marry well and live in a big city," I said in disbelief. "How did you let this happen?"

She wailed, "Go away. Leave me alone. Don't badger me. I've had enough of that to last me a lifetime. You'll hear about it from your father."

"I have a kitten here, so don't be surprised when she climbs up on the cot with you," I said as I closed the drape and went to serve the evening meal.

I delayed supper while Mother and Father whispered in the bedroom. My brothers were hungry, so I knocked on the door asking if I should serve the boys.

"Yes. Father and I will eat later. We don't have an appetite right now. Go ahead and clean up afterward as usual."

My mind was in turmoil as I went through the motions of supper. I wasn't hungry either, but ate a little chicken stew, canned fruit and fresh bread. While we ate, Father came from the bedroom, put on his coat and stomped out the front door. Mother went upstairs. Hattie wailed. Mother's soft yet stern voice tried to calm her.

I asked William to help me clean up and dry the dishes. He was very able to help, although he protested mightily about having to do women's work. Later, I read to the boys until their bedtime. We were tense and curious about why Hattie was in such distress, why Father had brought her here and what was going to happen next.

I was tired. I wanted to go to bed, but I didn't have a bed! I waited for Mother to tell me where to sleep and thought about the twists and turns of life. Mother was sure to find Marmalade in my room. If I had to put her out in the barn, I'd go there too. I was upset that, because Hattie had made a mistake, I might have to sleep in the barn. Our house was full even without Hattie and her child. If Lester came home the house would bulge.

Father returned well after dark. Brother McNeill, who had recently been appointed the Bishop of our ward, was with him. "Mary, what are you doing up so late?" Father asked.

"Hattie's on my bed and Mother is there with her. I didn't know what you wanted me to do. What's going on?" I asked.

Father said, "I know you're curious about Hattie, but this is something we grownups will sort out. You'll get your bed back in a few days. I'll make a pallet on the floor in your room and let you know when things are settled. Tell your Mother to come down, get your night clothes and go to bed in our room for now."

I did as he directed. Mother sat on my bed with Hattie's head in her lap. Marmalade lay on Hattie's chest purring while Hattie stroked her.

Mother said, "I see you have a new friend. You should have told me before I found out myself. That's a way of being false. I'm ashamed of you. The kitten is a comfort to Hattie, so I'll let her stay for now."

"I know I was wrong. Father wants you downstairs," I mumbled as I gathered my nightclothes and went to my parent's room.

I was so keyed up I couldn't fall asleep. Finally, I stopped straining to hear what was being talked about on the other side of the door and drifted off. Later, when Father carried me upstairs and lay me on the floor pallet, I barely woke. I was worn out and slept soundly. Marmalade crept from her basket and snuggled in the crook of my arm.

The next few days were punctuated by Hattie's fits of weeping and Lester's constant complaints about being dragged home from the mill. He liked being on his own to do what he wanted, when he wanted.

He told me, "I'm fifteen years old. I've been on my own for four years. I feel caged at home. I like playing cards, riding to the Fort or to Bluewater on my days off. My buddies and I have big plans. We're not going to be hicks from the boonies. Planting potatoes! I can't think of any thing duller."

Father fixed a place for him in the barn so he had privacy from his adoring little brothers. He was impatient with them and ignored their pleas to tell them stories of his doings at the mill. I still didn't know the circumstances of Hattie's disgrace. A week passed. Mother said no more about Marmalade.

Finally, Father gathered us and said, "A wedding is planned for Hattie and Hyrum Hunt, Bishop McNeill's nephew from Bluewater. He recently lost his wife to pneumonia leaving their three young children motherless. The wedding will be next Sunday, after which Hattie and Hyrum will depart for Bluewater."

I'd have to pry it out of Hattie, which would be hard to do because she continued to weep most of the time. When we retired for the night, I asked her how she felt about getting married to someone she'd never laid eyes on.

"I'll tell you if you'll go to the kitchen and get me one of those dill pickles in the crock. I'm craving them."

Everyone else in the house slept as I tiptoed down the stairs. A full moon shone through the window by the back door giving enough light to see by. I had just stuck a fork into the crock when there was a soft knock at the back door. I put the fork down peeked out the window and saw a man on the porch. A saddled black horse stood near the barn.

The man had a full dark beard and wore a black hat pulled down over his forehead. He seemed somehow familiar. I opened the door a crack.

He whispered, "Is that you, Mary? I must speak to your father. It's urgent. Get him."

I shut the door and went to wake Father. How did that man know my name? I tried to remember where I'd seen him. Father rose, pulled his coat over his long johns and went to the door. I followed to find out who the stranger was. The men whispered a few words, then Father invited him into the kitchen.

As the stranger took off his hat he smiled, "Mary, don't you remember me? I'm Pat Traynor."

Chapter Twenty

Ramah, New Mexico Territory Spring 1889

I was so startled I dropped the fork into the pickle crock. "Pat Traynor! You look different," I blurted. "Like an old ranch hand in that slouchy hat, grimy clothes, muddy boots and your bushy black beard."

Father said, "Shh, Mary, don't wake the whole household. What are you doing down here, anyway?"

"I was getting Hattie a pickle. She craves them."

"Get what you need and go to bed. Mr. Traynor and I must talk. You can visit in the morning."

I fished in the crock, found the fork, stabbed a pickle, wrapped it in a dishtowel and went to my nook. Hattie had fallen asleep but I woke her, "I went to a lot of trouble to get this pickle. Eat it and tell me what happened. I won't sleep if I don't satisfy my curiosity about at least one mystery."

Hattie took a bite of the dill and smacked her lips. "Your Mother makes the best pickles I ever ate. I'll ask for the recipe. Now that I'm going to be wife and mother, I'll need to learn the housewifely skills I previously scorned."

With Marmalade in my lap, I waited for her to begin. Moonlight flooded the room, changing Hattie into a silver, ghostly maiden. I expected a romantic tale of young lovers separated by tragic circumstances.

"You asked how I felt about marrying someone I've never met. I'm scared, that's what I am. I haven't even seen a picture of him. All I know is; he is twenty-five years old, has three children—two girls, two and five and a boy four years old. My child is due in October, so I will have four to care for. I don't know if I can do it," she moaned.

"What happened to Judd? You planned to marry next summer. You're going to be sixteen in June. Why couldn't you do it a few months early?" I asked.

Hattie finished the pickle, wiped her hands and blew her nose on the dishtowel. "Judd's not the father."

"Good heavens, Hattie! What happened? I thought this was between you and Judd. Now you're saying another fellow caused all this uproar. Tell me everything."

"As Judd and I got better acquainted, he began to think we weren't suited for marriage. He paid less and less attention to me and got really bossy. I did things to please him, but it didn't matter what I did. I was always wrong.

"Last fall he told me he was too young to be tied down. His parents wanted him to go to college in Utah. I thought his parents liked me and were happy about our plans. Now, I think they wanted to get him away from me so they used the excuse of school to send him to his grandmother in Salt Lake City."

"Why didn't you go to St. George to live with your folks after Judd left?"

"I wanted to, but the group I was to travel with changed their plans. They decided to remain in St. Johns until spring. Two women were pregnant and didn't want to give birth on the trail. Another group agreed to take me, but winter came early and their trip was postponed. Nothing went right," she wailed.

"So, who is the father and how did you get mixed up with him?"

"Last October, I went to the store to shop for Sister Selkirk. On my way home, I stepped in an icy puddle, slipped and fell. My groceries flew and I banged my shoulder. I struggled to get up. A young man came to help me. He gathered the groceries, put them back in the bags, then introduced himself. His English was poor but I understood most of what he said. His name was Marco Chavarria and he'd recently moved to St. Johns from Sonora, Mexico, to work on his older brother's sheep ranch.

"Marco wanted to learn good English so he could become a wealthy businessman. I offered to give him lessons and we met every afternoon after school. We'd go to the new hotel on Main Street, sit in the lobby and speak English. Sister Selkirk and other churchwomen were appalled to see me in public with a Mexican. I didn't care. Judd had deserted me, I was lonely and depressed. Marco cheered me up. He was polite and appreciated me. He brought little gifts; a bar of lavender soap, Belgian Chocolates and a lace and linen handkerchief from Spain.

"Get to the important part. The part about getting pregnant."

"One afternoon he asked if I'd like to see his brother's house. It was a cold, windy late November day. I was sad and homesick, the holidays were fast approaching and I wasn't thinking straight. His sweet talk, sincere attentions and gifts blinded me. No one was home; the servants were out and I succumbed to his advances. I was deflowered on the parlor floor on a Persian carpet. I thought my first time would be lovely and romantic. Actually it hurt and was disappointing."

"What did he say when you told him you were with child?" I was shocked and astonished. I couldn't believe my ears. I'd read stories about bad girls who let men have their way with them but I never thought my cousin would do that sort of thing.

"I never told him. The next time I saw him, he said he was going to Concho on business and would be back the next week. When he didn't meet me on the appointed day, I thought he'd been delayed. The days turned to weeks, my monthly didn't come and I was in a panic. I went to his brother's house and learned Marco had returned to Mexico.

"A few days later, while in Barth's, I overheard some young men talking about Marco seducing a Mormon girl. They laughed and made lewd remarks about how Mormon women were supposed to be so pure, but Marco had shown they could be sweet talked in to anything. They admired Marco for what he'd done. They didn't know I was the girl and I carried Marco's child. I wanted to die right in front of the candy counter. My wobbly legs barely carried me home. I took to my bed for three days, couldn't stop crying and vomited what little I ate. So here I am—a stupid girl who thought she knew everything. Actually, I know nothing about the world or men."

"Oh, Hattie, I'm so sorry. What can I do to help you?"

"Don't be as dumb as I was. Don't hate me. I'll be out of your nook and gone to Bluewater come Sunday." She put the pillow over her head and refused to say more.

By the time I got downstairs next morning, Mother was cooking breakfast. Father was in the barn with our midnight caller. I set the table, dressed the little ones and called the men and Lester to breakfast. While I ate, I listened to the adults talk, but learned nothing to explain Pat Traynor's visit. I hurried through my tasks, then left for school. Since my brothers had left earlier, I enjoyed my quiet walk with time to think about Hattie.

Was what I felt for Tom, love? Were Mother and Father in love? How about my love for Marmalade and the love I felt for my brothers? Sometimes love is all right and sometimes it leads you into dire circumstances. Some kinds of love are good and blessed by God, other kinds are condemned and are bad. How can I know the difference between the two? The older I get the more complicated life becomes. I vow to watch my step and not end up with a stranger like Hattie or in a marriage where husband and wife barely tolerate each other.

I was tired and the day passed in a haze. "Mary, are you all right?" the teacher asked. "Take this group outside for games. Maybe the fresh air will revive you."

Nothing would revive me except a return to normalcy. I muddled through the rest of the school day and was thankful when 3:00 P.M. came. After supper Father and Pat Traynor sat by the stove. I listened while I sat at the table practicing penmanship.

"Mr. Traynor, how did you know where we lived?" Father asked.

"Do you remember Pip Pipken, the man who brought Lester home from Becker Lake? When I came from Mexico last year, I met him in Columbus, New Mexico. I learned he'd been in the St. Johns/Springerville area, so I asked if he knew the George family. I told him about rescuing Mary and he said he'd heard you had moved to Ramah. I planned to pass this way, so I decided to stop and ask for help."

"Last night you said you were in a tight spot. Care to elaborate?"

"Both the Mexicans and the Cartwrights are on my trail. That cattle deal with Westbrook went sour and I've been running ever since. He told me that herd was out of Sonora. I discovered it was from Prescott and that Jackson Cartwright has a warrant out for me.

"I stopped in a mining camp near Silver City and saw a wanted poster tacked to a tree. It described me pretty good and offered a five-hundred dollar reward for my capture. I headed north that night. I need to lay low for a spell and then hightail it for Moab, Utah. Some old buddies are holed up there and I can throw in with them. I tried the straight life, but it never felt right. I guess a crooked tree can never straighten its branches."

I didn't realize I'd fallen asleep until Mother shook me. "Go to bed, Mary. Tomorrow we'll be busy getting ready for Hattie's wedding."

In the morning Hattie sorted through the few belongings she'd brought from St. Johns. After she discarded many of her old things, she had very little left.

Mother said, "Most brides have time to prepare for their weddings. I'll look through my trunk to see if I have some linens and family mementos you can have. If your mother was here, she'd do the same."

I asked, "Which dress are you going to wear tomorrow? There isn't time to make anything new."

"This dark blue wool will have to do. It has a nice lace collar and cuffs and isn't as old and shabby as the others. Sister Selkirk gave it to me when her daughter outgrew it. I have a cameo broach Mother gave me. She said my grandmother gave it to her. It will look nice pinned between the collar."

Mother returned, followed by William, who huffed up the stairs carrying a battered old trunk. "I hear you'll be going by wagon to Fort Wingate and then by train to Bluewater. Pack everything in the trunk except what you'll wear tomorrow. It was brought from England by your Grandmother Shelton. Take good care of it."

"You're going to wear the blue dress?" Mother asked. "That's the best choice. Here's a crocheted shawl my mother's sister, Aunt Rhoda, gave me as a wedding present. It will fancy up the dress. Make it look more festive."

Mother brought linen sheets and matching pillow cases, two goose down pillows, a cross stitched apron and a small silver cup which she put in the trunk. "The cup is for your baby. It's over one-hundred years old. I want you to know we bear no hard feelings toward you and your child. I just wish things had turned out better for you."

Mother had tears in her eyes as she said, "Mary, following the private ceremony we'll have a few guests for the wedding dinner. I need your help to prepare it. Hattie and Hyrum will spend the night in the Ashcroft's guest house and leave Monday for Bluewater."

Mother and I left Hattie to pack, went to the kitchen and set to work. Earlier, she'd killed two plump chickens, bled and gutted them. We plucked the feathers and saved them to make pillows. I held the scrawny carcasses by the feet while Mother singed each one with a pine torch to get rid of any small feathers. Tomorrow we would fry them, boil and mash the potatoes, make gravy and biscuits and open jars of fruit from down cellar.

"There's time to make a cake, Mary. Look in the pantry and see what we have. No wedding should be without a cake."

I found dried fruit, a little shortening, flour, salt, sugar, baking soda and some chocolate powder. We had plenty of eggs. Mother and I set to and made the cake. She made a drizzle of frosting to top it off.

On Hattie's wedding day I was in a tizzy of excitement to see what her husband-to-be looked like. Bishop McNeill and Hyrum Hunt arrived shortly after 9:00 a.m. All of us children had been told to stay outside to allow Hyrum and Hattie time alone. I watched from the side yard as they rode into the yard, dismounted and went to the door. I had a good look at Hyrum. He was taller than his six-foot uncle, had straight brown hair, a pleasant open face and walked like a man who spent a lot of time on a horse.

I wanted to be a fly on the wall when Hyrum and Hattie met. After half an hour the men came out, mounted their horses and left.

I rushed into the house, cornered Hattie, "So! What do you think? How do you feel? Will you be able to love him? Do you think he's handsome?"

Hattie turned and went upstairs without a word. Mother grabbed me by the arm, "Mary, your questions will get you in trouble some day. Things will work out in good time. Leave Hattie alone. She has enough questions of her own. Help me pull the table into the middle of the room and put these leaves in it. It was for times like these that Henry made a table that could be extended."

The wedding was scheduled for noon, after Sunday School. A few folks had been asked to stay for the brief ceremony. Then, they would come to our place for dinner.

When it was time to leave, Father drove our wagon into the front yard and we climbed on for the trip. Mother and Hattie sat on the driver's box with Father. Hattie looked nice, but too solemn for a bride.

When I get married I'll surely be happier than Hattie is today. I'll have a big wedding with all my friends and family in attendance. Afterwards there will be a dancing party with lots of fancy food. My husband and I will go off to some faraway exotic place for a royal honeymoon.

How could I have known that my wedding would be worse then Hattie's?

When we got to the church, Sunday School was over and most worshipers had left. We found the small invited group waiting to witness the wedding. Bishop McNeill was the Justice of the Peace. I was happy to see Tom, his sisters Jennie and Roxie, brother Joady and his mother, Mary Jane. Bishop McNeill's first wife, Phoebe and her two children were there also. Lissie, the third and much younger wife was ailing, so was not able to attend.

Afterwards, Tom asked, "Mary would you like to ride with us? Your family's wagon is full. Ride up here with me. Mother wants to ride in the wagon bed with Jenny, Joady and Roxie." Tom's mother showed by her expanding waist that she expected her child by early summer.

Lester didn't attend the wedding. He preferred spending time with Pat

Traynor who still hid in our barn. Pat and Lester had struck up a friendship. They spent a lot of time drawing maps on the ground in the corral and making lists.

Father had fetched Lester from the sawmill after he'd brought Hattie. He'd been busy marking out his future potato field. He and Lester, when he could get him away from Pat, put a cross pole fence around the plot to keep the cattle out of the field. Then they began plowing.

Lester complained constantly. "I will never be a farmer. I hate walking behind that damned plow, plodding behind those slow stupid mules."

Father didn't get mad often, but he'd finally had enough and took Lester to the woodshed to give him a couple of good whacks. Father and Lester yelled at each other. On top of all the stress over Hattie, it sent Mother to her bed for a day.

On the wedding day Lester was cheerful and pleasant at dinner. He was polite and tried to make conversation. I wondered if my parents noticed how strange he was acting. I was so busy serving, eating and cleaning up that I forgot my suspicions. Our guest in the barn didn't show his face.

I had no opportunity to talk privately with my cousin, but I whispered to her as I hugged her goodbye, "I love you, Hattie. All will be well. He needs you as much as you need him. Be happy."

After cleanup, there was a lull in the house. So much had been happening that now there was emptiness. Marmalade missed Hattie. She slept next to me all night instead of in her basket.

Father and Lester continued plowing and preparing the field for planting the seed potatoes Father had bought from Brother Bond. Following instructions, he'd built chitting boxes to prepare the potatoes for planting. They were put in the boxes, single layer, with the sprouting end up, then put in the barn where they wouldn't freeze. Every night Father covered them with a canvas and uncovered them during the day as they needed some light to sprout.

While the "seeds" were waiting, they mixed manure into the earth and dug a ditch from the creek to the field to irrigate if the rains didn't come.

By the first of April, the field was ready. I was glad Lester was home to help. Pat Traynor helped some but stuck close to the barn. Whenever he heard a horse on the road, he skedaddled up into the hayloft to his hidey-hole.

One day after school my brothers and I went to McNeill's store to shop for Mother. We liked to go to McNeill's. It smelled so good and there were always new things to look at in the glass-fronted counter. I gave Sister Phoebe Mother's list and while she gathered the things, I looked around. I stopped short and caught my breath when I spotted a poster tacked to the wall.

That's Pat Traynor! How long has it been on the wall?

I told my brothers to wait outside while I finished the transaction. I didn't want them asking questions and giving anything away. I said, "Sister McNeill, how long has that wanted poster been here? Who brought it in? That sounds like a real bad man. Wanted for cattle rustling and murder! Gives me goose bumps!"

"Deputies from Holbrook brought it in yesterday. They said he'd been spotted in Quemado a few weeks ago and thought he might have come through here on his way north."

"We'll keep an eye out for him. Got to get home. Thank you."

I rounded up my brothers who griped all the way home about having to leave the store before they'd had enough time to look around. I didn't say a word, just walked fast and thought about what to do next.

I gave Mother her purchases and went looking for Father. He and Lester were coming in from the potato field after a day of digging shallow trenches in which to plant the seed potatoes. They were hot, sweaty and tired. Again I was glad it was Lester and not me doing the farming.

"Father, I need to talk to you. It's very important."

"What is it Mary? A problem at school with one of your brothers?"

I waited until Lester was out of earshot. "I saw a wanted poster on the wall at the store. Some deputies put it up yesterday."

As I told Father the details, his face became grim. He scowled, his lips thinned and his jaw clenched. "I'd better stop in the barn and speak to our guest. Time he goes on his way. Our indebtedness to him for saving you has been repaid."

I don't know what transpired in the hayloft, or if Father told Mother, but everyone except Lester was subdued that evening. He was jumpy and grouchier than ever. I was glad when he went to the barn for the night.

About midnight, I was awakened by the sound of horses snuffling and moving out by the barn. It was the dark of the moon, so I couldn't see a thing. I drifted back to sleep thinking that something had spooked the horses in the corral and there was no cause for alarm.

The next thing I heard was a shriek from below. It was Mother. "Henry! He's gone. He left a note. Lester's left with that outlaw."

Chapter Twenty-One

Ramah, New Mexico Territory, Spring 1889

Father hastened to the barn. When he returned his face was ashen. He shuffled to a chair. He looked battered and weary. "Lester and Pat Traynor not only left, they took a horse and a mule. I don't mind that he took the horse and saddle but, dag nabbit, that mule was our hardest worker."

He sat at the table with his head in his hands. "I wish I knew what Lester expects to achieve by running away to join a gang of outlaws. When he was six he ran away with that old miner from Nevada. Took us a week to find and bring him home. Lester hankers for the treasure that lies over the next hill. The day he was born was already too late for him to have any common sense."

Mother wept and rocked. The boys stood on the stairs. William, Roy, Richard and Parley were bewildered to see the ones in charge in such a state. They didn't know whether to go back to the loft or continue down.

I heard Ezra crying and went into the bedroom to clean and dress him. Although only six months old he was standing, holding the top rail of his crib. He smiled and made baby sounds as he held up one arm to me. It was hard for me to imagine Lester ever being that sweet. My heart hardened toward my oldest brother. Not only had he devastated our parents, but I would have to help plant the potatoes.

Lester's leaving was deplorable, and on top of Hattie's hasty marriage, I was afraid of its effect on Mother. Not a day went by that she didn't mourn for her sister Jane. Having Hattie in the house reminded Mother of how much she missed Aunt Jane.

Father said, "Mary, get breakfast for the boys and all of you get busy with the chores. Because Lester is gone doesn't mean the chickens aren't hungry and the cow isn't waiting to be milked."

I asked, "Should the boys go to school? I'll stay home."

"Yes, after they do chores. I must write Reuben and tell him to come home. Bishop McNeill is going to St. Johns today or tomorrow and can deliver it."

When Father returned, he said, "Elizabeth, Mary and I will be in the potato field. If you need us, ring the cowbell."

She replied, "I want you to go after Lester. The potatoes will wait."

"Lester will come to no harm. When he gets a taste of being low man in a gang, he'll ride for home. They'll have him doing the dirty work. May teach him a lesson. We have no idea which way they went, I could spend a useless week searching. The first batch of seed potatoes must be planted today."

Mother's eyes sparked, "You never listen to me. Why does everything have to be your way? I'd go, but I don't know how to ride a horse."

"Take care of Parley and Ezra. That's your job. My job is to see that we don't starve next winter."

I changed into work clothes and went to the field. We carried the chitting boxes and planting tools through the gate setting them beside the furrows. Father showed me how to choose the four tallest sprouts and break off the others. We carefully sat each potato, sprouts up, a foot apart in the prepared furrow. When a row was filled we shoveled soil over the furrow to a depth of three to four inches. As the plants grew, we would hill more soil around their stems.

By noon I was sweaty, dirty and achy. The dry, dusty, manured soil hung suspended in the air. We had dark rings around our mouths, noses and eyes.

"That's enough for today, Mary. We'll plant two rows every five days so the potatoes can be harvested at different times. Let's wash up and have dinner. Need to check on Mother and the boys."

I said a silent prayer that Reuben would come home by the time the next rows were to be planted. I cursed Lester for running away. We returned the tools to the barn, carefully washed and dried them and hung them on hooks. Tools were valuable and hard to come by.

As we approached the back porch, we heard Ezra yelling and Parley bawling. "I can't feed you! I'm not a mother! Gum on this bread."

Father looked puzzled as we hurried into the kitchen. Ezra was gripping the top of his playpen with both hands while screaming at the top of his lungs. Tears wet his cheeks as snot ran down his chin. Parley was near tears as he tried to get Ezra to take a crust of bread.

"Where's your mother?" Father asked.

"I no know. She say she going walking an she lef," Parley mumbled.

My heart sank.

Not again. Mother's gone, Lester's run away, Reuben won't be home for at least a week and I'll be in charge. Aunt Jane's not here to help.

"I'll try to find Elizabeth. Hold the fort and hope for the best. If I can't find her, I'll ask for help in Ramah. I'll ride by Sister McNeill's place to ask if they've seen her and tell them you're here alone," Father said. "I'll be back by dark with or without her."

After washing up, I fixed a bottle for Ezra, comforted Parley and tried to calm myself. I felt forsaken. Maybe Tom or his mother would come.

My brothers came from school. I prepared and served supper and got them ready for bed. It was pitch dark by the time I heard father's horse on the road. I ran to the window to see if mother was with him, but it was too dark to tell. I pulled on my coat and ran to the barn. "Did you find her? Is she with you?" I called as I ran toward him.

"Found a few footprints in the canyon, but lost the trail near the river. I think she was walking on rocks or in the water. Lots of caves and old ruins where she could hide. Sorry. Tomorrow I'll get help and search again. I wish I knew what to do for her. I love your mother with all my heart, but she's not sturdy. Something's wrong with her. She was right when she said she wasn't cut out to be a pioneer."

Father left early the next morning for town. I sent the boys to school, did my chores and waited. The breadbox was empty so I set some dough to rise, ironed clothes, took Parley and Ezra outside to play and waited.

At mid afternoon Tom knocked on the door. "Mother sent fresh milk, butter and cheese. How can I help? Looks like the wood box is about empty."

What I wanted was for him to put his arms around me, but I wasn't going to ask. Wouldn't be seemly to ask for affection. "Yes, bring in some wood, then sit and keep me company. I'm heavy hearted about Mother. I'll never understand what gets into her."

Parley and Ezra were napping, the fragrance of baking bread filled the house and I heard the song of newly returned robins through the open window. My heartache eased. I snatched at the unexpected joy and smiled at

Tom as he came in with an armful of wood.

"I appreciate your help," I said. He smiled and sat at the table. "Would you like a cup of tea?"

"No, can't stay long. Mother isn't feeling well and I must finish the roof by tonight. I have an idea. A family of Navajos live far up the canyon in spring and summer. Ghosea Spino is a medicine chief. He has three wives with a passel of children. I go hunting with his boys, Shingle Head and Flat Nose. They know this country better than anyone. If I leave now, I can ride to their camp and ask if they've seen your mother. They may not have seen her, but they should be told she's missing."

Tom stood and I realized how fast he was growing. He'd turned fifteen in March and was already taller than many grown men. He'd be out and out tall by the time he got his full growth.

"I'll do what I can, Mary. Don't worry yourself sick. Your family needs you to be strong," he said. He patted me on my shoulder and left. I'd have to be satisfied with a pat instead of a hug.

After he left, I took the bread from the oven. My brothers returned from school and I set them to their evening chores. My spirits sank as the sun lowered and still no word of Mother.

Was I any different than Mother? Was I cut out to be a pioneer? I'll be twelve soon and I think about what kind of life I want. Do I have any choices? What if I want to be a teacher, a doctor, live in a city or be a writer?

The circumstances of my life tightened like the shrinking wet leather thongs that bind the reeds of a new basket.

A knock on the door interrupted my day dreaming. I was flabbergasted to find Grandma Burntwater standing on the porch. I flung my arms around her and started to cry. She set her bag down, returned my hug and said, "There, there child. Your father asked me to come. I saw him at the store this morning before the search party left."

I invited her in and started asking questions. She laughed, "You've grown since I last saw you but you still have many questions."

"How long can you stay? I never dreamed I'd see you again. I'm overwhelmed with worry and responsibilities. Then I feel guilty because I'm such a weak ninny," I mumbled through my tears of relief.

"I'm here for as long as your family needs me. I hope your mother will be found soon and will take hold of the reins after she returns. The hardest thing to do is wait while not knowing. What needs doing right now?" she asked as she went to the stove to help with supper.

Before bedtime she gathered the boys and told one of her stories. She took charge and calmed us. A weight lifted from my chest, I was able to breathe deeply and regain a sense of balance. She was delighted with Marmalade and spread her sleeping mat next to her basket. There was no sign of Father, but I slept soundly with my friend in the house.

On the third afternoon, while I was in the chicken house, I heard hoofbeats approaching from the canyon. When I got into the house, I found Grandma Burntwater sitting across the table from a Navajo man. He was short, thin and wiry, dressed in faded jeans and a sheepskin jacket. His raven black hair was twisted and tied in a bun at the back of his leathery neck. I knew some Navajo, but he talked too fast for me.

Grandma Burntwater made noises deep in her throat like "Uhmm, ahh, and hmm?" while the man, I supposed was Ghosea Spino, rambled on with his story. It took forever for him to get it all out while I waited for a translation.

Finally he stopped; Grandma Burntwater said, "Mary, get our guest a drink of water and a slice of fresh bread. Then I'll tell you what's happened."

I took a cup from the cupboard, dipped it into the water barrel and brought it to the table. I spread a slice of bread with butter and put it on a saucer. A jar of jam stood on the table so I put a knife on the saucer. Navajos enjoy sweets.

"This is Ghosea Spino, Mary. He said Tom McNeill rode to his camp a few days ago and asked him to be on the look out for your mother. Farther up the mountain is a place called Outlaw Canyon. In the past a group of rustlers used it for a hideout. The canyon is steep and isolated, making it a good place to hide. The clever outlaws built a series of wooden ramps from the rim of the gorge down into the heavily wooded canyon. The ramps allowed the men to lead their horses into their den. There's a stream and enough wild grass for them to water and feed their horses. They could stay holed up for weeks. He doesn't know if outlaws are using it now, but someone is there because he smelled and saw a wisp of smoke rising above the rim two days ago when he was hunting.

"The ramps are well hidden by boulders and bushes. A person on horseback would miss them. Someone on foot could find them. We need to get word to the search party about Outlaw Canyon."

"I'll get Tom McNeill. He can ask in town if anyone knows which way the search party went. He'll find them," I answered as I tied my sunbonnet under my chin and ran out the door.

Tom found the searchers returning from an unfruitful search near Zuni.

Father came home and talked with Ghosea Spino. He ate and went directly to bed to be ready to ride to Outlaw Canyon the next day. Ghosea Spino slept in the barn.

Before I fell asleep, I thought about Mother.

Will they find her in the canyon? Will Lester and Pat Traynor be with her? Will she want to come home? I wish I could go with them. Tom's going. I'll get the story from him. I need to write about this in my book.

The next day the sun crept across the sky, the hands of our clock hesitated at every minute and time moved like a tortoise. When I thought I was about to explode with not knowing, Tom raced into the yard on his horse, Doodle-Bug.

I ran to meet him with trepidation in my heart. "We found her. They're bringing her in a hammock slung between two horses; she has a broken leg. We didn't find anyone with her, but someone had splinted her leg. They may be outlaws, but they tried to care for her."

This time I hugged him and he hugged me back. As we pulled back from each other, Tom blushed and said in an offhand way, "Er, uhm-a, could you get me a drink of water?"

He does care for me! I know it in my heart.

"Oh, yes! Anything! When should we expect them? I'd better tell Grandma Burntwater to get ready. I'm sure they'll all be hungry. Mother will need special care. Did you talk to her?"

"They should be here in an hour. I didn't hear your Mother speak. She looked dazed and seemed to fade in and out. I'll stay and see if I can help. I stopped at our place so my mother knows I'm back."

I brought him water and told Grandma Burntwater. Tom and I sat side by side on the bench by the barn. He shyly took my hand in his and said, "I'm glad I can be here with you."

Tom told me about the search, finding the ramps, guiding the skittish horses down and finding Mother lying in a small cave at the bottom of the canyon. I listened, but all I could think about was the feel of Tom's hand holding mine.

When they arrived, Father carried Mother to their room. Grandma Burntwater followed and closed the door. There was no doctor in Ramah, so Grandma Burntwater and Father would set Mother's leg.

Father opened the door a crack, "Mary, put the big kettle of water to boil, ask Tom to ride to the Tietjens to ask Emma C to come. She's had bone setting experience."

Emma C came. I prepared and served supper for my brothers and Tom.

"Good biscuits, Mary," Tom said as he left the table. "You'll make a man a good wife someday. I have to get home to my chores."

It wasn't until after the boys bedded down that Father and the women came from the bedroom. He thanked Emma C. "I'll let you know in the morning how Elizabeth is doing. Really appreciate your help."

Grandma Burntwater sat the pot of chicken stew on the stove and I put biscuits, butter and jam on the table. She and Father ate in tired silence and for once, I held my tongue until they finished.

"Is Mother going to be all right? How bad is the break? Has she said anything?" I asked as Father polished his plate with the last biscuit.

"She may have one leg shorter than the other, but she'll be able to get around. She's lucky we found her when we did, before the leg developed gangrene. Amputation is no fun for the victim nor the one who does the cutting," he answered sternly. "I'll sleep on the floor in our room for the next few weeks. Goodnight."

I cleaned up the kitchen and then went to bed. Grandma Burntwater was in her bedroll. I asked, "Did Mother say anything?

"No, she's unconscious. I don't expect her to talk for several days. Try not to worry so much. Look at how relaxed Marmalade is. You should be more like her."

I'm not a cat! Grownups! They never want to tell me the important things. When I have children I'll talk to them about everything. I won't be like my parents.

Bishop McNeill came from St. Johns with Reuben and Jenny. Reuben said, "School was almost over for the year. Most students are needed for summer planting. Jenny decided to come so she can help her mother during the last months before the baby is due. Bishop McNeill said he had a lot on his mind and didn't feel like talking. Wonder what happened in St. Johns?"

I brought him up to date on Lester, Mother's disappearance and how happy I was he was home to help Father in the potato patch.

"I know that's dirty work and you're needed in the house. How is Mother doing?" I had brought him a glass of cold buttermilk, a favorite of his. After he drank it he had a white mustache.

"Wipe your mouth," I said. "Mother doesn't have a fever and the swelling in her foot has gone down. Emma C comes every day and I've heard them talking, but I haven't talked to her yet. Actually I'm put out at Mother. I don't understand how she can be so flighty and disappear like she does. Leaving Parley and Ezra without so much as a by your leave was scary. One of these times she won't come back. Thank goodness Grandma Burntwater is here."

"How long can she stay?" Ruben asked.

"Her daughter was here yesterday asking when she'd be home. They need her to watch their babies while they plant corn. I hope she'll stay another week," I said.

Reuben and Father planted another two rows of potatoes. We had gentle spring rains, which was encouraging. Green sprouts showed on the tops of the first rows. William and Roy were put in charge of walking the rows every day to pull weeds.

Saturday evening father said, "Bishop McNeill has an announcement and wants as many of us as possible to be there for a special meeting after Sunday School. I want all of us except Mother, of course, to be ready to leave tomorrow morning by nine o'clock. Grandma Burntwater will stay with Mother. Mary, you see to the boys' clothes. I'll bring in the tub and everyone will bathe."

It was a beautiful April Sunday. The swooping cliff swallows had returned and the robins busily built nests in the trees while they called and sang. I hoped to see Tom. The world was alive with possibilities. My heart lifted.

Maybe this afternoon I can talk with Mother. I don't like feeling put-out with her. I need her to tell me what happened in Outlaw Canyon, why she deserted Parley and Ezra, and does she know why she's so different?

The hall was packed for the meeting. Some men stood around the sides of the room. The windows and doors were open to let in the fresh spring air. Folks were buzzing with curiosity about what good news the bishop had brought from St. Johns. Special meetings were rare and we were sure something wonderful and exciting was about to be shared. Maybe we were going to get a real school teacher or a group of new residents were coming.

Bishop McNeill drank a glass of water and began. "Brothers and Sisters, while in St. Johns, I received by way of Bishop Udall, a distressing letter from Mr. E. A. Carr, the president of the Cebolla Cattle Company."

The mood in the room immediately shifted from excited expectation to apprehension. Everyone, including the courting teenagers, was silent and attentive. Sweat beaded on the Bishop's high forehead; he wiped his face with a handkerchief, drank another glass of water, took a deep breath and continued.

I was stunned by what he told us. My mind numbed and my hands and feet turned to ice. The gist of it was the Cattle Company claimed they had purchased the land in and around Ramah in 1886 for fifty cents an acre from the railroad. The Company said the settlers should have been paying rent to the Cattle Company for two years. No one seemed to have heard of or paid any attention to the demands for payment, which were said to have been sent through Salt Lake City. Now the Company offered Ramah a choice. Either pay the Company ten dollars an acre to buy the land, which came to around $7,000 or be evicted, lock stock and barrel by the end of June.

Chapter Twenty-Two

Ramah, New Mexico Territory, Summer & Fall 1889

The women and children were told to leave the room, while males over the age of thirteen discussed the problem. Since Reuben would turn thirteen in May, he was allowed to stay. Tom's mother invited me and my brothers to ride home with them. Jennie and I sat on the seat with Aunt Mary Jane while the younger ones rode in back. My brothers were fascinated by the way Joadie was able to do most everything with his right hand even though, except for little stubs, he didn't have fingers.

Joadie was born at Sunset Crossing. He was sickly and nearly died a couple of times. When he was two he fell into an open fireplace and was badly burned. His right hand fingers turned gangrenous. To save his arm, an elder cut them off with an ax.

I asked Aunt Mary Jane, "Do you think we'll have to move? I like it here, and until lately, Mother's been better than in St. Johns."

She replied, "Knowing my husband, I'm sure he'll do what he can to resolve this problem. I don't feel about him as I did about his brother, but he is a go-getter and a good talker. Go about your life and try not to fret."

I had wondered about her union with Bishop McNeill. They saw little of each other since she'd moved to the canyon. She was polite to her two co-wives, Phoebe and Lissie, but not friendly. "I'd rather spend what little spare time I have reading a good book than blathering," I'd heard her say when asked why she didn't attend more of the women's church meetings.

When we arrived at our place, she said, "I'll visit your mother soon. Does she like to read? I recently received my annual shipment of Family Library Books. What should I bring her?"

"She loves poetry. She'd enjoy getting to know you. Do you have any books about nursing the sick and caring for injuries? I feel helpless when one of my brothers is sick and I don't know what to do for him."

A week later Bishop McNeill left for Salt Lake City. Now that the railroads had connected with each other, his trip would take only a week instead of several months. Someday I'd like to ride on a train that ate up the miles as hungrily as a starving coyote gobbles a chicken.

Grandma Burntwater returned to her daughter's, the potato plants flourished, rain fell when it was needed, mother's leg healed and Aunt Mary Jane visited. She brought books about caring for the sick and wounded and poetry. It was easier for Tom's mother to get away since Jennie was home for the summer. She was very large and looked forward to the birth of her fifth child.

She said to Mother, "This will be my last baby. I won't have relations with any man ever again."

"How can you avoid it? James is your husband and surely he'll expect you to accommodate him," Mother said.

"I loved my first husband Thomas, James' older brother. We were sealed in the temple. I married James to provide for Tom and Jennie and because the church said it was a good thing to do. I don't love James. With Tom's help, I provide very well for my children," Aunt Mary Jane explained.

Mother went on, "What do you think of plural marriage? Henry says he isn't interested as I am a handful by myself. Sometimes I think it would be nice to have another woman to help with the work. I have depended on Mary so much that she hasn't had a childhood."

"Plural marriages work sometimes, but it isn't for me. A big problem develops when there are no young women left for the young men. Mary is a good girl. With her experience and her caring nature she'll make some man a fine wife. I hope Tom will find a girl half as suitable when the time comes for him to marry. I'm feeling crampy, so had better head home. The walk will do me good. Maybe my time is near."

When I heard Tom's mother praise me, I blushed and felt hot. My feelings for Tom perplexed me. I didn't understand why hearing his name or being around him affected me in such a strange way.

The next day, with the help of Sister Emma C, Tom's mother delivered a baby boy. They named him Henry Ballard and called him H B.

I fretted about the land problem, and one evening after supper, I asked Father, "I thought Ramah was so far away from anything that no one would ever want this land but us. What's going to happen if we have to move?"

"We were sent to settle places no one else wanted. That's why Brigham Young chose to bring the faithful to Utah. He thought it was so isolated that outsiders would leave us alone. He hoped to establish our own country of Deseret. But the Gentiles kept passing through and our people traded with them. The railroads were determined to cross the country come hell or high water. The dream of a separate country was abandoned.

"We were told to sell all we had and come south to spread the gospel of the church to the natives and to settle these isolated lands before they were taken by the Gentiles. The officials in Salt Lake City must help us in this dispute with the Cattle Company or they will have many homeless, faithful families on their conscience. Bishop McNeill will return in a few weeks with news. In the meantime all we can do is cultivate the potatoes and garden, pray that Elizabeth stays well and hope to hear from Lester."

I said, "Lester's been gone so much that I don't miss him. I know Mother worries. He doesn't care about us, why should we worry about him?"

"Lester's our first child. A good parent cares about all their children just as God cares about his people. Remember the story about Jesus looking for the one lost lamb?"

"That's all right in a story, but real life is different. When I have a family, I'll make sure they do things the right way. None of them will run away or leave the ways of the church the way Lester has."

"I pray you're right, Mary. Only time will tell and life has a way of sneaking up on us, giving us a swift kick in the pants now and then." Father laughed and gave me a hug. "Time for bed. Early day tomorrow. Reuben and I are going to harvest potatoes."

In July Bishop McNeill returned with good news. The authorities loaned the village $7,000 to pay the Cebolla Cattle Company. President Woodruff sent a message to us that was read at services. He cautioned that he expected families to stay in Ramah and make good on the loan. Some settlers who were ready to give up and leave were distressed by this "sentence in Hell."

Ramah isn't Hell. It's too cold most of the time.

Our potato crop was doing well and Father and Reuben regularly took a wagon load to Fort Wingate. They returned with cash and provisions we were unable to provide for ourselves. Families who'd planted wheat suffered a grasshopper disaster. The hordes flew in at mid August, just as harvesting approached. We spent days stomping on, burning piles of gathered hoppers and being vigilant not to allow any in the house. They'd eat the clothes right off your back. Wheat fields were destroyed while our potatoes were spared. For some reason they didn't like potato plants. Tom's family was all right as they made money from dairy products. They did have to take their cows higher up the canyon to graze and their supply of hay for the winter would be sparse.

A committee was formed to find ways to repay the loan. It was named "The Ramah Land Purchase Pay Off" and all proceeds from sponsored events went into that fund. An outdoor dance, bonfire and box supper was planned for the first of September. Tom shyly asked if he could escort me to the festivities. It was the rule of the church that all dances be held under their supervision, private parties were discouraged. There was concern among the leaders that several young women had recently married outside the church. The nearby cattle companies not only had tried to take Ramah's land, but their cowboys were rustling the future mothers of the faithful. Efforts to convert the cowboys had proven lackluster.

Mother altered one of her dresses so I would have a nice frock to wear. I prepared a box of fried chicken, baked beans, fresh tomatoes and sugar cookies. I decorated the box with a piece of plaid fabric from our old curtains. Tom knew which box to bid on.

That afternoon I bathed, washed and curled my long brown hair. I was in a tizzy. I was almost twelve years old and this was the first time I would go to an affair with an escort who was not one of my brothers. I waited eagerly for Tom to come. All day my goofy brothers teased me about my first date.

"Tom's courting Mary! Tom's courting Mary!" they chanted. "Are you going to let him kiss you? Will it be your first kiss? K-I-S-S-I-N-G, Tom and Mary sittin' under a tree!"

"Mother, make them stop," I wailed.

"Henry, take these boys out for a wagon ride and don't come back before seven. Go to the lake and let them swim off their energy," Mother instructed.

"Why don't they tease Reuben? He's taking Betsy Tietjen to the party and they don't poke fun at him," I said.

"You're their only sister, Mary. They love you and I think they're a little jealous of Tom," Mother said. "Maybe that will change next spring." I was in such a dither that it wasn't until days later that I remembered what Mother had said.

Tom looked handsome when he came for me. He wore a clean plaid shirt, blue jeans with a wide leather belt and polished cowboy boots. His red hair was neatly trimmed. He doffed his new straw hat, "Good evening, Miss Mary! May I help you into our carriage?"

I put my boxed supper under the seat and took the hand he offered to help me up. I was suddenly shy and could think of nothing to say so I smiled as I settled my long skirt around my legs.

"Cat got your tongue?" he asked.

"No, I just feel different tonight. Did your mother make your new hat?" Aunt Mary Jane was a hat maker and knew how to weave any kind of dried straw into fancy or plain hats.

"Yes, she finished it this afternoon. You undid your braids. First time I've seen it down. Looks soft and floaty around your face."

"Thank you. It's so plain and brown. I wish it was the color of yours," I mumbled.

"Wouldn't do to have two redheads in one family. Too much Scot temper to contend with."

Tom had to bid higher and higher to buy my box. Peter Ashcroft kept in the bidding until it reached two dollars. That was a lot of money and I was surprised that Peter even knew who I was. He was a year older than Tom and worked at the sawmill.

Tom bought my box for two dollars and twenty-five cents and we went to the picnic tables under the trees to eat. Lemonade, water and ice cream were served. Some cowboys came, which created a stir but they were welcomed and joined in the bidding. The loan committee was glad to take their money. Young and old alike enjoyed the evening picnic. It was a chance to visit folks we didn't often see.

As dusk deepened, a large pile of scrap lumber, dead tree limbs and other assorted wood that had been gathered was piled in the middle of the road for the bonfire. Four men rolled the piano from the church. Brother Bond tuned up his fiddle. Brother Lewis wiped his mouth with a white kerchief and blew on his mouth organ. All was ready for the dance to begin.

Round dancing was not allowed as it promoted wanton thoughts in the minds and bodies of the young. The elders didn't notice that while most were enjoying vigorous square and folk dances, some couples were busy in the shadows of the trees across the street promoting wanton thoughts on their own.

Tom and I danced with each other and changed partners when the call was given. This was also a way to keep couples from getting too familiar. I didn't lack for partners and I enjoyed them all. Eventually, I needed a break and went to the refreshment table for a glass of lemonade. While I listened to the music and watched the colors whirl in the firelight, Peter Ashcroft walked by.

"Mary, sorry I couldn't buy your box. Tom was determined to have supper with you. I knew he'd just keep outbidding me, so I ran the price up! We need to talk. I have a message from Lester."

I don't want Lester butting in and spoiling this evening.

I smiled and said, "Really? How nice. What a surprise. We've wondered when we'd hear from him."

"He told me to tell you. Whether you tell your parents is up to you. He knows he caused anger and grief, but he had to do it. Pat Traynor offered him a chance of a lifetime to experience the real Wild West. The kind of west he'd read about in books at the sheep ranch at Concho, about outlaws, train robbers and exciting escapes from the law," Peter said.

I was angrier than ever at my stupid brother.

He wants the real Wild West? What did he think we're living in? The west is about settlers, ranchers and daily living more than outlaws.

"Lester said he and Pat Traynor were headed north to the canyon lands of eastern Utah where they'd hook up with a gang of Mormon boys who specialize in polite train robberies. He'll write or come home when he's had his taste of the wild life."

"If he comes home it'll probably be because he's had his horse shot out from under him, been wounded or is starving. How can any person be so stupid? He doesn't have the sense God gave a goose," I said.

"Don't blame me, I'm just the messenger. Want to dance?" Peter asked.

"Not now. I need a chance to cool off. Think I'll sit down over by the trees. If you see Tom will you tell him where I am?"

I was hot inside and out. My mind churned and I felt sick to my stomach.

What right does my brother have to send his tale to me and make me be the one to decide who to tell?

The happy sounds of the music and the whoops and claps of the dancers collided with my feelings of anger and frustration. I took some deep breaths, dipped my hanky in a glass of water and wiped my face.

"What's the matter?" Tom asked as he sat beside me. "Aren't you having a good time?"

I leaned my head on his shoulder as he put his arm around my waist. He felt solid and down to earth. He'd never run away to become an outlaw. I sighed and Tom kissed me on the forehead.

"What's wrong? Are you going to tell me? Is there anything I can do for you?"

"I need a few minutes to collect my wits. There's nothing to be done. I'll be all right."

I won't let Lester ruin this night.

The music and the fire beckoned. I stood, took Tom by the hand and returned to the dance.

On the drive home, I shivered under my lightweight shawl. "Brrr, I feel fall in the air. Did you see those people standing back in the trees across from the church? I saw them dancing but I don't know who they were."

"Scoot over here next to me," Tom said. He held the reins of the team in both hands. "I'd put my arm around you, but that's risky in the dark. Need to keep tight reins on the team. Never know what might spook the horses. I've heard mountain lions screaming lately. Yes, I saw some Navajos in the shadows. They come to enjoy the music. I think they were some of Ghosea Spino's bunch."

"I wonder who this land really belongs to. They were here before the railroads, before the ranchers and now we've moved in. Do you think they hate us and wish we'd all go back to where we came from?" I asked.

"They resent us, but where would we go? Times are changing and we're caught in it. We need to learn more about the natives and try not to trample their way of life. Shingle Head's teaching me to speak Navajo and I help him with English. It helps if you can talk to them and explain why you're mad when their cows eat up half your field of corn or trample your young apple trees."

We rode in silence the rest of the way. Tom stopped the team, helped me down and walked me to the door. Both of us were struck by the bashfuls. Tom didn't know whether to shake my hand or kiss me on the mouth. I solved our dilemma by giving him a quick hug, opening the door and saying, "I had a good time. Thanks, Tom."

By morning I felt awful. My gut cramped, my head ached and I wanted to lie in bed and cry all day. When I got up I found blood on my nighty and realized I had become a woman. Mother helped me with some of her monthly cloths and I felt better after I moved around.

"So, my daughter, you've come of age. I've been expecting it. You've grown up a lot these past months and you'll be twelve next month. In another three years it will be time to think of finding a good husband for you."

"I wish I'd been born a boy," I wailed. "I don't want to mess with this every month. Boys have it all. They go to school, work outside, be what they want when they grow up and don't have to have babies."

"Now, now," Mother tried to calm me. "Do your chores and go with Sister McNeill to gather material for hats. Do you good to get away. Someday you'll learn men and boys don't have it as easy as you think."

I'd decided it would do no good to tell my parents about Lester. There was nothing they could do. Mother seemed happy and I didn't want to tilt the wagon. Thus, I began my role as a keeper of secrets.

Reuben and Jennie returned to St. Johns to attend fall session at the Academy. I stopped going to classes in Ramah. I was too old for the school. Reuben had brought me some school books and I studied them every evening. Days grew shorter, the wind had a bite to it and winter crept closer each week. We had an ample supply of bottled fruits, vegetables and meat, a bin full of potatoes in the cellar and plenty of flour in the large lidded tins in the pantry. It had been many years since we'd been so well prepared for winter.

Many other villagers weren't as fortunate. Every week at services a call was voiced for this family or the other who needed help. Father gave what we could spare while giving thanks that he'd planted potatoes instead of wheat.

One evening in October, Mother and Father told us we would have a new brother or sister next summer. It would be their ninth child.

In late November, we received a letter from Hattie. She'd delivered a healthy baby boy named Henry Lucas. She said she was happy and liked Bluewater. She wished we could come visit in the spring. That was the first part of the letter. The next part burned into my mind and I've never forgotten it.

"We had a bit of excitement in Bluewater last month. The train from Albuquerque was carrying the payroll for Fort Wingate and railroad workers in California. The men are paid in gold coin and greenbacks so there was a lot of cash aboard.

"East of Bluewater is an area called the Malapais, Spanish for bad rocks. Years ago there was a volcanic eruption near here and the sharp black rocks give the area its name. It has always been a maze of secret trails and caves for outlaws. A gang of bandits waited for the train to slow down as it started the climb westward toward the continental divide. According to what we heard, three men stormed the engine and stopped the train, while three others shot their way in to the payroll car.

"They got away with thirty-thousand dollars, injured two postal employees and in the darkness disappeared into the Malapais. Some sheep men think they saw the robbers the next day beyond Mt. Taylor riding hell bent for leather toward Colorado.

"One man was dressed in black and rode a black horse. It sounded like the sheepherder was describing the man who stayed in your barn last spring. Whatever became of him?" Hattie asked.

Mother turned as pale as an unbaked loaf of bread, cried out "My God, what has happened to my boy? Will I ever see him again?"

Her eyes rolled, she moaned, swooned and crumpled to the floor.

Chapter Twenty-Three

Ramah, New Mexico Territory, Winter, Spring, Summer 1889-1890

Mother spent three days in bed while winter blew in on a snowstorm. I was trapped by the weather and my family's demands. After recovering, Mother said, "I've made a decision. I must let Lester go. Whatever happens is of his choosing. I carry a new life and I'm positive it's a girl. I shouldn't neglect those I have by agonizing over the one who's gone. I've given Lester back to God."

Father made snowshoes for us so we could exercise in the fresh air and visit our neighbors. He and William shoveled paths to the barn and outhouse.

A friendship flowered between Mother and Aunt Mary Jane from the seedbed of their love of reading. They met once a week to share poems and stories from favorite books. One December day, Mother invited me to go to the McNeill's for their "Ladies Literary Society" meeting. Leaving Father in charge of the boys, we left in high spirits. The Society was so exclusive that it had only two members. Most town ladies were active in the Women's Relief Society and had no interest or time to read or discuss books. Besides, the officials of the church had issued a statement condemning "private gatherings."

Mother and Aunt Mary Jane occasionally went to the Society's programs concerning childcare, food preparation and preservation and devotionals. Mother needed more. "My brain needs feeding as much as my body and soul.

At times, I feel my mind is suffering a drought."

I thought them daring and brave to start a book club. I was flattered at being asked to join them and took one of Reuben's history books to share. Aunt Mary Jane was reading the history of the ancient world by Josephus and she shared things she'd learned about the Jewish people. I read a page in the history book about Colonial America and how the first English settlers got along with the Indians. Mother shared a poem.

When the afternoon was over, I felt very grownup. Mother and I bundled up, strapped on our snow shoes and started for home. As we walked along the snow covered road, I sniffed and said, "Mother, Something's burning."

"Look beyond our place, Mary. Is that a red glow towards the Tietjens?"

"Yes, and the church bell is ringing."

We arrived at our door as Father rushed out. " Fire at the Tietjens. Be back when it's out."

He returned tired, disheveled, smelling of smoke, with black smudges on his face, hands and clothing. "Fix me a cup of tea, Elizabeth. I'm half frozen and must get out of these sodden clothes before I tell you what's happened."

Later, he sat near the fireplace with a cup in his hand. "A tragedy has befallen the Tietjens. This afternoon Amanda Tietjen stepped into her yard for a brief walk. She'd been housebound and needed to be outside for a few minutes.

"The older children were in school. Two-year-old Sarah was napping. When Amanda walked back to the front of the house, flames were shooting from the front windows and smoke billowed from the roof. She cried, "FIRE! FIRE!" and Ernest, who was visiting at Emma C's place, came running. He broke in the back door and charged up the stairs to rescue Sarah. Others formed a bucket brigade and threw snow on the burning house. Two men held Amanda when she tried to run into the house."

We held our breath as Father continued. Fire was a constant danger. We could not survive without it but, when out of control, it was disaster. "Ernest found Sarah, without a burn on her. The smoke had killed her. The distraught father carried her out just before the roof fell in. The house is gone and Amanda is crazed with grief. They think a spark from the fireplace ignited some quilt pieces that lay nearby on the floor."

Services for Sarah were held three days later. Tom had built a large sled and he and his family came by for us. If it hadn't been such a sad occasion it would have been great fun riding smoothly between the snow covered trees, watching the sparkling snow diamonds that covered the ground.

Burial would be delayed until the spring thaw. In the meantime Sarah, in her little coffin, rested in the cold storage building back of McNeill's store. It had thick rock walls and was built into the side of a hill in order to keep milk, cheese and eggs cool in the summer. It was a safe place to hang frozen meat in the winter. Hunters stored their kills there to protect them from wild animals. Bears hibernated in the winter, but mountain lions prowled year round.

Another tragedy struck in February. It was only because we lived a distance from the village and had sufficient supplies that none of us got smallpox.

Relatives of the Pipken and Lewis families arrived from Arkansas in late January. They'd been traveling for three months and planned to settle in Ramah. They stopped near Albuquerque for two days while Mrs. Pipken gave birth. They gratefully accepted the use of a house that had recently been vacated by a family moving back to Utah. What they didn't know was that the family had died of or had become ill with smallpox by the time they reached the San Juan River.

The Pipkens and two families with them had been eagerly awaited and preparations had been made to welcome them. Instead of joy they brought death to Ramah.

We learned of this when Father came from a Priesthood meeting and said, "You will not go to town until I say so. Hopefully, we are far enough away to avoid catching smallpox. No one knows how it is spread, but being around someone who has it is a sure path to the grave.

"The Navajos near Grandma Burntwater's daughter have a full blown epidemic. The Pipken group stopped there for a day to water their stock. Several of their party were not well, but no one realized they had smallpox.

"Three Indians tried to prevent the emigrants from using water at the spring. They almost came to blows. The Navajos relented when Brother Pipken offered blankets in exchange for water. The Navajos left warm and happy, wrapped in their deadly blankets."

"Did you hear of Grandma Burntwater?" I asked fearfully.

"No. A cowboy who came in for supplies told Bishop McNeill he saw many empty hogans, families on the move and a pervasive outlook of despair. Navajos won't stay in a hogan after a death. Has to do with their beliefs about death. They pack up and move as soon as they bury the dead. They are so afraid of ghosts related to death that one of the greatest favors we can do for a Navajo is to bury their dead."

For a month, we isolated ourselves from Ramah. Father said we could visit with Tom's family because they weren't going into town either. He went to church once a week to hear the latest news.

Whenever Father returned, Mother made him undress in the barn, bathe himself and put on clean clothes before she'd let him in the house. She said she'd prefer to burn his clothes, but since he didn't have many, she picked them up with a stick and boiled them in hot vinegar water before washing them. We learned fourteen additional coffins were stored at McNeill's. Since the population of Ramah was only one-hundred and thirty three the losses were sorely felt.

One afternoon while Aunt Mary Jane was at our place for a meeting of the book club, Bishop McNeill rode into the yard. Father went to greet him, stopping a few yards short.

"What can I do for you, Bishop? I can't let you into the house for fear of contagion."

I had opened the front door and heard, "I need to talk to my wife, Mary Jane. Tom says she's here."

Aunt Mary Jane came to the door and they talked across the yard. "Phoebe and the twins are sick. Lissie and our baby Jamie, have died. You must come and care for what's left of my family. It is your duty."

"If I come, I risk losing my family. We are safe. Thank goodness Jennie is in St. Johns. I'm sorry about Lissie and the babe. I will not, in good conscience and common sense, go with you. You haven't been concerned about us until now when you need help. I'll keep you in my prayers. The children will pray for you and Phoebe," she said firmly.

I saw the determined set of her jaw, the glint of resolve in her eyes and was stunned by what she said. I had never heard a wife defy her husband in such a strong way. I looked at Father. His face was red with embarrassment. For once he was speechless. Mother sat in her rocker. Her white knuckled hands gripped the arms of the chair.

"When this is over, you and I are going to have a talk," the Bishop said as he mounted his horse and whipped it into a gallop.

Aunt Mary Jane closed the door, gathered her things and prepared to leave. "Well, I guess the meeting is over for this week. See you next week at my place," she said as she walked serenely down the front steps. "Mary, Tom asked me to tell you he'd be by after supper to go for a walk."

I am shocked while she's as calm as a biddy on a nest of eggs. How can grownups do that? In the blink of an eye they change from one person to another. One minute they're furious and the next they are sweet and smiley. It seems to depend on who they're speaking to.

The weather warmed, the ground thawed and graves dug. It was with a sigh of relief that the dear departed were buried. Two weeks later another grave was prepared. Amanda Tietjen, Sarah's mother, had dwindled away. After the fire, all she wanted was to join Sarah.

The folks from Arkansas were hard working people who quickly blended into Ramah. No one was openly angry or resentful toward them for bringing smallpox. Families who'd suffered losses grieved, but accepted the deaths as a risk of life.

I wondered if the man who'd helped Lester home from Becker Lake was any relation to these new Pipkens. One Sunday I asked Annie Pipken, "Are you any relation to a man named Pip Pipken?"

"Well," she drawled, (all of the new settlers drawled when they spoke) "he's my father's cousin. His real first name is Asa. We don't talk about him. What do you know about him? I heard he stole money from the government."

I told her the story of how he'd brought Lester home and spent the night with us. "We liked him. He's not been in Ramah since he was banned from the church."

That night before I fell asleep, I thought about Pip Pipken. He seemed like a nice man. Whatever made him steal money from his job? Where was he now? He was another mystery.

In early April, Reuben and Jennie came home for the summer. Father had had such success with the potatoes the previous summer that he and Reuben plowed and prepared another field in order to plant twice as many. William, Roy, and for the first time, Richard, were added to the work force. Father taught them how to plant, weed and hill the growing plants.

I had my regular chores, caring for Parley and Ezra and trying to ease Mother's burden as the time for her delivery drew near. Meetings of the Literary Society were put on hold for the summer. I missed them. I had come to look forward to them as much, if not more so, than Mother.

Tom often brought me a new book from his mother's shelf. She had a standing order from a book publisher and every six months a new selection arrived. The publisher chose the books. It was like Christmas when she received a crate from the Frontier Family Library.

Tom liked books about prehistoric fossils, lost treasures and daring explorers who risked life and limb to discover unknown tribes in remote parts of the world. I liked stories about English history, Indian tribes in the United States and women who worked hard and went against society to become doctors, writers or politicians.

When we walked through the long soft summer evenings, we talked about faraway lost worlds, people we'd read about and admired, what we wished we could do with our lives and now and then, Tom hinted about a future we might share.

One time he took me to a low hill near the lake. "This would be a nice place for a house. How do you like the view from here? This is part of Mother's homestead. When I'm twenty-one, I plan to claim the adjoining acres that go into those wooded hills. Lots of good timber up there."

I thought he was daydreaming. I said, "Great place for a home. Give me that stick and I'll draw a floor plan. How big of a mansion will you build? Will it have a tower for your princess to sit in while she eats candy and orders her servants around? Over here, you can put a glassed in room so she can have fresh fruits and vegetables year round."

Tom was silent while he watched me make a fool of myself. He wasn't laughing at my foolery. I saw the blush on his face and confusion in his eyes. He had been serious and I had hurt his feelings.

I threw down the stick, took his hand and said, "It will make a lovely place for a home—no matter who you choose as your princess."

He escorted me home in silence, kissed me on the cheek and murmured, "You are a princess. You just don't know it yet."

By mid June, Mother was so big that we teased her about giving birth to an elephant. All was in readiness for the birth. Emma O and Aunt Mary Jane planned to attend the "Birthday Party." Mother spent most of her time pacing the floor. She could sit for mere minutes at a time, lie down and sleep for only an hour or so and was miserable.

"I've never had a pregnancy like this. Usually, I keep going until the pains start, but this child has taken the starch out of me. Sure wish my time would come," she moaned.

"Aunt Mary Jane says she thinks you're going to have twins. Do twins run in our family?" I asked.

"Good heavens, I hope not. I don't remember any in my family but there may be some on Henry's side. Twins are so little that they need special care. At least it's warm weather. Babies born in the fall or winter have a harder time of it than those born in spring or summer."

240

Father brought her chair from the house and put it under a tree in the yard. I brought a cup of tea. She watched a pair of robins feeding their young in a nearby nest.

"It's my favorite time of year. Spring and early summer are full of possibilities. Remember, Mary, no matter what kind of predicament you find yourself in, there are always possibilities. I was only fourteen when I married, and my knowledge of the world was so limited that I didn't realize there might have been another way.

"My mother, Mary, who you're named after, wasn't married until she was nineteen. She worked in the mine superintendent's house. Her Father had died, leaving her mother with eight little ones to raise and they needed the pittance she earned. After she married, her younger sister took her job.

"She wanted me to wait until I was sixteen, but I was in love with your tall handsome father. He was twenty-one and I thought if I put him off some other girl would set her cap for him. He told me he stayed single for so long because he was waiting for the right girl. Lester was born a year later. I sometimes wish I had not been so smitten and had waited a few years before I married and started having babies."

It was the first time Mother talked to me about her feelings for Father. *How will she feel when I decide to marry? Will I listen to her advice?*

The summer rains came on July the first. The last two weeks of June had been miserably hot. The clear, blue skies had mocked us as we scanned the horizon each day for signs of thunderclouds. It was so dry that plants and people drooped by noon. Our vegetable garden wasn't on the irrigation ditch, so I carried water from the main ditch to keep everything from burning up. Father's efforts went into the potato fields.

Mother's discomfort grew. She'd stopped eating, but drank a lot of water. Her feet and legs swelled and she couldn't get out of her chair by herself.

At noon on July first, I heard the distant rumble of thunder. I ran to the door and looked toward the mountains. A puffy white cloud billowed and grew. A gust of wind brought the scent of rain. I hoped for rain, not hail. I helped Mother in from the yard and we watched at the window. Cooling breezes blew the white feed sack curtains as we laughed with delight at the end of the heat.

That first storm didn't bring us much moisture, but we all felt better. We received blessed rain each afternoon for the next couple of days. Father was happy, I was hopeful and Mother was resigned.

"If I stop thinking about this child, it may decide to make its appearance," she said. "Mary, bring me the new book of poetry that Mary Jane brought. Maybe it will take my mind off my misery."

During the wee hours of the morning on the Fourth of July, Father woke me saying, "I've sent Reuben for Emma O. Fetch Sister Mary Jane. Mother's time has come."

I ran through the predawn darkness, praying I wouldn't encounter a bear or a lion. I carried a big stick. The moon was full so the road was easy to see. I heard lots of rustling in the bushes, but if there were animals they were probably trying to get away from me.

I banged on the McNeill's door. "I thought this might be the day. My bag is packed and I'm dressed. Just have to pull on my shoes," Aunt Mary Jane said.

Tom looked half asleep as he came from his room. His red hair stood on end, his eyes were puffy and his nightshirt was rumpled and twisted above his knees. I had never seen him that way and thought he looked like a little boy. I had the urge to hug him, but his mother was ready to go.

"Tom, you and Jennie know what to do. Don't know when I'll be home. Goodbye." She took my arm and pulled me outside.

By seven o'clock, Father and the older boys had eaten breakfast and gone to work in the fields. After I did the dishes and swept the floor, Parley, Ezra and I went to the barn to milk our two cows and feed the pigs and chickens. We had a beautiful cream and white Buff Orpington rooster and a large, honking, male Toulouse goose, both of which hated everyone. I gave a stick to Parley and told him to keep the birds away from Ezra. The rooster and the goose patrolled what they reckoned was their territory and didn't hesitate to attack anyone who crossed the line. The path from the back door to the outhouse was their special ambush location. That's why we kept a big stick by the back door.

Actually, I wished Parley would give that Buff Orpington such a whack that he'd kill it and then I'd make stew out of him. On that day, both birds were off in the field or down by the lake and Parley didn't get to smack either one.

I had dinner on the table when the farmers came in from work. "Any news?" Father asked.

We could hear Mother's moans and an occasional shriek, Emma O's reassurances and Aunt Mary Jane's encouraging "That's the way! Now relax and wait for the next one!"

The older boys gulped their soup and scurried back outside. I put Parley to washing the dishes while I got Ezra down for a nap. Father went into the bedroom to see how things were progressing.

Shortly after he went in I heard a mewling cry and a hoot from Father. "Finally another girl! Look at all that black hair. She's a good size, but not as big as I thought she'd be considering how big you were."

Parley and I stopped and went to peek through the partially open door. I heard Emma O say, "That's not all. Here's her twin sister!"

Aunt Mary Jane ordered, "Henry, get out of here. You're in the way. Wait in the kitchen, we'll call you when things are under control."

Father beamed at Parley and I. "Mary, you finally have not just one sister, but two! No wonder Elizabeth was so large."

An hour later Father, Parley and I were invited into the bedroom. Mother looked pale and worn-out, but she smiled at me and said, "I finally did it. Two of them at one time—born on the Fourth of July. Now you have two sisters, Mary. They'll always have a big birthday party!"

They were little, red, wrinkled prunes. One had thick black hair, the other sparse blonde wisps. I knew that in a week they'd look better, so I made no comment about their appearance.

Aunt Mary Jane said, "I'm going to spend the night. Elizabeth is weak and weary. She may need help during the night. I want to be here for her. Emma O is going home to her family and will check back tomorrow. Mary, go tell Tom and Roxie I'll be here until tomorrow. They can manage with out me. Henry, you must make a cradle for the second baby."

Father and I left the room. "She sure can be bossy, can't she? Always speaks her mind and doesn't hesitate to tell others what to do."

I answered, "At least you know what she's saying. Makes no bones about things and doesn't make you guess what she means. I like that."

"Doesn't seem quite womanly to me. She's usually right, but she's too forward for my taste."

Mother recovered quickly from Emily and Anne's birthing. Both babies thrived and Mother had plenty of milk for both.

"I know Emily is Father's mother's name but where did you get Anne?" I asked Mother.

"Anne Ewan was my great grandmother's name. She was from Wales. I never knew her, she was long dead by the time I came along, but I remember my mother speaking of her grandmother, Anne Ewan. She wrote poems and songs and played the harp. I wish I had known her."

The summer moved into August and Father was worried. The potatoes weren't growing like they should. We had plenty of rain but the plants weren't thriving. The few potatoes he'd dug up were soft and mushy. What was wrong? He asked Brother Bond to come with his Farmer's Handbook. If the potatoes failed, we had little to fall back on. I had a nice vegetable garden but not enough to preserve for winter. We needed cash to buy staples.

When Father and Brother Bond returned from the field, they brought leaves to compare with the drawings in the book. The leaves had black mold growing on their undersides.

"Here it is, on page thirty-two," Brother Bond said. "Looks like Potato Blight. The mold drops from the leaves onto the soil and is washed down to the potatoes and turns them to mush."

"What can I do about it? What caused it?"

"Says it's caused by too much moisture. We've had a surfeit of rain and that's been good for the wheat and fruit trees, but bad for potatoes. Have to plow them under. Can't plant potatoes in that ground until after a couple of dry years. It's the blight that caused the famine in Ireland in the forties. Sorry, Henry."

Father took his hat from the peg by the door and walked out with Brother Bond. I heard him riding towards town. He was gone for two days. When he returned he stank like Coronado's Cantina.

Chapter Twenty-Four

Ramah, New Mexico Territory, Summer, Fall, Winter 1890-1891

Father's eyes were bloodshot, his hair and beard tangled, his clothes stank of sweat and vomit. Mother said, "Get into the bedroom and take off those filthy things. I'll ask Mary to prepare a bath. I should send you to the barn so you can enjoy your stink and headache by yourself."

He stumbled to their room, mumbling, "Never have I been so disgusted or disappointed in anyone like I am with myself. Sorry. The new saloon on the road to Zuni was my undoing."

"We'll discuss it later," Mother said, slamming the door behind him.

For the next week she refused to speak to him. The weather was nice with refreshing afternoon showers. The twins were healthy and fussed only when hungry. The potatoes rotted in the field. Their stench filled the air. Earnest Tietjen asked Father, "When do you aim to plow those stinking things into the ground?"

Father grinned, "Well, thought I'd let them dry before plowing them under. The worst is over. Can you stand the stink for a few days?"

"Hmmph!" Brother Tietjen replied. "Can't sit under my trees in the evening without smelling what I'd swear was a percolating still. Do you need help? I'll send my boys when you're ready to plow."

The odor took on a distinctly tangy essence. Were the fields fermenting?

The aroma reminded me of father when he'd returned from his jaunt. From then on, whenever I got a whiff of a rotten potato, I'd be in Ramah in the summer of 1890.

Father answered, "Reuben and I are leaving. When we return, we'll plow. I need cash for winter, so we've taken jobs at the sawmill. They've installed a steam boiler hoping to raise their output."

The tension eased after they left. "Will Reuben go to the Academy in September?" I asked Mother.

"Not this year. With Lester gone, the potatoes rotting in the field and no cash on hand, it's going to be a rough winter. We need Reuben here."

Tom and I continued our evening walks. He told me of the Pipken's troubles. "Do you know Abigail's older sister, Eve? She's married to Ebenezer Jones. They have two children."

"I met her one Sunday. She had a bruise on her cheek. Said she'd knocked a can of lard off the shelf. She's a pretty blonde with brown eyes. Her husband scares me though. Has a strange look about him."

The first time I saw Brother Jones was at a spring funeral. He was tall, loose limbed with long black hair. His eyes were so black that his pupils weren't visible. I felt uncomfortable when he looked at me. Abigail told me his grandmother was Cherokee. He's from Alabama and met Eve Pipken when he took a job with a freighting outfit that hauls cotton to the ports along the Gulf of Mexico. Eve was visiting her aunt in New Orleans and her uncle had business with the freight outfit. The freighters carried more than cotton. Hidden in the wagons was untaxed, top quality moonshine from the stills of Northern Alabama. It was in demand along the Mississippi River. Eve's uncle traded in legal and illegal spirits.

Eve and Eb fell in love and returned to Eve's home in Arkansas to marry. The Pipkens weren't happy with their son-in-law, but since the couple was expecting a child there wasn't much they could do about it.

"Why did you ask if I know Eve?"

"She's leaving her husband. After he's been to the saloon he beats her and roughs up the kids. He's not a church member and the Pipkens would be glad to see him go back to Alabama. They've decided to send Eve and her two children to Snowflake to Sister Pipken's family. Eve's brother, Polk, is going to take them. His friend, Hank Lewis, will go and help bring the wagon and team back."

"How sad. Why would any man beat his wife? Would you ever do something like that?"

"Alcohol does cruel things to people. Changes them. I have a temper, but don't think I'd ever hit a woman. Sometimes I get hot under the collar at Jenny, but then I get away for a while. A ride into the hills is good for my soul and temper. Any woman who marries me will have to put up with my jaunts into the wilderness, but that's better than hurting someone I love," Tom replied.

Father and Reuben came home from the mountain because the steam boiler blew up and the mill was shut for repairs. With help from the Tietjen boys they plowed the potatoes under.

By the middle of August it was still hot during the day, but early in the morning, I could feel autumn in the air. The sunlight was softer and leaves on the Aspens high on the mountain were turning. The sun moved south and shone through our front window at a different angle.

Soon after plowing the field, Father and Reuben received word the boiler was working. They hurried back up the mountain to earn as much as they could before the mill shut down for the winter.

Early one morning, I heard a horse galloping towards McNeill's. I didn't pay any attention but when, a short time later, I heard two horses going lickety split towards town, I looked to see who was in such a hurry. I saw Tom on his bay horse, Baldy, and Lars Tietjen on his black horse, Licorice, racing towards town.

I hoped Tom would come later in the day and tell us what was going on. Evening came, but Tom didn't. We spread our supper on a blanket under a tree and had a picnic. It was calm and pleasant at that time of day. I helped Parley, Ezra and Richard catch lightening bugs in jars.

William and Roy practiced throwing their pocketknives in a game they called mumbly peg. They drew a circle in the dirt and with the handle of their knife, drove a wooden peg into the dirt in the middle of the circle. They took turns flipping their knives into the circle. If a knife didn't land blade down and stick upright in the dirt the other player got to drive the peg further into the dirt. He got to hit the peg once and the loser had to pull the peg out with his teeth. They had great fun. Both ended with dirty faces.

The next morning Aunt Mary Jane visited Mother. "Tom didn't come home last night. I didn't want him to go, but he didn't want to miss the excitement. Have you heard what happened to Polk Pipken?" she asked.

"Haven't heard anything. Given that Henry's not here I don't get news unless I go to town. Is something wrong?" Mother asked.

"I know only the bare details. Lars Tietjen came early yesterday to fetch Tom to join a posse to find Eb Jones. While Tom saddled Baldy, Lars told me what he knew. The Pipken boy and his friend, Hank Lewis, helped Eve pack a wagon with her things; a bedstead, a sewing machine and two trunks. They left for Snowflake about noon. Polk was driving the team, with Hank riding alongside the wagon. A mile beyond the saloon, Eb was waiting behind the rocks with his rifle. He was liquored up and mad as a newly branded calf because his wife was leaving. He killed Polk then took off toward Zuni.

"Hank laid Polk's body in the bed of the wagon with his weeping sister and her children. He drove back to the saloon and left them in care of the owner's wife while he hightailed it for town. When Brother Pipken learned of his son's death he went to the saloon to get his family. He brought his son's body, his distraught daughter, and his grandchildren back to town. It was almost dark by the time they got to Ramah. When Bishop McNeill heard the news he formed a posse."

Mother gasped, "My Heavens! Cold blooded murder! Those poor people have had a time of it with the smallpox and now this. How many men went looking for Eb?"

"When he came for Tom, Lars said they had eight men preparing to ride out. Sure wish we had a sheriff. They have one in St. Johns now, but that's two days away and in Arizona. I'm always afraid a bunch of angry, rankled men will take the law into their own hands and cause even more trouble. I don't want my son starting his adult life as a killer."

"Nothing to do but wait. I hope there are some cool heads in the posse," Mother said.

"My husband has a temper, but he's good at thinking things through and making plans. Lars said that James, Brother Bond and Brother Merrill were leading the hunt. I'd better get home. Baby HB has a bad cold and I want to brew him some Mormon tea. That seems to do more good than anything to break up congestion."

Mother said, "Tom will be all right. We'll keep a listening ear and an open eye out for him. If he stops here we'll tell him you're worried and won't let him dawdle. He and Mary have taken a shine to one another and can shoot the breeze for hours. Wonder if anything will come of that?"

Tom's mother shrugged, hugged Mother and left. I felt tightness in my chest and my hands were cold as ice. Tom on a posse! I knew he could take care of himself on a horse and was a good shot, but accidents happened and a hunted, demented man was dangerous. I said a prayer for the men and the Pipken family.

Around noon, Emma O came to the door. Her eyes were swollen and her nose was red from weeping. "Elizabeth, come and help us prepare Emma C's son Lars and Brother Lewis for burial. It's a senseless calamity caused by that no good Eb Jones. I wish the Pipkens had never come to Ramah."

Mother said, "Mary you're in charge until I return. Keep the boys indoors, don't answer the door unless you know who it is and stay calm. I'll be home as soon as I can."

After they left, I tried to keep busy with the twins and other chores. I couldn't help wondering and worrying about what might have happened. My mind conjured up all kinds of tragedies and stories. Finally, I went upstairs to get my journal. It helped to write down my fears and get them out of my head. Otherwise they chased themselves round and round like a dog after its tail.

Mother returned after supper. I was glad to see her so I could learn what had happened and so she could nurse the hungry twins. She slumped tiredly into her rocker. I handed Emily, who was fussing the loudest, to Mother and busied myself fixing her a cup of tea. I sat beside her and waited to hear the story.

She gathered her thoughts for what seemed an eternity. When I was about to burst, I asked, "Is Tom all right? I've imagined terrible things. Ease my mind."

Mother sighed, blew her nose and began. "Tom's going to be all right. A bullet grazed his head and took the top off his left ear. Got a good scare.

"I don't know details. You'll have to ask Tom. Maybe he can tell the story straight. Everyone was upset about Eb Jones shooting his brother-in-law and on top of that, two of our men were killed. None of it makes sense.

"All I got was that one part of the posse thought they'd spotted Eb Jones on the opposite side of an arroyo and commenced firing. Turned out they were shooting at the other half of their own group. It's so sad, so sad," Mother sobbed.

"How dreadful. Where's Tom now?"

"I suppose he's home by now. There's going to be a meeting at the church as soon as the sheriff from St. Johns arrives. In the meantime, three graves must be dug and services held. I'm glad Henry and Reuben weren't here. They would have been right in the middle of it."

The next weeks were awful. Neighbor avoided neighbor. Former friends didn't speak. The bereaved families blamed themselves and each other. Bishop McNeill was so distraught he couldn't preside over the service for Lars, Polk and Jim. Brother Merrill held the services. Men wore pistols to town, to church and into the fields. The town lamented its loss. The pall of sorrow that hung in the air was as tangible as the stench of potatoes rotting in the field.

I longed to go to Tom and comfort him. Mother said the best thing was stay home and wait for him to come to me. So I waited. I saw him at the funeral from across the room. He had a bandage wrapped around his head and a haunted look in his eyes. He nodded, but didn't smile.

Two days later, Sheriff Upton and two of his deputies arrived. The Stake President, John Udall, came with them and they interviewed all parties involved, including the Pipken family.

Sheriff Upton and President Udall concluded the deaths of Lars and Brother Lewis were accidental, caused by darkness, tension and human error. Bishop McNeill offered to resign, but his offer was refused. President Udall asked him to stay for another year until things calmed down. He also admonished the men for taking the law into their own hands and counseled the members to stop talking about it in front of their children.

Sheriff Upton said they would distribute wanted posters and keep alert for any news of Eb Jones. He sent one of his deputies to Gallup and Fort Wingate to report what came to be known as the Ramah Rampage. Two weeks after their visit, Ira Bloomfield, one of the men in the posse, was beaten up by two of the Tietjen boys. The next week he moved his family to Bluewater.

Other families grumbled about leaving, but after a talk by Bishop McNeill asking the members to be firm and determined and not abandon Ramah in time of trial, tribulation and hardship, they stayed.

One evening in late September, nearly a month after the killings, Tom knocked at our door. "It's blustery out, Mary, but would you walk with me?"

We walked hand in hand in silence toward the lake. Scores of migrating ducks and geese were hunkered down for an overnight before continuing their journey south. The trees were turning color and the chilly breeze foretold winter as it blew down the collar of my coat. I shivered from the cold and from my joy that Tom had come.

I broke the silence. "I see where the bullet creased your skull. Took a little piece of your ear, didn't it?"

"It used to upset me when Mother told me I was hardheaded, but I'm thankful I am. Lady Luck was with me that night. I have nightmares about Lars falling dead beside me. I heard the zing of the bullet that killed my friend. The next shot scraped my ear and head. I heard Brother Lewis cry out and saw him clutch his chest. The third shot hit his head and he fell on Lars."

"Do you want to talk about what happened? I haven't heard the whole story and it might help if you get it out of your head."

"There was nothing I could do," Tom said tearfully. "I yelled for the men to stop shooting, but in the ruckus, they didn't hear me. Brother Merrill finally gave his loud pig-calling whistle and that got their attention. The only thing I know beyond a doubt is that two good men died that night beside the arroyo."

"Tell me what you remember."

Tom told a story of anger, confusion in the dark and nervous trigger happy men.

He finished by saying, "By the time all the hollering and shooting stopped, two of our men were dead and Eb Jones was nowhere to be found. Bishop McNeill sent Brother Bond to St. Johns to get the sheriff. He realized the situation was out of control and we needed help before someone else was killed. Three men are dead because of Eb Jones. They'll catch him someday and I hope they hang him straight to hell."

"Mother's glad Father and Reuben weren't here."

"We took the bodies to the saloon and learned, in addition to murder, Eb Jones is guilty of stealing a horse. He left his tired old plow horse tied to the hitching rail and stole a faster one, saddle and pack included."

"You'll never forget that awful night. Maybe talking about it has helped," I said as I hugged him and smoothed back his rough red hair. "Here, use my hanky."

My feelings for Tom grew deeper when, for the first time, I saw him cry. He never again spoke of that wrenching experience but he carried the scars for the rest of his life.

Daily life went on. Mother and I spent the days canning and preserving vegetables and fruit in preparation for winter. We killed and canned some chickens. With Tom's help, we slaughtered a hog and hung the meat in the smokehouse.

One morning on my way to the outhouse with a full chamber pot, the Buff Orpington rooster attacked. His sharp claws and spurs were aimed right at me. It was the last straw. My hands were full so I didn't have the stick. I kicked at him and felt a satisfying thunk as my foot connected with His Royal Highness. His head flopped to one side; he fell and rolled on his back with those vicious claws pointing skyward. Later I apologized to Mother for killing one of her favorites.

She said, with a tiny smile at the corner of her mouth, "Don't fash yourself, Mary, he was due."

Fash was a word from England that meant don't get in a tizzy. She used it when she was trying to be stern but funny at the same time. We enjoyed my thirteenth birthday dinner of chicken and dumplings courtesy of the rooster that got his comeuppance.

After the first heavy snow in the last week of October, we expected Father and Reuben to come home. There was work to be done in preparation for winter and we needed a man to do the heavy chores. William was eleven and good with animals, but not strong enough to cut the firewood we would need.

Late one afternoon, Father and Reuben rode into the yard. I was happy to see two fat deer tied across the rumps of their horses. They settled in, heard the news, got reacquainted with the twins and spent a week felling trees and cutting them to stove and fireplace size.

Father planned to ride to Fort Wingate before the trail was snowed in to buy staples for the cold months ahead. He asked, "Will, would you like to ride over the mountain to the fort? Reuben and I've been together for months and I'd like some time with you."

"Yes, Father! You bet. Can I ride my pony or will I need a horse?" William had a Shetland pony named Mack which he'd been given by Brother Merrill for helping with the corn harvest. He loved that wee steed and often, in warm weather, slept in the barn with Mack.

After the twins came, Mother had ousted Marmalade from the house. Many an early morning I'd find William, Mack and Marmalade snuggled together in Mack's stall. Any man I married would have to abide my cat in the house. I liked having Marmalade near me at night, but Mother said cats were dangerous around babies. She swore she knew about cats sneaking into a baby's basket and sucking its breath away and causing death.

Father said, "Will, we need two horses to pack the flour, sugar, beans and corn meal we require. You can ride Maggie. She's sturdy and gentle. Get to bed so you can be ready at first light. We'll get up and go. Mary, fix us up a sack of breakfast and lunch to carry along."

They left as the sky lightened. It was a clear, cold breezy day with no sign of the storm brewing in Arizona. By noon, when they should have been halfway to Ft Wingate, they returned. "Too risky to continue," Father said. "The snow was blowing in a gale so thick we could hardly see each other. Drifts were piling up and I knew we must return. We'll try again next week."

The winter weather continued for weeks. On Thanksgiving we had venison roast, applesauce, canned green beans, fresh baked rolls and a pumpkin pie. We had no potatoes. It was ironic, we had cash, but Father wasn't able to go get what we needed. McNeill's store had put in a supply of staples but they charged double what we would pay at the fort or in Gallup.

Soon we had no choice but to pay the price. The foul weather continued week after week and old timers said they'd never seen such continually awful weather. Even the road to St. Johns was blocked. Ramah was cut off from the world.

Each day we ate less and less. Mother's milk began to dry up. Any milk we got from our one remaining cow went to the twins. The other cow, Buttercup, had been our best milker. She got out of the barn one night and went looking for something to graze on. Two days later Reuben found her standing near the lake, frozen solid. Father tied a rope around her, pulled her home behind his horse and with Tom's help butchered her with a handsaw. Father gave Tom a hindquarter for his help. I loved Buttercup and had a hard time swallowing her flesh. If I hadn't been so hungry I wouldn't have been able to do it. Buttercup and all of her parts got us through December.

By New Year's Day 1891, the shelves at McNeill's store were bare. All of the villagers were in dire straits. No one could help their neighbor. People whispered that this or that family hoarded supplies. Spirits sagged. The flame of missionary and pioneer zeal flickered dangerously low.

In January Father returned from hunting with a porcupine in a burlap bag. He skinned and gutted it and I put it to boil in a pot of water. The first time we tried to eat the porcupine it was so tough we couldn't chew it. The broth wasn't bad, so for supper we had corn bread soaked in broth.

The porcupine simmered all the next day and smelled really good. The only thing good about it was its fragrance. It was still tougher than three-year-old dried jerky and nearly cracked my teeth when I tried to chew it. My jaws tired with the effort. It took more energy to eat it than it was worth, so we threw it out into the snow covered yard. Maybe a wild animal would eat it. The next day the boiled porcupine still lay on top of the snow with animal tracks circling around. Even hungry mountain lions and wolves didn't want it.

Father's next attempt to feed his family was when he took us hunting for prickly pear pads. Reuben, William and I went with him to the base of a nearby bluff where the cactus grew.

He told us, "I know the cattle eat these things and I've heard the Mexicans, who call them 'nopales,' think they are a delicacy. Surely, we can figure out how to fix them."

We gathered three gunny sacks full of flat, green, prickly, fleshy pads. The stickers weren't long sharp thorns but short fine, fuzzy, sneaky things that embedded themselves in our fingers and clothing and burned like fire. Following Father's instructions Reuben and I wore heavy gloves and destickered the pads by scraping them with a knife.

Mother was skeptical, but she cleaned the bark off some oak sticks Father provided. We would have a nopales roast. We felt quite festive as we each held our pad laden sticks to the fire. Would they be crispy or juicy? Our mouths watered as our empty stomachs grumbled.

Our anticipation quickly turned to disgust as the pads roasted to slimy green jelly and fell into the fire. The odor was sickening and I, who could usually stomach any taste or smell, ran to the back door and vomited.

The next morning, Father told us he and Reuben were going to St. Johns to let them know what dire straits Ramah was in. "The Bishop should have let President Udall know how bad off we are. He's not been himself since the Rampage. He's lost all of his get up and go. I fear for our lives if someone doesn't do something."

Mother said, "We have one loaf of bread, a half pound of corn meal, a jar of canned chicken and a few dried apples left. We'll do the best we can but I pray you aren't delayed by bad weather."

Father and Reuben dressed warmly, went to the door and prepared to leave. "Do we all agree the babies should get the last loaf of bread?" Father asked just before he left.

We nodded and murmured, "Yes, Father."

"I pray the Lord will watch over my flock while I'm gone," Father said. I saw the tears in his eyes and knew there was sorrow in his heart to be leaving us in near starvation.

I felt the emptiness of their absence as I listened to the hammer of hooves strike the anvil of ice on the road. Then silence.

Chapter Twenty-Five

Ramah, New Mexico Territory, Winter, Spring 1891

The bitter dark days echoed the mood at home. Mother cared for Emily and Anne while I kept the fires burning and rationed the food. William was disgruntled that Father had not taken him to St. Johns.

Father had carved a Cowboys and Indians chess set from ironwood and taught William to play. I asked him to teach Roy and Richard. He grudgingly agreed and soon they were enjoying a tournament. Parley could read and write and knew his numbers, so I coaxed him to teach Ezra.

We did our chores and tried to ignore our empty stomachs.

Mother looks weary and old. She is thirty-three. Giving birth to ten children has taken a lot out of her. Her mental state nags in the back of my mind. When she gets that far away look in her eyes, blows her nose, sighs and shrugs her shoulders, I sense she broods about Lester. She rarely mentions him. His absence is a silent sorrow.

On the third day after Father left, Mother didn't get out of bed. She lay pale and weak with Emily and Anne beside her. They fussed to be fed. Parley and Ezra were too weak to cry for food. The others were cranky and quarrelsome.

By noon, I knew I must go to McNeill's for help. I told Mother I was going, pulled on my coat, boots and gloves. I took my snowshoes from their peg in the pantry, tied them on and left.

The world was white. The pale winter sun gave no warmth, but glared painfully off the snow. After weeks of cloudy, dim days, the brightness almost blinded me. I was tired, weak and half frozen as I struggled through the powdery snow.

You cannot fall. You will not fall. Your family will die if you fall.

After two hours of floundering through the drifts, I saw the roof of Tom's barn. The house was just beyond. I had made it. I cried with relief, tears frozen on my cheeks.

"For Heavens sake!" Aunt Mary Jane said when she answered the door. "Poor dear. Get in here and sit down. Jennie, make Mary a cup of tea. What's wrong?"

Tom helped me remove the snowshoes. My face and lips were so numb that I couldn't smile or talk. I walked stiffly through the door to a chair by the stove and sat. Aunt Mary Jane quickly removed my wet boots, coat and gloves.

Jennie had come home from St Johns before Christmas and hadn't been able to return because of the weather. I forced my nearly frozen lips into what I hoped was a smile. I was glad to see her. Every summer she taught me things she had learned at the Academy and shared her books with me.

When warmed, I mumbled, "Do you have any food to spare? I'm afraid some of us will die before Father returns from St. Johns. He and Reuben went for help."

Aunt Mary Jane said, "Tom, check in the smokehouse for bacon or ham, then hitch up the sleigh. Jennie, there are a few jars of fruit in the cellar. We don't have wheat flour left, but I have oats for mush and some cornmeal left. Do you have any lard? Dodgers are easy to make. Make pasty dough with cornmeal and water. Roll the dough into oval shapes and fry in hot lard. They'll be crispy on the outside, soft and crumbly on the inside. I learned to make them from my Scot grandmother."

"We have lard. We don't expect Father back for a week. When he comes, we'll share whatever he brings."

Aunt Mary Jane said, "You look weak and peaked. You've lost weight haven't you? Sit and rest while we get things together. Joadie, get some of the leftover cornbread from dinner and bring it to Mary. How long has it been since you had a meal?"

"Two days," I sputtered through a mouthful of delicious cold cornbread.

Tom called through the door, "I'm ready, Mary. Get your things on. Don't forget your snowshoes."

The short day was darkening and long shadows lay across the road as Tom guided the team and sleigh. It was too cold to talk, but there was no need for words. When Tom looked at me, I saw admiration and affection in his green eyes. I sat close, held his arm and felt his strong young muscles through his coat.

I entered the frigid house. I smelled the acrid stench of a dead fire. No one had tended the stove or the fireplace all afternoon. It was quiet and still. Where was my family?

"They've died!" I shrieked to Tom as he came through the door with bundles of food in his arms.

I jerked open the door to Mother's room and saw an empty bed. Clambering up the ladder to the loft, I found no one. "My God, where are they? If they all died their bodies would be here," I said to Tom.

"Here's a note, Mary. Calm down, everything's all right. Brother Tietjen and one of his boys came and took your family home with them. Let's get a fire started, put this food away. I'll take you to Tietjens in a while."

It was the first time Tom and I had been alone together inside a house. Suddenly I was shy and awkward.

What I really want is for him to put his arms around me and tell me that not only am I a princess—I am his princess.

It wouldn't be proper to ask for affection, so I said nothing. I didn't know what Tom was feeling, but a blush started at his collar and rose to his cheeks.

Instead of looking at each other, we bustled around being careful to stay out of each other's way. He started the fires. I put the food away. No scavenging mouse would steal our precious rations.

When all was done, I said, "Well, shall we go? Mother will be anxious about me."

"Let's not be in a big hurry. Come and sit beside me in front of the fireplace. You look frazzled and pale. I'll be glad when spring comes and restores the pretty blush on your cheeks. I've missed you," Tom said as he put his arm around my shoulder and pulled me close.

"I've missed you too. I like our walks and our talks about books and the world."

"Hush now, sometimes words get in the way," he said as he put a hand under my chin and turned my face toward his.

I closed my eyes as he kissed me on the mouth. It wasn't at all like the brotherly pecks on the check he'd given me before. I turned, put my arms around him, and felt an inner warmth start in my chest and sink down to my thighs. We stood and he ran his hands down my back. I stretched to put my arms around his neck and ran my hands through his thick, wavy, red hair. He was getting so tall. I had stopped growing taller but was filling out in womanly ways.

We kissed again and he pulled away, "Now you know how I feel about you."

A green pine log in the fireplace spit and burst causing sparks and coals to fly onto the hearth. Tom had forgotten to put the fire screen in place. We rushed to brush the embers back into the fire and put up the screen. The mood was broken and we laughed.

"It's a good thing we were interrupted. I'd better get you to the Tietjens. Just one more kiss?"

I was happy to oblige. We bundled up, went to the sleigh, and were on our way. We glided over the snow. The only sounds were the soft sshh, sshh of the sleigh runners, the jingle of the horse harness bells and the soft plop, plop of hooves. I was warm yet shivery at the same time.

So, this is what people talk about when they speak of being in love! No wonder some lovers get carried away like Hattie did. That won't happen to Tom and me. I won't get married until I'm good and ready.

Tom guided the sleigh into Emma O's yard and kissed me one more time before we went in. "I have a secret name that I call you when I think about you at night. Can I call you Mame when we're alone? I'm reading a book on the Clans of Scotland. A clan leader had a beloved named Mary, he called her Mame."

"Yes," I murmured. "What can I call you? I need a secret name for you."

"Tom is good enough. Use Thomas James when you're mad at me! Brother Tietjen has opened the door and is beckoning to us to come in."

We enjoyed being with our friends, eating a hot meal of rabbit stew and pie made from dried apples. After supper, the children popped the last of the popcorn while the grownups discussed the weather, food shortage and Father's chances of success.

Tom and I sat together on a bench at the side of the room. We didn't hold hands or touch, but we were aware of the currents that collided between us.

Later, Tom loaded us into his sleigh and took us home. We carried the little ones into the house that was cool, but not cold because of the fires Tom and I had started. As Tom left, he turned and winked. "Hope to see you soon, Mary. Let us know when your Father and Reuben get home."

Between the supplies that Aunt Mary Jane had sent and some things the

Tietjens could spare, we were fine for the next week. Mother was up most days and that lifted our spirits. I had a warm glow in my heart and soul whenever I thought of Tom, which was nearly all the time.

"Mary," Mother called. "I asked you to bring the twins from the bedroom and put them in the playpen ten minutes ago. Didn't you hear me? If I didn't know better, I'd swear you were in love. Your mind seems to have disappeared into one of my fogs!"

"Sorry. I'm tired of being in the house so much. Tom brought me a book about Scotland and I keep thinking about it. When are you going to start Literary Society meetings again?" I asked, hoping to change the subject.

"I don't know if we'll continue. Henry thinks Mary Jane is a bad influence. He says she's headstrong and too independent for her own good. He has developed a dislike for her and it saddens me. She's become so precious that she has almost taken the place of my sister Jane. I haven't decided what to do about it. If it's not one problem it's another." Mother sighed.

On the evening of the tenth day after Father left, we heard horses in the yard, the squeak of the barn door opening and Mack's whinny as he greeted his friends. William threw on his coat and bounded into the yard whooping and hollering, "They're back! Father and Reuben are home!"

"Stay with the twins, Mary. I'm going to greet them and find out what they brought," Mother said.

I desperately wanted to run to the barn. Instead, I waited for what seemed hours until the two tired rescuers came in. Reuben had sprouted some straggly chin whiskers in the time they'd been gone. He looked ten years not just ten days, older. Father was hunched and cold. He shuffled into the kitchen and held his hands toward the stove. I saw in his face the temporary grooves of old age which would, with time, become permanent.

"Fix us a cup of tea, Elizabeth. I've been thinking of a hot cup all afternoon. God! It's good to be home," Father sighed as he motioned to me to help him out of his heavy coat. "Hang it in the pantry so it can thaw and drip. William and Roy, bring the sacks in from the barn. We've brought flour, sugar, corn meal and dried beans. More will come tomorrow. We never reached St. Johns. They knew of our dire straits and had sent supplies. We met the wagon and two drivers near the territory line. They gave us some bags to carry in our saddle packs. After they distribute supplies in town, they'll be here tomorrow with more for us and some for the McNeills. Wish that stubborn woman would move into town and live with her husband. Then I wouldn't have to worry about her."

Reuben asked, "Suppose we could have a hot bath before we turn in? I'd say I feel like a flea bitten mangy dog except it's too cold for fleas."

Mother said, "Mary and William, get buckets and bring in enough snow to make a hot bath. Heat it in the kettles so these poor, cold, brave men can get clean and warm before we tuck them in."

That night I slept without nightmares of starving. I looked forward to meeting the two men who'd driven the wagon through seventy miles of snow and ice to bring relief to Ramah.

I'll get up early and bake a treat for them. We don't have any eggs, but I can use baking soda to make it rise.

Father and Reuben slept late. We tiptoed as we did our chores so they could get a much-needed rest. When they finally got up they ate a hot breakfast of corn meal mush. They'd just put on their now dry, warm coats when we heard horses and a wagon in the yard.

I ran to the window and watched a man walk toward the door. "He looks familiar," flashed through my mind.

"My, my! Are you Mary? What a pretty young lady you are! By the look on your face, I can tell you don't recognize me," the tall bearded man said.

A younger man followed and I invited them in. Father greeted them with hugs and back slapping. "Good to see you. Have a good night's sleep? Pip, I bet your cousin was surprised to see you. Abner, welcome to our home. Family, this is Abner Lumpkins from Holbrook by way of St. Johns. He came along to help and to take a gander at our fair valley. He's looking for a place to settle, find a wife and start a family."

Abner grinned. He had a nice smile, even though his teeth were criss-crossed. His ears stuck out like the handles on a sugar bowl. His eyes were so pale blue they looked silver, and when he took off his cap, his straw colored hair stood straight up. He wasn't good looking but I liked him.

He held out a callused, chapped hand to Mother, "Glad to meet you, ma'am. Mighty fine family you have here. Proud to be of service."

While all were meeting and greeting, I gaped at the fellow Father called Pip. I thought, *How could it be? Is he Pip Pipken the embezzler and sometime outlaw? Nah, must be another man with the same name, but how many Pips could there be? He's the right height. His beard's longer and he's thicker through the middle. This is going to be a humdinger of a story!*

William had shot a jackrabbit so Mother and I hurried to fix a pot of rabbit soup. We had soaked some of the dried beans Father had brought and I added them to the soup. I wished we had some carrots and potatoes to add. I served soda cake with stewed dried peaches for dessert

"Mighty fine fare, Sister George," Pip said as he wiped his lips with a napkin. "Mary, you look like you're about to bust a gusset to learn why I'm in Ramah. Henry, shall I tell my story now?"

"Let's go to McNeills' and offload their things first. When we return, put your horses in our barn and spend the night here. Dark comes early even if it's almost February. Your adventurous tale is too good to be told in a hurry."

The men returned, cared for the horses, warmed themselves by the fireplace and Pip regaled us with his exploit that ended with his official reinstatement in the church and his return to Ramah. As best as I remember it went this way—

After leaving St. Johns, he had drifted around Arizona and New Mexico. He drank too much liquor, gambled away too many dollars, and made the acquaintance of more than a few fancy women. He was forty years old and saw the years slipping heedlessly away. When he landed a job at a mine down at Silver City, New Mexico, he was about at the end of his rope. The place was booming. The manager of the Molly B mine needed someone to keep track of ore shipments, payroll and supplies.

He felt he'd found a place to call home. He rented a room at Silver Sue's Boarding House, made friends, met a few respectable young women, and thought his rambling days were over. He missed Ramah and tried to keep informed of the doings here. He frequented the saloons more for companionship than liquor. He'd been there almost two years when, a month ago, he met an interesting fellow at the bar of the Silver Nugget. The man was new in town and tried to impress folks with his tales of smuggling moonshine from Alabama to New Orleans.

At first, Pip didn't pay attention but, his ears perked up when he heard the name of Pipken. Pip moved his chair closer and listened to the man brag.

He asked the stranger, "What did you say your name is?"

That's a question you don't ask a stranger in a saloon because many drifters are running away from something and take offense at being questioned. Pip took the chance because something about the stranger niggled at the back of his mind. He'd heard from one of the mail riders about a shooting near Ramah the previous fall. A man from Alabama had killed one of his cousin's boys.

The braggart ignored Pip's question. Pip bided his time and bought him more drinks. While the man drank Pip excused himself saying he had to see a man about a horse, meaning he intended to visit the outhouse. Instead, he spoke to friends who agreed to help find out if the stranger was the murderer.

If he was, they agreed to hog tie him, deliver him to the makeshift jail at the mortuary and send for the sheriff.

The evening wore on and the stranger bragged about his exploits in outwitting the Mormons who blundered around and shot their own men. Finally, he fell to the floor in an alcoholic stupor and Pip searched his pockets. Sure enough, in his vest pocket there was a watch inscribed *Eb Jones from Eve Pipken Love, Forever*. Pip and his friends delivered the unconscious Eb Jones to the jail. They found the sheriff asleep in his own bed and rousted him out to make a formal arrest.

The following day four men, including Pip, left to take Eb to St. Johns. Sheriff Upton could then deliver Eb to the authorities in Gallup or Fort Wingate for prosecution. After a three-day ride, they delivered the fugitive to the law.

Pip arranged to meet with President Udall to request that, in light of his willingness to repay what he'd stolen and his capture of Eb Jones, his expulsion from the church be reconsidered. He was tired of meandering and more than anything wanted to go home to Ramah. He was reinstated with two years probation and was assured he would be welcomed home. The town folk would be especially glad to see him if he arrived with a wagon of food. President Udall had heard from the cowboy grapevine that Ramah was on the verge of starvation and had been looking for someone willing to make the trip.

"Abner wanted to see Ramah, so he volunteered to help," Pip ended.

My brothers bombarded Pip with questions while Mother and I served cornbread and beans. I was happy Pip was back in the fold. He was a nice man and before long he and Widow Lula Haws, who had five children, found a meeting of the minds and were married.

Days grew longer; spring was on its way. Life fell into a routine and although we didn't have an abundance of food, we got by. McNeills store opened when regular deliveries began.

March second was Tom's seventeenth birthday. His mother invited us to share a dinner, a cake and their happiness. Father refused to go, "I'm very leery of them. I don't like Sister McNeill and I don't like Tom and Mary seeing so much of each other. I fear they are more than friends."

Mother replied, "All right, Henry. Stick your hidebound English nose up in the air. Mary Jane is my friend. You couldn't ask for a finer young man than Tom for Mary to cotton to. We're going."

Mother, Reuben, William and I walked to their house. I had made Tom three cotton handkerchiefs embroidered with his initials, T J M.

Tom and I had a few minutes alone when he took me to the barn to meet a new colt. "Someday, Mame, we'll have a barn and a herd of horses of our own. I have dreams that include you."

"I'll be fourteen in October, but I'm not ready to talk about that. I'm not like girls who think about marriage by the time they're my age. I think I love you, but how do I know? I feel uneasy when you talk like we plan to marry soon. Give me time to grow up."

"I'll wait no matter how long it takes. You're my love, Mame. I've known it since we met in St. Johns. You're different than other girls. You see beyond the ordinary, beyond the horizon. You aren't afraid to ask questions." Tom said, holding my hands and looking me in the eye. Tears welled in my eyes and I mutely nodded.

Several weeks later, I heard a knock at the door. I joyfully opened the door to Grandma Burntwater. "Good Morning, Mary! You've blossomed into a lovely young woman."

"Come in, come in! I haven't heard from you for so long I was afraid something bad had happened. I feared you'd died of smallpox. Would you take a cup of tea?"

"Yes, thank you. I need to talk to your mother. I only have a short time before I must return to my family. We're camping near the lake until we head to Gallup."

"Sit here. I'll fetch her from the hen house. She's checking on a biddy that should be hatching a clutch of eggs any day now."

When Mother and I returned, the kettle was steaming and I fixed three cups. Mother brought Anne and Emily from the bedroom. Grandma Burntwater oohed and ahhed. Anne had curly blonde hair, bright blue eyes and babbled constantly. Father called her "My Sunshine." She was his favorite. Emily's hair was straight, dark brown and her eyes were almost black. She was the quiet, sober one. Mother said she reminded her of a solemn judge and said she needed more care than Anne. Did Mother see herself in Emily?

Grandma Burntwater sipped her tea, "I urge you, Elizabeth, to get your family vaccinated for smallpox. It will prevent the disease and causes only mild discomfort. My children and I were vaccinated when I worked at Fort Wingate. Last winter I lost three grandchildren and one son-in-law.

"My family and I are moving to Window Rock. I will plead with the tribal council and the Indian agent to vaccinate all Navajos. It's the crusade of my old age," she concluded.

"I'll think about it," Mother said. "Now, how have you been?"

They visited for an hour. As Grandma Burntwater prepared to leave, she rummaged in the pocket of her three-tiered satin skirt and found a small newspaper wrapped item.

She held it out to me. "This is for you to remember me by, Mary. When you hold it in your hand and stroke its belly, remember the day you visited my hogan. We sat on the stoop and surveyed the world. Don't ever stop asking questions. This is a wonderful world no matter how hard your life becomes. The stars will twinkle, the sun will shine and castle clouds will float in the sky. I must go."

We hugged and without another word, she turned and was gone before I could properly thank her for all she'd done for me. I unfolded the yellowed paper and found a mottled brown and cream, stone horney toad with turquoise eyes. It sat in the palm of my hand, no bigger than a silver dollar. A miniature turquoise arrowhead was tied to its back with a thin leather cord. I never saw Grandma Burntwater again but she was with me each time I held and stroked her gift.

Bishop McNeill announced in church that he was resigning his position, selling the store and leaving in June for Utah. Tom leaving? I felt faint. I tried to catch Tom's eye as we left, but he kept his head down and hurried from the building.

Abigail Pipken, who knew how I felt about Tom, rushed to me. "Mary, you are as white as a sheet. Come over under the tree and sit down."

She pulled me into the shade. I sat on the ground and put my head down on my drawn up knees. By this time, what I'd heard was starting to sink in, causing tears to flow. I had done a lot of crying lately.

My cry bag must need mending.

"Here take my hanky." Abigail tried to console me.

"I have to help Mother," I said as I stood, brushed leaves and grass from my skirt and watched Tom drive away with his family.

That evening Tom came, "We need to talk. Can you come out for a walk?"

Without asking permission, I took my shawl from its peg and went. He led me toward the lake. The willows had leafed out and their pale green boughs offered us a secluded place. We leaned against a tree trunk.

"I know you were shocked by my stepfather's announcement. I am so angry and frustrated that I couldn't wait to get away. Sorry if I hurt your feelings."

"I thought I was going to faint. Abigail tried to comfort me but nothing helped. How long have you known?"

"Three evenings ago the Bishop came calling. I was reading a book on the porch. The window was open and I soon realized the conversation between Mother and her husband was heating up. I heard him say, "You are my wife. We have been married for eleven years and have three children. I married you and cared for your two children by my brother. You are indebted to me. Under the laws of God and man you are required to do what I say."

"What did your mother say?"

"She flat out told him she would not move to Utah. 'James Reid McNeill, I have tolerated you because I needed the protection and guidance of a man after my beloved Thomas died. I was only twenty-two, had two children and no knowledge of what kind of man you are. I am older, wiser and have come to realize you are not the same kind, loving man Thomas was. You are hard, scheming, and ambitious. You married me because it was decreed by the church that multiple wives were good. It was a feather in your cap to have two wives.

"Then you married poor, frail Lissie. Her death and the passing of her child was a shame but maybe she's better off in Heaven. Take Phoebe, who I love and admire and your two children and leave. My children are older. I have a profitable business. I will not go with you.'"

"Your mother has a mind of her own. What happened next?"

"When I heard the Bishop walk to the front door, I skedaddled off the porch. I didn't want to be in his way. He stormed out the door, slammed it hard enough to make the wall shake and mounted his horse. He took off like a jackrabbit chased by a coyote. I'm afraid to ask Mother about it because she stomps around looking like a tornado in search of a flimsy barn."

I laughed, "I hope you don't move. You've been the man of the house anyway for a couple of years. Things won't change."

Tom said, "May delay my own plans for a few years. Will you wait for me, Mame?"

In early May, Father was asked to manage the sawmill for the summer. He was delighted. He had never liked farming and it would allow him to earn money to provide for us. He never said it but I think he liked being away from the daily grind of home life. He loved to talk and joke with the lumbermen rather than listen to babies cry and boys fuss and feud. Reuben would go with him.

Late one night before Father was to leave, I was wakened by loud voices. "Elizabeth, I forbid you to have anything to do with that woman. She's a stubborn mule refusing to go with her lawful husband. I don't want Mary to have anything to do with her son, either."

"Henry George, don't back me into a corner. Mary Jane is my best friend and I refuse to obey your unreasonable demands. I will choose my own friends. As for Mary and Tom, I don't know if there will ever be anything serious between them. I do know that forbidden fruit is sweeter. Mary's a sensible girl. She won't make the mistake I made by marrying when she is fourteen. If she wanted to marry, I don't know of a better match for her than Tom."

"She has a choice. Abner Lumpkins is quite taken with her and has asked permission to come calling."

Chapter Twenty-Six

Ramah, New Mexico Territory, Summer1891—Summer 1892

I answered a knock on the door. Abner Lumpkins stood on the porch with a bouquet of wildflowers in one hand, a book in the other and a grin as wide as a jack-o-lantern on his face. He took off his hat and I saw his hair was slicked back. He wore clean overalls with a striped red and white long sleeved shirt. His boots were polished and his hands scrubbed. I could have committed mayhem on my Father.

Before he left, he told me why I should consider Abner's attentions favorably. "Abner is a fine young man who, despite adversities, is optimistic and ambitious. On their way to Utah from North Carolina, his parents were killed in a wagon accident. His mother was a McDonald from the Cape Fear River area. Many Scot families settled there before 1776. Abner's father was from Ireland."

"He's nice, but I resent your efforts to encourage him. How did he get to Holbrook?"

Father replied, "Abner, an only child, was sent to live with his mother's brother. He works for the AT & SF Railroad as a maintenance supervisor. He lives in a housekeeping car attached to the trains and travels the line checking the rails and their beds. Abner tired of not having a permanent home.

"They stopped at Holbrook and Abner inquired about the area. He liked what he heard and enjoyed the scenery, so told his uncle it was the end of the line for Abner. He wanted to settle with other Saints, marry and raise a family. He wanted to return to the fold and was baptized in our church. He has taken a shine to you and I like him," Father concluded.

"Why do you like him better than Tom?"

"Tom is too much like his mother: headstrong and stubborn. At times, he's imprudent and impulsive. It's said that Noah visited the ancestral home of the Clan McNeill, Barra Isle, off the coast of Scotland. He asked if they needed a place on the ark. The clan chieftain, Duncan McNeill replied, 'Thank ye kindly, but we've a boat a our aine.' They were pirates. Successful, but pirates just the same."

"I like Tom for those very reasons. The other side of stubbornness is loyalty and perseverance. You're drawn to Abner because he has no family and you think you could father him," I said.

I am shocked I talked that way to Father. He's in charge and I'm questioning his motives. I've never done that before. I've never even thought of doing it.

"Hmmph!" he grumped. "I don't want you to narrow your choices. You're going to be too busy this summer to see much of Tom. Another thing, if we leave Ramah, Tom couldn't come with us. He'll be the man of Mary Jane's house after James and Phoebe leave."

My jaw dropped.

Did Father realize how much he'd told me? Leaving Ramah? This had been home through thick and thin for four years. We struggled mightily to get here and now he's thinking of leaving? So, Aunt Mary Jane was staying. My heart raced. Tom would stay, but we might leave. It was all too much to grasp.

I invited Abner to sit on the porch. "It's a nice day. Let's enjoy the sun."

"Your father gave me leave to call so we could get to know each other. I brought flowers. Mayhap you'd put them in water."

"I'll get a jar," I said taking the white daisies, blue lupine and yellow daffodils. I returned with the flowers in a mason jar and set them on a table. "Thank you, Abner. They're sprightly and spring like. What is that book you're carrying?"

"Your Father said you l-l-liked to read. I borrowed this b-book of poems from my landlady. I thought we c-c-could read together." He stammered and blushed.

I am not about to encourage him in thinking I am open to courting. I'll change the subject.

"Who are you boarding with?" I didn't want to read poetry with him. It was too intimate a thing to do with a young man I barely knew.

"With the Ashcrofts. They have a lean-to on their barn. The food is good and I enjoy being in town so I can get to know folks."

While he talked, my mind whirled, seeking a way out of my predicament. I had a flash of inspiration. Last Sunday Abner sat behind me at church. When we sang, I heard his beautiful tenor voice rise above the voices of everyone else. I'd been amazed that such clear, pure tones came from this homely, friendly fellow. "Have you met Abigail Pipken? Pip is her father's cousin."

"Yes, after church one Sunday. Her family is so grieved by Polk's death. No one sees much of them. Why do you ask?"

"You sing so well and Abigail plays the piano. The two of you could do a number for the Fourth of July celebration. Polk was always in the holiday programs. He had a good voice and played his mouth organ. Do you play an instrument?"

"When I lived on the railroad I learned to pick a banjo. In the evenings the men swapped tall tales, got drunk or entertained each other by pickin' and singin.' I learned old Irish and Scottish songs from the railroad men. Does anyone in Ramah have a banjo?"

"Abigail will know. I plan to see her tomorrow. Are you still working at the store? I heard someone from Albuquerque bought it."

"Yes, the new owners are brothers. Their father owns a mercantile and he helped his sons buy McNeills. Both have families and will move to Ramah by fall. Last week they came to prepare to enlarge the store and have two houses built. They asked me to help with the construction and take charge of the new farm supply section. I have a future here!" he crowed.

"Congratulations! Will you be there tomorrow? I'll tell Abigail about your musical talents and ask her to come to the store with me. You two could share ideas about doing a number on the Fourth."

Mother continued to visit Aunt Mary Jane. I walked with Tom. We disobeyed Father's orders. I asked, "Mother, does he have the right to forbid us to see certain people? They aren't bad people or criminals. Others think highly of them."

"They scare him. He's afraid he will lose control of us if we think for ourselves."

On June tenth Brother and Sister McNeill's heavily loaded wagon passed. They were headed to Fort Wingate to catch the train to Utah. Tom told me they planned to stop at his house for dinner and goodbyes. I wished I could be a fly on the wall to see how that farewell played out.

By the end of June, our vegetable garden was in and up. Those first fresh carrots, sweet peas and lettuce were delicious after a winter of want and canned or dried food. The ex-potato fields lay fallow and grew a nice crop of weeds.

The mill shut down for the Fourth of July holiday, so Father and Reuben would be home. We would also celebrate Anne and Emily's first birthday. I enjoyed my baby sisters but they paid little attention to anyone but each other. They gabbled in some strange invented language no one else understood. They were happy as long as the other was nearby.

Father and Reuben arrived the day before the festivities. On July 4 we packed the picnic food we'd prepared, loaded the wagon and went to the church. I looked forward to an afternoon and evening of friendship, food, music and patriotic poems and declamations. Father hadn't brought up the subject of Aunt Mary Jane and Tom so Mother and I kept our mouths shut.

I endured the serious speeches and recitations which came first. Musical selections were next. Abigail and Abner had prepared a musical number. It tickled me pink that they had hit it off. Abner had transferred his affections to Abigail.

When their turn came, Abner walked to the center of the stage and said, "This is an old Scot song I learned from a friend on the railroad. It's about something we all like to do and is named 'The History of Kissing.' Please clap or join in the chorus."

Abigail sounded a chord on the piano and Abner began:

To compliment and kiss,
Some hold to be a sin,
But I can tell you first of all,
How kissing did begin.
First Adam he kissed Eve,
And so begot a son.
Tis about five-thousand years ago,
Since kissing first begun!

Abner stepped toward the audience, "I'll sing the first line of the chorus, you repeat and so on."

Since kissing first began, brave boys,
Since kissing first began,
'Tis above five-thousand years ago,
since kissing first began.

Abner sang, Abigail played the rousing tune and we clapped and laughed our way through ten verses. Abner twirled a cane, winked at the ladies and did a soft step shuffle. While performing, he wasn't homely or shy. It was magic. The presentation ended when Abigail stood, joined Abner and hand in hand, they illustrated the song by sharing a kiss. The audience clapped and cheered. Then, chairs, benches and tables were moved outside, under the trees for the picnic.

Frowning, Father watched Tom and me walk hand in hand to a group of friends and join them for supper. I laughed and chatted while I shook with foreboding inside. I tread on thin ice. Father wouldn't make a scene in public. My reckoning would come later. After supper, the furniture was taken inside and gathered wood was piled for the bonfire. It gave light to the dancers and inside its cone of brightness, we felt safe from prowling animals.

Tom took me home. I rode behind him on his horse, my arms around his waist with my head resting on his back. I loved the smell of him, the feel of his muscles moving under his shirt as he guided the horse and the sense of belonging he gave me.

I pulled his shirt out of his jeans and rested my face on his bare back.

"Mame, are you trying to get us in trouble?" He laughed. "Moves like that make me want to ride into the dark and throw you to the ground."

He was halfway serious but I couldn't help covering his shoulders with nipping kisses. We turned into my yard before any more passion could erupt. The lamp in the front window glowed. My parents had retired so there would be no tirade from Father to spoil the evening.

It happened two days before Father and Reuben were due to return to the mill. Mother was quieter than usual. She seemed resigned and submissive. I wondered why she gathered the twins clothing and toys into bags.

After supper on July sixth, Father dropped his bombshell. "Mary, Elizabeth is going to the mill. We'll also take Emily and Anne. The crew needs a cook.

271

on his pony, but sometimes I had to get away. Those walks were my entertainment.

My parents expected to be gone until the end of September, so I was surprised to see them the last week of August. We ran to the wagon, whooping and hollering our welcome. I was overjoyed to see Mother, but my elation vanished when I saw the look in her eyes. Father handed the twins to William and me. Anne had a dark bruise on her face and deep scratches on her arms. There were no marks on Emily. I looked questioningly at Father. He shook his head and helped Mother into the house. She stood in the middle of the room, looked at no one and spoke not a word. She was as wooden as a hitching post. Father led her to her rocker.

"Mary, feed the girls then put them to bed. We'll talk later," Father directed.

After all was in order, he asked me to walk with him. I dreaded what Father was about to tell me. "It was a mistake to take Elizabeth. She didn't want to go and agreed to it only if she could bring the twins. I didn't like the idea, but found I enjoyed them. Especially Anne. She is a sunny little thing and always makes me laugh and feel happy to be alive. Perhaps I dote on her too much. I think Elizabeth became jealous of Anne. I didn't see it happening, but afterward Reuben said that he'd noticed Mother slipping into one of her fogs."

"Where is Reuben? Why isn't he with you?"

"He's staying at the mill for another month. I have to return to fill my time as manager. He'll come home with me when the place shuts for the winter."

"What happened to Anne?"

"I think Elizabeth tried to kill her."

"Mother couldn't do such a thing! What happened to make you say something so far fetched?"

"Stop asking so many questions and I'll tell you."

"Four days ago Elizabeth said she needed a day off. She wanted to go into the woods with the girls and look for mushrooms and herbs to dry. I said it was all right if she'd prepare meals ahead for the crew. She packed a picnic lunch, put it in the small wagon with the twins and left.

"I was worried when she hadn't returned by evening. Morning came and she still hadn't come back. Reuben and I set off to look for them. We found her and Emily sleeping under an oak two miles from the mill. When I asked about Anne, she looked at me with those vacant eyes. She didn't speak. I sent them to the mill with Reuben while I continued to search.

"Three miles farther on, I heard a faint cry. I thought it was an animal, but when I drew near I realized it was a child. I found Anne at the bottom of a shallow ravine, covered with vomit, banged up from a fall and mewling like a sick kitten. In the vomit were chunks of mushroom. I know enough to know they were the poisonous kind. Your Mother knew that too."

"Is Anne going to be all right? What are we going to do about Mother? Do people with mental problems ever get well?"

"Anne's weak, but will be all right. As for Elizabeth, ask Sister McNeill for help. Maybe there's something in one of her books about mental problems. I wish we'd gone to St. George with Bill and Jane. I'd leave Ramah next week if I could find a way to pay our debts and outfit a wagon."

My heart sank.

Can I leave Tom? Should I stay and marry him? I love his family, I love him, but I'm not ready to jump from the frying pan into marriage. In the deepest part of me I want more. I want too much. What's wrong with me?

The weeks passed, Anne recovered, but had a touchy stomach from then on. She vomited easily. Aunt Mary Jane came as often as she could get away from her prospering dairy. She always brought a book and spent time reading to Mother. Mother rarely spoke and spent her time rocking back and forth. Sometimes the constant creak, creak drove me to distraction.

In October, shortly before my fourteenth birthday, Abigail and Abner married. I was her maid of honor and Pip Pipken was the best man. The Pipken family took Abner into their hearts. The newlyweds moved into living quarters above the Ramah Mercantile and Supply. Abner had found a family and a future in Ramah. I wished things looked as good for Tom and me

When Father and Reuben returned, Father commented, "You let a good one get away, Mary."

"You said I shouldn't limit my choices at my young age, Father."

It was a mild winter. The roads and trails were closed for days, instead of weeks at a time. Mother gradually improved and spent a lot of time playing with Emily. She ignored Anne. Our garden had produced prodigiously, so we had a cellar full of bottled fruits and vegetables. We slaughtered two hogs. Our smokehouse was well stocked with hams and bacon.

Tom's sister Jennie came home for Christmas. She had graduated from the Academy, taken the teachers test and passed. She was hired to teach the younger children at Ramah. Jennie had received the education I coveted.

The winter we lived in St. Johns was the only formal schooling I ever had. Everything else I learned as best I could. Sometimes I resented my situation in life. I was the only girl in a family of eight brothers for my first thirteen years. Mother was a hard worker but I never knew when she would disappear, leaving me with all the work.

The winter passed with no major crisis. We had food, money to buy what we needed and a store that stayed open all winter. Life was good. Father allowed Mother to see Aunt Mary Jane and he no longer griped about Tom. Little did I know a volcano was about to erupt and change our lives.

In March 1892, Tom celebrated his eighteenth birthday. I was surprised when Father agreed to attend the party. Had he resigned himself to Tom and I being sweethearts? I was unaware that my parents had received a letter from Lester offering them a way out of Ramah.

In early April, I learned of Father's plans. Mother let it slip. "I was so happy to hear from Lester and learn he's now happily and lawfully living in Idaho."

I looked at her in surprise. "I didn't know Lester had written. Why didn't you tell me? What's the big secret?"

"Oh my, I wasn't supposed to tell. I can tell some, but you'll have to talk to your father for the whole story."

With dread balling in my gut I listened. "Lester sent a money order for three-hundred dollars. I don't want to know how he got it. I was thankful to hear he's left the gang and moved to Dingle, Idaho, near some of my family. Dingle is a few miles south of Montpelier near the Utah border."

"Is Pat Traynor with him?"

"No, Pat was killed during a train robbery. Lester says he heard the fracas and decided to hightail it out of the area. He said he wasn't a bandit, but was the horse wrangler for the gang. He'd wait in a secluded place with fresh horses for them to make their getaway. I don't see how that was better than being an outlaw. He's settled down and wants us to come and live near him. Talk to your father about plans for this summer."

My first impulse was to run to Tom, tell him we must marry and forget my family. I was angry and frightened. I decided to confront Father before I rushed to Tom. I found him in the barn.

"Mother told me you'd heard from Lester and he sent money. What are your plans?"

He patted the bale of hay beside him and said, "Come and sit. I knew I must talk to you, but I don't relish the telling. I should never have forced Elizabeth to leave Mendon. It was the biggest mistake I've ever made. I've hated Ramah. Not just for me, but for what it's done to my wife and children. Winter before last was Hell. Watching my children cry for food tore me up. I swore it would never happen again."

"Am I right in thinking you plan to leave this summer? What if I want to stay?" I asked with a trembling voice.

My palms were sweaty and icy. My knees were shaking even though I was seated. I couldn't look Father in the eye. My world trembled. My head whirled.

"Nothing's going to happen overnight. Calm down and listen," he said as he tried to take my cold hand.

I yanked my hand away and turned my back to him.

"Mother said she'd never take another long wagon trip. It would be hard on Anne and Emily. How can you do this to us? You uproot us, drag us around like a bunch of gypsies and expect us to act like we love it. I feel at home here. I love Tom and someday I will marry him whether you like him or not."

"I know this is hard for all of you. I know another move will be difficult, but should we live with my mistake? A man has to be ready to admit he's been wrong and try to make things right. Whatever you decide will be with my blessing."

That night I tossed and turned. I'd never thought growing up would be so confusing, so full of decisions, so full of love and hate at the same time.

Mother would not take another wagon trip. She, the twins and Ezra would travel by train. They would go to Dingle where Lester said there was construction work for Father. Lester had met the young woman he planned to marry and was building them a home. When he finished, he would start on a place for us. Mother would leave in June.

Father and Reuben would go back to the mill to earn enough to pay off the debts Father still had on our house and land. I, with the rest of my brothers, would stay in Ramah. We'd show the place to prospective buyers, thin out our belongings, bake trail crackers and buy supplies for our wagon trip to Idaho.

I am in agony trying to make up my mind. Should I go with my family and never see Tom again? Should I stay and get married before I am fifteen? It's time to confide in Tom.

As we walked by the lake, I told him of my family's plans—of my anguish at having to make such a wrenching decision. I wept on his shoulder while he held me tight. When I finished, he remained silent for what seemed like hours.

Finally he wiped my face with his handkerchief, turned me to face him, held my hands and began, "Mame, I love you more than any other in this world. We will marry, but not now. I won't do that to you. You would grow to resent me. You need a chance to realize your ambitions. Montpelier is a good size town. Maybe you can go to a nurse's training school. Go with your family. I'll come for you when we are both ready for marriage."

"I can't bear the thought of leaving you," I blubbered. "Will you write to me?"

"As often as I can. We can still share books through the mail," Tom said. "Come stand by our willow tree.

"My Mother tells of a Scottish custom; handfasting. Couples who wanted to marry but had no priest or preacher nearby held a private ceremony and pledged themselves to each other. They lived together legally until a preacher came by. We'll do a handfast to pledge our devotion to one another as an engagement ceremony. Will you do this for me? Will you wait for me, Mame?"

We held hands and faced one another under our willow next to the lake. Tom vowed to remain faithful, to care for and protect and love me for the rest of his life. He promised to come for me when the time was right.

I said to Tom, "I, Mary George, swear to wait in love and with patience until Tom McNeill comes for me. I will marry no other and keep faith in Tom and his devotion to me."

Chapter Twenty-Seven

Dingle & Montpelier, Idaho, Autumn 1892—Spring 1895
I had made my decision, but I flip-flopped like a frantic fish. Mother packed, unpacked then packed again trying to decide what to take. Father planned to take only one wagon so space would be limited to the things we must have to survive.

On the morning of June fourteenth, Mother, Ezra, Anne and Emily embarked with bag and baggage on the first leg of their trip. Father came from the mill and drove them to Gallup. Two days later he returned and gave me instructions concerning preparations for our trip and selling the place.

I walked through the nearly empty house. My footsteps echoed. So many things were gone that the house seemed twice its former size. I tried not to think of leaving Tom. It was hard. Like my tongue seeking out a loose tooth, my thoughts relentlessly returned to him and our future. I was short with my brothers, grumpy with Tom and generally disagreeable.

I daydreamed that the place wouldn't sell. Father wouldn't be able to buy a wagon and team. We would stay. It was only a daydream. Our leaving was inevitable.

Mary George, don't be a ninny. Don't waste the last precious weeks with Tom grumbling about what is. Put a smile on your face and leave Tom with a memory he will cherish.

Having changed my outlook, preparations became easier. A problem was solved when Aunt Mary Jane agreed to keep Marmalade and her kitten, Lily. I named her Lily because she was pure white except for faint orange stripes on her tail and ears. Tom said, "They'll be here when we return together."

"I know they will. We must decide what to do with Mack. Father wants William to sell him. William says he won't go if Mack can't come."

William begged, pleaded and promised that his friend would cause no trouble. Father relented. Mack would accompany us. He wouldn't make it to Idaho.

July passed in a flurry of cleaning, discarding, giving away and packing. I carefully wrapped my treasures in old bed linens. I caressed each and remembered where I had received it and who had blessed me with it: the doll dishes from Mother at Tuba City, the Katsina from my Hopi friend, the storage pot from ruins that would later be called Wupatki, Sammy and Captain Jack's eagle feathers, the green stone buffalo from Tom and the Zuni horny toad from Grandma Burntwater.

I came upon my catechism book. I opened it and saw "Mary George, Her Book" written in childlike script. My eyes blurred as I held the precious book and thought of how far I had come since writing those words.

I've grown in body, spirit and mind, but I am determined to keep growing. I'm not finished yet.

Pip Pipken brought a family named Morris to look at our place. "Mary, these folks are just in from Texas. I met Brother Morris while I was wandering and told him about Ramah. He's decided to settle here and is looking for a place this size."

Mrs. Morris had a babe in her arms, one child hung on her skirt while three older children stood shyly beside their wagon. They looked tired.

"You're welcome to look around," I said. "Father will be home on Friday. If you're interested, come back then."

Mr. Morris and Pip inspected the fields. Mrs. Morris and the children went into the house while I waited in the yard. I knew they would buy. Mrs. Morris returned. We sat on the porch while the children played and chased around the yard. I heard the shouts and squeals of my brothers in their voices and knew I had already left this place behind.

Father returned and came to an agreement with Mr. Morris. Our home was sold. We outfitted our new wagon and made the acquaintance of four new mules. We were ready by the middle of August.

I made the rounds to say goodbye. No one knew of my pledge with Tom.

Some girls teased me saying, "Now that you're leaving I'm going to set my sights on handsome Tom McNeill. He's too good a catch to leave behind."

I tried to hide my emotions, rise above the teasing and not let doubts creep into my mind. The evening before we left, Tom and I said our private farewells under our willow tree. That night in my bedroll on the ground, I cried myself to sleep. We would leave at dawn. As we ate a hasty breakfast, I heard a horse approaching. Tom called, "I'm riding as far as Gallup with you."

Father and Reuben drove the wagon, William and I rode our saddle horses while Roy, Richard, and Parley walked or rode in the wagon. Mack was tied to the back of the wagon or was led by one of the boys. We hoped to make it to Idaho in six weeks.

When the time came to say my final farewell to Tom, I was glad others were near by. I had no choice but to contain myself and not blubber. Tom put his arms around me, kissed me gently and whispered, "I'll come for you, Mame." He turned, mounted his horse and rode toward the mountains. I took a deep breath, mounted my horse and said, "I'm ready."

Not one of my brothers laughed or teased. They knew if they wanted to eat they had better stay on my good side.

Our route would take us north through New Mexico to the San Juan River near the landmark called Shiprock. It resembled a ship under full sail. From Shiprock we'd follow the river as it flowed northwest. We'd cross it at Bluff where the river is wide, shallow and easy to ford. Bluff was one of the struggling Mormon communities in southeastern Utah. Father planned to stop and visit a boyhood friend.

I had my journal and wrote a few words at the end of each day. I hoped this would be the last long wagon trip I'd ever make, so I wanted a record of my experience. Seven years before, I had been too young to keep a journal.

The three day stretch from Gallup to the San Juan was hot, dry and miserable. By the time we reached the welcome shade along the river, our water barrels were empty and our tempers frayed. Father had pushed the team to get across the desert quickly.

The next three days the trail followed the winding river. On the third evening we made camp south of the river and Father rode across to Bluff to find his friend. I assumed Brother Taylor was there because Father didn't return until the next morning.

When I stopped to think about my responsibilities I was scared.

Here I am with Reuben, who had turned sixteen last winter and four younger brothers in the middle of Indian country. I pray none will get sick, fall off a horse or get an infection. Only the Good Lord watches over us. Father is casually confident in my ability to handle anything that might occur. I don't share his certainty.

Brother Taylor returned with Father to help us ford the river. We got good and wet but it felt delightful. He had a field of red ripe grapes and invited us to gather and eat our fill. I picked enough to make raisins. Roy ate too many and kept me up all night crying with a royal bellyache. After two days at Bluff we headed north toward Blanding, Monticello and Moab.

The country was strange and beautiful. We named the large red sandstone formations. One was Church Rock because of its spire of whorled stone. Another showed the profile of a woman lying on her back. It was Lazy Woman. We passed stone mushrooms each with a flat stone capping an upright pillar. We called it Toadstool Forest.

We stopped at Moab to visit another friend, Brother Burnham. He was a beekeeper and gave us three buckets of golden sweetness. I was careful not to eat too much at one time. At Moab, the Colorado River was a gentle, easy stream. We crossed it early in the morning and headed northwest towards the Green River.

The trip, though dry and hot, was uneventful. We came to a small settlement near the Green River where our church brethren welcomed us. Visitors brought news and welcome diversion to these exiled, lonely villagers. Father carried letters from Ramah to Brother Lewis' sister. She invited us for supper and the home cooked meal would be a welcome change.

We did our chores, hobbled the horses, washed faces and hands and walked to Sister Markson's home. Upon returning, we checked the livestock. Mack had pulled up his hobble. Father said, "He won't go far. He'll be back by morning. Let's turn in and hope for the best. Too dark to hunt for him now, anyhow."

William grumbled, but he was as tired as the rest of us so we bedded down. During the night I heard wolves howling but thought nothing of it. Wolves and coyotes were constant companions on the trail. They served a purpose by scavenging dead animals. We saw many bony remains of mules and horses beside the trail.

William was up at dawn to look for Mack. We were finishing breakfast and loading up when he returned. Tears ran down his freckled face. "I found Mack stuck in quicksand near the river. The wolves had torn him to bits. If I'd left him in Ramah he'd be happily carting the Morris children around. They offered to buy him, but I was selfish and dragged him along. It's my fault."

Father hugged William. "No amount of fretting will undo what's done. We all have better hindsight than foresight. Get a bite and let's be on our way. Long way to go today. We have to ferry across, so must get to the landing early. I don't have time to waste waiting for others to cross."

The crossing went smoothly and we continued angling northwest toward the Price River. We camped on the banks of the Price that evening and followed it for the next three days. We re-provisioned at the settlement named Price and continued due north to a town called Helper.

I remarked, "Helper is a strange name for a town. Why is it called that?"

We found the railroad had a switching yard at Helper. It was here they hooked an extra engine, a helper, to the trains to get them over the mountains. The clamor, acrid odor of coal smoke and air of excitement in the little town were a welcome change from the isolated country we'd been through.

Reuben said, "You're pushing the mules too hard. We're climbing as we move into the mountains. Bessie, the lead mule, is favoring her right fore leg. We need to slow down."

"We've been on the trail for four weeks. It's the middle of September and we could get an early storm any time. If Bessie quits, we'll put a saddle horse in her place. I want to be in Logan in ten days."

Three mornings later, we found Bessie lying on her side. She would not get up so Father shot her and left her beside the road. "Sometimes you have to be ruthless. I can't risk our lives for a mule."

We pulled into Father's sister Emma's place in Logan in a cold driving rain. We were chilled, worn out and another mule had died. We arrived with no animals to spare but we had made it to family.

Father sent Reuben to Dingle to get Lester and fresh mules. I enjoyed four days of rest and getting to know my cousins. Aunt Emma and Uncle Bradley had ten children. Ruthella, was my age. She was engaged to marry at Christmas. I felt a tiny bit envious, but knew my time would come when I was ready.

Father's meeting with Lester, the prodigal, was emotional. They stayed up late talking. Lester was not my favorite. He made fun of me, teased me mercilessly and at times was cruel, but he was my brother. I was friendly, but cautious.

The weather cleared and we set off for Dingle with high hopes and four fresh mules. The trail followed the western shore of Bear Lake at the base of rugged mountains. The autumn sun was soft, the meadows full of sunflowers and I saw many elk and deer. I wished Tom could share the beauty.

Our reunion with Mother, Ezra, Anne and Emily was joyful. We were together, near family, living in a snug log and stone cabin, ready to begin again. Lester found a job for Father helping build a large dairy farm with an attached butter and cheese factory.

I turned sixteen in October. In December Mother delivered her eleventh child, Carl. He dallied one day too long to be a Christmas baby.

As 1893 began, I began to search for ways to reach my goals. A hospital in Montpelier sponsored a nurses training program. I wrote for information and an application. Their reply was discouraging. To enter, one had to be at least eighteen years old, hold a high school diploma and be a young woman of high moral standards. I met only one requirement, so I threw the papers away and looked elsewhere.

Without telling anyone, I applied at the cheese factory. As part of their salary, young women lived in small cottages and took their meals in a dining room. I wanted to be a Dingle Dairy Maid. When I told my parents I was moving to the dairy, they were livid.

Father's face turned beet red, his mouth thinned into a straight line, his brow furrowed and lowered, while his jaw jutted forward a full inch. "Mary George, what on earth do you think you're doing? We need you here. Carl is only a month old and Mother is still recuperating from his difficult birth. Why are you doing this to us?"

I trembled and my knees turned to water, but I stood my ground. "I'm not doing this to you. I'm doing it for myself. All my life I've taken care of others. Now it's my turn. The Willard's are good church members. Their women workers are sheltered and cared for. I'll earn three dollars a week and will give two to you. I am sixteen and do not need your written permission to work outside my home."

Mother, who was speechless, finally found her voice, "Mary, I understand your need. I sometimes wish I had done the same. Will you visit? I hoped you would meet a nice Dingle boy and learn that Tom McNeill isn't the only man you can love."

"Elizabeth, how can you say such things. Our daughter working in a dairy with strangers? I refuse to condone it. Who knows what corroding influences she will be exposed to?"

"I start Monday. I'll have most weekends off, so I will usually be home on Sunday," I said.

Father stomped out. "I have to go to work. I'm sorry I helped build that damn dairy."

Mother smiled, "He'll get over it. I'll get my cousin's girl to live in and help."

My first week at the dairy was hectic. I moved into a cottage that I shared with four other girls. My job was easy as I had made butter and cheese for as long as I could remember. The food was plain, but good and filling. I enjoyed the conversation around the large tables and soon made friends and felt at home. Most men workers were married and went home for supper. At noon, many of them sat in the dining room at a separate table. One young man learned my name and often greeted me as we passed at work or at dinner.

"Learning the ropes are you, Mary? How do you like it?" he'd ask.

I had no idea who he was. My friends teased me about the boss's son. I asked, "Who is he? What is his name and why do you call him the boss's son?"

LaPreal replied, "You're kidding! Right? I can't believe you don't know who Kayle Willard is."

"Is he really the owner's son? What's he doing working with the hired help?" I asked.

"He's starting at the bottom learning the business. Just came from two years college in Salt Lake City. Someday he'll run this place."

"He's nice and good looking, but I'm not interested. I have other things on my mind," I said as the end of dinner bell rang.

One morning in April, the dining room supervisor handed me a note telling me to report to Mr. Willard's office. I hurried to respond.

What have I done wrong? I hope I'm not fired. This job is easy as pie compared to other things I've done. I'll miss my friends and my freedom if I'm let go. For the first time I've saved some money of my own.

I knocked on the glass windowed door and was invited in, "Sit down, Mary. I need to talk to you about an opportunity. One of the clerks in our retail store has given notice. She finds she must marry as soon as possible. Our son, Kayle, has suggested you as her replacement. Would you be interested? The pay is more; five dollars a week instead of three. You will remain in the same cottage and have the same dining privileges. Do you need to think it over?"

I took a deep breath, "I will do a good job. Thank you for offering me the position. When will I start?"

"Go to my wife's office and tell her you need a new uniform. As soon as it's ready, hopefully by tomorrow, you can start on the 10:00 a.m. to 5:00 p.m. shift. You may work some Saturdays as that is a busy day in retail. I hope that won't be a problem?"

"None at all. Thank you, Mr. Willard."

I felt like skipping, but I walked sedately to arrange for my uniform. I started in the shop the next day and enjoyed it. I met many nice people and learned about their likes and dislikes so I could recommend certain products to them. The only problem was Kayle Willard. He kept asking me to the Saturday night dances at the church.

One weekend, Father, who had started speaking to his wayward, headstrong daughter again said, "I met Kayle Willard at a church meeting. He said he'd met you at the dairy and was impressed with your hard work and friendly smile. He wondered if you are seeing anyone. He asked permission to escort you to a dance or to dinner some evening."

"Did you tell him I have a sweetheart? I do not intend to encourage Kayle. He's a nice fellow, good looking and someday will be well off, but I'm not interested."

"I said you had had a beau in New Mexico, but that we've been here for a year and New Mexico is very far away. Aren't your feelings for Tom fading?"

"Father, you know Tom and I write regularly. I do and always will love him. He'll come for me when the time is right. You wait and see."

"In the meantime, it wouldn't hurt you to have a social life. You're sixteen and it's time you looked around. I want you to accept Kayle's invitation. Won't you do it for me?"

"I'm going to talk to Mother. Curfew on Sundays is 9:00 p.m. Nice to talk with you, Father."

The dairy sold most products wholesale. Milkmen in horse drawn wagons delivered milk to homes. The shop at the front gate sold retail. Dr. Eldridge from Montpelier was a regular customer. Whenever he was in Dingle, he stopped on his way home to buy cheese curds, butter, or a wheel of white cheddar.

Dr. Eldridge and I chatted while I filled his orders. He asked me where I was from and how old I was. He asked if I planned to spend the rest of my life selling cheese.

I told him of my disappointment with nurse training. When I shared my dream of becoming a nurse midwife, he looked thoughtful and said, "Hmmm."

In June, LaPreal asked if I'd like to go with her family to Logan for the weekend. I arranged to have Saturday off and told my parents I wouldn't be home on Sunday. Tom's grandmother, Jessie McNeill, lived in Logan and he wrote that she would like to meet me.

I was apprehensive, yet eager to meet Tom's grandmother. Tom had told me some of her life story. I admired her for overcoming the many hardships encountered while crossing the country by wagon in 1856. She and her party were among the first pioneers to emigrate from Scotland to Utah.

Tom's cousin welcomed me at the door and led me to the back parlor. Grandmother Jessie was in her seventies. She was a wiry, little white haired woman with piercing green eyes. She spoke with a Scottish accent, "Well, lassie, Tom writes ye want to marry him. Are ye sure you're up ta marryin' a McNeill?"

"I love Tom and will devote my life to him and to helping the Saints in New Mexico fulfill their mission."

She took my hand. "I can tell you're a hard worker by the sturdiness of your hand. Ye must be strong to stand up to marryin' a stubborn Scott. The McNeill's have a reputation of always bein' right, never compromising and knowin' the right way ta do everthing. Their motto is Victory or Death. No middle ground. I gie ye my blessin'. Just hope ye can keep ahold a some a yourself!"

I assured her I would do my best. We enjoyed a cup of tea before I left to join LaPreal at her aunt's home.

The next time Dr.Eldridge came to the shop he asked if he could speak to me privately. With a nod and a 'just a minute' gesture to the other clerk I took him to the empty dining room.

"My wife and I have six children. The oldest is eleven and the youngest three months. Selma needs help with our brood and I need help in my office. We offer you this proposition. Mornings, you work with the children. Afternoons, I'll train you in nursing procedures in my home office. You will have a room of your own, take your meals with the family and have two days off every week. I propose to pay you five dollars a week in addition to your room, board and the training. You're pale. Are you all right? Do you need time to think about this?"

He was right. I was so surprised to have this opportunity drop unexpectedly into my life that all the blood left my head and I shook with excitement.

I took a deep breath. "I accept. I don't need time to think it over. I must give the dairy a week's notice. That's only fair. When will I start?"

He extended his hand, "Fine, it's settled. Selma will be pleased. I'll come for you next Wednesday morning. Bring your personal things. I'll provide your uniform."

On Sunday, I went to Dingle to tell my parents. I found Mother resting in bed while Father sat beside her with a worried look on his face. I stood in the doorway and for the first time, saw that my parents had aged. Father was only forty-one but there were gray streaks in his dark beard and hair. His shoulders sagged as he held Mother's hand. He sighed and shook his head. Mother's eyes were closed and she was pale. Furrows between her eyes and along her cheeks made her look older than thirty-five.

I coughed to draw their attention. Father turned and smiled. "Elizabeth, Mary's come for her visit. Now we can tell her our news."

"What news?" I asked as I tried to swallow the lump in my throat. "Is it good or bad? I have good news."

"Mother's going to have another child. This little one will make twelve fine children."

"Mother, why are you in bed? You don't look well."

She opened her eyes. "Just a little tired, Mary. Did a big laundry and ironing yesterday. Guess it was a bit much. I'll be all right. This babe comes as a big surprise, but God sends them to those who can care for them."

"Isn't Margaret coming in to help anymore?" I asked.

"Off and on. She's busy with her social life. I wish you were here. I never had a better helper than you. I want things to be the way they were when I could count on you."

I felt the steel trap tightening. I had to say what I'd come to say. "Mother, there are plenty of girls in Dingle who would be willing to live in. Father is making a good living with his construction business. You can afford it."

"Yes, but it wouldn't be the same as having you here. I miss you, Mary."

I took a deep breath and blurted, "Dr. Eldridge and his wife have hired me to help with their children. Part of my salary will be training in nursing and midwifery. It is important to me. I know you love me and would like to have me here, but I must do this. This is my chance. When Tom comes I will be ready to help the Saints in New Mexico."

Father stood and knocked over his chair. "Who do you think you are to refuse your parents? That stubborn Scot will never come. You delude yourself. Love! You have no idea what love is. I forbid you to go to Montpelier or to marry Tom. There are young men right here in Dingle who want to court you. Any one of them would make a better husband than that pirate."

Mother pleaded, "Mary don't cause this disruption. I've bided my time thinking you would come to your senses."

I trembled, knowing that what I was about to do would change my life. There would be no going back. I refused to let the silken threads of love that bound me to my family strangle me.

"I start next Wednesday at Dr. Eldridge's. I hope things go well with this child and you will find it possible to understand what I am doing. Lester ran off with a gang of outlaws and you have forgiven him. I will make something good of myself and my life. I'd hoped you would be proud of me."

Father followed me to the door. "Mary George, if you leave now, you cannot come back. We will refuse to take you in when you need a place to come home to. The years will pass and you'll find yourself an old maid. Your precious Tom will never come for you. This is your last chance. What is your answer?"

I turned and walked out the door, down the front walk, through the gate to the road. I had made my choice.

Reuben worked for a freighting company and occasionally came to visit. I asked him to bring my treasure trunk, which I'd left at our parent's home. I enjoyed my attic room and displayed my things on shelves next to the large window. I felt at home.

I stopped sharing my salary with my family. I saved as much as possible to have a nest egg when Tom came. The doctor provided me with two blue cotton dresses and white aprons. One of the aprons had a red cross sewn on the bib and I wore it in the office.

In addition to my training, I studied the doctor's medical books. I helped with the patients by taking their history, listening to their complaints and listening to their heart. Under the doctor's supervision I sutured cuts and treated minor infections. I learned about sterilization of instruments, sheets and bandages.

I began accompanying the doctor to deliveries. Giving birth was not considered an illness and babies were born at home. Some mothers-to-be began asking for me to preside over their deliveries which they called "Birthday Parties." They felt easier with a woman than a man.

I was happy, but lonely. I went to visit Mother after Udell's birth. He was her twelfth child. A stranger opened the door, told me to wait in the hall.

She returned, "I'm sorry, Mrs. George does not wish to speak to you."

I left and did not return. This time Mother had made the choice.

Letters from Tom came regularly, and every time I opened an envelope, I hoped it would bring news that he was preparing to come to Idaho. Two years passed and I was an old maid at eighteen.

I had learned as much as I could from Dr. Eldridge and thought of applying at the hospital or advertising my services as a midwife. The children were growing up. The family could easily do without me.

The lilacs beside the back door were in full bloom. Their scent drifted through the open kitchen window. For the rest of my life the perfume of lilacs would take me back to that evening in early May. I sat at the table reading a book instead of a letter from Tom. I had not heard from him in weeks. The house was quiet as the family had gone to a church supper. They had invited me, but I was discouraged and apprehensive about the choices I'd made. I needed to be alone.

There was a knock on the back door. I saw the dark outline of a tall man in a slouchy hat. The setting sun was in my eyes. I smelled dirt, sweat, horse and leather.

"I'm sorry, we don't have any work that needs doing," I said. I thought the fellow was looking for work or a handout.

He chuckled, pushed his hat back on his forehead and held his hand out to me. I saw the flash of green eyes as he said, "I've come for you, Mame."

Epilogue

Bluewater, New Mexico, March 1964
The day is ending as surely as my life is nearing its end. Marmalade XII cuddles and comforts me as all my orange tabbies have done.

Tom and I married on May 15, 1895 at the Logan LDS Temple. In the custom of the church, we were sealed for life and eternity. Reuben and William attended.

Tom sold his horse and saddle and we took the train to New Mexico. We lived at Ramah for a year, then homesteaded in Bluewater. This valley, this village, these people were our lives. We had four boys and two girls. The second boy died two days after birth.

For over forty years, I provided medical care for the area. I amputated limbs, dug bullets out of feuding cowboys, saved hundreds of lives during the 1918 flu epidemic and attended over three-hundred "Birthday Parties." I delivered twenty-three sets of twins and one set of triplets. I lost nary mother nor child. Many of my babies bring their children to visit.

I weep tears of grief and loss for what has gone. I weep tears of joy for love and family that is remembered and for those who remain to carry on.

I've given away many of my treasures—the dishes to a daughter, the Thunderbird Kachina to a son, the stone carvings are in a museum and the many pots to family and friends. I still have my books and maybe someday a grandchild will read the fabric covered journal and let others know about all those adventures I had when I was young and curious.

Now, Tom has gone ahead. When my time comes, I'll hear him say, "I've been waiting. It's about time you came to me, Mame.